"You'll need a protection detail for the drive back and forth, too."

More manpower. But Raleigh's tone seemed to suggest something else. "You don't want me here for the interviews?"

"No, I do. You know more about Hannah's case than I do, and you know Warren. You might hear something that helps us figure this out." He paused, groaned softly. "If and when we eventually make it out of here tonight, you could stay at my place. It's not far."

"With you?" she blurted out.

The corner of his mouth lifted, but the slight smile didn't last long. "We're former lovers. I can't change that. But I don't want it to get in the way of us doing what needs to be done."

THE COWBOY'S WATCH

USA TODAY BESTSELLING AUTHOR

Delores Fossen

&

Nicole Helm

Previously published as *Under the Cowboy's Protection*
and *Wyoming Cowboy Ranger*

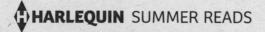 HARLEQUIN SUMMER READS

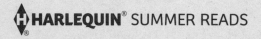 **HARLEQUIN**® SUMMER READS

ISBN-13: 978-1-335-45518-5
The Cowboy's Watch
Copyright © 2021 by Harlequin Books S.A.

Recycling programs for this product may not exist in your area.

Under the Cowboy's Protection
First published in 2019. This edition published in 2021.
Copyright © 2019 by Delores Fossen

Wyoming Cowboy Ranger
First published in 2019. This edition published in 2021.
Copyright © 2019 by Nicole Helm

This edition published by arrangement with Harlequin Books S.A.

For questions and comments about the quality of this book, please contact us at CustomerService@Harlequin.com.

Harlequin Enterprises ULC
22 Adelaide St. West, 40th Floor
Toronto, Ontario M5H 4E3, Canada
www.Harlequin.com

Printed in U.S.A.

CONTENTS

Delores Fossen, a *USA TODAY* bestselling author, has written over one hundred novels, with millions of copies of her books in print worldwide. She's received a Booksellers' Best Award and an RT Reviewers' Choice Best Book Award. She was also a finalist for a prestigious RITA® Award. You can contact the author through her website at deloresfossen.com.

Books by Delores Fossen

Harlequin Intrigue

Longview Ridge Ranch
Safety Breach
A Threat to His Family
Settling an Old Score
His Brand of Justice

HQN Books

Lone Star Ridge
Tangled Up in Texas
Chasing Trouble in Texas

A Coldwater Texas Novel
Lone Star Christmas
Hot Texas Sunrise
Sweet Summer Sunset
A Coldwater Christmas

Visit the Author Profile page at Harlequin.com for more titles.

UNDER THE COWBOY'S PROTECTION

Delores Fossen

Chapter 1

Sheriff Raleigh Lawton didn't like the looks of this.

The glass on the front door of the house had been shattered, and the chairs on the porch were toppled over. Both could be signs that maybe there'd been some kind of struggle here.

That kicked up his heart rate a huge notch, and he drew his gun, hoping he didn't need to use it. While he was hoping, he added that maybe there was some explanation for the glass and chairs. Maybe the woman who lived in this small one-story house was okay. Raleigh had a double reason for wishing that.

Because the woman, Sonya Burney, was nine months pregnant.

He'd known her all his life, and that's why Raleigh hadn't hesitated to go check on her when the doctor from the OB clinic had called him to say that Sonya had missed her appointment. In a big city, something like that would have gone practically unnoticed, but in a small ranching town like Durango Ridge, it got noticed all right.

The rain spat at him when he stepped from his truck. It was coming down hard now, with an even heavier downpour in the forecast. He had a raincoat, but he didn't want to take the time to put it on. However, he did keep watch around him as he hurried up the steps and onto the porch.

"Sonya?" he called out and immediately listened for anyone or anything.

Nothing.

He tested the doorknob. Unlocked. And he cursed when he stepped inside. The furniture had been tossed here, too. There was a broken lamp on the floor, and the coffee table was on its side. Raleigh reached for his phone, ready to call one of his deputies for backup, but something caught his eye.

Drops of what appeared to be blood on the floor.

Raleigh had a closer look. Not blood. Judging from the smell, it was paint. And he soon got more proof of that. There was a still-open can in the hall just off the living room, and a discarded brush was next to it. However, it wasn't the can or brush that grabbed his attention. It was what someone had scrawled on the wall.

This is for Sheriff Warren McCall.

Hell.

That felt like a punch to the gut. Because he'd seen a message identical to that one almost a year ago. A message that'd been written in the apartment of a woman who had been murdered. Unlike Sonya, that particular woman had been a stranger to him.

The memories came. Images Raleigh wished that time would have blurred. But they were still crystal clear. The woman. Her limp, lifeless body, and the baby she'd been carrying was missing—it still was.

He prayed that Sonya and the baby wouldn't have similar fates.

Raleigh didn't have any proof of who'd killed that other woman, stolen the child or written that message. But he had always thought the message had been left for him. And Warren, of course.

Warren was his father.

Biologically anyway. Raleigh had never considered the man to be his actual dad. Never would.

He made the call for backup and used his phone to take a quick picture of the message. Actually, it was a threat. Raleigh just hoped that Sonya hadn't gotten caught up in this tangled mess between Warren and him.

"Sonya?" he called out again.

Still nothing, but Raleigh continued to look for her. The house wasn't huge, a combined living and kitchen area, two bedrooms and a bath. He went through each one and didn't see her. But there was another message, and it'd been slopped in red paint on one of the bedroom walls. A repeat of the other one.

The repeat hadn't been necessary. Raleigh had gotten it the first time.

This is for Sheriff Warren McCall.

Warren was retired now, but he'd once indeed been the sheriff of McCall Canyon, a town one county over. He'd also carried on an affair with Raleigh's mom for nearly three and a half decades. Or rather, Warren had *carried on* with her until his secret had come out into the open after someone had tried to kill him. Raleigh's mother had been a suspect in that attack. And Warren's "real" family—his wife, two sons and his daughter—hated Raleigh and her.

Was one of them responsible for this?

Maybe. That was something he would definitely investigate, but first he had to find Sonya.

Since it would take a good twenty minutes for his deputy to get all the way out to Sonya's house, Raleigh kept looking, and he made his way out through the kitchen and to the back porch. The moment he stepped outside, he heard something. At first he thought it was the cool October rain hitting the tin roof.

It wasn't.

There was a woman dressed in jeans and a raincoat. She was facedown, on the end of the porch, and she was moaning. Raleigh ran to her and turned her over, but it wasn't Sonya. However, it was someone he knew.

Deputy Thea Morris.

Seeing her gave his heart rate another jolt. Of course, Thea usually had that effect on him. Not in a good way, either, and it certainly wasn't good now. What the hell was she doing here, and what was wrong with her?

Raleigh didn't see any obvious injuries. Not at first. Then he pushed aside her dark blond hair and saw the two small circular burn marks on her neck. Someone had used a stun gun on her.

"Where's Sonya?" he asked.

Thea opened her eyes, but she was clearly having trouble focusing because she blinked several times. Then she groaned again. She didn't answer him, but he saw the alarm on her face, and she started struggling to sit up. He helped her with that. Too bad it meant putting his arms around her to do that.

And Raleigh immediately got another dose of too-clear memories that he didn't want.

Of Thea being not just in his arms but in his bed. But that was an *old water, old bridge* situation.

"Where's Sonya?" Raleigh repeated. "And what happened to you?" He had other questions, but those were enough of a start, since finding Sonya was his priority right now.

"Sonya," Thea repeated in a mutter. She lifted her hand—not easily because it was practically limp—and she touched her fingers to her head. "Sonya."

"Yeah, that's right. *Sonya.* She's pregnant, and I'm worried about her." *Worried* was an understatement. "What happened to her? What happened to *you*?"

Thea blinked some more, looked up at him, and the concern was obvious in her deep green eyes. "A man. I think he took her."

That got Raleigh's attention, and he fired glances around them, trying to see if he could spot her. But there was still no sign of Sonya.

"The man had a gun," Thea added, and she groaned, trying to get to her feet. She failed and dropped right back down on the porch. She also reached for her own gun, but her shoulder holster was empty. Since she was wearing her badge, Raleigh doubted she'd come here without her gun.

"What man?" Raleigh demanded. "And where did he take her?"

Thea groaned again and shook her head. "I don't know, but he said he was doing this because of Warren."

Raleigh hadn't actually needed that last bit of info to

raise the alarm inside him. With the signs of struggle and those stun gun marks on Thea's neck, he decided it wasn't a good idea for them to be out in the open like this. Sonya's place was an old farmhouse with a barn and a storage shed, but the woods were only a short walk away. It would give an attacker plenty of places to hide.

If the man was indeed hiding, that is. If someone had actually taken Sonya, he could be long gone by now.

"We need to get inside." Raleigh hooked his arm around Thea's waist, pulling her to her feet. She wobbled, landing against him. Specifically against his chest. He shoved aside the next dose of memories that came with that close contact.

"You have to go after the man," Thea said. Her voice was as shaky as the rest of her. "You have to get Sonya."

"I will."

His deputy would be here in ten minutes or so, and Raleigh would start searching as soon as he had someone to watch Thea. She wasn't in any shape to defend herself if her attacker returned. At the moment though, he was much more concerned about Sonya. After all, Thea was alive and okay, for the most part anyway, but Sonya could be in the hands of a kidnapper.

Or a killer.

But that didn't make sense. Who would want to hurt her, and what did any of this have to do with Warren? Unless...

A very unsettling thought came to mind.

"Did this happen because Sonya's a surrogate?" Raleigh asked. He helped Thea into a chair at the kitchen table and then went back to the window to see if he could spot any sign of the woman or the person who'd taken her.

"I don't know. Maybe..." Thea's voice trailed off, and that's when Raleigh noticed that Thea's attention had landed on the painted message on the wall. She shuddered, but she didn't turn away. "I don't suppose you put that there?" But she shook her head, waving off her question. "No. You and Sonya were friends."

Raleigh wasn't sure how Thea knew that, but then he wasn't sure of a lot of things right now. "Start talking. I want to know everything that happened." Though it was hard to stand there and listen to anything Thea had to say when his instincts were screaming for him to go after Sonya.

Thea didn't jump right into that explanation; instead, she got to her feet. "We can talk while we look for her. Do you have a backup gun you can lend me?"

Raleigh frowned. Thea didn't look at all steady on her feet, which meant her aim would probably suck, too. Still, she was a cop.

Warren's star deputy, in fact.

Warren had not only trained her and given Thea her start in law enforcement, his father had made it clear that he loved Thea like a daughter. That was convenient, since Thea loved him like a father.

Raleigh wasn't sure how Thea had managed to overlook the fact that Warren was a lying, cheating snake, and he really didn't care. Heck, at the moment he didn't care if Thea was having trouble standing. She had the right idea about looking for Sonya as they talked, so Raleigh gave her his backup gun from his boot holster.

"I got here about a half hour ago," Thea said, glancing at the clock on the microwave. While she held on to the kitchen counter, she made her way to the back door. "Sonya didn't answer my call this morning, so I came over to check on her." She paused. "I've been checking on her a lot lately."

"I didn't know Sonya and you were that close," Raleigh commented. Sonya had only moved to Durango Ridge about ten years ago, so it was possible she'd known Thea before then. Or maybe they'd recently become friends. But after one look in Thea's eyes, he knew that wasn't the case.

Raleigh groaned. "This has to do with Sonya being a surrogate."

Thea nodded and managed to get the back door open. "I haven't given up on finding Hannah Neal's killer."

Neither had Raleigh. And he especially wasn't forgetting her now, because that message on Sonya's wall was identical to the one found at Hannah's apartment a year ago. Hannah had been murdered only a couple of hours after she'd given birth. That same person who'd killed Hannah had almost certainly been the one who had taken the newborn.

"Sonya didn't know Hannah," Thea continued, "but they were both surrogates, and they used the same doctor for the in vitro procedures that got them pregnant."

Raleigh's gut twisted. Because he'd known that. And he had dismissed it as being something unimportant. Of course, he sure wasn't dismissing it now.

Still, it didn't make sense. Why would someone go after two surrogates to get back at Warren? Especially since Sonya had no personal connection to Warren.

Or did she?

Raleigh didn't have the answer to that, either, but he soon would.

Thea stepped out onto the back porch, and like Raleigh, she looked around. She also caught on to the porch railing to keep herself from falling. Raleigh nearly had her sit down on the step, but babysitting Thea wasn't his job. His job was to find Sonya.

"Tell me about this man who took Sonya," Raleigh demanded. "Was he here when you arrived?"

Thea nodded and followed him into the yard. Not easily, but she made it while still wobbling and using every last inch of the porch railing. "I saw him. He wore a ski mask and was holding her at gunpoint. He was about six-one and about two hundred pounds."

That tightened his stomach even more. Sonya was barely five-three and had a petite build. She wouldn't have stood a chance against a guy that size. Especially if he had a gun.

Thea stopped once she was in the yard, and with the rain pouring down on her, she looked back at him. "Sonya had the baby. Not with her," she added when she must have seen the shock on his face. "But she was no longer pregnant."

That didn't make sense, either. Sonya's doctor was in town. So was the hospital she'd intended to use to deliver. If she'd had the baby there, Raleigh would have certainly heard about it.

"Did she say anything about the baby? About the man?" Raleigh pressed.

"No. He had her gagged and already in the yard when I got here. I moved toward him, but there must have been a second man. Or a second person. He hit me with a stun gun when I came onto the porch. I think they took Sonya that way." She tipped her head to the woods.

Thea was lucky the guy hadn't killed her. Or maybe

luck didn't have anything to do with it. Maybe keeping her alive had been part of the plan.

"I would tell you to wait here, but I doubt you will," Raleigh grumbled to her, and he started for those woods.

He didn't get far though, because he heard the sound of a car engine. At first he thought it might be the deputy, but it was a woman who came running out the back door, and Raleigh recognized the tall brunette.

Yvette O'Hara.

The woman who'd hired Sonya to be a surrogate. Like Thea and him, Yvette was wet from the rain. The woman was breathing through her mouth, her eyes were wide and her forehead was bunched up.

"Where's Sonya?" Yvette blurted out.

"We're not sure." Raleigh figured Yvette wasn't going to like that answer. Judging from her huff, she didn't. But it was the best he could do. "Stay here. Deputy Morris and I were about to look for her."

Yvette glanced at Thea. "What's going on? Did something happen to Sonya, to the baby?" She was right to be concerned—especially if she'd noticed the toppled furniture and messages on the walls.

"Stay put," he warned her again.

But Yvette didn't listen. She barreled down the steps, and also like Thea, she had some trouble staying steady. In her case though, it was because she was wearing high heels.

"Sonya's doctor called me," Yvette said, her words running together. "She missed her appointment. She wouldn't have done that if everything was all right."

Probably not. But Raleigh kept that to himself. Yvette already looked to be in alarm-overload mode, and it was best if he didn't add to that. He didn't want her getting hysterical.

"Just stay here," he said. "That way, if Sonya comes back, she won't be here alone."

Yvette finally gave a shaky nod to that and sank down onto the porch steps. Good. It was bad enough that he had Thea to watch, and he didn't want to have to keep an eye on Yvette, too. If those armed thugs were still in the area, it was too dangerous for Yvette to follow them.

Thea didn't stay back though. Despite her unsteady gait, she kept on walking, straight toward the woods, and Raleigh had to run to catch up with her. He'd just managed that when he heard someone call out to him.

"Raleigh?" It was Deputy Dalton Kane. Since Raleigh hadn't heard a siren, it meant Dalton had done a silent approach, and Raleigh was glad he was there. He needed some backup right now.

"Stay with Mrs. O'Hara," Raleigh told him. "The woman on the porch," he added in case Dalton didn't know who Yvette was. "And get more backup and some CSIs out here. I want the house processed ASAP."

Again, Thea got ahead of him, and Raleigh had to catch up with her. She didn't even pause when she made it to the trees; she just walked right in. Since it was obvious that she wasn't going to be cautious, Raleigh moved in front of her.

"I think the thugs were parked back here somewhere," Thea said. "Shortly after the one hit me with the stun gun, I believe I heard a vehicle leaving."

Raleigh silently groaned. If that was true, then there was no telling where Sonya could be. "Is it possible one of the men had the baby with him?" he asked.

"No." But Thea paused and shook her head. "Maybe.

I didn't get even a glimpse of him. After the stun gun hit, I fell on the porch, and I think I passed out."

Perhaps because she'd hit her head. Raleigh could see the bruise forming on her right cheekbone. Of course, if this was a kidnapping, the person could have even drugged Thea to make sure she didn't come after them.

But who would want to kidnap Sonya?

Raleigh drew a blank. Sonya hadn't been romantically involved with anyone. At least he didn't think she had been, but it was possible she'd met someone. It was something Raleigh hoped he could ask her as soon as they found her.

They kept walking, and it didn't take long for Raleigh to spot the clearing just ahead. He'd been born and raised in Durango Ridge, but he hadn't been in this part of the woods. However, like the rest of the area, there were paths and old ranch trails like this one that led to the creek.

"The rain is washing away the tracks," Thea mumbled, and she sped up.

She was right—if there were any tracks to be found, that is. And there were. Despite the rain, Raleigh could still see the grooves in the dirt and gravel surface. A vehicle had been here recently. He took out his phone to get photos of the tracks just in case they were gone before the CSI team could arrive. He'd managed to click a few shots when he heard Thea make a loud gasp.

Raleigh snapped in her direction, following her gaze to see what had captured her attention. There, in the bushes, he saw something that he definitely hadn't wanted to see.

Sonya's lifeless body.

Chapter 2

Thea fought the effects of the adrenaline crash. Or rather she tried. But while she was waiting on Sonya's front porch, she was also fighting off the remnants of that stun gun, along with the sickening dread that another woman was dead.

Oh, God. She was dead.

For a few seconds after she'd seen the body, Thea had tried to hold out hope that it wasn't Sonya. That it was some stranger, but that had been an unrealistic hope to have. After all, she'd seen the gunman taking Sonya. She'd known the woman was in extreme danger.

"Why did the gunman even take Sonya from the house?" Thea mumbled. "If he was just going to kill her, why didn't he do that when he first broke in?"

She hadn't intended for anyone to actually hear those questions. Not with all the chaos going on. But Raleigh obviously heard her, since he looked at her. What he didn't do was attempt an answer, because he was standing in the front doorway while giving instructions to the CSIs, who were now processing Sonya's yard and house.

Because it was a crime scene.

One that wasn't in Thea's jurisdiction.

That's why she just sat there on the front porch, waiting for Raleigh to give her some task to do. *Any* task. Anything that would help them find out who'd done this. That wouldn't stop this crushing feeling in her heart though, and it couldn't bring back Sonya. But maybe Thea could help get justice for the dead woman.

"Please tell me you found the baby," she said when Raleigh finished with the CSIs and started toward her.

He shook his head. "But there's some evidence that Sonya delivered the child here, at her house." Raleigh added a weary sigh to that, and he stopped directly in front of her. "There were some bloody sheets in the washer, and a package of newborn diapers had been opened. So had a case of premade formula bottles. Three of the bottles and four of the diapers were missing."

Well, Sonya had obviously had the baby somewhere, so the delivery could have easily happened here in her home, but that just led Thea to yet another question. Why wouldn't Sonya have gone to the hospital to deliver the child?

However, Thea instantly thought of a bad answer to that.

Maybe the gunman was here when the baby had been born. Those thugs could have stopped her from getting the medical attention she needed.

She looked up at Raleigh, and he was staring at her. His lawman's stare. That meant his comment about the sheets and diapers hadn't been just to catch her up on what they'd found. This was the start of his official interview, since she'd actually seen the man who was likely responsible for murdering Sonya.

Of course, Thea had already told him some details when Raleigh had found her on the back porch, and she had added other bits of info while they'd waited for the CSIs and ME to arrive. Obviously though, he wanted a lot more now.

But Thea didn't have more.

"You should be inside the house with Yvette," Raleigh reminded her. It wasn't the first time he'd mentioned that. "Whoever killed Sonya is still at large, and you could be a target."

"So could you." Best not to mention that the gunmen might want him dead because he was Warren's son.

No.

That would only make matters worse. And as for going inside with Yvette, obviously neither of them wanted to do that, because they both stayed put.

Thea's heart was breaking for Yvette, since the missing baby was her biological child—a daughter, from what Sonya had told her a couple months ago—but Thea didn't have the emotional energy to deal with Yvette just yet. Besides, she didn't even know what to say to the woman. The only thing they could do was hope they found the baby soon, along with finding Sonya's killer.

"I had at least a dozen conversations with Sonya," Thea explained to Raleigh. "I visited her here at her house three times, and not once did she ever hint that she was in any kind of danger."

He made a sound that could have meant anything and kept up the intense stare. He was good at it, too. Unfor-

tunately, looking at him reminded her of other things
that had nothing to do with the murder and missing baby.

Once Raleigh had been attracted to her. Obviously
not now though. There wasn't a trace of attraction in
his stormy blue eyes or on that handsome face. He was
all cowboy cop now.

"And you visited Sonya because of Hannah Neal,"
he said.

It wasn't a question, but Thea nodded to confirm that.
"Hannah was my friend, and it eats away at me that I
haven't been able to find her killer."

She caught something in his eyes. A glimmer that
she recognized. It ate away at Raleigh, too.

Raleigh hadn't known Hannah, but Hannah's body
had been dumped just at the edge of Durango Ridge.
That meant it was Raleigh's case, but then, despite his
retirement, Sheriff Warren McCall had gotten involved
because Hannah had lived in their hometown of McCall
Canyon. Plus, Hannah had been murdered in McCall
Canyon, too. Murdered, and her killer had left the same
obscene message on her wall that he had on Sonya's.

At the time of that investigation, Warren hadn't
mentioned a word about Raleigh being his illegitimate
son. Neither had Thea, though she had known. She had
found out Warren's secret a few months before that, but
she hadn't told anyone. And that was the reason she no
longer saw the attraction in Raleigh's eyes. He hated
her now because she'd kept that from him.

But not nearly as much as she hated herself for doing
it.

Thea shook her head to clear it, forcing her mind off
Hannah and back onto Sonya. Hannah's case was cold,

but what they uncovered here today could maybe help them solve both murders.

"Why exactly did you become friends with Sonya?" Raleigh asked.

It wasn't an easy question. "It didn't start out as friendship. I'd been keeping tabs on the doctor who did the in vitro on Hannah." Actually, she'd kept tabs on anything related to her late friend. "So, when I found out this same doctor, Bryce Sheridan, had done this procedure on another surrogate, I wanted to talk to her. I wanted to see if there were any…irregularities."

Raleigh's eyebrow came up. "You think Dr. Sheridan had something to do with Hannah's murder?"

"No. I mean, I didn't know. I was just trying to find any kind of lead." Thea had to take a deep breath before she could continue. "But after I met and talked to Sonya, I didn't see any obvious red flags. Especially not any red flags about Dr. Sheridan."

That ate away at Thea even more. Because she should have seen something. She should have been able to stop this from happening.

"Both Hannah and Sonya were surrogates," Raleigh said, "and both were connected to you. According to the messages left at the crime scenes, the women were linked to Warren, too."

She couldn't deny that. Thea knew both women and had worked for Warren for three years before he'd retired and turned the reins of the sheriff's office over to his son Egan. It was ironic that all three of Warren's sons had become lawmen, but Thea seriously doubted that Raleigh would ever say that he had followed in his father's footsteps.

"You think I'm the reason these women were killed?" Thea came out and asked him.

Just saying the question aloud robbed her of her breath, and Raleigh didn't even get a chance to answer, because his deputy Dalton came out of the house and onto the porch. He wasn't alone, either. Yvette was with him. The woman was no longer crying, but her eyes were red and swollen, and she had her phone gripped in her hand so hard that her knuckles were white.

"We have to find my daughter, so I hired some private investigators," Yvette immediately said.

"I told her I didn't think that was a good idea," Dalton mumbled.

It wasn't. PIs, even well-meaning ones, could interfere with an investigation to the point of slowing it down, but Thea couldn't fault Yvette for doing this. The woman had to be desperate because her baby could be in the hands of a killer.

"You saw Sonya," Yvette said to Thea. "How was she? Was she weak? Did she say anything about the baby?"

Yvette had already asked these questions several times and in a couple of different ways. So had Raleigh. But Thea didn't mind answering them again. Maybe if she kept going over what she'd seen, she would remember something else. It was a tactic that cops used to try to get more info from witnesses.

"Yes, she looked weak," Thea admitted. "And scared. The man who took her had his arm around her waist as if holding her up."

Even though that wasn't new information, it caused fresh tears to spring to Yvette's eyes. "What about the second man, the one who had the stun gun. Is it possible he had the baby with him?"

Thea had already considered that and had mentally walked through every moment of the attack. "It's possible. I didn't even see him. In fact, as I said earlier, it could have been a woman."

Yes, she had indeed said that earlier, but this time it caused Raleigh to shift his attention to Yvette. And Yvette noticed the abrupt shift, too.

"Well, it wasn't me," Yvette snapped. "I'd have no reason to take my own child and murder the woman who carried her for nine months."

No obvious reason anyway, but it was odd that the woman had assumed they were thinking the worst about her.

"Do you have anyone with a grudge against you?" Raleigh asked Yvette. "Someone who might want to try to kidnap the baby and hold her for ransom?"

Yvette was shaking her head before he even finished the question. "Of course not. My husband and I manage my late father's successful real estate company. We've never even had a serious complaint from a customer."

No, but that didn't mean someone hadn't kidnapped the baby for ransom. That's the reason Raleigh had told the woman to keep her phone close to her. Yvette had. In fact, she was doing everything a frantic mother would do to find her child. But something was missing here.

Or rather *someone*.

"Where's your husband?" Thea asked. "You called him right after we discovered the body, so shouldn't he have been here by now?"

Since Yvette was still looking a little defensive, Thea expected the woman to blast her for even hinting that Mr. O'Hara wasn't doing all he could to be there to comfort his wife or look for their child. But Yvette's reaction was a little surprising. She glanced away, dodging Thea's gaze.

Now, this was a red flag.

"Nick had some things to tie up at work," Yvette answered after several long moments.

Raleigh made one of those vague sounds of agreement. "Yeah, Sonya mentioned to me that your husband wasn't completely on board with having this baby."

Thea tried not to look too surprised, but she suspected that was a lie. She'd had a lot of conversations with Sonya, and never once had the surrogate brought up anything like that. If Sonya had, it would have been one of those red flags that Thea had been searching so hard to find.

What was equally surprising though was that Yvette didn't even deny it.

"Nick had a troubled childhood," Yvette said, still not looking at either Thea or Raleigh. She stared past them and into the yard. "He was hesitant about us having a baby because of all the money it would cost for a surrogate. And because of all the time I'd have to take off from the business to be a stay-at-home mom. But he finally agreed to it."

Maybe. And maybe Nick hadn't actually agreed the way that Yvette thought. It seemed extreme though to kill a surrogate so that he wouldn't have to be a father, especially since the baby had already been conceived. And born. Still, Thea would look into it, and she was certain Raleigh would, as well.

"Call your husband again," Raleigh told the woman. "I want him to come to the sheriff's office on Main Street in Durango Ridge in thirty minutes. I'll take Thea and you there now in the cruiser, and he can meet us."

Yvette started shaking her head again, and alarm

went through her eyes. "He had nothing to do with this, and it'll only upset him if you start interrogating him the way you did me."

Thea had watched that so-called interrogation, and Raleigh had handled the woman with kid gloves. He'd treated her like a distraught mother whose child had been stolen. She doubted Raleigh would show that same consideration to Nick. Because Nick apparently had a motive for this nightmare that'd just happened.

Raleigh checked the time and motioned for Yvette to make the call. The woman hesitated, but she finally went to the other end of the porch to do that. Too bad Yvette didn't put it on speaker, because Thea would have loved to hear Nick's response to Raleigh's order.

While Yvette was still on the phone, Raleigh turned back to Thea. "I'll need you to give me a statement, of course." He hesitated, too. "And you should be in protective custody."

He was right, but it riled her a little that he thought she couldn't take care of herself. After all, she was a cop, and she could point out to him that the thug hadn't murdered her when he or she had the chance. Still, she needed to take some precautions.

Once Yvette had finished her call, Thea stood, ready to go to the cruiser, but she stopped when she heard the approaching vehicle. Raleigh and Dalton must have heard it, too, because they automatically stepped in front of her and Yvette. Thea slid her hand over the gun that she'd borrowed from Raleigh. But it wasn't the threat they were all obviously bracing themselves for.

It was Warren.

He pulled his familiar black truck to a stop behind

the trio of cruisers and the other vehicles, and he got out and started for the house.

"What the hell is he doing here?" Raleigh asked, turning his glare back on Thea.

"I didn't call him," Thea said, but it would have been easy enough for Warren to hear about it. After all, most law enforcement agencies in the state had been alerted to the missing baby.

"Raleigh," Warren greeted. He obviously ignored the glare his son now had aimed at him, and he walked right past Raleigh to pull Thea into his arms.

It certainly wasn't the first time that Warren had hugged her. He'd always treated her like family and had practically raised her and her brother, Griff. But it felt awkward now in front of Raleigh—who hadn't gotten that same family treatment from the man.

"Are you okay?" Warren asked her when he pulled back from the hug.

His attention went to the stun gun marks on her neck, and it looked as if he had to bite back some profanity. When she'd been his deputy, he had always hated whenever she'd gotten hurt or been put in danger, and he still apparently felt that way. Thea appreciated the concern, especially since she'd never gotten any from her own parents, but it made the situation with Raleigh seem even more awkward.

"I'm fine," Thea assured him. She didn't especially want to bring this up, but Warren would soon learn it anyway. "Whoever did this also took the newborn, and he left a message on the wall—"

"Two messages," Raleigh corrected. "There was a second in Sonya's bedroom. They were both written in red paint and used identical wording to what was left at Hannah's place. 'This is for Sheriff Warren McCall.'"

"This man is Sheriff McCall?" Yvette asked. Warren nodded, and she went to him, catching on to his arms. "Who did this? Why would someone take my baby because of you?"

Warren's face tightened. "I don't know."

"But you must have some—" Yvette started, but Raleigh moved her away when her grip tightened on Warren.

"This is the missing baby's mother," Raleigh explained. "Yvette O'Hara."

Warren tipped the brim of his Stetson as a greeting. "I'm really sorry for what happened, but I honestly don't know who took your child." He turned to Raleigh. "Are you sure this is connected to Hannah, or is it a copycat?"

A muscle flickered in Raleigh's jaw. "Too early to tell. Do you have a reason for being here?" There definitely was nothing friendly about his tone.

Warren sighed. "Yes. I was worried about Thea and thought she might need a ride home because she's so shaken up."

"She will, but only after she's given her statement about the attack." Again, there was no friendliness from Raleigh. "I was about to take her to my office now. No reason that I know of for you to be there for that, but you can wait for her at the café across the street."

Warren would do that if he couldn't get Raleigh to relent and let him stay with her in the sheriff's office. And Raleigh wouldn't back down on this.

They started down the steps, and Thea didn't miss it when she saw Warren wince and slide his fingers over his chest. He quickly moved his hand away, but she knew he'd been touching the scar beneath his shirt. The scar he'd gotten from a gunshot wound six months ago.

The wound itself had healed, but the muscles there had been damaged enough that Warren would always have pain. Something he obviously didn't want to discuss because he shook his head when Thea opened her mouth to ask if he was okay. Maybe it was a guy thing not to want to admit that he was in pain, or maybe he just didn't want to talk about it in front of Raleigh.

"Ride in the cruiser with Raleigh," Warren whispered to her, and he made a lawman's glance around them. "There are a lot of places for a killer to lie in wait on the road that leads into Durango Ridge."

She nodded, but his reminder only gave her another jolt of adrenaline. So did the sound of her phone ringing. Not a reaction she wanted to have as a deputy. Nor was the reaction she had next.

Her stomach went to her knees when she looked at her phone screen.

"Unknown caller," she said.

That stopped Raleigh and Warren, and Yvette eventually stopped, too, when she realized they were no longer moving toward the cruiser.

It could be nothing, maybe even a telemarketer, but Raleigh must have realized it could be something important because he took out his own phone to record the call, and he motioned for her to answer it. She did, and unlike what Yvette had done earlier, Thea put it on speaker.

"I'm guessing you're looking for the kid," a man immediately said. Thea didn't recognize his voice, but it was possible that it was the same man who'd taken Sonya.

Yvette gasped, and Warren motioned for her to stay

quiet. Good move because it wouldn't do any good to have Yvette start yelling at this thug.

"Where's the baby?" Thea demanded. Of course, she wanted to ask the snake why he'd murdered Sonya, but right now, the baby had to come first. It was too late to save Sonya, but maybe they could still help the child.

"I'll give her to you. All you have to do is come and get her."

Thea looked at Raleigh to get his take on this. Like her, he was clearly skeptical, but at the moment, this was all they had. Maybe it was a matter of paying a ransom. If so, she figured they could scrape together whatever amount they needed to get the child safely away from a killer.

The conversation must have alerted Dalton because he came down the steps and into the yard with them.

"Where's the baby?" Thea repeated to the man.

"I'll text you the time and the place where you can get her. Oh, and I'll text you the rules, too. Don't forget those or you won't get the kid." He sounded arrogant, and Thea wished she could reach through the phone and make him pay for what he'd done.

She tamped down the anger so she could speak. "How do I know you actually have her? This could be a trap."

"Sweetcakes, if I'd wanted you dead, you already would be. You wouldn't have made it off that back porch of Sonya's house."

Since Thea had already realized that, she knew it was true. But there were plenty of other things that didn't make sense. "How do I know for certain that you have the newborn?" she pressed.

The man didn't answer. Not with words anyway. But Thea heard the sound in the background.

A baby crying.

Chapter 3

Raleigh cursed and snatched the phone from Thea. "Tell me the location of the baby now!" he demanded. But he was talking to the air, because the kidnapper had already ended the call.

"Oh, God." Yvette grabbed the phone, too, and she hit Redial.

No answer.

A hoarse sob tore from Yvette's mouth, and she would have likely fallen to the ground if Warren hadn't caught her. Raleigh didn't thank him for doing that because he didn't want the man anywhere around here. Raleigh had enough distractions with Thea and Yvette, and he didn't need to add his so-called father to the mix.

Raleigh turned to Dalton. "Take Yvette to the station. Call a doctor for her, too. She might need some meds to calm her down."

"The only thing I need is my baby!" Yvette shouted.

The woman tried Redial again, and she was gripping Thea's phone so hard that Raleigh thought she might break it. That wouldn't be good since it was obviously the way the kidnapper had chosen to communicate with them.

"She's a newborn," Yvette went on. "She has to be fed. Someone has to take care of her."

"And the men who have her will do that," Thea said. "They'll want to keep the baby safe and well. Remember, they took formula so she won't be hungry."

True, but that didn't mean a newborn was going to get expert care from the thugs who'd snatched her. That's why they had to find her ASAP.

Dalton gently took Yvette by the arm. "Once we get to the station," he told the woman, "I'll examine the call. I might be able to get a match on his voice, because Raleigh will send me the recording of the conversation."

Raleigh would do that, but he wasn't holding out any hope for a match. Or that the call would be traced for that matter. The kidnapper had almost certainly used a burner cell, a disposable one that couldn't be traced. Still, they'd try.

"What can I do?" Warren asked him.

"You can go home to your wife and family in McCall Canyon until I've got time to interrogate you. After all, it was your name on that wall, and there had to be a reason for it."

That was a knee-jerk reaction. One that Raleigh instantly regretted. Not because he hadn't meant it—he had. But it was the wrong time to vent.

Raleigh took a deep breath to steady himself. "My people have the scene secured," he added to Warren.

There was much less emotion in his voice now, which was a good thing. "Give me a couple of hours so I can deal with this kidnapper, and then I can question you."

Warren didn't balk at any part of that, but judging from his tight expression, something was on his mind. "What about Thea?" Warren asked.

Of course. Thea. Warren was worried about the woman he'd practically raised.

"I'll take Thea to the station so we can wait on this thug to call us back," Raleigh answered.

Warren stood there, his hands on his hips while he volleyed glances between them as if he was trying to figure out if that was the wise thing to do. The man didn't budge until Thea nodded.

"I'll be okay," she assured Warren.

"Call me if you need anything," Warren finally said, and he hugged her again. After he pulled away from her, he looked at Raleigh, maybe trying to figure out what to say to him, but he settled for another tip of his hat. This one was a farewell, and he headed to his truck.

Raleigh and Thea were right behind him, and the moment Raleigh had her in the cruiser, he started toward town. It wouldn't be a long drive, only about twenty minutes, but he could use that time to get some things straight.

"The kidnapper said there'd be rules," he reminded her. "That probably means a ransom demand with instructions for the payout so we can get the baby. You won't be involved in that. If I haven't worked out a protective custody arrangement by then, you can wait in my office."

She shook her head. "The kidnapper said I was to come and get her."

"That won't be happening." At least he hoped not anyway. Raleigh didn't want to involve Thea in this any more than she already was.

But obviously Thea wasn't giving up. "I'm the person best suited to make an exchange like that. The kidnapper said if he wanted me dead, he would have killed me on the porch. And he could have done just that."

Raleigh wasn't giving up, either. "Maybe because the person standing next to you was holding a baby, and he didn't want to risk hurting her. That could have been the sole reason he didn't kill you."

She opened her mouth as if she might disagree with that, but she must have realized it could be the truth because Thea huffed and leaned back against the seat.

"I'll get Yvette's husband in for questioning," Raleigh added a moment later. "Right now, he's a person of interest. He could have orchestrated all of this because he doesn't want to be a father."

Though it did seem extreme—unless he hadn't intended for Sonya to die. Maybe the thugs hadn't had orders to kill Sonya or anyone else who showed up. That would explain why they'd had a stun gun with them. It would also explain why the one that Thea had seen was wearing a ski mask. He didn't want his identity known because he hadn't intended to kill any witnesses.

That was the best-case scenario though. It was still possible that the goons wanted Thea dead.

"Warren is a person of interest, too?" she asked.

"Of course." Raleigh would love nothing more than to charge the man with something. Anything.

"And what about your mother?" Thea pressed. "Will you also question her?"

Raleigh's gaze slashed to her, and he nearly had another of those knee-jerk reactions. But he forced himself to see this through her cop's perspective. His mother, Alma, no longer loved Warren. In fact, she might actually hate him.

"Alma thought Warren was going to leave his wife to be with her," Thea continued when he didn't say anything. "That didn't happen, and when he broke off things with her six months ago—"

"Don't finish that," Raleigh warned her. "I know how upset my mother was, and I don't have to hear a recap from you."

Hell, she was still upset. Alma had carried on an affair with a married man, gotten pregnant and had basically lived her life waiting for the emotional scraps that Warren might toss her. Now that the secret was out, she was just seething in anger.

Raleigh hated to admit it, but he was seething, too. Because his mother had lied to him about his father. She'd lied all because she didn't want Warren's secret life exposed. Well, it was sure as hell exposed now.

"Did your mother know Sonya well?" Thea asked. It was a cop's kind of question, because Thea was again trying to link his mom to what was going on.

"Everyone in town knew Sonya," Raleigh snarled. But his mom had known Sonya better than most because Sonya had done some office work at his mother's ranch. "Don't worry. I'll question my mom," Raleigh added. "But there are plenty of other ways for her to get back at Warren. Ways that don't involve kidnapping a newborn baby and killing a surrogate."

It surprised him a little when Thea made a sound of agreement. After all, Warren's wife, Helen, had raised

Thea, too, and that meant Thea and the McCalls likely thought of his mother as the villain in all of this.

"There doesn't seem to be a connection between Warren and Sonya," Thea added. "If your mother was going to try to get back at him in some way, she would go after him or someone he cared about."

True. But his mother would only do that if she'd finally gone off the deep end. There were times when Raleigh thought she might be headed there, and he was doing his damnedest to make sure that didn't happen.

"I also want to talk to the doctor who did the in vitro procedures for both Hannah and Sonya," Raleigh continued, and he was about to ask Thea what she knew about the man, but her phone rang.

Unknown Caller.

Raleigh immediately pulled onto the shoulder of the road so he could again use his phone to record the conversation. Once he had it ready, Thea took the call. The first thing Raleigh heard was the baby crying again. It was like taking hard punches to the gut. It sickened him to think of these monsters having that little girl.

"All right, you ready to do this?" the kidnapper asked.

"We are," Raleigh answered, and he waited a moment to see if the guy would ask who he was. He didn't. Which meant the thug likely knew all the players in this. That wasn't much of a surprise since whoever was behind this had probably done their homework.

"Good. Because I'm gonna make this real easy. Transfer fifty thousand into the account number that I'm about to text to you."

In the grand scheme of things, fifty thousand wasn't much for a ransom demand, which made Raleigh instantly suspicious. Then again, maybe these guys just wanted some quick cash so they could make a getaway. After all, they were killers now, and if arrested, they'd be looking at the death penalty. Fifty would be more than enough to escape.

"If you do it right," the kidnapper went on, "it'll only take a couple of minutes at most for the money to show up. Then you can have the kid."

Raleigh huffed. "How do we know you even have the child? The crying we heard could be any baby. Or a recording. And if you do have her, what stops you from taking the money and running?"

"I figured you'd ask that. Well, I'm sending you a picture of the kid, and since Thea's using her cell for this call, I'll text it to your phone."

The guy didn't ask for Raleigh's number, and several moments later Raleigh's phone did indeed ding with a text message. Two of them, in fact. The first was the routing number for a bank account. Probably an offshore one that would be out of reach of law enforcement.

Raleigh went to the second text. A photo. It was indeed a baby wrapped in a blanket, and seeing her was like another punch. He reminded himself though that the picture could be fake. But this didn't feel like a ruse. Raleigh was certain these snakes had that little girl.

He showed the photo to Thea, and he saw the raw emotions go through her eyes. "Oh, God," she whispered, her voice mostly breath.

She obviously didn't think it was a ruse, either. And that led Raleigh back to his second issue with this ransom arrangement.

"I'll transfer twenty grand," Raleigh told the kidnapper. He could take that from his own personal checking account. "You'll get the rest when I actually see the baby. And Thea will have no part in the drop. It'll be between you and me."

Along with some backup deputies that Raleigh would have in place. The plan was to catch these idiots and make them pay for what they'd done. First though, he had to make sure the baby was safe.

The guy didn't say anything, and the silence went on for what seemed to be an eternity. "All right," the kidnapper finally answered. "Get that money to me in the next five minutes, and then I'll give you the location of the kid."

Before Raleigh could ask for any more time, the kidnapper ended the call. Raleigh didn't bother to hit Redial because it would just eat up precious time.

He had a quick debate with himself as to how to handle this, and the one thing he knew was that he didn't want Thea anywhere near this. That meant getting her to the station.

"Call the emergency dispatcher," Raleigh said as he used his own phone to access his bank account. "Have him connect you to Dalton. Tell him to gather up as many deputies as he can because I might need them. I also need Dalton to get the remaining thirty grand of the ransom money." If nothing went wrong with the first part of this plan, Raleigh wanted to be ready.

"I could do backup," Thea insisted. "I still have your gun, and I'm not woozy anymore from the stun gun."

Raleigh dismissed that with a headshake and motioned for her to make the call. She did, and he continued with his own task.

It took several moments for him to get access to his account, several more for Raleigh to put in the number the kidnapper had given him. The transfer went through without any hitches.

He had more money in investment accounts, but he doubted those would be as easy to tap into. That's why he'd wanted Dalton to come up with the rest. That would involve getting some help from fellow law enforcement, maybe even the DA. Somehow though, they'd come up with that money.

"Dalton said to tell you that he'll get to work right away on all of that," Thea relayed to him the moment she finished her call. She also took his phone and had another look at the photo the kidnapper had sent. "I'm just trying to figure out if there's any resemblance between the baby and Yvette."

"And?" He started driving again so he could get Thea to the station. They were still ten minutes out, so Raleigh sped up. After everything that'd happened, he didn't want to be on this rural stretch of road any longer than necessary.

"I can't tell. You think we should send it to Yvette to see if she recognizes any features? The baby could resemble her husband since it was Yvette's and his fertilized embryo that was implanted in Sonya."

He had another short debate about that and dismissed it. The woman had been so frantic that this might push her over the edge. Raleigh wanted her to stay put with Dalton at least until he could get there.

"Egan would send backup if you need it," Thea reminded him.

She probably hadn't suggested that to rile him. After all, *Egan* was Sheriff Egan McCall of McCall Canyon. Along with being Thea's boss, he was Raleigh's half brother and Warren's son. Raleigh wasn't so stubborn that he would refuse help and therefore put the baby at even greater risk, but he didn't think he would have to rely on McCall help just yet.

Only a short distance ahead, Raleigh spotted a dark blue SUV. It wasn't on the road but had pulled off onto one of the ranch trails. A trail with a lot of trees and wild shrubs. Normally, seeing a vehicle parked there wouldn't have alarmed him. After all, there was pasture land out here for sale, and this could be a potential buyer. But this day was far from normal.

"You recognize the SUV?" Thea asked. She drew her gun, which meant this had put her on edge, too.

"No." And it was parked in such a way that he couldn't see the license plates.

Raleigh considered just speeding up, and once he passed the vehicle, he could get the plates and call them in. But he saw something else. Something on the ground next to the passenger's side door.

"Is that what I think it is?" Thea muttered. "It looks like a baby carrier."

It did. Raleigh had already had a bad feeling about this, and that feeling went up a significant notch when the SUV came flying off the trail and onto the road just ahead of Thea and him. The driver sped away, heading in the direction of town.

Raleigh hit his brakes and slowed so he could have a better look. At first, he thought the carrier was empty, that this was some kind of trick. But then he saw the baby's tiny hand moving away. He heard the cries, too.

His phone dinged with another text. Since Thea still had hold of it, she read it to him. "Change of plans. The kid is all yours. Thanks for the twenty grand."

Raleigh wanted to know what had happened to make

them flee like that. He also wanted to go in pursuit, but that would mean leaving the baby out here.

"Call Dalton back," he told Thea. "Let him know what's happening. I want that SUV stopped."

While she did that, Raleigh drew his gun and got out. He fired glances all around them but didn't see anyone. However, the baby's cries seemed to be even more frantic now. She could be hungry or scared.

Still keeping watch, Raleigh went closer, and he prayed this wasn't some elaborate dummy. It wasn't. The baby was real. And there was what appeared to be a note on the blanket that was loosely draped over her.

Raleigh went to her, stooping down, and he touched her cheek, hoping to soothe her. It didn't work. She kept crying, and he was about to pick her up when he saw what was written on the note.

He read the note out loud, so Thea could hear. "'Warren's going to be so sad when he finds out she's dead.'"

Raleigh shook his head, not understanding what it meant. Who was the *she*? Certainly not the baby because she was very much alive. It hit him then. Another she, and this one was definitely connected to Warren. He whipped back around, his attention going to the cruiser.

What he saw caused his heart to go to his knees.

Because there was a guy wearing a ski mask, and he had a gun pointed right at Thea's head.

Chapter 4

Thea was certain that Raleigh was cursing her as he was diving for cover with the baby. She was cursing herself for letting this snake get the drop on her and knocking the gun from her hand. Yes, she was still wobbly from the other attack, but that was no excuse. She was a cop, and she shouldn't have let this happen.

Especially because it could end up getting Raleigh and the baby hurt.

Raleigh was obviously trying to prevent that from happening because he dropped down into the shallow ditch with the baby. It wouldn't be much protection if shots were fired, but it was better than being out in the open. And much better than having the baby in the hands of this thug.

She had no idea who was holding her at gunpoint, but one thing was for certain—if he'd wanted her dead, she already would be. Instead of grabbing her when she stepped from the truck, he could have just put a bullet in her head and then escaped. Raleigh would have had a hard time going after him with a baby in tow.

So, what did the thug want?

Thea prayed that whatever it was, the baby wouldn't be put in any more danger. The newborn had already been through enough.

"Why are you doing this?" Thea managed to ask.

It was hard for her to talk though because he had her in a choke hold, and the barrel of the gun was digging so hard against her skin that she'd probably have a fresh cut to go along with the one she'd gotten when she fell on Sonya's porch after being hit with the stun gun.

Was this the same attacker?

She didn't know, and even if she got a chance to see his face beneath that ski mask, she still probably wouldn't recognize him.

And that only left her with another question. Where was his partner? He had almost certainly been the one to drive away in the SUV—probably after this thug had gotten out and hidden in a ditch to wait for them. But the partner would come back. No doubt soon. That meant Raleigh and she didn't have much time.

"Let her go," Raleigh called out, though he certainly knew that wasn't going to stop this thug. However, he had positioned himself in front of the baby, and he had his gun ready.

Not that he had a shot.

The guy behind her was hunched down just enough that Raleigh wouldn't be able to shoot him. She certainly wouldn't be able to do that, either, not with the backup weapon that Raleigh had given her on the ground. She was only about five feet away from where it had fallen when the guy bashed his own weapon against her hand to send the gun flying. But despite it being that close, there wasn't much of a chance she could get to it without getting shot. Still, she would have to go for it if he tried to hurt the baby. First though, Thea wanted to know what the heck was going on.

"Did you bring the baby here?" she demanded, and she hoped she sounded a lot stronger than she actually felt. Thea was scared. Not for herself but for the baby.

"Nope. It wasn't me. But this is how this is going to work," the guy said in a voice plenty loud enough for Raleigh to hear. "First you're gonna use your phone to transfer the rest of the money. All thirty grand of it. Then, you're gonna bring the kid to me."

Raleigh cursed. "Why the hell would I do that?"

"Because if you don't, I'm gonna shoot this pretty lady here. Warren's going to be so sad if that happens."

It was similar wording to what had been in the note, but Thea didn't take either it or this snake's threat at face value. He could be lying so he could connect Warren to this. Of course, Thea didn't know why he would do that, but it was still a possibility. None of this had felt right from the beginning.

"Did Nick O'Hara hire you to do this?" she snapped. "Is that why you want the baby?"

The thug didn't answer, but she thought maybe he tensed more than he already was. Hard to tell though because he was wired and practically fidgeting. Definitely not someone she wanted with his finger on the trigger.

"Transfer the money now!" he shouted to Raleigh.

Raleigh had his famous glare aimed at the thug, but she also saw him do something with his phone. Even though there hadn't been a lot of time to do it, maybe Raleigh's deputy had managed to get the money. If not, perhaps she could bargain with her captor to let her call Warren for the funds. That could also buy her some time so she could figure out what to do.

"Once you have me and the money," she said to the guy, "there's no reason for you to have the baby, too. She's a newborn, and she needs to be at the hospital."

"What the kid needs is for the sheriff to cooperate," he snarled. She felt him fumbling around and realized he was checking his phone. No doubt looking to see if the transfer had been made.

Raleigh lifted his head enough for Thea to make eye contact with him, and for a moment she thought he was going to say he hadn't been able to get the money. But the thug made a sound of approval.

"Good job," he told Raleigh. "I knew you'd come through for me."

Thea didn't breathe easier, because she figured what was coming next, and she didn't have to wait long for it.

"Now the kid," the guy said. "Me and Thea are going to walk closer to you to get her. That means you toss out your gun and keep your hands where I can see them."

"So you can kill me? I don't think so. Tell me, why didn't you just take the baby and run?"

"Oh, I will be doing that." He chuckled and started walking with her. "First though, I had to fix a screwup."

Thea wasn't sure if he meant her or not. Maybe his partner and he thought she could ID them. She couldn't. But since a murder charge was on the table, they might not want to risk it. Or it could be something more than that. They could want to use her to get to Warren.

Or make it look as if they were using her for that.

She heard the sound of a car engine, and moments later the blue SUV came into view. It was creeping toward them, the driver probably looking to make sure his partner had what they'd come for—the baby and her. And in a few more seconds, that might happen if she didn't do something.

Raleigh still didn't have a shot, but since he still hadn't tossed out his gun, there was a chance that her captor would shift his position enough for Raleigh to take him out.

"Are you deaf?" the man shouted to Raleigh. "I told you to drop the gun."

There was no way Thea could let that happen, not with the SUV getting closer and closer. Right now the thug holding her was outnumbered, but that wouldn't be true once his partner arrived onto the scene.

She looked at Raleigh again, hoping that he was ready for what she was about to do. If not, it could get them both killed.

Thea dragged in a deep breath, and just as the thug pushed her forward another step, she rammed her elbow into his stomach. In the same motion, she dropped down her weight. She didn't get far though because he still had her in a choke hold.

But she did something about that, too.

Thea twisted her body, ramming him again with her elbow until he loosened his grip enough for her to drop down low enough to give Raleigh a chance at a shot. She prayed it was one he would take.

And he did.

Raleigh already had his gun lifted, and the bullets blasted through the air. One shot, quickly followed by another.

Time seemed to stop. Thea thought maybe her heart had, as well. She could only wait to see what had happened, and several long moments later, the thug's grip on her melted away as he collapsed to the ground. She glanced back at him and saw the blood and his blank, already lifeless eyes. Raleigh's shot had killed him.

"Get down!" Raleigh shouted to her.

Thea scrambled away from the thug, snatching up the gun as she ran, and she dropped down into the ditch. It wasn't a second too soon. Because more shots came. Not from Raleigh this time but from the person who was in the SUV.

The bullets slammed into the surface of the road, just inches from where she was. That told her that she was the target since the shooter didn't try to take out Raleigh even though he also had a gun. But what she still didn't know was why this attack was even happening.

The gunman fired two more shots, both of them slamming into the dirt bank of the ditch just above her head. If he changed the angle just a little or got closer, he'd have a much easier time killing her. However, as bad of a thought as that was, at least this snake wasn't shooting in the direction of the baby.

Thea waited for a lull in the shooting, and she lifted her head enough to take aim at the shooter. He was wearing a ski mask and was leaning out of the driver's-side window. She fired right at him.

So did Raleigh.

She wasn't sure which of their bullets hit the windshield, but one slammed into the glass. It also sent the shooter ducking back into the SUV. Almost immediately, he threw the SUV into Reverse and hit the accelerator.

He was getting away.

Thea definitely didn't want that, because they needed him to get answers. She came out of the ditch, aiming at the tires, and she fired. The SUV was already moving too fast though, and before she could even take a second shot, it was already out of sight.

Raleigh stood in the doorway of the ER examination room while he waited for his deputy Dalton to come back on the line. If they got lucky, then maybe Dalton would tell him that the driver of that SUV had been caught and was ready for interrogation.

Because Raleigh very much wanted to question him.

Then he'd arrest him for not only murder and kidnapping, but also for the attempted murder of two law enforcement officers, as well.

Thea looked up at him, no doubt checking to see if he knew anything yet, but Raleigh just shook his head. He also kept watch in the hall and ER to make sure a gunman didn't come rushing in to try to finish what he'd started.

There was a lot to distract Raleigh though, and he knew he had to be mindful of that. Thea was holding the baby while Dr. Halvorson, the pediatrician, finished up his exam. An exam that Raleigh hoped would let them know that the baby was all right. It would be somewhat of a miracle if she was, considering the ordeal she'd been through. At least she was too young to know what was going on, but maybe she could still sense the stress.

And there was plenty of that.

Thea's face was etched with worry, and Raleigh was certain his was, too. Because as long as the shooter was at large, then they were probably still in danger. It was too much to hope that the shooter would have fled and had no plans to return.

The doctor pushed his rolling chair away from Thea and the baby, and he stood. Raleigh turned so he could see the doctor but also keep watch.

"She seems to be just fine," Dr. Halvorson said, causing Raleigh to release a breath of relief. "Of course, I'll still run tests to make sure nothing shows up."

The tests would include a blood sample that a nurse had taken from the heel of the baby's foot. The newborn had definitely made a fuss about that, and Raleigh didn't intend to admit that it'd put a knot in his stomach. But when Thea had given her the bottle that the hospital had provided, the little girl had drifted off to sleep.

Thea had had to collect the baby's clothes and diaper. Since the items could have fibers and such on them, they'd been sent to the crime lab, along with the infant carrier. Thankfully, the hospital had had newborn gowns, fresh diapers and a blanket.

"I'm guessing it'll be a problem if we admit her to the hospital?" the doctor asked.

Raleigh had to think about that for a second. "It would, but if she needs to be here, we'll make it work."

The doctor shook his head. "I don't see a reason to admit her other than for observation. She's a healthy weight—seven pounds, four ounces. No breathing issues or signs of injury."

That was somewhat of a miracle. Too bad Sonya hadn't gotten a miracle of her own.

"Are there any indications that the baby was born from a forced labor?" Raleigh asked the doctor. "Like maybe some kind of drug?"

"I doubt we'd be able to tell that from the newborn, but something like that might be in Sonya's body."

The doctor's voice cracked a little on the last word. That was because he knew Sonya. Most people in Durango Ridge did. And it was hard to lose one of their own. Especially to murder.

"Raleigh, you still there?" Dalton asked when he came back on.

"Yeah." And he stepped out into the hall. He didn't put the call on speaker, because he didn't want anyone who happened to walk by to hear any grisly details. That meant he'd have to fill Thea in on whatever he learned.

"The other deputies didn't catch the guy," Dalton said, sounding as frustrated as Raleigh felt. "The APB is out on the blue SUV, so someone might spot it and call it in."

That could happen, but it was beyond a long shot. There hadn't been any plates on the SUV, so they couldn't try to trace the vehicle. And by now, the driver could have either ditched it or else put on some plates so that it wouldn't draw any attention from law enforcement.

"What about Nick and Yvette O'Hara?" Raleigh asked. "Are they still at the station?"

"She is. I've got her in an interview room, and she's pitching a fit to leave to go to the hospital and see the baby. I told her she shouldn't be out and about, not with the killer at large, but she's insisting."

Raleigh couldn't blame her. All indications were that this was Yvette's daughter, and she was acting the way a distraught mother would. Her husband though was a different story. "See if you can find someone to escort her here." The hospital was only a couple of minutes from the station, so maybe there wouldn't be enough time for a killer to take shots at her. "And get Nick in for questioning ASAP."

Though he figured Dalton already had a list of things that fell into that *as soon as possible* category.

"Will do. We ran the prints on the dead guy, and we got an ID," Dalton went on a moment later. "His name was Marco Slater. Ring any bells?"

Raleigh mentally repeated it a couple of times and came up blank. "No. Should it?"

"According to Slater's record, Warren McCall arrested him for an outstanding warrant on a parole violation. That happened shortly before Warren retired when Slater was driving through McCall Canyon. Warren apparently recognized him from his mug shots."

Now, that was luck. Well, unless Slater had been on parole because of a crime he'd committed in or around Warren's town. Either way, Slater could have a grudge against Warren, and that could be motive for what had gone on today.

"Text me a copy of Slater's record," he instructed Dalton. "Was there anything on the body to tell us why he went after Thea and the baby?"

"Nothing. The guy wasn't even carrying a wallet, and other than extra ammo and a burner cell, there wasn't anything in his pockets."

So he was probably a hired gun, but maybe the lab would be able to get something from the phone. "Anything new from the ME on Sonya?"

"Not yet, but he said he would call as soon as he had something."

Raleigh needed the info, especially if there was any fiber or trace evidence on the body that could lead them to the driver of that SUV. Or the person who'd put the dead guy up to kidnapping the baby and killing Sonya. The driver could be the boss or just another hired gun.

"How's the kid?" Dalton asked. "And where will you be taking her?"

"She's fine." But Raleigh didn't have an answer for the second question. Since she could still be a target, she would need to be in protective custody. Ditto for Thea and maybe even Yvette. "I'll get back to you on the details," Raleigh added before he ended the call.

He put his phone away and stepped back into the doorway. Of course, Thea's attention went right to him. "The gunman got away."

"For now." He hoped like the devil that would change soon.

"I need to check on another patient," the doctor said. Maybe he sensed that Raleigh needed to talk business with Thea. "Let me know what your plans are for the baby."

He would—as soon as he figured it out.

"You look as if you've had a lot of experience with kids," Raleigh said to Thea while the doctor was clearing out.

"Several of my friends have babies." With the newborn cradled in her arms, she brushed a kiss on the baby's head but kept her attention on Raleigh. Since she was a cop, she obviously knew he'd been discussing the specifics of the case, and there were a couple of the specifics that he wanted to go over with her.

"Marco Slater is the dead guy who tried to kill us. You know him?" he asked.

Raleigh saw the instant recognition in her eyes. "Marco Slater," she repeated. "He had a run-in with

Warren years ago. He was supposed to be serving a ten-year sentence."

Well, the guy had apparently gotten an early release. Raleigh would find out more about that when he had Marco's records. "Did Marco hate Warren enough to put together a scheme that involves murder?"

She shook her head. "I remember Marco resisting arrest, and he took a swing at Warren. That's why he ended up with some extra jail time. I don't remember Marco vowing to get revenge though."

Maybe the man hadn't said it, but that didn't mean he hadn't attempted it. It could tie everything up in a neat little package, and Raleigh might not have to investigate anyone else who could have a grudge against Warren.

Like Raleigh's mother.

"There's more," Raleigh went on. "The CSIs are going through Sonya's house, and they found a tape recorder. Apparently, she was recording her calls. Did she happen to mention anything about that?"

"No," Thea answered without hesitation. She paused though. "She did say she'd had a bad relationship a couple of years ago. Maybe the old boyfriend was harassing her or something."

Now it was Raleigh's turn to say, "No. She did have a relationship, and it didn't end especially well, but I know the guy, and he's moved on. He's married, and they've got a baby." Though it was an angle he would check just in case. "I've got one of my deputies skimming through the recording just to see if anything stands out. If not, then I'll go over them more closely tonight."

At least he would do that if he wasn't still dealing with the O'Haras and a kidnapper.

Thea looked up at him again. "I know you're anxious to put some distance between us," she said. "But I'd rather work on this investigation than be tucked away at a safe house, in protective custody."

Yes, he was ready for them not to be under the same roof, but Thea probably believed that was because of the bad blood between them. And there was indeed some of that. But the attraction was stirring again, and Raleigh definitely didn't have time to deal with it. However, he seriously doubted that this would be a situation of out of sight, out of mind. No, now that she'd come back into his life, it wouldn't be easy to forget what they'd once had together.

She kept staring at him, obviously waiting for him to agree or disagree about the safe house. But Raleigh didn't get a chance to say anything, because he heard hurried footsteps.

Someone was running toward them.

Raleigh automatically drew his gun, but the person rushing to the room wasn't armed. It was Yvette, and she was ahead of one of his deputies, Alice Rowe, who was trying to keep up with her. Alice had no doubt escorted the woman there.

"Where is she?" Yvette asked the moment she spotted Raleigh. "Is she all right? I need to see her."

"The baby's fine," Raleigh assured her, and he stepped back so that Yvette could come in.

Yvette didn't take him at his word. No good mother probably would have. She went straight to Thea. Thea glanced at Raleigh, probably to make sure it was okay for her to hand over the baby, and Raleigh nodded. He wouldn't allow Yvette to take the newborn from the room, but he could see no harm in Yvette holding her. Thea eased the baby into Yvette's waiting arms.

Much as Thea had done on the ride to the hospital, Yvette pulled open the blanket and checked the baby. The little girl opened her eyes and looked out for a moment before she went back to sleep.

"Oh, she's perfect," Yvette said, and tears filled her eyes. She ran her fingers over the baby's dark brown hair. "Please tell me those kidnappers didn't hurt her."

"They didn't," Raleigh assured her, and he was about to fill her in on what the doctor had said, but he heard Alice in the hall.

"Stop right there," Alice warned someone.

That sent Raleigh hurrying to see what had caused his deputy to say that, and he soon spotted the bulky, sandy-haired man trying to push his way past the deputy. "I'm Nick O'Hara," the man snarled. "I know my wife is here because I saw her come into the building. Where is she?"

"That's my husband," Yvette said on a rise of breath. She would have stepped out into the hall if Raleigh hadn't moved in front of her. "Stay put. One of the kidnappers is still at large, and he could come here."

That put a huge amount of concern in Yvette's eyes. She gave a shaky nod and stayed where she was. Raleigh stepped outside, his gaze connecting first with Nick and then with Alice. "Frisk him," he told Alice.

That earned him a glare from Nick, but Raleigh didn't care. Yvette had been checked for weapons when she'd been taken to the sheriff's office, and Raleigh wanted the same to happen to Nick.

"He's clean," Alice relayed when she'd finished patting him down, and she let go of the man so he could come into the room. Nick's glare was still razor-sharp when he looked at Raleigh and Thea. And the look continued when he turned to his wife.

"Nick," Yvette said, smiling. "It's our daughter. She's safe."

The man went closer, peering down at the baby's face, and he shook his head. "That's not our kid." He snapped back toward Raleigh. "I don't know what kind of game you're playing, but it won't work. You can't pass that kid off as mine."

Raleigh glanced at Yvette to see if she had a clue what her husband was talking about, but she seemed just as confused as Raleigh. Thea, too, because she huffed.

"What are you talking about?" Thea asked.

"This," Nick snarled, and he whipped his phone from his pocket. He lifted it so they could see the picture of a baby on the screen. It was a blonde-haired newborn wrapped in a pink blanket.

Yvette shook her head. "Who is that? Why do you have that picture?"

"Because someone texted it to me about ten minutes ago. Probably the same person who called me from an unknown number a few seconds later and demanded a quarter-of-a-million-dollar ransom."

"A ransom?" Yvette repeated. "Why?"

Nick tipped his head to the baby in her arms. "Because that's not our kid." He took the little girl from his wife and handed her back to Thea. "The kidnappers still have our baby, and we need to find her now."

Chapter 5

Thea had been so sure that Raleigh and she would have answers by the time they left the hospital, but that hadn't happened. And to make matters worse, they had to deal with the possibility that the O'Hara newborn was still out there.

In the hands of kidnappers.

But if that was true, then whose baby was in Thea's arms?

Thea was hoping they'd learn that now that they were at the sheriff's office. Yvette clearly wanted to know the same thing, and for the past hour since they'd left the hospital, she'd kept eyeing the child as if she might snatch her back from Thea. Since Yvette had been giving her that same look from the moment her husband had delivered that bombshell, Thea doubted the woman would try to take the baby and run. Still, she was keeping watch just in case. Yvette definitely looked ready to come unglued.

Thankfully, the baby was staying calm. Now that she'd been fed and changed anyway. Thea had done that as well, figuring that she was perhaps the only person in the building who'd actually had any experience doing it. Plus, she wanted to do it. It felt safer having the baby next to her.

"If the kidnappers really had our daughter, they would have called back by now," Yvette muttered.

That wasn't the first time she'd said something similar, and like the other times, her husband ignored her. Instead, Nick kept his attention on Dalton, who was setting up a recording device in the squad room. A recorder that would be used when and if the kidnappers called back. Before that, Nick had been on the phone, working out arrangements for a loan from Yvette's grandfather. The grandfather had agreed, though the man was apparently too frail to come to Durango Ridge to give his granddaughter some emotional support.

Something that Yvette seemed to definitely need.

Thea knew how she felt. She was still on edge from the attack and Sonya's murder, but she had to tamp down her nerves and focus on the investigation. Just as Raleigh was doing. He had his phone sandwiched between his shoulder and ear as he spoke to someone at the lab. While he was doing that, he was also checking something on his computer.

Thea wanted to help, but Raleigh had already made it crystal clear that she was not to let the baby out of her sight, or arms. He'd been insistent, too, that she stay away from the windows in case their attacker returned. Thea had had no problem with that, but it was the reason that she—and therefore Yvette and Nick—had ended up in Raleigh's office.

Soon though—very soon—they'd need to figure out if this second ransom demand was some kind of hoax. The baby in the photo Nick had shown them could be anyone's child, and this could be an attempt to milk the O'Hara's out of all that money. If so, it might work, too, since it was obvious that Nick and Yvette were planning on paying the demand.

When Raleigh finished his latest call, he brought his laptop to where Thea was seated, and he sank down in the chair next to her. "I had to have Alice call social services to tell them about the baby," he said, looking down at the newborn. "They're on the way here to take her."

That hit her a lot harder than Thea had expected, though Raleigh was right. There had been no choice about contacting them.

"What?" Yvette questioned. "You can't let them take her. Not until we're sure she's not ours."

"It's the law," Raleigh explained, "now that the baby's identity is in question."

Yvette shook her head and moved as if to take the baby, but her husband stepped in front of her. "This child has parents out there," he said. "Parents who are probably looking for her."

That was true, but there were no other missing baby reports. As a cop, that made Thea think the worst because if there was indeed a second baby, then the kidnappers could have murdered the parents when they took the child.

"But she could stay here with us until we sort it all out," Yvette argued. "And what about her safety? Can they protect her?"

"They know there's potential danger and will bring in the marshals." Raleigh paused, groaned softly. "It's out of my hands."

Apparently, it had hit Raleigh hard, too. But a police station was no place for a newborn. Especially when they had no idea if she was even a target.

More tears sprang into Yvette's eyes. Obviously, she didn't want this baby out of her sight, but she quit arguing and sank back down into the chair.

"The courier arrived at the lab with the DNA swabs," Raleigh added a moment later. "It'll be a day or two though before we have the DNA results on the baby."

That wasn't a surprise, though Thea wished they could have them sooner. Yvette probably felt the same way. Maybe even Nick, too, since he hadn't protested about giving a sample of his DNA, even though he seemed pretty certain that this little girl wasn't his child.

Once Yvette had her attention back on her husband, Raleigh shifted the laptop so Thea could see the screen, and she immediately saw Marco's records. "He did get an early release," Raleigh pointed out. "He's been out nearly a month now."

Plenty of time to plan the attacks, the kidnapping and even Sonya's murder. But had he done that? Marco certainly had a criminal history. Four arrests for breaking and entering, robbery and even assault. Those were serious enough charges, considering they showed a pattern of illegal behavior, but nothing on the rap sheet jumped out that this man could be a killer.

Of course, maybe Sonya's murder hadn't been planned. Heck, maybe Marco hadn't even had a part in that if it had been premeditated. Everything was in question now because of the second ransom demand.

"Did Marco have the funds to put together something like this?" she asked.

Raleigh lifted his shoulder and set his laptop aside. "If he did, he had it stashed away somewhere, maybe even under an alias. But it wouldn't have taken that much cash—not really. The SUV could have been a rental— Alice is checking on that now. And the driver could have been one of Marco's cronies who was working for a share of the first ransom."

A ransom that he didn't get because the FBI had managed to freeze the account where Raleigh had transferred the money. That was good that he wouldn't be out any cash.

"Dr. Bryce Sheridan is coming in first thing tomorrow morning," Raleigh went on. "I spoke to him briefly, and he claims he only did Sonya and Hannah's in vitro procedures, that he had no contact with either of the women once they were pregnant."

Thea thought about that a moment. "But you're bringing him in anyway?"

"This is a murder investigation. We're in *leave no stone unturned* territory." He paused. "That's why my mother is coming in tomorrow, as well. Sonya worked for her for a while. You didn't know?" he asked, no doubt when he saw the surprise in her eyes.

Thea shook her head. "Sonya didn't mention it."

"It was a few years ago. I'm not sure exactly why Sonya quit or even if she was fired, but those are questions I need to ask my mother."

Apparently, he didn't want to do that unofficially, either, because it could make it seem as if he was giving her preferential treatment.

Nick's phone rang, the sound immediately getting everyone's attention. Raleigh and Yvette stood, and Dalton put his finger on the record button. But Nick shook his head when he glanced at the screen.

"Sorry, it's a business associate," Nick grumbled, and he let the call go to voice mail as he turned toward Raleigh. "Is this normal for the kidnappers to wait so long before calling back?"

Raleigh shrugged. "They could be doing this to put you even more on edge. Their logic could be the more frantic and desperate you are, the more you'll cooperate."

Thea hoped that was what was going on, but this didn't feel right. The O'Haras could pay the ransom only to discover the newborn with them was their child after all.

There were sounds of voices in the squad room, and Raleigh stepped in front of Thea and the baby. Protecting them again. But Thea realized this wasn't a threat when she recognized one of the voices. Her brother, Texas Ranger Griff Morris.

Thea got up and went to the door to look out, and she immediately spotted not only Griff but another familiar face. Rachel McCall Morris. Rachel wasn't only Griff's wife though.

She was also Warren's daughter and Raleigh's half sister.

There was a marshal standing behind her, and Thea made the connection then. Rachel was a social worker, and she'd come here to take the baby.

"Raleigh," Griff greeted.

They'd met when Thea and Raleigh were dating, but Thea wasn't sure if Raleigh knew Rachel or not. Apparently, he did because he pulled back his shoulders and looked past Griff to stare at her.

The family resemblance was definitely there between the two, and Thea figured if there was anyone in the McCall family who could start mending the rift, it was Rachel. She looked like his kid sister. Plus, she was four months pregnant.

"I volunteered to do this," Rachel said, walking closer. She kept her eyes locked with Raleigh, too.

Even though Rachel and she were close friends, Thea could only guess what was going on in Rachel's mind. Part of her probably resented Raleigh because he was proof of Warren's affair, but then Rachel wasn't exactly on friendly terms with her father after news of that affair had ripped their family apart.

Rachel went to her, tearing her gaze from Raleigh so she could look at the baby. "Are you okay?" Rachel whispered to Thea, and she gave her a gentle hug.

"I've had better days," Thea whispered back.

Griff came to the doorway of the crowded office, and he took in everything with a sweeping glance before his attention settled on her. He didn't hug her, but Thea could see the concern in his eyes. Followed by the relief that she was okay.

"Anything from the kidnappers yet?" Griff asked.

She shook her head and gently transferred the baby to Rachel's arms. Yvette was right there, watching their every move. And still crying.

"Can't you just wait with her here?" Yvette asked. "We might know something soon."

Soon was being optimistic. Rachel and the rest of them knew that. "We'll take good care of her, I promise. She'll be under guard from Marshal McKinney and a Texas Ranger."

Yvette wiped some tears from her cheek. "Where will you take her?"

Rachel looked at Griff to answer that. "To a safe house. And no, I won't be able to tell you the location," he added before Yvette could ask. "We'll keep Sheriff Lawton informed though, and if anything develops, I'm sure he'll pass it on to you."

It wasn't much of a surprise that Yvette didn't seem pleased about that, either, and Raleigh must have decided it was best not to have the woman around when Rachel and the others actually left with the baby.

"Go ahead and take the O'Haras and the recorder to the break room," Raleigh instructed Dalton. "Have the diner bring them over something to eat, too."

Of course, Yvette protested that, saying she didn't want to leave and that she wasn't hungry, but her husband put his arm around her waist to get her moving. Yvette kissed the little girl, but her husband barely spared the baby a glance before Dalton led them away.

"I'm guessing Nick O'Hara thinks there's no chance that this baby is the one their surrogate delivered?" Griff asked Raleigh.

"It appears that way." Raleigh kept his hard stare on Nick until he was out of sight. "Either that or he's a jerk. I'm not sure which yet. Yvette admitted that he was having second thoughts about fatherhood."

That caused Griff to mumble some profanity.

Rachel adjusted the baby's blanket while she stepped closer to her brother. She opened her mouth and then closed it as if she'd changed her mind about what to say. "I'm glad Thea and you weren't hurt," Rachel finally said.

Raleigh nodded. Stared at her. Then he huffed. "Thanks for coming."

Even though the conversation was only a handful of words, it seemed to have set some kind of truce in motion. One that Thea was thankful for. It was a start, but she wasn't under any illusions that this would repair what she'd once had with Raleigh. No. Rachel hadn't known about her father's affair until it had come to light after his shooting. But Thea had known. And she'd kept it a secret. That was something Raleigh might never be able to get past.

When Rachel moved to the side, Griff came closer to Thea, giving her a once-over. The kind of look that only a big brother could manage. He respected her wishes to be a cop, but that didn't mean he didn't worry about her.

"You'll make sure she's okay?" Griff said to Raleigh.

Thea huffed and tapped her badge.

Griff huffed and motioned toward the stun gun marks on her neck.

She wanted to remind him that there were times when he'd been hurt, too, in the line of duty, but she didn't want to get into an argument with her hardheaded brother. Instead, she hugged him and gave the baby a goodbye kiss on the cheek.

Rachel turned to go but then stopped and looked at Raleigh again. "Maybe when this is over, we can meet for lunch or something. And yes, I know you don't like or trust us," she added before Raleigh could speak. "But I'm just as upset about what our father did as you are."

"Does that mean we're on the same side?" Raleigh asked, and it had some sarcasm in it. Some of the old wounds, too.

"Yes," Rachel said without hesitation. "And even if

we weren't, we're still kin." She smiled and followed Griff out of the room.

"I don't need a family. Or siblings," Raleigh grumbled.

He didn't, but he had them whether he wanted them or not. Besides, one of those siblings might be able to help them with this investigation.

"Egan has the old case files on Hannah's murder," Thea reminded Raleigh. "If Sonya's murder is connected to hers, then it might not hurt to go through everything again." She paused, waiting for him to answer, but when he didn't say anything, she added, "I can ask Egan to send a copy here."

"No." That time Raleigh didn't hesitate. "I'll ask him myself. But you've read everything in Hannah's file. Other than using the same doctor, do they have anything concrete in common?"

Obviously, he was putting aside the nearly identical threats left at Sonya's and Hannah's crime scenes. The threat that mentioned Warren. Thea wanted to put it aside, too, for now anyway, since the latest one could be a ploy to throw them off track.

"No," she answered. "But maybe Dr. Bryce Sheridan is behind this. Maybe there was something illegal going on at the fertility clinic, and he wanted to cover it up?"

Raleigh made a sound of agreement so quickly that he'd obviously already considered that. "But the murders happened a year apart. That's a long time for Dr. Sheridan to wait to cover up something. Unless, of course, he's committed several different crimes." He tipped his head toward the break room. "Right now though, Nick's high up on my list of persons of interest."

She agreed. The man certainly seemed to be anxious

to hear from the kidnappers, but it also felt like there was an emotional disconnect. He could be that way though because his marriage was falling apart over his wife's insistence on having a child.

Raleigh dragged in a long breath. "I need to get back to Marco's rap sheet, and then I can make arrangements for a place for you to stay. Unless you want me to take you to the McCall Ranch."

"No." She didn't have to even think about that. "If the gunman that was in the SUV comes after me again, I don't want him to follow me to the ranch. Warren's still recovering from his injuries, and he could get killed trying to protect me."

She wanted to kick herself for putting it that way. It had to be a reminder that Warren had never done anything for Raleigh other than keeping the secret that he was his father. Raleigh had learned the truth about that only after Warren's affair with Raleigh's mother had been exposed.

"You have several people willing to protect you," Raleigh said.

She looked up at him just as he looked down at her. "Yes. But don't listen to what Griff told you. There's no need for you to make sure I'm okay." She added that just in case Raleigh considered himself one of those *several people*.

He continued to stare at her, and that's when Thea realized she was probably standing too close to him. She went to step back, but he took hold of her arm, keeping her in place.

"I think your brother was smart to tell me what he did," Raleigh said. "I believe you're in danger. I believe the driver of that SUV will come after you again. Why,

I don't know, but Marco made it pretty clear that you were the target. And even if you're the target only to make us believe it's connected to Warren, that won't stop you from being gunned down."

She knew that, of course, but it sent a chill through her to hear it spelled out like that. Thea hadn't meant for her mouth to tremble and definitely hadn't wanted Raleigh to see it.

"Just because you're a cop, it doesn't mean you shouldn't be scared," he went on. "You should be. And while I understand you not wanting to go to the McCall Ranch so you can keep Warren safe, you'll need to be someplace where you have backup."

Thea clamped her teeth over her bottom lip for just a moment until she could regain her bearing. "I could go back to my office." Egan would make sure she had someone to help protect her, and he would do that even if it stretched his manpower thin. "Then I could come back in the morning when you question your mother and the doctor."

"You'll need a protection detail for the drive back and forth, too."

More manpower. But Raleigh's tone seemed to suggest something else. "You don't want me here for the interviews?"

"No. I do. You know more about Hannah's case than I do, and you know Warren. You might hear something that helps us figure this out." He paused, groaned softly. "If and when we eventually make it out of here tonight, you could stay at my place. It's not far."

"With you?" she blurted out.

The corner of his mouth lifted, but the slight smile didn't last long. "We're former lovers. I can't change that. But I don't want it to get in the way of us doing what needs to be done."

Neither did she, but Thea had to give this some more thought. She'd been to Raleigh's horse ranch and knew his mom wouldn't be there. Alma had her own home and ranch just up the road from his. But still, she'd be under the same roof, and the attraction between them was still there. It was for her anyway.

Thea was so caught up in her own thoughts that the sound of the knock behind her nearly caused her to gasp. She whirled around, but it wasn't the threat that her body had believed it might be. It was Raleigh's deputy Alice, and even though the deputy didn't pose any danger, Thea could tell from her expression that something was wrong.

"Raleigh, you need to hear this." Alice was carrying a laptop that she sat on Raleigh's desk. "I had all of Sonya's recordings of her phone conversations transferred to an audio file that I could share with the lab, and I found something."

That definitely got Thea's and Raleigh's attention.

"It's the last one Sonya recorded," Alice continued. "Unfortunately, they're not date stamped, and she doesn't mention a date or time, so I don't know when the call came in."

Thea and Raleigh both moved closer to the laptop when Alice pressed the play button. It didn't take long for Thea to hear Sonya's voice.

"I swear I didn't know," Sonya said, her voice trembling. "I went in for the in vitro, and I thought that's what I got."

The sense of dread washed over Thea. Because obviously something had gone wrong at the clinic. Or at least Sonya thought something had.

"I'm not sure I can go through with this," Sonya went on. "Now that I know the baby is actually mine, how could I give her up?"

Oh, mercy. Yes, something had indeed gone wrong, and Raleigh was clearly just as stunned as she was.

"Who is she talking to?" Raleigh asked Alice.

But it wasn't necessary for the deputy to answer because the person spoke.

"We had an agreement," the other woman snapped. Thea easily recognized her voice, too.

It was Yvette.

"You're not backing out of our deal," Yvette insisted. "I've paid you plenty of money, thousands, and I'm not going to be punished because the clinic messed up." Unlike Sonya's voice, Yvette's wasn't shaking, but the anger came through loud and clear. "One way or another, Sonya, you will give me that child."

Chapter 6

At least Raleigh didn't have far to go to confront Yvette with what he'd just heard. And he would confront her and demand to know what the heck was going on.

With Thea and Alice right behind him, he went to the break room, where he immediately spotted Dalton and Nick seated at the table. Yvette was pacing, and her gaze zoomed to them when Raleigh stepped into the room.

"Did the kidnapper call you?" she blurted out. She continued to study his expression. "Oh, God. Did something happen to the baby?"

"The baby's fine," Raleigh assured her, "but I'm thinking you might want to have your lawyer come out here."

Yvette pulled back her shoulders. "What are you talking about?"

"This," he said. Raleigh had the laptop in his hands,

and he rewound the recording to the last part of the conversation.

One way or another, Sonya, you will give me that child.

Yvette gasped and stormed toward him as if she were about to take the laptop, but Raleigh handed it to Thea in case he had to restrain Yvette.

"Where did you get that?" Yvette demanded. It was the same angry voice she'd used to threaten Sonya.

Before Raleigh asked her anything, he read Yvette her rights. Obviously, that didn't go over well, and her husband went to her side.

"What's this all about?" Nick asked as he volleyed glances between Yvette and Raleigh.

Raleigh just waited for Yvette to answer.

"Oh, God." Yvette pressed her fingers to her mouth a moment. And she started crying again.

But those tears didn't have the same heart-tugging effect they'd had on him earlier. Judging from Thea's huff, she felt the same way.

"Sonya recorded your whole conversation," Raleigh told the crying woman.

That wasn't exactly the truth. It was only a partial recording. Since Yvette didn't know that though, he was hoping she'd fill in the blanks. Maybe along with confessing that she was the one who'd set up this deadly chain of events.

"What's going on," Nick growled, and this time the demand was aimed at his wife. "What did you do?"

Yvette snapped toward him, her eyes suddenly wide. She started shaking her head. "I didn't kill Sonya if that's what you're suggesting."

"Then what the hell did you do?" Nick asked, taking the question right out of Raleigh's mouth.

Even with all of them staring at her and waiting, Yvette didn't answer right away. Still shaking her head, still crying, she sank down into the chair. "Sonya called me this morning and told me she'd found out something."

She looked up at Raleigh as if pleading with him not to make her explain this, but he motioned for her to keep talking. But Yvette had already given him something critical. The timing of the call. It meant the call could have been the trigger for Yvette to send in kidnappers to get the baby.

Yvette swallowed hard before she continued. "Sonya said she got an anonymous tip that there'd been a serious mix-up when she had the in vitro procedure. The person claimed that my stored eggs were lost prior to fertilization, so the clinic decided to do an artificial insemination on Sonya instead."

Raleigh watched Nick as he processed that. It took him several long moments. "Are you saying the baby is Sonya's?"

Yvette nodded. "And yours. The baby is yours," she quickly repeated. She got to her feet and took hold of his arms when he cursed and tried to move away. "It doesn't matter to me that she's not my biological child. I'll still love her. We can still have the child we've always wanted."

Nick cursed some more and threw off her grip with more force than necessary. "A child *you've* always wanted," he corrected in a snarl. He groaned, squeezed his eyes shut and put his hands on the sides of his head.

The man was clearly shaken by this and was probably seeing the irony. He hadn't especially wanted a child but had apparently fathered one. And Yvette wasn't the biological mother.

It took several more moments for the shock to wear off enough for Nick to whirl back around and face his wife. "What did you do? Did you hire those kidnappers?"

"No!" Yvette certainly didn't hesitate, and she repeated the denial to Thea and Raleigh. "I was upset when I said that to Sonya, but I would have never done anything to hurt the baby or her."

Maybe. But Raleigh still wasn't convinced. "Are there two babies?"

"I don't know. I swear, I don't."

Raleigh had to add another unspoken *maybe* to that. "Who told Sonya about what had gone on at the clinic?"

"I told you already that it was an anonymous tip. Whoever it was sent her results of an amniocentesis to prove it. That's a test of the amniotic fluid around the baby. It can tell if there's something wrong." Yvette swallowed hard again. "And it can also tell the baby's DNA."

Interesting. Raleigh looked at Thea to get her take on this, and she was staring at Yvette. "Why was a test like that done? Was Sonya having medical problems?"

"She'd got an infection early on in the pregnancy, and the fertility clinic had her do the test just to make sure. We never heard back from them, so we assumed all was well."

That didn't mesh with what Dr. Sheridan had told them, that he hadn't had any involvement with Hannah or Sonya after the in vitro procedures. That was almost certainly a lie, one that Raleigh would definitely question him about. But it was possible that someone else in the clinic was responsible for the test and the botched procedure.

"I can't believe you didn't tell me this," Nick said, the anger etched all over his face. "And now Sonya's dead, and we don't know where the hell her baby is. *My baby*," he emphasized.

Yeah, and they didn't know if Yvette was responsible. It was time to move this past the chatting stage and make it a full-fledged interview. Before Raleigh did that though, he wanted to talk to Dr. Sheridan, and as late as it already was, that wasn't going to happen until morning.

"We're holding you for questioning," Raleigh told Yvette. "You aren't leaving the sheriff's office until I have some answers."

"Uh, you want me to put her in a holding cell?" Dalton asked.

If Nick was the least bit concerned about that happening, he didn't show it. In fact, he was looking at his wife with disgust. However, Yvette was definitely concerned.

"But I didn't do anything wrong," she practically shouted.

"You obstructed justice by not telling me the truth in a murder investigation," Raleigh explained. "The murder of a woman you hired as a surrogate. And now I have a recording of you arguing with that very woman just hours before she was killed."

"I didn't kill her." Now it was a shout, and she repeated it to her husband.

Nick huffed again. "You lied to me, too," he said after getting his teeth unclenched. "Hell, you even gave the cops a DNA sample to compare to the baby they found. You did that even though you knew you weren't going to be a match."

She tried to take hold of him again, but he pushed her away. "I thought once you learned the child was yours, that you'd love her. And that we would still be able to raise her. It doesn't matter that she's not a child of my own blood. She would have been *our* child. She still can be."

The anger tightened Nick's face so much that it was obvious he was having trouble reining in his temper. He cursed, groaned and went to stand in the doorway. "I don't even know if there's another baby. Or any real kidnappers." He kept going despite Yvette's continued denials. "Is there somewhere else I can wait for a kidnapper's call? Someplace where my *wife* won't be?"

Well, at least the man was willing to hang around in case there truly was a kidnapper. At this point, Raleigh had no idea if there was one, or if this was part of Yvette's scheme to cover up her crime.

But that didn't make sense.

If Yvette had hired thugs to murder Sonya, then why would there be a second baby? Maybe the thugs had gone rogue and were now trying to milk as much money out of this situation as possible.

"Do you and your wife have joint bank accounts?" Raleigh asked Nick.

Nick nodded. For a moment it seemed as if he was going to ask why, but then his mouth tightened. "You want to examine them to see if she withdrew funds for this nightmare that's going on. Well, you're welcome to do that. I'll get you the account numbers and the passwords. In the morning, I'll call the bank and tell them you can have access to our safe-deposit box. There should be some family jewelry and cash in there."

He figured it was Nick's anger at his wife that was making him so cooperative, but Raleigh was thankful for it. This would save him from getting a court order and a search warrant.

"Take Mr. O'Hara to an interview room," Raleigh instructed Dalton. "Set up the recorder in there in case a kidnapper does call. The night deputies will be in soon so you can turn things over to them."

Dalton nodded, immediately picked up his equipment and started leading Nick out of the break room. Yvette didn't follow, but she did start sobbing again.

"Keep her here and instruct the night deputies to lock her up if she tries to leave," Raleigh added to Alice, and then he turned to Yvette. "Remember that part about you having a right to an attorney. You might need it."

Since that only caused Yvette's sobbing to get worse, Raleigh led Thea back to his office. "You really believe she had Sonya killed?" Thea asked.

"Maybe. And maybe not intentionally." He glanced at Alice's laptop. "I want to go through all the recordings Sonya left. I need to know who gave her that anonymous tip. I'd also like to see if there's something to prove why she started the recordings in the first place."

While he was at it, Raleigh was also hoping he could find a connection between Yvette and Marco. The bank records could possibly help with that. If not, at least he would know if there'd been any recent cash withdrawals that Nick couldn't account for. If there was something like that, then it would be another circumstantial piece of evidence against Yvette.

"How much did Sonya know about Hannah's murder?" Raleigh asked Thea. "Did she know about the message that'd been left at the crime scene?"

There was no need for him to clarify which message

because it was no doubt etched in their memories. *This is for Sheriff Warren McCall.*

Thea's forehead bunched up a moment while she gave that some thought. "Probably. When I told Sonya about Hannah and her using the same doctor, Sonya did an internet check to see if there were any other similarities between them."

Then yes, Sonya would have known about the message and could have mentioned it to Yvette. Yvette, in turn, could have had her hired henchmen write that on Sonya's wall to throw suspicion off herself. But there was plenty of suspicion on the woman right now.

Thea tipped her head to the laptop. "If you get me a copy of Sonya's audio recordings, I can go through them, too. I might hear something that I can connect to a conversation I had with her."

Good idea. They could work on that until they found out if Yvette's lawyer was going to show tonight. If he did, then he could start the interview. He still had the kidnapper-ransom issue to deal with, too, if the guy ever called back.

"I'll get you a laptop and the recordings," Raleigh said, heading out of his office.

With a deputy still at Sonya's house and with Dalton and Alice tied up, that only left him with two deputies in the squad room, Miguel Sanchez and Zeb Hooper. Miguel had his phone in his hand, and he was already making his way to Raleigh.

"Sheriff Egan McCall just found an abandoned vehicle on the outskirts of McCall Canyon," Miguel said. "It's a blue SUV matching the description of the one used in your attack."

Good. Because now they could process it for any

evidence. Though he doubted it was a coincidence that the vehicle had been found in Warren's town. No. This could be another attempt to connect the murders to him.

Or maybe there really was a connection.

If so, Raleigh needed to find it before Thea and he landed again in the path of a would-be killer.

"There's more," Miguel added a moment later. "There was a dead body in the SUV, and according to his ID, it's someone you know."

Miguel handed him a note with the name, and the moment Raleigh saw it, he cursed.

Hell.

Thea wished she could turn her mind off for just a couple of seconds. She was exhausted from the spent adrenaline, the late hour and the events of the day, but she couldn't stop the thoughts from coming.

Another body.

And this time, it was Dr. Bryce Sheridan. He'd died from a single gunshot wound to the head that appeared to be self-inflicted.

Appeared.

Egan wasn't convinced it was a suicide though, and therefore neither was Thea. Egan was a good cop, and he had probably seen something with the positioning of the body or the gun that had made him believe this could be a setup.

Until Egan had found the body in the SUV, the doctor had been a person of interest in Sonya's murder. He was also someone that Raleigh and she had counted on to give them answers about Sonya's botched in vitro. But now that he was dead, they would have to wait until morning to get into the fertility clinic so they could access anything they could find.

Maybe before then, Raleigh and she could even manage to get some sleep. But Thea immediately dismissed that notion when she stepped into Raleigh's house. A different set of thoughts hit her then.

Scalding-hot memories of the nights she'd spent here with Raleigh.

Great. Just what she didn't need when she already felt so beaten down from the fatigue. So she had no choice but to stand there and let the memories run their course. Even when the most vivid images and sensations faded though, the thoughts still lingered.

Raleigh had kissed her right in the foyer. That'd been the start of some frantic foreplay that had led them straight to his bed. In those days, their whole relationship had seemed frantic. As if they were starved for each other and couldn't get enough. But that had all come crashing down when Raleigh had found out she'd kept Warren's secret about the affair.

And the secret that he was Warren's son.

When Thea's hand started to hurt, she glanced down and realized she had a too-tight grip on the overnight bag that Griff had packed for her and then sent to Raleigh's office. A bag that hopefully contained the things on the list she'd given him since she'd need a change of clothes and toiletries.

Too bad the bag wouldn't contain something to make her immune to Raleigh.

And speaking of Raleigh, he came in behind her, closing the door and setting the security system. He looked at her, and maybe because he saw something in her eyes, there was suddenly some alarm in his expression. Then he got it.

"Oh," he grumbled. "Yeah."

Thea could practically see the wall he'd just put up between them. A wall that hadn't been there as they'd worked together on the recordings and while waiting for the kidnapper to call back.

A call that hadn't come.

But now that they were back here, at the scene of their affair, then he probably knew it wasn't a good idea for them to be so chummy. With the attraction still simmering between them, even chumminess could lead to sex. Heck, maybe breathing could.

Another couple that definitely wouldn't be getting chummy tonight was Nick and Yvette. Nick had refused to leave the sheriff's office because he wanted to be there in case the kidnapper did call. Since her lawyer wasn't arriving until morning, Yvette was still in the break room, where she'd stay until Raleigh either released her or charged her with obstruction of justice. Maybe even murder for hire, along with other assorted felonies.

Without the evidence that Dr. Sheridan could have possibly given them, Raleigh was in a wait-and-see mode. There was a lot riding on those banking records because even if Yvette was guilty, Thea doubted the woman would just confess to the growing list of crimes.

It was also possible they'd get something from the crime lab. But they, too, had a mountain of stuff to process. Not just any possible evidence they'd gathered from Sonya and the woods where her body had been found, but also the baby's clothes and carrier. And now the SUV might turn up something, too.

Unless…

"What if Dr. Sheridan was the gunman who shot at us from the SUV?" she asked. It was a question that had been going through her head, along with all those other thoughts, and she was certain that Raleigh had considered it, too.

"I'm sure your boss will have the body tested for gunshot residue," he said, and he didn't add as much venom to the word *boss* as he probably could have, considering that her boss, Egan, was also his half brother. "If Sheridan has GSR on him, then we'll know he fired a gun."

True, but it wouldn't necessarily prove he was the one who'd tried to kill them. Someone could have set up the doctor.

"I can call Egan if you like," she offered.

Raleigh paused as if considering that, but he certainly didn't decline. That's because finding the killer was far more important than their family troubles. "Yeah, if I haven't heard from him by morning."

"If Egan has anything, he'll call," she assured him. "He's a cop through and through like you."

Raleigh opened his mouth, maybe to say he was nothing like Egan, but then he stopped and dragged in a long breath. "I talked to him earlier when you were in the bathroom at the sheriff's office." He paused and gave her a flat look. "He told me to make sure that you were okay."

Thea groaned. Good grief. That was almost identical to what her brother had told Raleigh. "They forget that I'm a cop with just as much training as they have." Well, almost as much.

"No, they remember that. They care about you and are worried because I haven't been able to ID the killer."

She hated that Raleigh was putting all of this on his shoulders. "If I'm the target, then I'm the one responsible for this. I'm the one who dragged you and all of your deputies into the path of a killer."

A possibility that ate away at her as much as Sonya's death. Thea prayed she wasn't the reason for that, too.

The one saving grace in all of this was that the baby was safe. Griff had let them know that when they'd arrived at the safe house, and there'd been no incidents along the way. Now they needed to make sure there wasn't a second baby out there who needed to be rescued from the monsters who'd taken her.

"You should try to get some rest," Raleigh said, pulling her out of her thoughts. "You remember where the guest room is?"

Thea nodded. She remembered though she'd never actually been in it. Whenever she'd stayed over, she'd always been in Raleigh's bed. With both of them naked.

Probably best not to remember that now though.

"I'll need to get back to the office by seven," Raleigh added, already heading in the direction of his bedroom. But he stopped when his phone rang.

Thea didn't groan, but considering the late hour, she figured this was probably bad news. Still, she hoped it was merely an update on the investigation.

"It's Miguel," Raleigh mumbled when he looked at the screen. He hit the answer button and put the call on speaker. It didn't take long for Thea to hear his deputy's voice.

"A detective from San Antonio PD just called," Miguel said. "A woman, Madison Travers, just walked in and confessed to botching the in vitro procedure done on Sonya. And this woman says she believes she knows who tried to kill you."

Chapter 7

Raleigh wished he'd managed to get a little more sleep. Two hours didn't seem nearly enough, considering the hellish day he was about to face. Still, he was glad he'd managed to get any sleep at all since he'd spent a good deal of the night on the phone with SAPD and his deputies.

Unfortunately, he'd spent some of the night thinking about Thea, too.

He cursed himself for that. He didn't have the time or mental energy to rehash the past, but that's exactly what he'd done anyway.

Having Thea under the same roof with him was a bad reminder of when they'd been lovers. Worse, Raleigh was certain it was the same for her. He hadn't missed the heated looks she'd given him. Also hadn't missed her expression that told him she was just as frustrated as he was about this.

He forced his attention back where it belonged—on the drive to the sheriff's office. No one was following Thea and him, but he needed to make sure it stayed that way. He needed to get to work in one piece so he could question Madison Travers. At least that was one of the things he had to do.

But at the moment the woman was his top priority.

She had not only confessed to the in vitro snafu but also claimed to know who wanted to kill them. Unfortunately, she hadn't wanted to share that info with the San Antonio cops but had insisted instead on talking to Raleigh. He very much wanted to talk to Madison, too, but Raleigh hoped this wasn't some kind of ruse to get at Thea and him again. That's why he hadn't taken Thea to San Antonio to question the woman. Instead, SAPD had waited until morning to bring Madison to Durango Ridge, and she was now waiting for them in an interview room.

Thea was keeping watch as well, even though she was on the phone with Egan to get an update on the Dr. Sheridan murder investigation. She hadn't put the call on speaker, maybe because she hadn't wanted to emphasize to her boss that she was in a cruiser with his illegitimate half brother. But judging from the way her forehead was bunched up, she didn't like what she was hearing from Egan.

"A problem?" Raleigh asked as soon as she'd finished the call.

"No. But it wasn't the answers we wanted."

Hell. As much as he disliked the idea of having his half brother connected to this case, Raleigh had hoped that Egan would be able to clear up some things. Raleigh would take all the help he could get.

"There was gunshot residue on Dr. Sheridan's jacket but not his hands," Thea continued a moment later. "Egan thinks the pattern indicates that it was transferred from the actual shooter to the doctor."

And that meant someone had tried to make it look as if Sheridan had killed himself in the SUV. If the doctor had actually done that, then the GSR should have been on his hands.

"So he was murdered," Raleigh concluded.

Thea nodded. "Egan said the placement of the gun was wrong, too. Sheridan was left-handed, and the gun was in his right."

So they were dealing with a sloppy killer. Or one that had panicked.

"There's more," she went on. "One of Sheridan's neighbors saw him yesterday afternoon with two men that she didn't recognize. She said she didn't think anything of it at the time, but after she heard about his death, she called SAPD. She didn't see a gun or anything, but she thought the men looked menacing."

"Did she give the cops a description of the men?" he asked.

Another nod just as her phone dinged with a message. "They're having her work with a sketch artist, too, so we might have something we can put out to the media."

That was a long shot, but it was all he had right now.

"There was a picture on Sheridan's phone," Thea went on when he pulled to a stop in front of the sheriff's office. "Egan just texted it to me. It's the same photo that the kidnappers sent Nick."

She showed him the photo on the screen, and it was indeed a match. But what did it mean? Had Sheridan been involved with the second kidnapping? Or had it all been a hoax? Raleigh was thinking hoax since the kidnapper still hadn't called back. Although if Sheridan was the kidnapper, that would explain why Nick had never gotten a call back.

"I'm hoping one of your deputies made lots of coffee," Thea grumbled as they hurried inside.

Raleigh was hoping the same thing, though it was asking a lot of mere caffeine to get rid of the headache he already had. The headache got worse when he immediately saw Nick and Yvette coming toward them. There was a guy in a suit behind Yvette. Her lawyer, no doubt, and he cut ahead of the pair. He didn't stop until he was practically right in Raleigh's face.

"You either need to charge my client or let her go," the man insisted. According to the business card he handed Raleigh, his name was Vernon Cutler. And yeah, he was a lawyer all right.

Raleigh was just ornery enough to say he was charging her, but he looked at Dalton to see if anything had come back on the bank records or the safe-deposit box.

Dalton shook his head. "If Mrs. O'Hara paid off hired guns, she didn't use those bank accounts, and there was nothing missing from the safe-deposit box. Mr. O'Hara gave us a list of the contents, and everything was there."

"What about any activity on Yvette's cell phone?" Raleigh pressed. He'd asked his deputies to check that to see if there were any irregularities.

"She made eight calls to Sonya yesterday. Two before the body was discovered and the rest came after."

"I call Sonya every day," Yvette argued. *"Called,"* she corrected, her voice cracking. "When she didn't answer, I kept trying to reach her because I was worried about her."

Raleigh heard every word of that, but it wasn't those calls that interested him. "Did she have any new contacts over the past week or so?" he pressed.

"No," Dalton answered. "Every call on her phone checked out."

That didn't mean the woman hadn't used a disposable cell phone, or a burner as it was called, but if she had, there was no proof.

"We got the search warrant for the O'Haras' house," Dalton explained. "Miguel's on the way there now to go through it with SAPD."

Good. But a search like that could take hours, and Raleigh doubted they'd find a murder weapon or anything else incriminating that Yvette had just happened to leave lying around.

So basically the only thing Raleigh had against the woman was the recorded argument that she'd had with Sonya. A recording that likely wouldn't be admissible in court since Sonya hadn't informed Yvette that the conversation was being recorded. Of course, the obstruction of justice charge was still on the table, but Raleigh had other more immediate issues.

Madison Travers, for one.

And there was his mother. He saw Alma in his office with her lawyer and longtime friend, Simon Lindley. Neither looked especially happy, and Simon was likely going to pitch a fit that Raleigh was questioning Alma.

"Your client is free to go," Raleigh told Vernon Cutler. "For now," he tacked on to that.

"But I don't want to go," Yvette said. "I want to stay here in case the kidnapper calls."

"You'll have to wait elsewhere," Raleigh told her. "This place is getting pretty crowded."

"Come on," Yvette's lawyer insisted, but he had to practically drag the woman out of the building.

"You should probably try to get some rest, too," Raleigh told Nick. No way though would he force the man to go.

"I managed a nap in the break room. I'd like to stay just in case."

Raleigh nodded and was about to make his way to the coffeepot, but then he saw Thea coming toward him with two cups of coffee in her hand. She was already sipping one and handed the other to him. He thanked her and downed as much of it as he could, even though it was scalding hot. Thea seemed to be doing the same thing.

"Thanks," he said to Thea, and he glanced at his mom. She wasn't glaring. Alma had a sad, how-could-you-do-this-to-me expression on her face. It was very effective at making Raleigh feel like a jerk and a bad son. But since he was a son with a badge, he had no choice about bringing her in.

"I didn't know about the search warrant," Nick said.

Since Nick had been cooperative so far, Raleigh hadn't expected to hear or see any hesitation, but he sure as heck saw it now. "Why? Is that a problem?"

Nick didn't jump to answer that. "No." But that didn't sound like the truth. And it was something Raleigh would need to dig a little deeper into once he dealt with the other issues. However, he kept his eyes on Nick as he headed back down the hall. The man also took out his phone and made a call.

"You think he doesn't want us to find something in

his house?" Thea asked. She'd obviously picked up on the bad vibe, too.

"Maybe." And maybe the guy was just acting punchy because he was exhausted. Something that Raleigh totally understood.

"I'll have Dalton do the interview with my mother," Raleigh explained to Thea, "but I need to speak to her first. You don't have to be part of that unless you're a glutton for punishment."

"Consider me a glutton." She gave him a half smile, but then she quickly got serious again. "I want to hear what anyone has to say about what's gone on. We need to catch Sonya's killer."

Yeah, they did, but he wished he'd had more sleep and more coffee before dealing with this. His mom was only half the problem. She was usually civil, even when Raleigh was calling her into question, but Simon could be a protective SOB. Part of Raleigh was pleased that Simon was so protective, but sometimes that got in the way.

Raleigh was certain it would now, too.

"Why are you doing this?" Simon snapped the moment Raleigh went into his office.

He looked Simon straight in the eyes. "Because a woman was murdered and a baby was kidnapped. A second baby might be missing, as well. I'm sure my mother would want to help with that in any way she could."

"I would." Alma got to her feet, and he saw the concern in her eyes. "Are the babies all right?"

"One of them is. She's with social services. I'm not sure about the other. That's what I'm trying to find out." Along with learning if the still-kidnapped baby even existed.

"I'll help any way I can," his mother said, and then she looked past him and at Thea. They'd met when Thea and he had been dating and while his mom had still been with Warren, and his mother had been friendly to Thea then.

Not so much now though.

Alma didn't glare at Thea or anything, but she quickly turned back to Raleigh, putting her attention solely on him. "You think I know something that could help with this case?" Alma asked.

Simon huffed. "You're a person of interest, Alma. Because Sonya worked for you, and you fired her."

This was the first Raleigh was hearing about the firing, so he stared at his mother, waiting for her to fill him in.

"You really don't think I'd kill Sonya because of what went on two years ago?" His mother patted her chest as if to steady her heart.

Raleigh answered that with a question of his own. "Why'd you fire her?"

"Because she stole some money from Alma, that's why," Simon barked.

"Because she *might* have stolen it," Alma corrected. "Some money went missing. And no, I didn't feel the need to tell you. I handled it myself."

"She didn't tell you because you would have arrested Sonya," Simon interrupted. "Especially if you'd heard the way Sonya talked to your mother. She yelled at her."

Sonya did have a temper, but he hadn't known about her being a possible thief. He hoped that was the extent of the woman's criminal behavior. He definitely didn't want her connected to the mix-up at the fertility clinic, but that was something he could ask Madison Travers.

"Sonya yelled at you?" Thea repeated.

His mother nodded, but Raleigh saw Simon's eyes narrow. "Oh, no. You're not going to pin Sonya's murder on Alma."

Maybe not, but Simon had just provided a motive for his mother to be part of this. It wasn't a strong motive, but it wasn't one he could just overlook, either.

"Did you bring him here?" Simon snapped.

It took Raleigh a moment to realize that Simon was looking over his shoulder. And his attention was on the man who'd just walked into the squad room.

Warren.

Hell.

"I need another cup of coffee for this," Raleigh grumbled, and he turned around to face the man. "It's not a good time," he warned Warren.

Warren acknowledged that with a nod. "I just wanted to check on Thea. And you."

Raleigh hadn't wanted to be included in that, though Warren's concern did seem genuine. As genuine as his mother's hurt and Simon's anger. Raleigh's anger, too.

"Come on, Alma." Simon took her by the arm. "We're leaving."

Alma didn't put up a fuss about that, but Raleigh had to. "You can take her to the interview room, but you can't leave. Not just yet. I need you to give Dalton your statement about the time Sonya worked for you," he added to his mother.

"She can do that another time, when he's not here," Simon spat out, his venom obviously aimed at Warren.

"I'll go," Warren said.

"No." Alma spoke up. "Simon and I can go to the interview room." She aimed a sharp look at Simon. "Let's just get this done."

Raleigh was glad that his mom had stood up to Simon. It was something she had to do often since Simon always seemed to be trying to control her. Not just in legal situations but in the rest of her life, too.

"Thanks," Raleigh told his mom. He didn't say anything to Simon, but the man glared at Thea, Warren and him on the way out of the office and all the way to the interview room.

"I didn't mean to cause trouble," Warren said. "I was just worried about Thea." He had his hands crammed in his pockets, but he looked as if he wanted to hug her.

"I'm all right," Thea assured him. "I'll be back in McCall Canyon soon, but Raleigh and I need to work this case."

Warren nodded and took out his phone from his pocket. "I've been studying it, too, and I know you probably don't want my help," he added to Raleigh, "but I might have found something."

Warren showed them the photos on his phone. Photos that Raleigh knew well because they were side-by-side shots of the two scrawled warnings that had been left at the scenes of Hannah's and Sonya's murders.

"Egan got the second photo of Sonya's wall from the lab," Warren explained. "He showed it to me since I'm still working to solve Hannah's case."

"*Unofficially* working," Raleigh automatically snapped, but then he waved that off.

He didn't like Warren, but if he'd been a retired cop with an unsolved murder, he would have kept at it, as well. Especially if he'd known the victim the way that Warren had known Hannah. This was personal for Warren, and Raleigh couldn't fault the man for putting his heart into the investigation.

"I have a friend who's a handwriting expert," Warren went on, "and I had him compare the two messages. As you know, it's hard to do a handwriting analysis on something like this, but he believes it's a match, that the same person wrote both messages."

Raleigh had another look at the photos and the warning. *This is for Sheriff Warren McCall.* They certainly looked the same.

"The killer could have used the same hired thug for both," Raleigh pointed out. "It wouldn't have been Marco though since he was in jail a year ago."

Warren made a sound of agreement. "But what if the killer himself wrote these? If this is someone with a grudge this big against me, maybe he or she wanted to do it himself?"

Raleigh nearly snapped at the addition of "she" because it referred to his mother. And while Raleigh couldn't see Alma killing two women, maybe someone close to her had.

Someone like Simon.

"I'll make sure Dalton asks Simon his whereabouts for both murders," Raleigh assured Warren.

"You really think Simon could be a killer?" Thea asked.

Raleigh lifted his shoulder. "I think he loves my mother enough to do pretty much anything. He was questioned about your shooting," he added to Warren. And even though Simon's name had been cleared, at the time he had been at the top of Raleigh's suspect list.

Warren certainly knew that because he'd probably studied every aspect of that investigation. "I… We," he amended, "need to get Hannah's killer so we can try to locate her missing child. The baby would be a year old now, and the biological parents need answers. *I* need answers. Maybe I'll get them if you can find who murdered Sonya."

Raleigh intended to do everything possible to make sure the killer was caught. "Sonya's murder could have been a copycat," he reminded Warren. "If so, then the person who left that message on her wall could have studied the one on Hannah's and made sure the signatures were similar."

"Yes," Warren readily admitted. "And if so, then I've wasted your time. Either way, catch this SOB."

Warren brushed his hand along Thea's arm, and then he headed out, leaving Raleigh with a boatload of feelings that he didn't want. He definitely didn't want to feel anything but disgust for this married man who'd carried on a secret affair with his mother.

Thea shut the door after Warren left. "Are you okay?" she asked. Since that simple question could cover a lot of territory, Raleigh just waited for her to add more. "I know it can't be easy for you to be around Warren."

"It's not." And that was all he intended to say about it.

But it apparently wasn't all that Thea intended to do. She slipped her arm around him and eased him to her. "Yes, I know this isn't smart, but if anyone needs a hug right now, it's you."

The cowboy in him wouldn't admit that, but the hug did feel, well, good. Comforting, even. At least it did for a couple of seconds, and then it turned to something else when that brainless part of him behind the zipper of his jeans reminded him that this was Thea.

And that he still wanted her.

He pulled back, intending to step away, but he made the mistake of looking down at her. Oh, man. It felt as if the air had caught fire. Something was certainly blazing, and he made the mistake even worse by leaning in and brushing his mouth over hers.

That sure didn't help cool the heat any.

And even though he realized that it wasn't helping, he didn't stop. He would have just stood there and kept on kissing her until things went well beyond the comforting-hug stage. Thankfully though, Thea seemed to still have some common sense because she's the one who moved away from him.

"I was right," she said, her voice silky and filled with breath. "That wasn't smart."

Yeah, but it was good. Which, of course, made it bad. Especially bad because he had other things he should be doing. Things that could end up keeping Thea out of the path of a killer.

"I need to talk to Madison Travers," Raleigh grumbled.

He didn't wait around, partly because he didn't want to talk about the kiss that shouldn't have happened and also because he was anxious to see if the woman had any information they could use. Thea followed him, of course, but he wanted her to hear this just in case she picked up on something he might miss. After all, she knew more about the fertility clinic than he did, since she'd been investigating it for a year.

Madison Travers was waiting for them in the interview room, and she immediately got to her feet. She was petite, right at five-feet tall, and she immediately made nervous glances at both Thea and him.

She didn't have a lawyer with her, but there was a uniformed cop at the table. He'd obviously escorted Madison there from SAPD headquarters, and he introduced himself as Dewayne Rodriquez.

"I've read Ms. Travers her rights," Officer Rodriquez said. "And she waived her right to an attorney."

"Because I don't need a lawyer to tell the truth," Madison blurted out. Judging from her red eyes and puffy face, she'd been crying.

Raleigh could have argued that she might indeed need an attorney because if she had done something illegal, then she could be arrested.

"You're Sheriff Lawton?" Madison asked.

He nodded and tipped his head to Thea. "And this is Deputy Morris from the McCall Canyon Sheriff's office. I understand you're responsible for the botched in vitro procedure for Sonya Burney?" Raleigh started. Both Thea and he took a seat at the table, and Madison sat across from them. "I want to hear all about that, but I'm especially interested in who tried to kill us and how you came by that information."

Madison seemed to lose even more color in her already pale face, but then Raleigh had made sure he sounded like a tough lawman. He wasn't going to let the woman skate just because she'd voluntarily gone to the cops. That's because she hadn't come clean for nearly nine months.

"Yes, I'm the one who messed up Sonya's in vitro. I misplaced Mrs. O'Hara's eggs. At least I guess I did because I couldn't find them when we got ready to do the procedure. I told Dr. Bryce Sheridan, and he said he'd take care of it."

"Dr. Sheridan?" Raleigh questioned. "So he knew about this?"

"Of course," Madison answered without hesitating. "He did an insemination instead. That means he just used Mr. O'Hara's semen to inject into Sonya, not the fertilized eggs as originally planned." She paused. "We didn't think it would be successful. Usually it isn't. So we thought we'd have time to find Mrs. O'Hara's eggs before we did the real in vitro in a couple of months."

"Why didn't you just come clean with Sonya and the O'Haras?" Thea asked, taking the question right out of Raleigh's mouth.

Now she hesitated. "I'd already gotten in trouble for improperly storing another sample, and I would have been fired. Bryce was covering for me." Madison started crying again when she said the doctor's name. *Bryce.* "Plus, the clinic is being sued by a former client who's claiming we illegally released medical information about her to her ex-husband. We couldn't have handled another lawsuit. It would have closed us down."

From everything Raleigh was hearing, closing them down wouldn't be a bad thing. Two errors made by Madison and a lawsuit weren't a stellar track record.

"You and Dr. Sheridan were lovers?" Raleigh pressed.

She nodded, wiped away her tears, but kept sobbing. "And now he's dead. Murdered. That's the reason I went to the cops. I thought somebody might try to kill me, too. Those men did this to him, didn't they?"

"Men?" Thea and Raleigh said in unison.

Madison grabbed some tissues from a box on the table, nodding while she blew her nose. "Two of them. They were wearing suits and had badges. They came to the clinic and asked to speak to Bryce. I told them it was his day off, and then they said they wanted to know the names of all his current patients."

Well, that was interesting. "Were the men cops?"

Madison shook her head. "They said they were FBI. But after they left, I got to thinking that there was something suspicious about them. I mean, they should have known I couldn't just give them the names without a court order."

"The FBI didn't send anyone to the clinic," Officer Rodriquez verified.

So the guys were posing as law enforcement. "When was this?" Raleigh asked Madison.

"About a week ago."

Raleigh figured that was plenty of time for someone who'd planned on attacking Sonya. "Describe the men."

Madison wiped her eyes again while she continued. "I only got a good look at one of them. The other stayed in the waiting room, and he had on a hat and dark glasses. But the other one, the one who talked to me, was bald. Oh, and he had a tattoo on his neck, but he'd tried to cover it up with makeup. I could see the makeup on the collar of his shirt."

Raleigh texted Dalton to bring him a picture of Marco, but he continued with the questions while he waited. "Does the clinic have security cameras?"

"Not inside the building, but we have one in the parking lot."

Raleigh looked at Officer Rodriquez again. "We asked the security company who monitors the camera to provide us with footage," the cop answered. "But they're stalling because they say it could violate patients' rights to release it. We're working on a court order, but it could take a while if they keep fighting it—especially since the murder didn't take place on the grounds or inside the clinic."

Well, hell. That complicated things. "Would it do any good if I talked to them?" Raleigh asked.

Officer Rodriquez lifted his shoulder. "It wouldn't hurt. Their office is in San Antonio. Maybe you could show them a picture of the murdered patient so they can see that the footage is part of an active murder investigation."

Raleigh looked at Thea, and she nodded. "We need that footage."

He couldn't argue with her about that, but he was worried about the risks of being out in the open with Thea. Still, this was the best shot they had right now. Well, unless he could convince SAPD to put more pressure on the security company.

There was a knock at the door, and a moment later Dalton came in with Marco's mug shot. When Raleigh turned the screen in Madison's direction, the woman shook her head.

"Who is he?" Madison demanded, the fear in her voice. "Is he the one who killed Bryce?"

No, he'd been dead by then, but Marco had certainly been willing to murder Thea.

"Is this one of the men who visited you at the clinic?" Raleigh asked.

"No. I've never seen that guy. Why would you think he was there?"

Raleigh was hoping Marco had been there so it would tie everything up, linking Marco to both Sonya's attack and the clinic. He needed to find out if Dr. Sheridan had been murdered because the killers/kidnappers thought he was onto them. If so, they might consider Madison a loose end, too.

And of course, Thea also fell into that same loose-end category.

But Madison had admitted she hadn't gotten a good look at the man with the hat who'd stayed in the waiting room, so maybe that one had been Marco.

"Sonya knew the child she was carrying was hers," Thea said to Madison. "Did you tell her?"

Again, Madison took her time answering. "Yes. I called her yesterday and then sent her results of the amnio to prove it. I just couldn't stay quiet after I got that visit from Nick O'Hara."

Even Officer Rodriquez seemed surprised by that. "When did Nick visit you?" Raleigh pressed.

"Two days ago." Madison's voice cracked. "He had a meeting with Bryce, and I didn't mean to overhear what they said, but Mr. O'Hara was talking pretty loud. He told Bryce that he was leaving his wife, Yvette."

Raleigh had thought that might happen. He certainly hadn't seen a lot of affection between Yvette and Nick. But something about this didn't make sense.

"Why would Nick go to Dr. Sheridan with this?" Raleigh asked.

"He wanted to see the surrogacy agreement. He said he couldn't find his copy but that he thought he remembered there being a way out of the arrangement. Mr. O'Hara didn't want to share custody with his wife. He wanted full custody for himself."

That didn't mesh with what Yvette had told them. She'd claimed that Nick was having second thoughts about the baby, but maybe he was just having second thoughts about having a baby with her.

"After I heard Mr. O'Hara say that," Madison went on, "I knew I had to tell Sonya the truth, so I called her."

"What phone did you use to do that?" Thea immediately asked.

"The one in my office."

Raleigh jumped right on that. "The office where those two men visited you?" He waited for Madison to confirm that with a nod. "Were you with the two men the whole time they were there?"

"No. I went up the hall to see if I could find our other doctor to talk to them, but he was with a patient." Madison's eyes widened. "Do you think they planted a bug or something?"

Yes, he did. Apparently so did Officer Rodriquez because he called someone to ask them to search the clinic for an eavesdropping device.

"Oh, God," Madison blurted out. "If they heard that, then they heard me say I was suspicious of them. They heard everything I said to Sonya."

Raleigh leaned in closer. "What exactly did you say to Sonya?"

The tears started up again. "I told her what I did about the botched procedure, and she was upset. She said that she was going to call you and that you would probably help her go someplace else to have the baby. A place where she could think about what she was going to do. I liked Sonya, and she said she trusted you. That's why I insisted on talking to you."

So, if Sonya was thinking about leaving town, that might have prompted her killer to spring into action. But it still didn't tell Raleigh who'd murdered her.

Sonya had told Yvette. They had the recording to prove that. But Raleigh wasn't sure if Sonya had had time to phone Nick or not. If she had, the man certainly hadn't mentioned it.

There was another knock at the door. His other deputy Alice this time. She was holding a tablet, and Raleigh could tell from her expression that she had something important to tell him.

"Excuse me for a moment," Raleigh said to Officer Rodriquez and Madison, and both Thea and he went out into the hall with his deputy.

"The lab called," Alice explained, "and they found a fingerprint on the bottom of the carrier seat that the baby was in when you found her." She glanced at the notes on her tablet. "They got a match on the print. A guy name Buck Tanner. He's a career criminal, and that's why his prints were in the system."

Raleigh felt some of the pressure leave his chest. They finally had a name, which meant they could locate this snake and bring him in.

"Is Buck a bald guy with a neck tattoo?" Thea asked.

Alice nodded and pulled up a picture of him. He matched Madison's description of one of her visitors, and Raleigh was about to take the photo in to have her confirm it when Alice stopped him.

"There's more," Alice went on. "I found the name of Buck's lawyer for his last two arrests. It was Simon."

Chapter 8

Thea knew Raleigh was on edge about this decision to go to Shaw's Security Company in San Antonio to try to get the camera footage from the fertility clinic. She was on edge about it, too, but this was the fastest way they had of finding out who'd visited the clinic with Buck Tanner.

If it was his lawyer, Simon, then Raleigh would be able to make an arrest.

Of course, that alone wouldn't be enough to convict Simon of Sonya's murder. Simon could always claim that he went to the clinic with his client, maybe to discuss something totally unrelated to Sonya. Simon could even dispute what Madison had said. After all, Madison had botched the in vitro procedure and then lied about it. She wasn't exactly a credible witness.

It would have helped if Sonya had recorded her chat

with Madison, but if she had done that, it wasn't with the other recordings. In fact, the only conversations that Sonya had taped were with Yvette, and that hadn't started until six weeks into Sonya's pregnancy.

Why?

Maybe Sonya hadn't trusted the woman. But that only brought Thea back to another *why*.

Even though the questions were important, Thea made sure she kept watch around them while Alice drove Raleigh and her to San Antonio. It wasn't a long trip—less than an hour—but they'd taken precautions. They were in the bullet-resistant cruiser, and Alice could give them backup. Raleigh had even considered sending just Alice and Dalton, but he had decided he, as the sheriff, stood a better chance of talking the security company owner into letting him view the footage. Thea agreed.

The visit was a risk, and it also ate up a good chunk of the morning, but Raleigh and she weren't being idle. Thea was reading through the report that the lab had sent them on the evidence that had been processed, and Raleigh was on the phone with his deputy Miguel.

"No, don't ask Simon anything about the visit to the fertility clinic," Raleigh said to Miguel. The call wasn't on speaker, but since Raleigh and she were side by side, Thea could still hear bits and pieces of the conversation. "Just keep looking for Buck Tanner and any financial links between him and Simon. Links that can't be explained as payment for Simon's legal services."

Raleigh and she had already started looking for Buck before they left Durango Ridge, but the man wasn't answering his phone, nor had he been at his house when SAPD had sent an officer out to bring him in for questioning. If Buck was responsible for the murders and the attack, then he had probably gone into hiding.

"Madison's in protective custody," Raleigh relayed to her as soon as he finished his call with Miguel. "She went willingly because she's convinced she could be a target."

She could be. Ditto for Raleigh and her. And Warren. Since Warren seemed to be at the center of the two dead surrogates, he was perhaps in danger, but unlike Madison, he'd refused any kind of protection. Thea only hoped that Egan and his brother, Court, would keep an eye on him. At least Rachel and the baby were safe, and Thea wanted to make sure it stayed that way.

"What about Nick?" she asked. "Was Miguel able to get in touch with him to ask about the meeting he had with Dr. Sheridan?"

Raleigh shook his head and made a sound of frustration. "He's not answering his phone, either. Someone's on the way to check on him."

Good. Because of all the bad stuff that'd gone on, it was possible that Nick was in danger, too. Besides, it was odd that the man wasn't answering his phone, because he'd seemed so anxious for a call from the kidnapper. Maybe though he'd given up hope about them calling back.

"I don't suppose there have been any reports of missing babies similar to the one in the picture that the kidnappers sent him?" Thea continued.

Another headshake. "But we still don't know how old the picture is. Or where it was taken. It could be a photo of a baby that was taken off the internet."

True. The baby in the photo might not even be missing, much less kidnapped and being held for ransom.

They'd done an image search on the internet to find possible matches, but that hadn't turned up anything, either.

Raleigh tipped his head to the report Thea had been reading. "Anything new in that lab report?"

"Not really new, but Buck's print wasn't from a single finger. It was actually a handprint, and it was in the right position for someone who was maybe holding the baby carrier to keep it steady. In other words, the print wasn't planted."

Not that Thea thought it had been, but it would be nice to rule it out if that's what Buck claimed had happened.

"I also brought these," she said, taking the hard copy photos from the file. They were pictures of Simon, Marco, Nick and even Yvette. "I wanted to see if anyone from the security company recognized them. That way, if they don't let us view the footage, then maybe they'll look at it and compare it to the photos."

Raleigh made another sound of approval, though she was sure he preferred to review the footage himself.

His phone dinged with a text, and he frowned when he read it and showed her the screen. It was from Dalton.

SAPD found an eavesdropping device in Madison's office.

Thea groaned. "That means the visitors—and perhaps the killer, too—knew that Madison had told Sonya about the botched in vitro." She paused, giving that some thought. "You think that was the trigger that caused the kidnapper/killer to go after Sonya?"

He paused, too. "Maybe. And if so, then it points to Yvette as being the killer."

"Yes, it does. Once we're back in Durango Ridge, we need to bring the woman back in for questioning."

Thea saw the sudden change in Raleigh's eyes, and it didn't take her long to figure out why. It was the "we" in that comment. It made it sound as if they were a team. Which they were. But that didn't mean he was comfortable with it.

"About that kiss," he said a moment later. He kept his voice low, probably so that Alice wouldn't hear. "It really shouldn't have happened."

"I won't argue with that." But for some stupid reason, Thea found herself fighting back a smile. There was nothing to smile about, even though the kiss had been pretty amazing. Of course, every kiss she'd ever had with Raleigh fell into that category.

"It's not just because we're working this case," he went on. "It's the baggage."

No need for him to remind her of that. "Because of Warren. Any kiss between us involves him, too."

Raleigh's eyebrow came up. "Trust me. I wasn't thinking about Warren during that."

She lost her fight with the smile, causing Raleigh to add some profanity under his breath. "Neither was I."

Thea would have liked to have promised that there wouldn't be another kiss, but she wasn't in the habit of lying to herself. If Raleigh and she were thrown together, they'd likely kiss again. And perhaps even do more. That was the reason she shouldn't stay at his house another night. The fatigue and adrenaline were already sky-high and that could bring down their already low defenses even more.

Best not to complicate things by having sex with

Raleigh. Even if that was something that sounded darn good to her.

She was about to tell him that she would call Court or one of her other fellow deputies to escort her home tonight and stay with her, but Alice took the turn into the parking lot of the security company. That conversation would have to wait.

As Thea had been doing the whole time they'd been on the road, she glanced around, looking for any signs of trouble. It wasn't a large building at all, and there were only two vehicles in the parking lot.

Raleigh had given the owner, Dan Shaw, a heads-up call that they were on the way to see him, and she hoped that one of the two cars belonged to Shaw. Thea didn't want him stalling them by ducking out on this visit.

Alice didn't park in any of the spots. Instead, she pulled directly in front of the door. "You want me to go in with you?" Alice asked Raleigh.

"No. Wait here and make sure no one else comes inside."

Thea hadn't needed a reminder of the possible danger that came with a visit like this, but that caused her heartbeat to kick up a significant notch. She didn't draw her gun, but she kept her hand in position as Raleigh and she got out and hurried inside.

There was a reception desk just a couple of yards from the door, but there was no one seated at it. In fact, there was no one in the room. Despite that, nothing seemed out of order. There was a cup of coffee and a sandwich still in its plastic wrapper next to an open laptop on the desk.

"Mr. Shaw?" Raleigh called out.

Nothing. But Thea didn't go into alarm mode just

yet. There was an office to the right, just off the reception area, and a hall to the left, where there were several other rooms.

Raleigh shouted the man's name again, and when Shaw didn't answer, Raleigh took out his phone and called him. Almost immediately, Thea heard the ringing sound in one of the back rooms off the hall.

Thea looked up at Raleigh and saw that he was just as concerned as she was. Maybe this was just a case of the man trying to hide from them, but it could be something much worse.

Raleigh and Thea drew their guns.

They started toward the hall, but she heard another sound in the room across from the reception desk. Someone was in there, and it sounded as if the person moaned.

Raleigh put his phone away and positioned himself in front of her. "Watch our backs," he told her.

Thea would because, after all, the owner's phone was on the other end of the building. Maybe the owner, too. But it was suspicious that he hadn't come out when Raleigh had called out for him. Suspicious, too, that someone else was nearby in the other room and hadn't said anything.

Raleigh walked closer to the room, keeping his steps slow and cautious, and once he reached the door, he readied his gun.

Then he cursed.

Thea had to lean to the side to see what had caused that reaction, and she soon spotted the woman on the floor. She was on her stomach, her arms and legs flung out in an awkward pose.

And there was blood on her head.

* * *

Raleigh felt that kick of emotion. A mix of dread and adrenaline. There was also some fear, since he figured that Thea and he had just walked into a crime scene.

His gaze slashed to every corner of the room. It was an office with a desk, but there was no one at the desk or beneath it. Only the woman on the floor.

"Is she still alive?" Thea asked, automatically taking out her phone. No doubt to call for an ambulance.

While he continued to keep watch, Raleigh stooped down and put his fingers to the woman's throat. "She's got a pulse." But in addition to what appeared to be blunt-force trauma to the head, she also had two distinctive marks on her neck.

Someone had used a stun gun on her.

Just as they had on Thea when she'd been at Sonya's house.

"Get Alice in here," Raleigh told Thea as she continued to make the call. "I need to check those back rooms where we heard the phone ringing."

And he didn't want to do that unless he had someone to help him protect Thea. Of course, Thea wouldn't appreciate him thinking like that, but she'd already come too close to dying, not once but twice.

Thea nodded and headed for the door but stopped when they heard another sound. Not a moan or a phone ringing this time. Someone was moving around in the room at the end of the hall. There was a sign next to that particular door, and it had Shaw's name on it, which meant that was his office.

"Call Alice and tell her to get in here," Raleigh repeated to Thea. She started to do that, but again the sound interrupted her.

But it was more than an interruption this time.

Shaw's office door flew open, and before Raleigh could even get a glimpse of the person who'd opened it, a shot blasted through the air. The bullet slammed into the wall right next to where Raleigh was standing. Another quarter of an inch, and he'd have been dead.

Raleigh hooked his arm around Thea, dragging her to the floor, but she'd already started in that direction anyway. Good thing, too, because more shots came. Thick, loud blasts that tore apart not just the wall behind them but also the reception desk. Since the desk wasn't much of a barrier at all, Raleigh pulled Thea into the room with the unconscious woman.

The woman moaned as if trying to warn them, but it was too late for that. Thea and he were under fire, and if Raleigh lifted his head to shoot back, he'd be an easy target.

Since the injured woman was too close to the door, Thea dragged her to the side so she wouldn't get hit by a stray bullet, and then Thea hurried back to him. A place he wished she wouldn't be, but he doubted there was any way he could talk her out of it. Plus, he needed the backup.

His phone buzzed, and when Raleigh saw Alice's name on the screen, he handed it to Thea. "Tell her to call SAPD if she hasn't already, but I don't want her coming through that door." She'd be too easy of a target for the shooter.

Thea did as he said, but her attention stayed in the direction of the gunman. So did Raleigh's. Judging from the angle of the shot, it was just one guy, but he could have brought a buddy with him who was holding Shaw. And Raleigh didn't have to guess what the thugs wanted.

They didn't want Thea and him to see the footage from the security camera.

That told Raleigh plenty about this situation—that he would almost certainly recognize the other man who'd gone to the fertility clinic to try to get a list of Dr. Sheridan's patients.

Maybe it was Nick or Simon.

Of course, it could be someone who could be linked to one of those two. And that's why it was important for Raleigh to get his hands on that footage.

"SAPDs on the way," Thea said when she finished her call to Alice.

Good. Because the angle of the shots changed. This thug was moving closer, no doubt trying to get in position to kill them both. That meant it was time for Raleigh to do something about that.

He stayed down, but he levered himself up just enough to send a bullet in the shooter's direction. Raleigh doubted he'd hit the guy, but it caused the man to growl out some raw curse words, and he kept shooting. However, Raleigh had gotten a decent look at the guy, and he was wearing a ski mask.

Raleigh fired another shot, too, and quickly moved back to cover. Well, as much cover as he had. The bullets were tearing through the wall, and it wouldn't be long before Thea and he couldn't use it for cover.

"Let's shoot at him together," Thea said.

He hated the idea because it would mean her being in the open. For a few seconds anyway. But SAPD or an ambulance wouldn't be able to get in and help until they'd contained the gunman. The woman definitely needed medical attention, and it was possible Shaw did, too.

"Fire now?" Thea asked.

She waited for Raleigh to nod, and together they leaned out, both of them pulling their triggers at the same time. Raleigh braced himself for the guy to shoot back. But he didn't. In fact, there were no gunshots from him, no profanity. Just the sound of someone running.

Hell, now the snake was trying to get away.

Raleigh got up, ready to fire, but the man was already ducking back into the office, and he slammed the door.

"If you want Shaw dead," the man shouted, "then go ahead and try to come back here."

Raleigh didn't want Shaw to die, but he couldn't trust that this goon would just keep him alive. In fact, he might use Shaw as a human shield so he could get out of the building.

The woman on the floor moaned again, a reminder to Raleigh that time wasn't on their side. She could bleed out and die if he didn't do something.

"Stay here with her," he told Thea. Of course, Thea probably didn't mind doing that part, but she knew what this meant.

"You're going out there," she said. Not a question. She knew it had to be done, but he could see the worry all over her face.

Raleigh tried to give her a reassuring nod, but he didn't want to waste another second. With his gun ready, he hurried out of the room, hunkering down behind the reception desk so he could get a better look at the hall. It wasn't long—less that twenty feet—but at any point the thug could open the door and start firing again. If Raleigh couldn't get into one of the other rooms, he'd be a sitting duck.

Even knowing that, he started moving. He ran to the wall right next to the hall and peered around. There was still no sign of the gunman. No sound of him, either. But there was something.

The smell of smoke.

Raleigh got a whiff of it just as it started to seep under and around the sides of the office door. The SOB had set the place on fire.

That gave Raleigh an even greater sense of urgency to do something.

"You might have to get the woman out of here," he called back to Thea, and he prayed that Alice and maybe even SAPD were out there to give her immediate backup.

Raleigh took a deep breath and started running up the hall. The smoke was already getting thicker, and he could smell something burning inside. He put his hand on the door to make sure there'd be no backdraft, but it was still cool to the touch, so he kicked it open.

There were flames all right, and they were already spreading across the wall and ceiling. But that wasn't the only thing that caught Raleigh's attention. It was the back door.

It was wide-open.

And there was no one in the room.

Chapter 9

Thea sat at Raleigh's desk in the Durango Ridge Sheriff's Office and tried to make sure she didn't show any signs of the raw nerves that were just beneath her skin. She had to be strong. Because Raleigh was already blaming himself enough. If she fell apart, that blame would skyrocket.

No way would he believe this attack wasn't his fault. He was kicking himself for taking her right into the middle of a gunfight. But he'd been in the middle of it, too, and that was one of the main reasons for Thea's raw nerves.

Again, he could have been killed, while trying to protect her.

And now they were in the middle of another round of chaos. One more layer to add to their already complicated investigation. It was more than just a *layer* though to Dan Shaw. He was missing, and his assistant, Sandra Millington, was in the hospital, in critical condition from a cracked skull and blood loss.

Raleigh was pacing in the squad room just outside his office door while he talked to someone in the San Antonio Fire Department. Apparently, he didn't like what he was hearing, which meant she wouldn't like it, either. Still, Thea tried not to focus on what was likely soon-to-be-revealed bad news and instead continued to read Madison's statement.

There wasn't anything new in the statement. At least Thea didn't think there was. But it was hard to concentrate when she could still hear the sound of those gunshots and see the blood on the injured woman.

Mercy.

She prayed Sandra Millington didn't die. There'd already been too many deaths connected to this investigation. Deaths maybe because of her. She couldn't forget that she'd been Marco's target, and that might mean all of this could be happening because of her or something she'd done.

Her phone rang, and Thea was so on edge that she gasped at the unexpected sound. And Raleigh noticed her reaction, too, because it caused his frown to deepen. But Thea wasn't frowning when she saw the name on the screen. Her heart went to her throat.

Because it was Rachel.

"Is the baby all right?" Thea blurted out as soon as she could hit the answer button.

"She's fine. We're all fine," Rachel quickly reassured her. "I was calling to check on you."

It took Thea a moment to get her voice and her breathing back under control. Despite all the horrible things that had happened, it would be a thousand times worse if the baby had been hurt or kidnapped again.

"I'm okay," Thea lied.

Judging from Rachel's huff, she knew it was a lie. "And is Raleigh *okay*?"

"I think so. Neither of us were hurt."

"No, you were just in a burning building with a gunman shooting at you." Rachel mumbled something Thea didn't catch. "I've always worried about Griff, Egan, Court and you. It's a strange feeling to add Raleigh to that worry list."

Thea didn't have any doubts about that. Didn't doubt, either, that Rachel would soon accept Raleigh as her brother. The question was, would Raleigh accept her as his sister? The bitterness he felt for Warren might get in the way of that.

"I do have another reason for calling," Rachel went on. "Griff's been pressuring the lab to get the DNA results on the baby, and we should have those back later today. Depending on what the test says, we have a decision to make. If the baby is Nick and Sonya's biological child, is there a reason for us not to hand over the baby to Nick?"

Thea groaned. Nick was still a person of interest in the attacks, and they certainly hadn't been able to rule him out. "When you have the results, just call Raleigh and me, and we'll go from there."

They might not be able to keep the child out of Nick's custody, but Thea wanted to delay that until they had some answers.

"Will do. Stay safe," Rachel added before she said goodbye.

Thea put her phone away at the same time that Raleigh finished his call with the fire department. He stepped inside the office and shut the door.

"The fire gutted the security company, destroying all the files and computers," he explained. His forehead was still bunched up, and even though he'd stopped pacing, he looked as if he needed to do something to burn off a lot of restless energy. "It's possible that Dan Shaw had files off-site or in an online storage, but we won't know that until we've talked to him or his assistant."

That tightened the muscles in her stomach and chest. Because they might not get a chance to ask either of them. They'd have to find Dan before they could question him, and as much as Thea hated to admit it, he could be dead. Their attacker could have killed him after he'd used Dan to help him escape.

Thea got up from the desk and went closer to Raleigh. "Any news on Sandra Millington?" she asked.

"She's still unconscious and in the ICU, but the hospital will call if there's any change. There's more," Raleigh said after he paused. "Someone torched the fertility clinic, too. No one was hurt," he quickly added. "But since the fire started in the records' room, whatever evidence was there was likely destroyed."

Mercy. No wonder Raleigh had been scowling and frowning when he'd been on the phone with the fire department. This definitely qualified as bad news. However, it did make her wonder...

"What could have been in those records that the killer didn't want us to find?" she asked. "I mean, Madison's already confessed to the botched in vitro, so what else could have been in there?"

"Maybe something to incriminate Yvette or Nick?

Exactly what that might be, I'm not sure, and we might never know."

True, and that led her to the call with Rachel. "Rachel said we should have the baby's DNA results today."

Raleigh cursed, which meant she didn't need to fill him in on the rest. "Nick's still not answering his phone. We don't know if that's because he was the person in the security company shooting, if he's a victim or if he's just lying low. Whichever it is, he's not at his house. We know that because SAPD is there now, carrying out a search order, and the only one around is Yvette."

Thea had known about the search order, but she hadn't realized it was already going on. Good. If there was anything incriminating, maybe the cops would find it so they wouldn't have to turn over the baby to Nick. Thea wanted the man to have his child only after he'd been cleared of any suspicion.

Raleigh looked at her, his gaze sliding from her face to her shirt. At first she thought there might be something sexual in that look, but then he cursed. "You have blood on you. Is it yours?"

She looked down at her sleeve and saw the small rip, along with the blood. Thea had noticed it earlier but had forgotten about it. "It's just a scratch." She'd gotten it when one of the gunman's bullets had shattered part of the door frame and had sent some splinters flying right at her.

It might have only been a scratch, but it seemed to be the final straw for Raleigh. He cursed, groaned and scrubbed his hand over his face. He was obviously about to deepen the guilt trip he was already on.

"That's not a good idea," he said when Thea slid her arm around his waist and pulled him to her.

"I know. A lot of what we do isn't a good idea. But going to the security company was," she added.

He eased back enough to look down at her and frown.

"Sandra's alive because we went there," Thea explained. "If we hadn't gotten to her, she could have been unconscious and trapped in that fire."

Raleigh's frown softened just a little. That was the only part of him soft though. His muscles were so tight that it felt as if she was hugging stone.

"The shooter might not have set the fire if we hadn't shown up," Raleigh pointed out, but he groaned again, maybe dismissing that. Because Thea was betting the gunman would indeed have burned down the place just to make sure they didn't get their hands on any evidence.

Since they had dozens of things to do, Thea was a little surprised when Raleigh stayed put. Surprised, too, at the gentle way he used just his fingertips to push her hair from her face. She figured the gentleness was a real effort for him with all that tension in his body.

She got yet another surprise when he leaned in even closer and kissed her. She felt the stubble on his jaw brush over her face. She took in his scent. And his taste.

The kiss packed a punch. A huge one. Maybe it was her frayed nerves, but she found herself leaning right into that kiss. She moved into the rhythm of it until her pulse was thick and throbbing. Until she remembered why she'd gotten involved with Raleigh in the first place.

When he finally pulled back, Thea didn't have to worry that he would see what a wreck she was from the attack. That's because now he was almost certainly seeing the heat in her eyes. Heat that he'd put there from that sizzling kiss.

Raleigh opened his mouth, maybe to apologize, but he didn't get a chance to say anything. That's because they heard Dalton shout out from the squad room.

"Hey, you can't just go in there," Dalton snarled.

But apparently the person thought the deputy's order didn't apply to him because the door flew open, and Simon was there with Dalton right behind him.

"Sorry about this," Dalton said to Raleigh, and he aimed a cop's glare at Simon. "Some people don't listen."

"*Some people* need to talk to the sheriff," Simon fired back.

But Simon didn't even look at Dalton when he spoke. His attention was on Raleigh and her. Specifically, Simon was noticing the way Thea had her arm around his waist and the fact that their bodies were practically touching. If Simon had come in just seconds earlier, he would have seen more than a touch, but even without that visual, Thea figured the man knew what had gone on.

And he didn't like it.

Maybe because she was close to Warren. However, Simon's anger was directed at Raleigh, too.

"Nice to see you're working so hard to find Sonya's killer," Simon grumbled.

He couldn't have said anything that would have made Raleigh and her move faster to get away from each other. Because it was true. They shouldn't be kissing when they were in the middle of a murder investigation. And Simon was part of that particular investigation.

"Your deputy called and said you wanted to see me," Simon went on. "Well, I'm a busy man. Busier than you are obviously. So what the heck do you want?"

Raleigh took a moment, maybe to rein in his temper, but he used that time to send a withering glare at

Simon. "Where were you at the times of Sonya's and Hannah Neal's murders?"

"What?" Simon howled. And he repeated it. "You think I had something to do with that?"

"I won't know until you've answered the question. It's a simple question, and I'd like an answer—now." There was no sign of a temper in Raleigh's tone, but he was all lawman now.

Dalton must have realized that Raleigh had this under control because he walked away, back toward his desk in the squad room.

"I was at home most of the day when Sonya was killed. And no, I doubt anyone can verify that. I didn't realize at the time that I would need an alibi since I'm not a criminal, and I don't have a criminal record."

Raleigh ignored that mini-tirade and kept on. "What about the day Hannah died? And don't say you don't know who she is, because her murder made front-page news around here."

"That was a year ago," Simon snapped. "No way could I remember something like that off the top of my head."

"Then check your calendar and appointment book and get back to me. I'd like an answer ASAP."

She hadn't thought Simon's glare could get worse, but it did. "What the hell is this about?"

"Buck Tanner," Raleigh immediately answered.

Thea watched Simon's expression, and she was certain that Raleigh was doing the same. The man's eyes widened for just a fraction of a second, and then his mouth tightened. "My former client. What about him?"

"Former?" Raleigh challenged. "You were his law-

yer of record for his last two arrests, one of them only about six months ago."

"We had a parting of the ways. Now, what's this about?" Simon included her in his volleyed glances, though Thea had no intentions of answering him.

"Buck Tanner's prints were on the kidnapped baby's carrier seat that Thea and I found," Raleigh explained. "I'm guessing you'll insist you don't know anything about that?"

"Of course I don't." But Simon definitely seemed uncomfortable. "Have you talked to him?"

"There's an APB out on him. We'll find him," Raleigh assured him. "Did he have a connection to Sonya? Did he know her?"

"I have no idea." The angry tone was back, but there was still plenty of concern in his eyes. "Are you suggesting that I put him up to something illegal?" Simon didn't wait for an answer. "Because I was his lawyer—that's all."

Raleigh made a *hmm* sound that let Simon know he wasn't exactly buying that. "I'll let you know what Buck says when we find him. And, oh, we're monitoring his phone and bank accounts. Just thought you should know that if you were planning on calling him."

If looks could kill, Simon would have blasted Raleigh and her off the planet. Simon belted out some profanity, turned and stormed out.

"You believe he's innocent?" Thea immediately asked Raleigh.

"I don't know. But something's going on with him."

Thea agreed. Too bad they couldn't find out if that *something* was Simon's plan to get back at Warren. Raleigh must have been thinking the same thing because he took out his phone.

"I'll call my mother and ask her if she ever heard Simon mention Buck," Raleigh explained.

But he didn't get a chance to make the call, because Dalton stepped into the doorway of the office. "SAPD found something when they were searching Yvette and Nick's house. A burner cell that was tucked between the mattresses. They'll send it to the lab to see if they can find out if it was used to make any calls."

"Did Yvette or Nick admit the phone was theirs?" she asked.

Dalton shook his head. "Nick wasn't there, and Yvette left shortly before they found it. You want me to get her in for questioning?"

"Not yet," Raleigh answered. "Wait until we hear back from the lab."

"There's more," Dalton went on. "There was also an envelope underneath a bunch of things in the bottom drawer of the nightstand. The kind of envelope that banks use sometimes when they give you a lot of cash. Someone had marked three thousand dollars on the outside of it, but inside there were only two one-hundred-dollar bills."

Three grand probably wasn't enough to hire two thugs to do your dirty work—like kidnap your surrogate's baby—but maybe it had been some kind of down payment. But the question was, where had Yvette or Nick gotten the money?

Thea looked up at Dalton. "Was there a withdrawal from their bank account in that amount?"

The deputy shook his head. "No cash withdrawal over two-hundred dollars."

It was possible that one of them had made the smaller withdrawals and stashed the money away in those increments, but it would have taken a while for that amount to accumulate. Still, it was doable.

"The lab is going to check for prints on the money," Dalton added.

Good. Then they would know if Nick or Yvette had put it there. Or maybe they both had. This could be their emergency fund, along with the cell phone. Maybe there was no criminal intent whatsoever.

"Let me know what the lab says," Raleigh reminded Dalton. "And make sure someone is keeping a close watch for Buck."

Dalton nodded. "His cell phone isn't in a service area, but if he gets or receives any calls, we'll know about it."

Since Buck was a career criminal, he'd probably ditched the cell. Too bad there wasn't a way for them to legally monitor Simon's phone, but they would need a court order for that. One they wouldn't be able to get because there wasn't enough evidence against him.

Dalton went back to his desk, leaving Raleigh and her standing there in the suddenly awkward silence. "I need to talk to my mom," he finally said. "Not just to ask her about Buck but because Simon will tell her that he saw you in my arms."

Sweet heaven. With everything else going on, Thea hadn't even considered that. But yes, Simon would tell her, and she didn't have to guess how Alma would handle the news because there was no way Raleigh's mom would approve of her son getting involved with her again.

Raleigh took out his phone, but before he could press

in Alma's number, he got another call. Her chest tightened when she saw the words *Unknown Caller* on the screen.

"Use your phone to record this," Raleigh insisted, and he waited until she had hit the recording function.

"Sheriff Lawton," a man said when Raleigh answered.

It wasn't a voice she recognized, and apparently neither did Raleigh because he snapped, "Who is this?"

"I'm the man who's going to make your day. You know that missing kid? The one that Hannah Neal was carrying for that couple who hired her to be a surrogate," he added. "Well, I got the kid. And before you ask, she's just fine."

Thea certainly hadn't expected that. Nor was she sure it was true.

"You've got the baby that's been missing?" Raleigh challenged. "You're sure about that, or is this some kind of hoax to extort some ransom money?"

"No hoax, and yeah, I'm sure."

"If that's true, where has the baby been all this time? She's been missing for a year."

"She's been in good hands with a nanny," the man said.

Thea prayed that was true. But that didn't mean the baby would remain in good hands, because this thug probably had demands. Money for sure. But maybe something more—like exchanging the baby for her. That's what Marco had wanted anyway, and this could be Buck, Marco's partner on the other end of the line.

If Buck or this snake did indeed want her, then Thea would try to make that happen. This had nothing to do with her being a cop. There was just no way she could allow the baby to be in the hands of a killer.

"You probably got questions," the man went on, "but you must know that I'm not gonna be real keen on answering them, especially since you're probably taping this and all. But here's the deal. You get the kid, no strings attached."

"Really? No strings?" Raleigh challenged.

"Not a one. If you want the kid, she's right outside the back door of the diner, the one that leads into the alley. My advice? Get there fast before I change my mind."

And with that, the caller hung up.

"You're not going out there," Raleigh said to Thea before she could even volunteer. "Stay put, and that's not up for negotiation."

Thea understood his concern. They'd nearly been killed just hours earlier, but she hadn't been the only one in the middle of that attack. Raleigh had been, too. Still, she didn't say anything because she knew it wasn't an argument she could win.

Raleigh drew his gun and hurried into the squad room. "Call the diner," he told Alice. "I don't want any of the employees or customers going outside the building, but there could be a baby at their back door."

Alice was in the process of making that call when Thea saw the front entrance of the diner open, and a woman in a waitress uniform started walking toward the sheriff's office.

She was holding an infant car seat, and there was indeed a baby strapped inside it.

Raleigh ran to the door, threw it open, and the moment the waitress reached him, he pulled her inside. "I heard a baby crying," she said, "and when I went to check it out, I found her. There's an envelope taped to the side of the seat, but I didn't touch it. I didn't unhook the straps, either."

That was smart of her, but Thea doubted there'd be any evidence to recover from it. Still, they had something that might link them back to who'd done this.

"Did you see anyone else back there or in the alley?" Raleigh asked the woman.

She shook her head. "Just the baby. Why would someone leave a precious little girl out there like that?"

"I don't know, but I'll find out," Raleigh assured her.

Thea went into the squad room so she could have a better look. The baby was wearing a pink dress and had blond curls. She was fussing and kicking her feet, but she seemed to be unharmed. Thank God.

"I need gloves," Raleigh told Alice, and the deputy ran to the supply cabinet to get him a pair.

Once Raleigh had them on, he took the car seat from the waitress, moving it to one of the desk tops. He clicked a picture of the carrier and baby before he removed the envelope. There was no letter or note inside, just two photos. And the sight of them caused Thea's breath to stall in her throat.

Because the first was a picture of Hannah. Alive. And she was holding a newborn baby. Judging from the looks of it, it was the baby she'd just delivered.

Raleigh moved on to the second photo, and even though Thea had tried to steel herself up for whatever it would be, the steeling didn't work. The sickening feeling of dread washed over her.

In this picture, Hannah was dead. Her lifeless body was sprawled out. And next to her was a man in a ski mask, holding the precious baby in his arms.

Chapter 10

The nightmare woke Raleigh, and he jackknifed in the bed. The images of an attack had been so real that his body had kicked up a huge amount of adrenaline, preparing itself for a fight. But there was no threat. He was alone in his bed, and his house was quiet.

Quiet but with the smell of coffee in the air.

He threw back the covers and checked the time. It was barely 6:00 a.m., which meant he'd gotten about five hours of sleep. Apparently though, Thea had gotten even less than that, since she was almost certainly the reason for the coffee scent. That meant she was probably up, working, something he should be doing.

Raleigh grabbed a quick shower, threw on some clothes and hurried into the kitchen. Thea was there all right, and there was a half-filled pot of coffee on the kitchen counter. But she was sacked out, her head on the table next to her open laptop and her phone.

The sound of his footsteps must have alerted her though because her eyes flew open, and she reached for her gun. Which wasn't there. Because she was wearing his pj's. Or rather pj's that belonged to him. Her brother hadn't packed her a pair of her own, so she'd had to use a pair of his.

For all of his adult life, Raleigh had only slept in boxers or gone commando, but for some reason his mother always gave him pajamas, slippers and robes as gifts. He'd never used any of them, but they looked darn good on Thea.

"Sorry," she mumbled. She stood and stretched, causing the blue plaid fabric to tighten across her breasts. Plus, she'd missed the two bottom buttons on the top, so he got a nice peep show of her stomach.

Yeah, the pj's looked good on her.

Raleigh felt his body clench, and to stop himself from ogling her, he got his mind on something else. "You couldn't sleep?" he asked, pouring himself a cup of coffee.

"I managed to get in a couple of hours, but I wanted to check on the baby. Well, both babies, actually. Rachel's an early riser because her pregnancy is getting to the uncomfortable stage, so she emailed me some updates. Sonya's baby is fine. And the baby that the waitress found yesterday is with social services and has had her DNA tested."

That was a start, but in addition to keeping both girls safe, they needed to know the identities of their parents. If the older baby was indeed the one that Hannah had carried, then the child would be given to the birth parents, the couple who'd hired Hannah to be their surrogate. It could be wonderful news for them.

Of course, that didn't change the fact that Hannah was dead.

Since Thea had already started her work day, Raleigh did, too. He took his laptop to the table and loaded his email, and he immediately saw one from the lab. According to the test they'd run, there were no prints on the car seat other than those of the waitress. And none on the envelope or the photos. Along with that, there were no fibers or trace evidence. Not good, but the photos would still be analyzed though to see if there was any visual evidence in the background.

Something that Raleigh had already been looking at.

Too bad he'd found nothing. However, he'd had the photos scanned, and he downloaded them from the storage files.

"Griff has been in touch with the San Antonio Fire Department," Thea continued. She got up to pour herself more coffee. "Both fires at the security company and fertility clinic were set with accelerants. Something we'd already suspected."

They had. Ditto for suspecting that Yvette would claim the money in the nightstand drawer was for emergencies, that there was no way she'd ever used the cash to pay a kidnapper. Yvette had also claimed that once there had been three grand in the envelope, but they'd tapped into it for various things.

As for the phone, Yvette insisted she had no idea why it was there. Since they still hadn't been able to get in touch with Nick, Raleigh didn't have anyone to confirm or deny what she'd said. And the phone wasn't going to be of much help because if it had been used to make or receive calls, all of that had been erased, and it had been wiped of any prints.

"I don't suppose you have any news about Buck?" Thea asked, sitting back down beside him again. "*Good news*—like the cops found and arrested him."

She looked at his laptop screen and groaned softly. That's because he had the photo of Hannah dead on the screen. Thea had seen it before, of course, but it never got easier to look at something like that.

"The killer was sick to take her picture," she mumbled and looked away.

Yeah, he was sick, but the ski-mask-wearing thug might have done that in case he ever had to prove that the baby was the one Hannah had delivered. A photo would have come in handy if there'd been a ransom demand. But there hadn't been.

Well, not until two days ago.

Raleigh pulled up the third picture, the one that'd been sent to Nick on his phone, and he positioned it side by side with the photo taken of Hannah when she was still alive. And holding the newborn that she'd almost certainly just delivered.

"They look like the same baby," Thea muttered.

Raleigh agreed, though the lab should be able to determine that. DNA, too. But that wouldn't answer his question of why the kidnapper/killer waited a year to return the little girl.

"At least the baby is healthy," Thea added. "The hospital said she's been well taken care of."

That was something at least, but it wouldn't erase the hell the biological parents had gone through worrying about their missing child.

"Dalton's coordinating all the security cameras for that block around the diner," Raleigh said after glancing at his next email update.

No one had seen anyone leave the baby, but it was possible one of the cameras had picked up something. But even if they had footage of the person, Raleigh figured the guy was long gone. Something had caused him to give up the child—without collecting a penny—and that meant he was likely going on the run.

But why?

Maybe the guy felt that he was close to being caught. Or if it was Buck, he could have known about the APB and that he would be arrested for murder if he stayed around.

"We need to find the nanny who took care of the baby," Thea said. "If she's alive, that is."

Thea's voice cracked a little on those last words, and she got up again, turning away from him. Since she wasn't looking at anything in particular, Raleigh figured she was dodging his gaze. That's why he stood, too. He took hold of her hand and eased her back around to face him.

There were tears in her eyes.

"Sometimes, it just gets to be too much," she whispered.

He felt the same way. The murders, the kidnappings, the fires and the attacks. And they still didn't know why this was happening. The problem was that it could get a whole lot worse.

Knowing it was a mistake, Raleigh pulled her into his arms and brushed a kiss on the top of her head. He kept it chaste. Well, as much as something like that could be between Thea and him. Which wasn't very chaste at all. He felt the immediate punch from the heat.

And tried to rein it in.

After all, they weren't in his office, where someone

could come walking in at any minute. They were in his house, behind closed doors and alone. Plus, there were the memories of when they'd had sex just a few yards away on the sofa in the living room.

Thea looked up at him and frowned. "Should we try to talk ourselves out of this?" The corners of her mouth lifted, and it seemed as if she was going to use that half joke to move away from him.

She didn't.

That's because she kept staring at his mouth, and her body seemed to be issuing this silent invitation for him to kiss her. So that's what he did. Raleigh snapped her to him, and he pushed common sense right out the window when he pressed his mouth to hers.

There it was. More than just a mere kick of attraction. As it always was with Thea, it started out scalding and just got hotter from there. That would have been good if this had been leading to sex. But it couldn't.

Raleigh repeated that.

Though he probably could have repeated it a hundred times and it wouldn't have helped. That's because Thea slipped her arms around his neck and pulled him down even lower so he could deepen the kiss.

The need came, sliding right through him and making him want to take this up a notch. So he did. Without breaking the kiss, Raleigh turned her, backing her against the wall, and he made that need even more urgent when he slid his hand beneath her top.

No bra.

Hell, he was in trouble.

And he kept creating the trouble when he cupped her right breast and flicked his thumb over her nipple. It wasn't hard to find because it was already puckered and tight from arousal. He made that worse, too, by lowering his head and taking it into his mouth.

Thea made a moaning sound. It was all pleasure. She definitely didn't move away from him. In fact, she ran her hands down his back, pulling him closer and closer.

Raleigh lingered there awhile, tasting her, and he took the kisses lower. To her stomach. The waist of the pj's bottoms was loose on her, making it very easy for him to push down the fabric and keep kissing until he reached the top of her panties. A sane man would have stopped there, but he just pushed them down and kept kissing.

Thea cursed, the profanity probably aimed at him. Maybe at herself. But those sounds of pleasure kept urging him on. So did the sight of her when he got her panties low enough. He'd made love to her this way before, but it'd been a long time.

Too long.

And maybe if he kept it to just this, he could convince himself that he hadn't crossed every line that shouldn't be crossed between them. But before Raleigh could take things to the next step, he heard a different sound. One he didn't want to hear. Because his phone was ringing.

Hell. Talk about losing focus.

Thea scrambled away from him and started fixing her clothes. Raleigh did some scrambling, too, and he whipped out his phone to see Dalton's name on the screen. Since it was too early for routine business, he knew this had to be important for his deputy to call him at home.

"What happened?" Raleigh asked when he hit the

answer button. And he hoped someone else wasn't dead or had been kidnapped.

"Nick O'Hara just walked in."

Well, at least the man was alive. Since no one had heard from him in twenty-four hours, Raleigh had started to think he was either dead or had fled because he was guilty of something.

"Mr. O'Hara's asking to talk to you," Dalton added a moment later. "I think you should come in because he says he needs to make a confession."

Even though it was only a short drive from Raleigh's house to the sheriff's office, Thea was on edge for every second of the trip. But at least they might have answers soon. Well, they would if Nick's confession led them to a killer—either himself or someone he'd hired.

"We never did find a connection between Nick and Hannah," Thea reminded Raleigh.

Even though Raleigh's attention seemed to be on keeping watch around them, he made an immediate sound of agreement. "Maybe there isn't one. Sonya's murder could be a copycat killing. One that doesn't have anything to do with Hannah. Or Warren."

She wished that would turn out to be true. It wouldn't bring back either woman, but it might ease the guilt Warren was no doubt feeling since he believed he was the reason for both women dying.

"About what happened right before I got Dalton's call…" Raleigh tossed out there.

Thea certainly hadn't forgotten about it. They were within a heartbeat of having some form of sex. And Raleigh was almost certainly regretting it.

She was about to give him an out. To tell him that

being under the same roof had just stirred some old memories. But Raleigh continued before she could say anything.

"If we're together, alone, it'll happen again." He mumbled some profanity to go along with that.

Thea couldn't deny that, and she took a moment to try to figure out how to answer that. "I should stay at my own place tonight. Griff can arrange a protection detail—"

"No," Raleigh interrupted. He looked at her. It was barely a glance, but he managed to put a lot of emotions into such a brief look. She saw the frustration. Even some anger. But she also saw the heat. "I want you in my bed, and your being somewhere else isn't going to change that."

Well, the man certainly knew how to take her breath away. And complicate things. Especially since it was obvious that neither of them should be thinking about sex right now. It was also obvious that it was going to happen whether or not it made a mess out of this situation.

Thankfully, Thea didn't have to say anything else because Raleigh pulled to a stop in front of the sheriff's office. Later though, there'd need to be a discussion about this. Or perhaps this attraction was past the discussion point.

Maybe she should just go for it. A hot, sweaty round of ex-sex with Raleigh might burn up some of this energy and cool down some of this fire between them. But then she looked at him and decided it was best if she didn't lie to herself. Sex wouldn't cool down anything. It would only remind her of what she'd once had with Raleigh.

And she wanted that again.

"Yeah," he said as if he knew exactly what she was thinking.

He didn't add more. Instead, Raleigh hurried her out of the cruiser and into the squad room, where she immediately spotted Nick. Not alone, either.

Simon was standing next to him.

"My client wants to talk to you," Simon greeted.

"Your client?" Raleigh challenged.

Nick nodded and rubbed his hand over his face. He definitely didn't look like the polished businessman who'd first shown up in Durango Ridge. No. Judging from his rumpled hair and clothes, he'd had a rough time. Thea knew exactly how he felt. But what she didn't understand was why he'd hired Simon.

Simon definitely seemed to be all right with the arrangement though.

The man was practically gloating, maybe because he believed this was some kind of dig against Raleigh and her. However, Thea was far less interested in Nick's choice of attorney than she was in why he felt he needed a lawyer in the first place. Maybe he did intend on confessing to murder.

"This way," Raleigh said, leading Simon and Nick toward an interview room. He motioned for Thea to come, as well.

She braced herself for Simon or even Nick to object to her being there. After all, this wasn't her jurisdiction. But neither man brought it up when she followed them into the room.

Simon and Nick sat at the table, and Raleigh took the seat across from them. "What's this all about?" Raleigh asked.

Despite the fact that Nick had been the one to ask for this meeting, he didn't jump right into an explanation. He groaned. "I was having an affair with Sonya," he finally blurted out.

Along with the shock of hearing that, Thea got a heavy feeling in her stomach. Sonya had never hinted of an affair. Of course, that didn't mean it hadn't happened.

"I'm going to want to hear a lot more about this," Raleigh insisted.

Nick didn't continue though until Simon whispered something in his ear. "The affair started shortly after we met. Right after Sonya got confirmation that she was pregnant."

Raleigh glanced at her, probably to see if she'd had any inkling, but Thea had to shake her head.

"I fell in love with Sonya," Nick went on. "And that's the reason I wasn't too enthusiastic when I thought I'd be raising my and Yvette's child. My marriage was in trouble—and don't blame Sonya for that. I had fallen out of love with my wife before I even met Sonya."

Thea couldn't believe what she was hearing. "Then why the heck did you agree to a surrogate pregnancy?"

Again, Simon whispered something to Nick, and it was Simon who continued. "Mr. O'Hara has come here in good faith, to set the record straight. I won't tolerate either of you judging him for his extramarital involvement."

Raleigh gave both of them a blank stare. "No judging. I'll leave that to a jury."

"A jury?" Nick snapped, jumping to his feet, but Simon pulled him right back in the chair.

"Are you saying you're going to arrest my client?" Simon asked, his tone smug because he knew an affair alone wouldn't be enough of a motive to charge Nick with Sonya's murder.

But maybe there was something else here.

"No arrest. Not yet," Raleigh added. "Right now though, I see a big red flag for *your client*. He's just admitted to an affair with a woman who was murdered. An affair he waited two days to tell us about. And now he admits to a rocky marriage. Is he here to confess to murder or to point the finger at his wife?"

"I didn't kill Sonya," Nick insisted, and he left it at that. Which meant he likely was going to try to pin this on Yvette.

And she might have done it, too.

"Yvette knew about the affair?" Thea asked.

Nick took his time answering. "I never told her, but I believe she found out and killed Sonya."

Raleigh didn't take that at face value. With his raised eyebrows, he looked skeptical. "You got any proof that Yvette did it?"

"She argued with Sonya the morning of the murder," Nick was quick to remind them.

"Yes, because Yvette found out the baby wasn't hers and that Sonya was thinking about keeping the child," Raleigh reminded him right back. "In that case, I think it was justified for Yvette to be upset." He leaned forward, his cop's stare on Nick. "So, how did you react when you found out the baby was yours and Sonya's?"

Nick exchanged glances with Simon before he said anything. "I was, well, shocked."

It was an interesting reaction, considering Nick had just talked about being in love with Sonya. There was something else going on here, and Raleigh picked up on it, too.

"I'm going out on a limb here, but I don't think you had plans to ever divorce Yvette," Raleigh started. "Maybe because she comes from money? I remember her saying you two ran her late father's successful real estate company. So, did you sign a prenup?"

Bingo. Nick didn't have to verbally confirm that for Thea to know it was true, and that led her to a problem that Sonya's pregnancy could have created.

"If Yvette found out Sonya was carrying your baby, she might have thought the child was the result of your affair," Thea suggested. "That would have given her grounds for a divorce. Of course, the affair alone would have also done that, but the baby would be proof that she could use in a court battle. And if she divorced you, you'd be broke and without a job."

That lit an angry fire in Nick's eyes. It didn't have Simon remaining calm, either. "Are you accusing me of setting up Yvette to take the blame for Sonya's murder?" Nick snarled.

"If Deputy Morris isn't accusing you, then I am," Raleigh fired back. "You've got a big motive for wanting Yvette behind bars. Plus, you lied to us. And let's get into the part about you knowing that Sonya's baby was yours, and yet you claimed it wasn't, that Thea and I had gotten the wrong child from Marco."

Nick huffed. "That was an honest mistake. The baby didn't look like Sonya and me, and I thought the other baby did. I didn't know it was a hoax to milk money from me."

Any money would have come from Yvette. If she had fallen for the hoax, that is. She hadn't. Yvette had continued to try to stake her claim to the baby Raleigh and she had rescued. And she'd done that despite the fact that the baby wasn't biologically hers. Maybe because she was desperate to be a mother, but Thea wondered if there was another reason.

Yvette could have somehow planned to use the child to get back at her cheating husband.

"My client has voluntarily explained everything to you," Simon concluded, and he stood. "I'm assuming he's free to go."

"No, he's not." Raleigh motioned for Nick to sit back down. "Tell me about the money that SAPD found in your nightstand drawer. And the phone between the mattresses."

Nick had already opened his mouth to answer until Raleigh added the last part. His mouth tightened, telling them that the man hadn't *explained everything* after all. "The money is for emergencies," Nick said after a long pause. "The phone was the one I used to call Sonya. I couldn't use my regular cell because Yvette would have seen Sonya's number on the bill."

"Now, are you satisfied?" Simon snapped at Raleigh.

"No. I'm more than a little concerned that you're the attorney for two suspects in this murder investigation."

"A suspect?" Nick howled.

Raleigh looked him straight in the eyes. "You heard me. If you're innocent, I'll apologize, but there'll be an asterisk by it because you withheld information about your affair with the victim." Raleigh stood. "Now you're free to go."

Thea and Raleigh walked out, leaving Nick still grumbling about being a suspect. Too bad they didn't have anything to hold the man, but other than circumstantial evidence, there was nothing to tie him to the crime of either Sonya's murder or the kidnapping.

"I'll call the lab and ask them to take another look at that cell phone the cops found between the mattresses," Raleigh said as they went back toward his office. "The calls were all erased, but maybe there's a storage cache they can find. I also need to have another chat with Yvette about the prenup and to find out if she knew anything about the affair."

Yes, because the affair could give Yvette motive for murdering Sonya.

Raleigh reached for his phone, but he stopped when they got to his office. That's because it wasn't empty.

His mother was there.

Thea checked the time to make sure it wasn't later than she thought. It wasn't. It wasn't even seven thirty yet. Pretty early for a visit, which meant something could be wrong.

"Dalton said Simon was here." Alma's voice was a little shaky. Actually, the same applied to her, too. She had a wadded up tissue in her hand, and Thea thought she might have been crying.

Raleigh nodded. "He's with a new client."

"I'll wait out here while you two talk," Thea offered.

But Alma immediately shook her head. "No. Please come in. Both of you. But shut the door. I don't want Simon to know I'm here."

Well, this was interesting, considering that Simon was not only Alma's longtime friend but her lawyer.

"Did something happen?" Raleigh asked once Thea and he were inside the office. He also shut the door.

His mother volleyed some nervous glances at him. "It's about Warren," Alma said after a very long hesitation.

Thea wanted to groan, and she hoped Alma wasn't about to try to accuse Warren of some crime.

"I wrote a letter to Warren," Alma went on when Raleigh and Thea just stared at her. "It was something I didn't want him to read until after my death."

Raleigh's forehead bunched up, and Thea's was certain that hers did, too. "What kind of letter?" Raleigh pressed. He wasn't using the same rough tone he did with Nick, but he was clearly concerned about this.

Alma was concerned, too, because she needed to use that tissue to dab at her eyes. "You're not going to like it, but I told Warren that I loved him. And I still do."

Raleigh mumbled some profanity. "He hurt you."

Alma nodded, blinked back tears. "And I'm sure I hurt his wife. Remember, I knew he was married, and I still kept seeing him."

Thea had to wonder if Sonya had felt the same way about Nick. She hoped it was love anyway and that the love hadn't soured to the point that it would make Nick want to kill her.

When Alma's tears continued, Raleigh went to her and pulled her into his arms. He brushed a kiss on the top of her head. "Why are you telling me this? Did something happen with the letter?"

"Yes, I believe something did."

Thea prayed that Warren's wife hadn't seen it. She was just now back on her feet, recovering from a mental breakdown, and it wouldn't help for her to see something like that.

Alma eased back from Raleigh to face both of them. "I was going to put the letter in the safe in my office, but I got busy doing something else and left it on my desk when I went out to meet with one of the new hands.

While I was gone, Ruby said that Simon arrived, and he went into my office."

"Ruby?" Thea asked.

"My housekeeper. She said, when she looked in my office, that Simon was reading the letter, and that he got very mad and stormed out. Ruby was going to tell me, but then her daughter got sick, and she had to leave. It must have slipped her mind because she didn't tell me about it until this morning."

So Simon had seen, in writing, that Alma still had feelings for Warren. That definitely wouldn't have sit well with him. But maybe it had done something much, much more.

"When did all this happen?" Raleigh asked. "When did Simon read the letter?"

Alma's mouth began to tremble. "The same morning that Sonya was murdered."

Oh, mercy. Maybe that was a coincidence, but it was too strong of a connection to dismiss it.

"I suppose you'll have to ask Simon about it?" Alma said to her son.

"Yes." Obviously giving that some thought, Raleigh stayed quiet a moment. "But not now. Not while you're here." He hugged her. "Just go on home, and I'll take care of it."

But Alma didn't budge. "Are you disappointed with me?" she asked him.

"No. I'm not disappointed," Raleigh assured her. And Thea believed that was the truth.

"Do you think I'm a fool for still having these feelings for Warren?" Alma aimed that second question at Thea.

Thea sighed and repeated Raleigh's "no." Alma

wasn't a fool. She was just a woman who couldn't get over her feelings for a man—something Thea could certainly relate to.

Raleigh opened the door and looked out, no doubt checking to make sure Simon wasn't out there. He wasn't, so Raleigh opened the door even wider. "You want me to have one of the deputies drive you home?" he asked her.

His mother shook her head and gave his hand a gentle squeeze. "I'll be fine. I just need some time to myself."

Thea watched the woman walk out, and she felt a strange mix of feelings. Resentment at the part Alma had played in nearly destroying Warren's marriage. But Thea felt empathy, too. She looked at Raleigh to tell him that, but Dalton came toward them.

"The lab just sent over the DNA results on the newborn," Dalton said. He handed Raleigh the report. "And as you can see, it's not what we were expecting."

Chapter 11

Raleigh read through the lab report, shook his head and read it again. What the heck was going on?

"The baby isn't Nick's," Thea said as she looked at the DNA results. "She's Sonya and Dr. Sheridan's."

Dalton had been right about them not expecting this. "How did the lab even have Dr. Sheridan's DNA to do the comparison?" Raleigh asked Dalton. And that was just the first of many questions he had.

"He was in the system because he worked in a federal prison for a short time, so when the baby's DNA didn't match Nick's, the lab tech just fed the results through the database. Dr. Sheridan fathered that baby."

It didn't take Raleigh long to figure out how this could have happened. Madison had already told them that Yvette's harvested eggs had been misplaced. Well, maybe Nick's semen had been, too. Dr. Sheridan could have substituted his own to make up for the mistake.

Or he'd been asked to do that by someone.

The only person in this equation who wasn't so eager for that baby to be conceived was Nick. That could mean he was in on this, and if so, he'd have a strong motive to kill the doctor if Sheridan had decided to come clean with Yvette.

"In case Nick's the one behind this, we need to dig into Dr. Sheridan's bank account and see if he was paid off for his part in the botched in vitro," Raleigh told Dalton. "We know there were no large sums of money taken from the O'Haras' bank account, but see if you can figure out another way for Nick to have gotten his hands on some cash about nine months ago."

"I'll get right on that," Dalton said as he went back to his desk.

"You really think Nick killed Sonya?" Thea asked.

"Maybe. If she'd tried to break things off with him, he could have been enraged enough to do something like that. There weren't any recordings of her and Nick's conversations, so we really don't know how things were between them."

She made a sound of agreement. "And then Nick could have killed Dr. Sheridan and burned down the clinic and the security company to cover his tracks." She paused. "Of course, Yvette could have hired someone to do the murders to set up her husband. If she was upset enough about the affair, she might have wanted to get revenge."

True. But it was also possible that the botched in vitro had nothing to do with the murders or the attacks. If so, then this all went back to Simon. And unlike Nick and Yvette, Simon did have a connection to one of the hired guns.

Raleigh's phone rang, and considering everything that was going on, he halfway expected to see *Unknown Caller* on the screen. But it was a familiar name.

Warren.

Raleigh wasn't especially eager to talk to him, but since this could be about the investigation, he answered it right away.

"I was driving into Durango Ridge to check on Thea," Warren immediately said, "and I saw your mom's car parked on the side of the road."

Raleigh's heart went into overdrive, especially when he heard his mother yelling in the background. "Is she all right?" He couldn't ask that fast enough.

"She's not hurt or anything like that, but she's crying and clearly upset. She tried to drive off, but I took away her keys. I didn't think she should be behind the wheel like that." Warren paused. "And now she's pulled a gun on me."

Raleigh didn't even bother to hold back the profanity. "I'm on the way. Where are you exactly?"

"About a quarter of a mile south of the turn for Alma's ranch."

Raleigh knew the spot. "Tell her not to do anything stupid, that I'll be right there."

He put away his phone and took out the keys for the cruiser parked right out front, but that's when he realized Thea was following him.

"You're not going out there alone," she insisted.

Hell. Now he had to worry about both his mother and Thea. And Warren. He didn't like the man, but he darn sure didn't want his mother to end up in jail for shooting him. Later, he'd kick himself for not having one of the deputies escort Alma home, but for now, he needed to get to her and hopefully defuse a bad situation.

"Come with us," Raleigh told Dalton. He hated to pull Dalton away from the pile of work that was on his desk, but after what happened at the security company, Raleigh didn't want to take any chances.

After Raleigh told Alice what was going on, Dalton, Thea and he hurried outside to the cruiser. Raleigh got behind the wheel, and with Dalton at shotgun, Thea got in the back. Raleigh turned on the flashing lights and siren so he could get down Main Street as fast as possible.

"What do you think happened to your mom?" Thea asked.

He doubted it was anything other than what Alma had already told them. That she was worried about Simon having read the letter. That had already brought his mother to tears before she'd come to the sheriff's office, and those tears had obviously continued after she left.

"I think my mom is worried that Simon murdered Sonya, maybe Hannah, too, and now she's blaming herself." Of course, that didn't explain why she'd pull a gun on a man she still loved, but it could be she'd gotten so hysterical that she didn't know what she was doing. Which made this situation even more dangerous.

Even though it was only a couple of miles, it seemed to take forever for them to get there, and by the time they arrived, Raleigh could feel his pulse drumming in his ears. What he saw sure didn't help with that, either.

Alma's car was indeed there. His mom had pulled off into a narrow clearing that was in front of a cattle gate and pasture. At least she hadn't stopped on the road.

Warren's truck was parked just behind Alma's car, and Dalton pulled to a stop behind it since the road shoulder was too narrow to park ahead of the vehicles.

Warren was there, too. He was standing by the driver's-side door of Alma's car. He had his hands raised in the air. Alma was inside, still behind the wheel, and she did indeed have a gun aimed at Warren. The gun was a Smith & Wesson that he knew his mom kept in her glove compartment.

Raleigh's first instinct was to bolt from the cruiser, but he glanced around first. Something he'd been doing during the whole drive. But he didn't see anyone. Maybe it would stay that way, though this was the road that led into town, so someone would no doubt eventually drive by.

He glanced back at Thea to tell her to stay put, but she was already getting out. And he couldn't blame her. She loved Warren and was probably afraid for his life.

Raleigh and Dalton got out as well, and Raleigh maneuvered himself in front of Thea. He didn't draw his gun, but Dalton did.

"I didn't want Warren to call you," his mom immediately said.

"Then you shouldn't have pulled a gun on him. Put it away, *now*," Raleigh ordered, and he was sure he sounded more like a sheriff than her son. "What the heck is going on here?"

Alma was crying all right, the tears streaming down her face, and she shook her head. "I just want my keys so I can go home, and he wouldn't give them to me."

But Warren handed them to Raleigh just as Thea went to Warren's side.

"You're not driving home like this," Raleigh told his mother. "And Warren was right to do what he did."

And no, hell didn't freeze over because he'd taken his *father's* side on this.

"Alma's not thinking straight. She wouldn't have shot me though," Warren insisted.

Probably not, but it was too big of a risk to take. That's why Raleigh held out his hand for his mother to give him the gun. She didn't jump to do that, but he didn't want to try to wrench it from her hand and end up risking her pulling the trigger by accident. She finally gave it to him and then collapsed with a hoarse sob against the steering wheel.

"This is all my fault," Alma managed to say, though it had to be hard to talk with her having to drag in her breath like that. "Simon did this for me."

Warren didn't seem surprised by that comment, which meant it'd likely been the topic of their conversation before things had taken a very bad turn.

"Simon might not have done anything wrong," Raleigh explained. "Especially nothing that had anything to do with you. We have two other solid suspects in Sonya's murder."

His mother lifted her head, blinked and stared at him. "Are you just saying that to make me feel better?"

"No. I'm saying it because it's true. And even if it wasn't, you aren't responsible for what Simon does or doesn't do."

She shook her head again. "But the letter…"

Now, Warren did show some surprise. He frowned when he looked at Raleigh. "What letter?"

Since it wasn't his place to answer that, Raleigh just waited for his mom to say something, but she waved it off. "It doesn't matter. I shouldn't have written the letter in the first place."

Alma wiped away her tears and sat up straight. She was probably trying to look strong enough to drive, but Raleigh wasn't buying it.

"Are you going to press charges for her pulling the gun on you?" Raleigh asked Warren.

"No." He fixed his gaze on Alma. "I did wrong by her. By you," he added to Raleigh. "I deserve anything the two of you dish out."

Well, he didn't deserve to be shot, and Raleigh considered it progress that he felt that way. He mumbled a thanks for Warren not pressing those charges, and then he had a quick debate about how to handle this. He couldn't allow his mother to go home alone, and he didn't think handing her off to Dalton was a good idea.

"I need to drive my mother home," Raleigh finally said to Thea. "You can go back to town with Dalton. Or Warren."

Thea seemed to have a debate with herself, too. She volleyed glances at all of them. "Why don't Dalton and I go with you to take Alma home? We could use the cruiser."

Raleigh didn't have to guess why she would suggest that. It was bullet resistant, and they could be attacked along the way. It was a good idea, but what wasn't good was extending the invitation for Warren to go with them. Warren must have sensed what Raleigh was thinking because he tipped his head to his truck.

"I'll be going," Warren said. "Now that I know Thea's okay, I need to be getting home." He hugged her and headed to his truck.

"I made a fool of myself," Alma mumbled, and the tears started again when Warren drove away.

Despite the crying, Raleigh didn't want to wait

around to calm her down again, so he opened her door. "Come on. I'll have someone from the ranch come back and get your car."

His mom didn't argue with him about that, thank God, and he got her moving to the cruiser. However, he didn't get far. Only a few steps. Before Raleigh heard something that he didn't want to hear.

A gunshot.

At first Thea thought the sound was a car backfiring, but she glanced up the road and saw that Warren's truck was already out of sight. And there wasn't another vehicle with a running engine anywhere around.

Raleigh obviously knew what it was though because, in the split second that followed the shot, he hooked his arms around her and his mother, and he pulled them to the ground.

Alma made a sharp gasp of pain, and Thea immediately had a terrifying thought—that the woman had been shot. But Alma had hit her head during the fall. She'd have a scrape on her cheek, but it was far better than the alternative.

Another shot came, and this one slammed into the ground, much too close to where they were.

Raleigh's gaze was firing all around. He was obviously trying to pinpoint the location of the shooter. Since Dalton was doing the same thing, Thea hooked her arm around Alma's waist and pulled the woman behind the back of her car. It wasn't ideal cover, but at least they weren't out in the open.

But Raleigh and Dalton were.

"Get down!" Thea shouted to them just as two more

shots came right at them. The bullets tore into the asphalt and the gravel shoulder of the road.

Raleigh and Dalton stayed low and they scrambled toward the back of the vehicle with Alma and her. Thea had already drawn her gun, but she had no idea where to even return fire.

"You see the shooter?" she asked Raleigh.

"He's somewhere across the road. Call for backup."

Thea did that. She called the sheriff's office and got Alice. The deputy assured her that she'd come right out, but Thea reminded her to approach with caution. She didn't want anyone else killed.

Mercy. This confirmed to Thea she was the target.

Of course, Thea had known that when Marco had taken her at gunpoint, but this reminder hit her like a Mack truck slamming into her. This wasn't just about cops being in the line of fire. Raleigh's mom could be hurt, or worse.

"Raleigh!" Alma shouted. "Don't let those bullets hit you."

Easier said than done. Three more shots came, one right behind the other.

While she positioned her body over Alma's to keep the woman on the ground, Thea lifted her head enough to glance at the direction of the shots. And she groaned. Because there were way too many trees and even some large rocks. The shooter could be behind any one of them.

"I swear, I didn't see a gunman," Alma insisted. "Where did he come from?"

Thea figured he'd parked on a ranch trail just off the pasture and then used the rocks and trees for cover to get into position. Maybe he'd even been following Alma because it would have been easier to get to the older woman than it was Raleigh and her. With Alma's state of mind, she might not have even noticed if a stranger was behind her vehicle.

The next bullet slammed into Alma's car, shattering the window on the rear-passenger's side, and it sent glass flying at Dalton. He moved even farther back, but it wasn't enough. Dalton, and the rest of them, could still be hit.

Thea glanced behind them to try to figure out what to do. Now that Warren's truck was gone, there was an open space between the car and the cruiser. It was plenty big enough for them to be easy targets if they went running out there. But there might be another way around this.

"I can get to the cruiser and pull it up in front of you," Thea suggested.

Raleigh looked back at her, and even though he didn't give her a flat look, it was close. "You're not going there. And if you ignore my order and try it, I will go after you. That means, we'd both get shot."

Thea wanted to believe he was bluffing, but she doubted that he was. No way could she risk something like that. She couldn't lose Raleigh.

Even if he wasn't hers to lose.

"Stay down," Raleigh told her. "And make sure my mom stays put, too."

Thea was trying to do just that, but Alma kept calling out to Raleigh to be careful, and she was squirming so she could look at him, probably to make sure he was okay. Thea couldn't fault the woman for that. Raleigh was her only son, but she needed Alma to cooperate so she could help Raleigh return fire—if they got a chance to do that.

"Raleigh's a good cop," Thea reminded Alma. "Please stay down so I can help him."

Alma looked up at her, their gazes connecting, and even though it seemed to be the last thing the woman wanted to do, she nodded and quit struggling. She practically went limp on the ground.

Thea pivoted, still staying close to Alma but moving to the side so she stood a chance of having a clean shot. She tried again to pinpoint the shooter.

And she did.

Just as Raleigh and Dalton did, too—thanks to the sunlight glinting off the shooter's gun. He was in the center of the pasture, behind one of the big rocks. The rock was the perfect cover, but he had to lean out to shoot at them.

She waited, her heart pounding and her breath so thin that her chest was hurting. But Thea reminded herself that she'd been trained for this, and the stakes were too high for her to fail.

Dalton and Raleigh were obviously waiting, too, and both had their guns pointed in the direction of the shooter. The seconds crawled by, maybe because the guy was reloading, but Thea finally saw him. He moved out from behind the rock, already taking aim at them.

But Dalton, Raleigh and Thea all fired, their shots blending into a loud, thick blast that was deafening. They each fired several more times before she saw a man wearing a ski mask tumble out onto the ground.

They waited with the silence closing in around them. Raleigh was no doubt waiting to make sure the guy was actually dead and that he didn't have a partner waiting in the wings to gun them down when they moved.

She heard the sirens and glanced at the road to see

the cruiser flying toward them. Alice, probably. Dalton verified that with a call to his fellow deputy, and Alice pulled to a stop directly in front of them.

Raleigh moved fast to get Alma into the cruiser. "Stay with her," he added to Thea. "I need to see if this guy is alive. If he is, we might finally know who's been trying to kill us."

Chapter 12

Raleigh stood at his kitchen counter and tossed back the shot of straight whiskey. It wasn't enough alcohol to cloud his head, but he hoped it would take off the edge. The adrenaline from the attack hadn't zapped nearly enough of this raw energy he was feeling.

Along with the frustration.

Because the shooter, Buck Tanner, was dead.

And that meant he hadn't been able to tell them who'd hired him. Not that he necessarily would have wanted to do that, but Raleigh would have figured out a way to get him to talk.

But now that option was gone, and they were back to square one. Well, with the exception that the two men who'd killed Sonya and kidnapped the baby were dead. That would have felt like some kind of justice if they'd managed to catch the hired thugs' boss, too.

"Did it help?" he heard Thea ask. He glanced over his shoulder to see Thea walking into the living room.

She was in his pj's again.

Obviously, she'd just gotten out of the shower because she was using a towel to dry her wet hair, and she tipped her head to the glass he was still holding.

"The jury's out on that," he said. He lifted the bottle. "You want a shot?"

"No, thanks. I'll probably just grab something to eat and crash. Unless you think we'll need to go back into your office tonight."

He shook his head. With the exception of the DNA on the second baby, they weren't waiting on any lab results, and there were no reports from SAPD on the fires at the security company and fertility clinic.

But there was some bad news he needed to tell Thea.

Since there was no easy way to put this, Raleigh just turned to face her and blurted it out. "Dan Shaw's body turned up about a mile from the security company." The very one the man had owned. "He died from two gunshots to the head."

Thea's breath hitched, and her shoulders dropped. Even though she hadn't personally known him, that didn't matter. Dan Shaw was dead because someone, probably Buck Tanner, had taken him hostage so he could escape.

"I think I'll have that drink now," she said, her voice shaky. She didn't look too steady, either.

Raleigh grabbed another glass from the cabinet, poured her a shot, and when she reached for it, that's when he noticed the bandage on the palm of her hand. She quickly tried to hide it beneath the sleeve of the bulky pj's, but he caught on to her wrist and had a better look.

"It's nothing." She pulled back her hand. "I just cut it on a rock or something when I fell. I didn't even notice it until we were away from the scene."

Even though Raleigh knew it could have been much worse, it twisted his stomach to know she'd been hurt. He'd seen the blood on her clothes, of course. That's why she'd taken a shower and put her clothes in the washer as soon as they'd gotten to his house, but he'd thought the blood was his mom's—from the scrape she gotten when he'd pushed them to the ground.

"It's nothing," Thea repeated. She had a sip of the whiskey and grimaced, but that bad reaction didn't stop her from finishing off the rest of the shot.

Since looking at that bandage wasn't helping with that raw energy bubbling inside him, he opened the bag of takeout he'd gotten from the diner. Burgers and fries. It smelled good, but Raleigh doubted it would sit well with the knots in his stomach. Still, he wanted Thea to eat, so he put the food on some plates and set them on the table.

Thea glanced at the food and made another face. Not quite a grimace this time, but it was close. But she sat down and picked up one of the fries.

"Did you call your mom while I was in the shower?" she asked.

He nodded. "Like you, she's insisting she's okay. I doubt it's true in either your case or hers."

Thea lifted her shoulder. "My offer still stands. If you want to stay the night with her, I can go to my brother's."

She had indeed made that offer, but Sonya's baby was with Griff, Rachel and a Texas Ranger for extra protection. There'd been no attacks directed at the new-born, and Raleigh wanted to keep it that way. If Thea went there or to the McCall Ranch, the danger might go with her.

Of course, an attack could happen here, too, and that's why Raleigh had closed the gate that led to his house. He'd also alerted the hands who worked with his horses to report anything suspicious to him. Added to that, he'd turned on his security system.

Because the killer was still out there.

Raleigh didn't believe for a second that Marco and Buck had put this together themselves. No. Their boss was probably gathering another team of hired guns, and Raleigh had to be ready for whatever the snake threw at them.

"Alice is staying with my mom," he added. "And the ranch hands there will keep watch."

She nodded, took a tiny bite of the french fry and put it back on the plate. "What will happen to Sonya's baby?" she asked. "Both of her biological parents are dead, and Yvette and Nick don't have a claim on her, thank goodness."

Yeah, that definitely qualified as a *thank goodness*. Both the O'Haras were suspects, and he didn't want them getting anywhere near the baby.

"Social services is contacting Sonya's and Dr. Sheridan's next of kin. Sonya has an aunt who she was close to, and she's already asked about taking the baby."

Thea made a sound of approval but then frowned. Maybe because she'd gotten attached to the little girl when she'd been taking care of her. She tried the fry again, tossed it right back down and got up to go to the window. He'd closed all the blinds and curtains, but she lifted the edge of the blind and looked out.

"We can't live like this," she said. There'd been weariness in her voice earlier, but it had gone up a notch. "We have to know who's behind the attacks." She stayed quiet a moment and then turned back to him. "Why don't we set a trap, using me as bait."

Hell. Raleigh had figured this was coming, and Thea had to know he was going to nix it. He pushed back his plate and went to her. "I'm not going to watch you die so I can catch a killer."

"He or she wouldn't be able to kill me if we did this right. Just hear me out," she added when he opened his mouth to argue. "We could get the word out that I need to go see Warren, that it's some kind of emergency. The killer would probably set up another attack somewhere on the road. But we'd be ready. We could have some of the deputies hiding in the cruiser."

That wouldn't stop her from being killed. Heck, it could get the deputies killed, too.

"This could work," she went on, and he could tell that she wasn't just going to give up on this.

And that's why Raleigh kissed her.

It was playing dirty, but he couldn't listen to Thea talk about sacrificing herself to put an end to this. He kept the kiss short, and he eased back, fully expecting her to yell or even push him away.

She didn't.

Thea stared at him. A long time. And with their gazes locked, she caught on to the front of his shirt, wadding it up in her left hand as she dragged him back to her.

It was Thea who continued the kiss.

* * *

From the moment Thea had seen Raleigh in the kitchen, she'd known this kiss was going to happen. There was just too much energy sizzling between them. Too much emotion.

And too much frustration.

Raleigh seemed to try to cure all of that with the kiss. In one quick motion, she was in his arms, and the urgency of his mouth on hers let her know that neither of them were going to stop this. Even if they regretted it. Which they would.

Well, Raleigh would anyway.

Thea wasn't sure she could regret something like this that felt so right. Of course, it'd always felt right when she was with Raleigh. It'd been that way for her even when she'd been with him after learning the truth about Warren's affair. Not telling Raleigh had caused her to lose him, and she'd thought she would never be with him like this again. But she was wrong. It was happening, and it was happening fast.

The kiss became hotter, more intense, and it didn't take minutes but rather mere seconds. Thea just let herself go with it when he pulled her deeper into his arms so that their bodies were touching. It was an incredible sensation with him touching her, but it soon wasn't enough. She needed more.

Thankfully, Raleigh didn't have trouble giving her that.

He popped open the buttons on the loose pajama top she was wearing, and he slipped his hand inside. She hadn't put on a bra after her shower, and without the barrier of any clothes, Raleigh lowered his head and moved the kisses to her breasts.

Yes, this was *more*.

Raleigh kept on giving, too, when he pushed down the bottom of the pj's. She was wearing panties, but he also slid them down her legs, leaving her practically naked. If she hadn't been so desperate for him, that might have bothered her, but Raleigh didn't give her a chance to remember who she was much less the fact that she was undressed, and he wasn't.

He kissed her. In many places. Touched her, too. And Thea let herself be swept up into the sensations that came wave after wave. Every inch of her wanted him more than her next breath, but despite the burning need, Raleigh just kept up with the maddening foreplay.

When she could take no more, Thea did something about his clothes. It was hard to get his buttons undone while still kissing, but she managed it and got a very nice reward. Her hands on his bare chest.

He wasn't overly muscled, but he was toned and tight. Perfect. But then, she thought that "perfect" label applied to many things when it came to Raleigh. Thea kissed his neck and chest.

She would have kept going as he'd done, but he pulled her back up to him, and when their eyes met, Thea recognized the look he gave her. He was giving her an out if she wanted to stop.

She didn't.

So she went straight back to him. This time though, there was no more foreplay—something that her on-fire body was thankful for. Raleigh scooped her up and carried her straight to his room. The moment he had her on the bed, he took a condom from his nightstand drawer.

He moved onto the bed with her, the mattress giving way to their combined weight, and she helped him slide off his boots and jeans. His boxers, too. Everything was frantic now, their movements feverish from the need. He didn't waste a second after he put on the condom.

Raleigh pushed into her.

The pleasure raced through her, leaving her speechless. And breathless. But she could certainly feel, and the feelings soared when he started to move inside her.

The memories came. No way to stop them. They'd been together like this many times, but each of those times had always had the same intensity as the first. This was no different. Except Thea knew that it might be their last. Once Raleigh came to his senses, he might regret this enough that it would never happen again.

A heartbreaking thought.

But it was a thought that quickly went out the window when his thrusts inside her got faster. Harder. Until the need and tension climbed higher and higher.

When Thea couldn't hang on any longer, when she could take no more, she let herself surrender to the pleasure. The climax rippled through her, and the only thing she could do was hold on and let it consume her.

Moments later, as he whispered her name, Raleigh buried his face against her neck, and he finished what they'd started.

Chapter 13

Raleigh closed his eyes and tried to sleep—something that usually happened easily after great sex. And this had indeed been *great*. But the sleep wouldn't come because his mind wasn't nearly as satisfied as the rest of him.

Sex was going to complicate things between Thea and him. Of course, the kissing had already done that, but this would send it through the roof. If the timing had been better, he might have just gone back in for another round of sex and put his worries on the back burner. But the timing only added to the complication.

He got up, but he tried to be as quiet as possible so that he wouldn't wake Thea. However, when he glanced at her, she was wide-awake and staring at the ceiling. Judging from the expression on her face, she was having more than just doubts and regrets.

"Was it that bad?" he joked, and because he was stupid, he brushed one of those complicating kisses on her mouth.

"No." She looked him straight in the eyes. "The frown is because it wasn't bad."

Unfortunately, he understood that. If the old chemistry between them had gone cold, it would have made leaving the bed easier. The kiss she gave him back in return certainly didn't help, either, but Raleigh forced himself to move away from her so he could get dressed.

"I should be keeping watch," he reminded her. "And checking for updates. You should try to get some sleep though."

But Raleigh knew that probably wasn't going to happen, and he was right. Thea immediately got up, and she headed to the guest room. A few minutes later, when she came out, she had dressed. Not in pj's, either, but her jeans and shirt.

"I'll make us a pot of coffee," she said, heading for the kitchen.

Raleigh considered asking Thea if she wanted to talk about what happened, but she was probably just as unsettled about this as he was. Plus, there wasn't time to launch into a conversation because his phone rang.

The call got Thea's attention, and she turned away from the coffee maker to hurry toward him. She was probably expecting it to be bad news, and when Raleigh saw the name on the screen, he considered that, as well. That's because it was Alice calling, and since she was staying with Alma, this could mean his mother was upset again. Maybe this time though, Alma hadn't pulled a gun on the deputy.

When Raleigh answered the call, the first thing he

heard was the loud clanging noise. It definitely wasn't something he wanted to hear because he was pretty sure it was the security alarm.

"I think someone broke into the house," Alice immediately said.

The news hit him hard, but Raleigh reminded himself that it could be a glitch in the system. Or maybe his mom had accidentally set it off. Still, it was hard not to feel the fear and panic.

"I've gone into your mom's bedroom with her," Alice added, "and I've locked the door."

"I'm on the way there right now," Raleigh assured her. "Text or call me with what's happening." Though for now he wanted Alice to focus only on keeping his mother safe.

He ended the call and reached for his holster and keys. Thea obviously heard what Alice had said because she, too, grabbed her gun and her phone. Raleigh didn't especially want her coming with him since they'd already been attacked twice while on the road, but he didn't have time to make other arrangements.

He went to the window and looked out. Nothing out of the ordinary, and he hoped it stayed that way.

"Hurry," he told Thea, and the moment he had his own security system disengaged, he got them out the door and into the cruiser that he'd parked right by his porch.

He half expected someone to shoot at them, but thankfully no bullets came their way. So he sped off, while keeping watch to make sure they weren't ambushed. Thea was keeping watch, too, but he handed her his phone. He didn't have to tell her to answer it right away if Alice called back. Thea would. But Raleigh hoped that when Alice did contact them that it would be to say that it was a false alarm.

"Text my deputy Miguel," he instructed. "His number is in my contacts. He'll be at the office, and tell him I want him out at my mom's place."

It might be overkill, but that was better than being short of backup if this turned out to be an attack.

"How many ranch hands does Alma have on the grounds?" Thea asked after she'd fired off a text to Miguel.

"Two right now. She has a lot more who work for her, but they don't live there." Though he might end up calling a couple of them, too.

It was pitch-black, just a sliver of a moon, and there were no lights out on this rural road. No traffic, either, thank goodness, and that's why Raleigh went much faster than he would normally go.

His mom's ranch was only about five miles from his, so it didn't take long to get there. When he took the turn, the house came into view. All looked well, but Thea and he had to drive past some dark pastures. Since Buck Tanner had used a pasture to hide for his attack, that possibility was still fresh in Raleigh's mind.

His phone dinged with a text message. Then almost immediately dinged again. "Miguel's on the way," Thea relayed. "The second text is from Alice. She says no one has tried to break into the room, and she doesn't hear anyone in the house."

That was good, but it might be hard for his deputy to hear much of anything with the alarm still blaring. The only way to turn it off would be for her to go to the keypads at the front and back doors, and Raleigh preferred that she stay put.

Raleigh was about to tell Thea to let Alice know they were nearby, but he caught some movement from the corner of his eye. Thea must have seen it, too, because they both pivoted in that direction and took aim. Raleigh had braced himself for a ski-mask-wearing thug, but it wasn't.

It was Warren.

"Don't shoot," Warren said, leaning out from a tree that was right next to the road.

Raleigh lowered his window and glanced around to see if Warren was alone. He appeared to be.

"What are you doing here?" Thea asked, taking the question right out of Raleigh's mouth.

"I got a call from a criminal informant of mine. He said one of his buddies had been hired to kidnap Alma. That the person who hired the buddy wanted to do that to get back at me."

Raleigh huffed. "And you didn't call me with information like that?"

"I wasn't sure it was accurate. The guy isn't always reliable if he needs money for a fix. He needed money," Warren added.

And despite the tip not being reliable, Warren had come anyway. Later, Raleigh would press him as to why he'd done that and where he'd parked his truck, since it was nowhere in sight, but for now he needed to get to the house.

"My mom's with one of my deputies, but someone broke in. Thea and I are headed there now."

That put some alarm on Warren's face. "I didn't

see anyone come onto the grounds, and I was keeping watch."

Later, Raleigh would want to know about that, too. Because if there was indeed an intruder, it was possible he'd been there for a while, before Warren's arrival.

"Let me go with you," Warren offered. "In case you need backup."

Raleigh wasn't sure he wanted that, but he also didn't want to sit around here while his mom was in danger. Nor did he want to leave Warren out here by himself. He unlocked the back door of the cruiser and motioned for Warren to get in. The moment he did that, Raleigh sped toward the house.

He didn't see anyone else along the way, but there was a truck in front of the house that belonged to one of the ranch hands who was supposed to be keeping watch. He pulled the cruiser to a stop next to it. And cursed. Because the driver's-side door was open, but the ranch hand wasn't inside.

Raleigh hated to think the worst, but with all the other attacks, it was the first possibility that came to mind. If someone had wanted to break into the house, they could have eliminated the ranch hands.

Since the driveway was on the side of the house and went all the way to the back, Raleigh kept driving. Kept looking. No one. But even from outside, he could hear the blare of the security system.

He pulled to a stop directly next to the back porch. "Wait here," Raleigh told Warren. "And let us know if anyone tries to come up behind us. Thea and I will go in and check on things." Maybe, just maybe, there'd be nothing wrong.

Raleigh glanced at Thea to make sure she was ready. She was. She had a firm grip on her gun as she opened the cruiser door. Raleigh did the same, but before he could even step out, he heard a hissing sound.

That was the only warning he got before the flames shot up in front of him.

Thea automatically jumped back from the flames and put her hand in front of her face to shield it. But she was on full alert, too, because she knew that this could be some kind of diversion so that gunmen could kill them.

However, it also confirmed that this wasn't just a false alarm.

The threat was real, and that meant not only were they in danger but so were Alma and Alice.

Raleigh ran to her and pulled her back even farther. Like her, he shot glances all around them. So did Warren when he got out of the cruiser.

"The fire isn't touching the house," Raleigh let them know.

At least it wasn't yet. It appeared that someone had poured a line of accelerant and had lit it with perhaps a remote control. But if the breeze blew the flames into the house, it could catch the place on fire.

The fire was creating another problem, too. The smoke. It was thick and dark, and it seemed to come right at them, causing them all to cough. Worse, it was burning her eyes and making it hard to see. Definitely what she didn't want since someone could be out there.

Someone with plans to kill them.

Thea had figured there'd be another attack, but she'd thought it would come down to Raleigh and her against the person responsible for so much chaos. But now Warren was here, and that meant he was in danger, too. Maybe that had been part of the plan all along though.

"Cover me," Raleigh told Thea.

He headed to the far back right corner of the house, where there was some kind of control box. For the automatic sprinkler system, she soon realized. Raleigh hit the button to turn on all the nozzles, and they immediately began to pop up and start spraying water. It meant the three of them were getting wet, but it might keep the flames under control.

"I'll call the fire department," Warren offered, taking out his phone.

Good. And Dalton was on the way, too, but Thea didn't intend to wait. Especially not wait out in the open. With Raleigh ahead of her and Warren right behind, they started up the porch steps.

And they immediately stopped.

"Those are the two ranch hands who were supposed to be keeping watch," Raleigh whispered.

Oh, God. This wasn't good. Because she soon spotted the two men sprawled out on the porch.

"Are they dead?" she asked, afraid to hear the answer.

While Thea and Warren kept watch, Raleigh touched his fingers to one of the men's necks and then the other. "They're alive. It looks as if someone used a stun gun on them. Maybe drugged them, too."

The relief came, but it didn't last because someone had obviously gotten close enough to the hands to incapacitate them. And that someone could now be inside, doing the same, or worse, to Raleigh's mother and his deputy.

"I'll call for an ambulance," Warren volunteered.

Maybe the men wouldn't need medical attention right away, because an ambulance wouldn't be able to get onto the ranch until they were sure there wasn't a shooter nearby.

Raleigh went to the door. "Locked," he said, and he fished through his pocket for the keys.

Maybe the person who'd attacked the hands hadn't gone in through the back, but if he had, he'd clearly locked it behind him. Maybe to slow them down.

Or ambush them when they went in.

Once he had the door unlocked, Raleigh used the barrel of his gun to ease it open a couple of inches. Thea steeled herself up for some kind of attack.

But nothing happened.

Raleigh reached inside to the keypad, hit some buttons and the alarm stopped. Thea immediately tried to listen for any sounds coming from inside, but she heard nothing.

"According to the light on the security panel, the alarm was tripped with this door," Raleigh explained, his voice barely louder than a whisper.

So whoever had broken in had locked the door behind him. There were no obvious signs of forced entry, but someone skilled at picking a lock would be able to get in without leaving any obvious damage. Certainly though, an intruder would have guessed there'd be a security system. But maybe he didn't care, especially since the alarm would have masked his movements in the house.

But there was another possibility.

One that Thea hoped was what had actually happened. That the alarm had scared the guy off, and that he'd gone running. She wanted to confront this monster and stop him—or her—but she didn't want that to happen with Raleigh's mother or Warren around.

"Text Alice and tell her we're here and about to come in," Raleigh told her. "Ask her if they're okay."

Since Thea still had his phone, she did that and got a quick response back from Alice that Thea relayed to Raleigh. "They're fine. No one's tried to get into the room where they are."

Maybe it would stay that way.

Raleigh stepped into the kitchen. He didn't turn on the lights and looked around before he motioned for Warren and her to join him. No smoke inside, thank goodness, but if the sprinkler didn't put out the flames, there soon would be. That meant they'd need to evacuate Alma and Alice. They didn't have a choice about that, but it came with huge risks since it meant they'd be outside, where they could be gunned down.

Raleigh's phone dinged with a message. At first, Thea thought it was Alice again, but it was Dalton this time.

When Thea read the text, her stomach clenched. "Someone put a spike strip on the road after we drove through. Dalton hit it and all the tires on his cruiser are flat. He'll have to wait for Miguel to come and give him a ride out here."

Raleigh mumbled some profanity. Whoever was behind this had wanted to make sure Dalton didn't arrive to help them. And it had worked. But what did this monster have planned for them?

"Tell Dalton not to come on foot," Raleigh instructed. "I don't want someone gunning him down."

Neither did she. Enough people had been hurt or killed.

"After Miguel picks him up," Raleigh went on, "Dalton and he can secure the perimeter of the house and get the two hands into the cruiser."

Thea sent the response to the deputy and then lifted her head to try to detect any trace of accelerant in the house. She didn't want a new fire trapping them inside, but there were no unusual smells. No unusual sounds, either.

Since this was the first time she'd been in Alma's house, she had no idea where the bedroom was, but Raleigh started out of the kitchen. But first he motioned for Warren to keep watch behind them. Thea made sure no one was on the sides of them. Hard to do though because the house was dark.

Raleigh led them through a family room and then a foyer. He tested the knob on the front door. "It's still locked," he whispered to them.

That was good because hopefully it meant no one could get in that way while they were walking up to the second floor. Raleigh went up the first three steps of the curved staircase and looked up, no doubt hoping to get a glimpse of whoever had broken in.

Thea certainly didn't see anything, but she heard something. Not a sound from the second floor or stairs, either. This had come from the living room on the other side of the foyer. Warren and Raleigh must have heard it, too, because they pivoted in that direction.

Just as someone fired a shot right at them.

Chapter 14

"Get down!" Raleigh shouted.

And he prayed Thea and Warren could do that before they got shot.

Warren didn't get down though. He fired in the direction of the shooter.

Even though Raleigh couldn't see the gunman and Warren probably couldn't, either, the shot paid off because their attacker didn't pull the trigger again. Raleigh did hear him scrambling for cover in the living room though. That was good because it gave the three of them a chance to get off the stairs and out of the foyer and into the living room.

It wasn't ideal, but at least there was a partial wall they could use that might prevent them from being gunned down.

From the moment that Thea and he arrived at the ranch, Raleigh had been steeling himself up for an attack. An attack that he had hoped to prevent, but obviously it was too late for that.

But who was behind this?

Raleigh silently cursed that it was something he still didn't know. And he might not find it out anytime soon. Because the person who'd shot at them could be just another hired gun, someone doing the dirty work for Simon, Nick or Yvette.

Another shot came, and it slammed into the half wall. Since a bullet could easily go through it, Raleigh motioned for Thea and Warren to get to the side of the sofa. That would serve two purposes. Not only would it put some distance between the shooter and them, it would give them a better vantage point to make sure someone didn't sneak up on them by coming through the kitchen. The ranch hands were on the back porch, but even if they had regained consciousness, they still might not be able to stop someone else from getting inside.

His phone dinged just as there was another shot, and this bullet did rip through the drywall and went God knew where in the living room. Raleigh glanced back to make sure Thea and Warren were okay. They were. For now. But he motioned for them to get down.

"Alice texted," Thea whispered. "She heard the shots."

Of course she had. They were deafening, so that meant his mother had heard them, too, and she was probably terrified. Raleigh was feeling some fear of his own because he had to consider that this thug downstairs was just a distraction so his partner could get to Alma.

But if Alma was the target, why hadn't the person just bashed down the bedroom door after he'd broken in?

Why wait?

He couldn't think of a good reason for doing that. So that meant Thea, he or Warren was the target. Or maybe all three. But hopefully his mom would be out of harm's way while he figured out how to safely get to her.

Raleigh scrambled closer to Thea so the gunman wouldn't hear what he wanted her to text Alice. "Tell her that I want Mom and her in the bathtub."

That way, if this clown started shooting at the ceiling, Alice and his mother wouldn't get hit with stray shots.

While Thea sent off the message, Raleigh moved again so he could maybe catch of glimpse of the shooter. He hurried to the other side of the sofa, where he still had some cover, but he was also in a better position to take this guy out.

When the gunman leaned out to fire, Raleigh sent two bullets right at him. He couldn't tell though if he hit him, but at least it stopped the gunfire. Raleigh doubted that would last though.

And it didn't.

It only took a few seconds before the man leaned out again. This time, Raleigh didn't miss. His shot slammed into the guy, and he made a loud groan of pain before he collapsed onto the floor.

While he watched to make sure no one was at the top of the stairs, ready to shoot him, Raleigh went to the thug. The guy had on a ski mask, but Raleigh pulled it off him and checked for a pulse. Nothing.

"He's dead," Raleigh told the others. He made a quick study of the dead man's face, but didn't recognize him.

"You smell that?" Thea asked.

Raleigh was so focused on the shooter that it took him a moment to realize what she meant.

Smoke.

And it didn't seem to be coming from outside.

"Stay put," Warren told Thea.

Before Raleigh could figure out if it was a good idea or not, Warren ran back toward the kitchen. Thea clearly didn't like that any better than Raleigh did, but they needed to know what was going on. And what was going on wasn't good. Raleigh could tell that from Warren's stark expression when he came back into the living room.

"Someone set a fire in the pantry." Warren's words rushed out with his frantic breath. "You have to get Alma and your deputy out of the house. And I need to move those hands off the porch in case the fire spreads back there."

Yes, he did. But that left Raleigh with a huge problem. He didn't want Warren on the porch without backup, especially when the man was trying to move the unconscious hands. But Raleigh didn't think it was a good idea for Thea to be outside, either. Still, that might be better than her being inside a house that was now on fire.

"Go with him," Raleigh told her.

She didn't argue, but he could practically feel the hesitation before she nodded. She tossed him his phone and followed Warren to the back.

Raleigh hated that it had come down to this. Yes, it was her job as a cop, but that didn't make this easier to swallow. He was afraid for Thea. Afraid he might never see her again. And angry with himself for not telling her just how much she meant to him.

He pushed those feelings aside so he could go up the stairs and rescue his mother, but his phone dinged after he'd made it only a few steps. It was another text from Alice.

Someone's breaking into the bedroom.

Hell. For just a few words, they packed a wallop, and Raleigh practically ran up the stairs. Of course, he had to stop when he got to the top because whoever was trying to break into his mother's room would see him the moment he was in the hall.

Unfortunately, there were no lights on in the hall, so it took Raleigh a moment to pick through the darkness and see the shadowy figure outside the bedroom. And it appeared he was trying to get the door unlocked. Raleigh didn't shoot the guy because he couldn't even tell if he was armed.

"I'm Sheriff Lawton," Raleigh called out. "Put your hands in the air."

The man pivoted, and that's when Raleigh caught a glimpse of his gun. A gun he pointed at Raleigh. He didn't give the thug a chance to fire though because Raleigh pulled the trigger first. Two shots slammed into the man's chest, causing him to drop just as fast as his partner had minutes earlier.

Raleigh hurried to him. The guy was dead all right. That felt like a hard rock in his stomach, but he hadn't had another option. He couldn't let the guy shoot him. Nor could he let him break into the bedroom.

"Alice, it's me," Raleigh called out, knocking on the

door. While he waited, he sent off a quick text to Thea to let her know he was okay. "There's a fire," he added to Alice, "and both of you need to get out of the house."

Almost immediately, he heard the sound of running footsteps, and a moment later, Alice opened the door. Alma was right behind her, and while his mom did indeed look terrified, he couldn't take the time to console her. The smoke was already making its way up the stairs, and he didn't want them trapped.

Alice hooked her arm around Alma's waist to get her moving, and both women glanced at the dead guy in the hall. Alma looked away, a hoarse sob coming from her throat.

"My house is on fire?" Alma asked. She was clearly alarmed by not just the dead man but also the fact that she might lose everything. Too bad that everything might include her life if there were other hired guns waiting outside.

"The fire department's on the way," Raleigh said.

Later, once he had everyone safe, he would make sure that was true and fill her in on everything else that'd happened. Of course, the fire department was almost certainly nearby, or soon would be, but they were no doubt waiting on word from him to make sure it was safe to come onto the grounds. Right now, it definitely wasn't safe.

"Keep watch behind us," Raleigh told Alice just in case someone was hiding in another one of the bedrooms off the hall.

With Raleigh ahead of them, he led them to the stairs, hurrying as much as he could. But he also had to watch and listen to make certain they weren't about to be ambushed. He didn't see anyone at the bottom of the stairs or in the foyer, but that didn't mean someone wasn't there.

"The cruiser's parked right outside," he told Alice. "Get Mom inside, and I'll find the others." Including those two hands who could be hurt.

Opening the door was a risk, but everything he did at this point would be. Still, the cruiser was the safest place for his mother.

He eased open the door and looked out. No one. So Raleigh unlocked the cruiser and then handed the keys to Alice.

"You're not coming with us?" Alma asked. Her voice and the rest of her were shaking.

"I'll be there soon," he told her and hoped that was true. "Move fast," he added to Alice in a whisper. "And if something goes wrong, drive out of here as quickly as you can."

Alice nodded, and Raleigh stepped out onto the porch to give them cover as they ran to the cruiser. However, Alice and his mom hadn't even gotten in yet when he heard something that caused his heart to slam against his chest.

"No!" someone shouted, and Raleigh was pretty sure that someone was Warren, who was at the back of the house.

And the shout was followed by another sound Raleigh didn't want to hear.

A gunshot.

Thea tried to keep watch of the backyard as she pulled one of the hands off the porch and away from the fire. It wasn't easy. He was a big guy, and since she couldn't lift him, she had no choice but to drag him down the steps and toward the grassy area behind the house.

Warren was doing the same thing to the second hand, and he was struggling as much as Thea was. She only hoped this wasn't doing more damage to Warren's already injured body, but even if it had, it wouldn't have stopped him.

The sprinklers didn't help the situation, either. They were still going full blast, and while that appeared to be containing the fire in the yard, it was also soaking Warren and her. Plus, the combination of water and smoke in her eyes made it even harder to see.

She'd just made it to the bottom step when she heard the two shots from inside the house. It caused her pulse to skyrocket because they had almost certainly come from the second floor, where Raleigh would be rescuing his mom and Alice.

Thea looked up at the windows but couldn't see anything, and she forced herself not to run inside. However, the second her phone dinged with a text message, she stopped dragging the ranch hand and looked at the screen. It was from Raleigh. We're okay.

The breath of relief rushed out of her, and she prayed it was true, that Raleigh hadn't told her that just to stop her from going inside. She would though. As soon as she'd finished moving the hand, she needed to make sure Raleigh, Alice and his mom had made it out. That meant going inside.

Thea kept dragging the hand. She had to get the man far enough away from the house in case the fire caused it to collapse. He still hadn't regained consciousness, and there was no way he'd be able to move to save himself.

"Over here," Warren told her.

He motioned toward the front of a small barn, where he was heading. It wasn't ideal cover because both ends were wide-open, but it would give them some protection from the sides. As it was now, they were out in the open, where anyone could gun them down.

"Was Raleigh hurt?" Warren asked, and he didn't sound like a lawman but rather a concerned father.

She shook her head. "He said they were all okay."

Thea's arms were aching by the time she reached the barn, but she got the hand in. It was like stepping into a cave since it was so dark. Too dark for her to see any of the corners. Plus, there was a tractor and some other equipment, plenty of places for someone to hide. That's why she took a moment to listen and made sure no one was inside. If someone was, he or she wasn't making a sound.

Since Warren was struggling, she went out to help him drag in the second hand, and she positioned him next to the other one.

"Wait here with them in case the fire comes this way and they need to be moved again," she told Warren. She tried to wipe some of the water off her face. "I need to check on Raleigh to see if he needs any help getting Alma out."

She expected Warren to argue with that because he didn't like her going out there without backup. And he no doubt wanted to argue, but he probably knew it wouldn't do any good. Instead, he huffed.

"Don't go in through the back," he warned her.

She wouldn't. By now, the fire had probably spread into the kitchen. Or maybe even farther into the house. That meant she'd need to go on the side so she could get to the front porch. But hopefully that's where Raleigh would be if he had indeed managed to get his mom and Alice out of the house.

Before she could start running, Warren caught on to her hand and made eye contact with her. It was so dark that it was hard to fully see his expression, but his forehead was bunched up with worry.

"Be careful," he said.

She was about to remind him to do the same thing, but then she saw the change in Warren's body language. His shoulders went back, and he started lifting his gun.

"No!" Warren shouted, his attention on the area behind her.

That was the only warning Thea got before the gunshot blasted through the air.

For a horrifying moment, she thought Warren or she had been shot. But the bullet went into the barn just as Warren grabbed hold of her and yanked her to the floor.

At least that's what he tried to do.

But someone took hold of her from behind, hooking his arm around her throat. In the same motion, he knocked her Glock from her hand and put a gun to her head.

The fear and adrenaline slammed into her, and her body went into fight mode. She rammed her elbow into his stomach, but it didn't work. The man was wearing some kind of body armor, and he didn't loosen his grip. In fact, he tightened it and dug the barrel of the gun into her temple.

Warren cursed and froze, his weapon aimed at an attacker she couldn't see, but he must have realized he didn't have a shot, because Warren scrambled to the side of the tractor. Good. At least he wouldn't be gunned down—which was probably what her attacker had planned to do because he fired another bullet in Warren's direction.

"Let go of her," Warren demanded.

Thea doubted that would work, and it didn't. The man held on. But he didn't start to move as if to escape, and he didn't fire any other shots at Warren. He seemed to be waiting for something. But what did he want and why was he doing this?

"Not much longer now," he growled in her ear. His voice was a raspy whisper. Maybe it was Nick or Simon, but it could be just another hired thug. One that maybe Yvette had sent to attack them.

When she heard someone running toward them, the man shifted her body so that she was facing the opening of the barn. He stayed behind her, using her as a shield.

Just as Raleigh came into view.

He'd obviously run through the sprinklers because he was wet, and even though he had his gun aimed and ready, he didn't have a clean shot. However, he must have been able to see her attacker's face because Raleigh cursed.

"What the hell do you think you're doing?" Raleigh snapped.

"Finishing this," the man readily answered. He didn't whisper this time though, and Thea had no trouble recognizing his voice.

It was Simon.

A dozen thoughts went through Raleigh's head, and none of them were good.

First and foremost though was that Thea was in grave danger. He could lose her right here, right now, to this sick piece of work. Raleigh had to stay alive to try to save her, and that's why he took cover by the side of the barn door.

Thea had to be terrified, but she was clearly trying to rein in her fear. Warren wasn't even attempting the facade. Raleigh could practically feel Warren's rage, and he shook his head, hoping it would keep Warren from launching himself at Simon. Raleigh wanted to try to defuse this, and that wouldn't happen if gunfire broke out.

And it wasn't just Thea and Warren he had to be concerned about. The two hands were on the barn floor, and they could easily be hit with gunfire. Simon basically had five people's lives in his hands.

"I thought you were in love with my mother," Raleigh reminded Simon. He kept watch around them, trying to make sure Simon didn't have another goon who would try to sneak up on them. "You've got a funny way of showing it since you nearly killed her with the fire you had your hired thug set. And now her house is burning down."

No way for Raleigh to save the house. Because it was too risky for him to get the fire department on the grounds. Hopefully Alice had managed to get his mother far from here.

"I *was* in love with Alma," Simon snapped. "Until I read that letter about her still having feelings for Warren. I've waited in the wings for years for her to be through with him, and just when I finally thought it had happened, Alma does something like this."

So that letter was the motive, and Raleigh could fill in the rest. "You killed Sonya and Hannah to get back at Warren, to punish him."

"And it worked. Warren nearly went crazy blaming himself and trying to figure out who killed Hannah." Simon smiled, but it quickly faded. "Except Sonya wasn't supposed to die. The men were supposed to kidnap her, but they overreacted when she escaped and ran."

"They murdered her," Raleigh pointed out. "Since you hired them, you're guilty of murder, too. And endangering the babies. How the hell could you do something like that to them?"

"I didn't endanger them, and I sure as heck didn't hurt them," Simon yelled. He glanced around, too, as if looking for something. Or someone. "Hannah's baby was well cared for, and Thea would have already been dead, but she was too close to Sonya's kid, so Marco couldn't shoot her."

That's why Thea had been spared. All because she was in the wrong place at the wrong time. Another minute before or after, and the baby might not have been close enough to her, and Marco or Buck would have gunned her down. Like Simon was planning to do.

Or not.

Simon obviously had already had a chance to kill her, so why hadn't he? Was he waiting for Warren to come out from cover so he could shoot him first?

Or did Simon plan to kill both Thea and him in front of Warren?

That way, Warren would lose his son and the woman he loved like a daughter. If that was what Simon had in mind, then Raleigh had to stop him. That meant buying himself some time so he could figure out how to safely launch himself at Simon.

"Why involve Sonya, Hannah and Thea in this? Why didn't you just kill me?" Warren growled.

Simon's mouth tightened into a sneer. "Because I

loved Alma enough that I didn't want her to grieve. I wanted her over and done with you, and if you'd been murdered, you would have become a martyr to her. That's why I didn't rat you out to your wife and kids. To Raleigh," he added.

Maybe. But Simon might have been worried that Warren would have chosen Alma instead of his wife and family. That definitely wouldn't have worked in Simon's favor to try to win Alma's heart.

"Everything I've done has been for Alma," Simon insisted. "That should prove to you how much I loved her."

No, it only proved that Simon was pathetic. And a killer.

A killer who clearly planned to murder Thea, but he wasn't trying to do that. Why? Simon had Warren right where he wanted him.

A moment later, Raleigh had his answer to that, and it wasn't an answer he liked.

"Finally," Simon snapped.

Raleigh heard the movement behind him, and he turned in that direction. And his heart skipped a couple of beats. Because there was a ski-mask-wearing thug coming toward him, and he wasn't alone.

He had Alma with him.

Hell. This was the reason Simon hadn't already added more murders to his list of crimes. He wanted to kill Alma in front of Warren. Or vice versa. Either way, Simon would almost certainly then try to murder all of them since he couldn't leave this many witnesses alive.

"Where's Alice?" Raleigh asked.

"This jerk used a stun gun on her," Alma answered, her voice cracking. "We didn't see him in time. Before Alice could drive away, he pulled her from the cruiser and left her on the driveway when he took me. Raleigh, I'm so sorry."

He hated that his mom felt the need to apologize for a thug assaulting a deputy and then manhandling her. Hated even more that this was happening. One way or another though, he would stop it. He just had to make sure he didn't get anyone killed in the process.

"Simon," his mother said, her voice quivering even more. She shifted her attention to Thea, then Raleigh and finally Warren. With each shift, her eyes got wider, and he could see the horror on her face when she realized what was happening. "Simon," she repeated.

"Don't look at me like that," Simon growled at her. "You're responsible for this."

"He read the letter," Raleigh told her.

Alma shook her head. "And you felt you had to do this because I still love Warren?" She didn't wait for an answer. "Because Warren doesn't love me. He's back with his wife, and it's over between us."

The glare that Simon gave Alma was scalpel sharp. "It'll never be over between you. Never. But it ends now. Everything ends."

Simon tipped his head to the masked thug, and the man shoved Alma forward, right into Raleigh. Raleigh didn't catch her because it would have meant taking his aim off Simon, but he used his body to help break the fall, and then he maneuvered himself in front of her.

Raleigh braced himself for Simon and his hired gun to start shooting, but the thug took off running. He ran past them and to the back opening of the barn, where Raleigh saw him press something he took from his pocket. Moments later, there was a hissing sound, and the flames shot up in front of the barn.

Alma screamed, and Raleigh prayed it wasn't because the fire had burned her. Even if it had, he couldn't take the time to check because he had to get her out of there. Not in the direction of the fire, either. Raleigh dragged her into the barn.

"If any of you move, Thea will be the first to die," Simon warned them.

Raleigh looked at Simon's face, and that's when he knew. Simon intended for all of them to die.

Warren moved closer to the end of the tractor. No doubt so he'd be in a better position to return fire if he got the chance. Right now, neither Warren nor he had a clean shot, so he had to do something to tip the odds in their favor.

"Get down," Raleigh whispered to his mom, and he hoped she listened. If not, Simon might try to shoot her.

Warren came out from behind the tractor, causing Simon to turn his gun in his direction. Thea took full advantage of no longer having the barrel pressed to her head. She shoved her weight against Simon, causing him to become off-balanced just enough so that when he pulled the trigger, his shot missed.

Simon fired again.

And again.

Thea scrambled away from Simon, making a beeline to her gun that was on the floor. But before she could even reach it, the shot rang out.

It seemed as if time had frozen. Raleigh thought maybe his heart had, too. He knew he hadn't been the one to pull the trigger, but obviously someone had.

This time, it wasn't Simon.

Raleigh saw the shock register on the man's face. Then saw the blood spread across the front of his shirt.

Clutching his chest, Simon dropped to his knees, his stare frozen on the person who'd just put a bullet in him.

Alma.

His mother had snatched up Thea's gun. And she hadn't missed. If the shot hadn't killed him, it soon would because he was bleeding out fast.

Despite what had played out in front of him, Raleigh quickly shifted his attention to the thug at the back of the barn. The man had already lifted his gun and was about to fire. But Raleigh fired first. The guy didn't fall on his knees but rather face-first onto the ground.

The adrenaline was still slamming hard through Raleigh, but he checked to make sure everyone was okay. He pulled Thea to her feet. No blood, thank God. It was the same for Warren. But when he looked back at his mother, the adrenaline spun right out of control.

Because his mother had been shot.

Chapter 15

Everyone who mattered was alive. That's what Raleigh kept reminding himself as they sat in the ER waiting room. Thea, his deputies, the drugged ranch hands and yes, even Warren had made it through the hellish nightmare. But at the moment, it didn't feel like a victory.

Because his mother might not make it.

That wasn't easy for him to consider. Especially since the man who'd put the bullet in her had been her friend for as long as Raleigh could remember. At least the *friend* was now dead, and so were all the thugs he'd hired to carry out his sick plan of revenge against Warren and Alma.

Thea was seated next to Raleigh, resting her head against his shoulder. Her hair and clothes were still damp from the soaking they'd gotten with the sprinklers, and she smelled like smoke. No physical injuries, but she had that stark look in her eyes. The one that told Raleigh that what'd happened this night would stay with her forever. It might be something she could never get past. And since he was part of those nightmarish memories, too, Thea might be done with him, as well.

Warren wasn't faring much better. He was sitting across from Thea and him. Again, no injuries, but he had his head in his hands, and every now and then he made a soft groaning sound. He definitely looked as if he needed some rest. And maybe some pain meds since Raleigh knew Warren was still recovering from his own shooting that'd happened a while back.

"If you want to go on home to your wife and kids," Raleigh told him, "I'll call you with any updates."

Raleigh immediately wished he hadn't worded it like that. It sounded bitter. Which he wasn't. Well, not bitter about Warren anyway. It was going to take a while before he didn't feel such things about Simon.

"Helen knows I'm here," Warren said.

Helen was his wife, and Raleigh knew Warren had called both his son Egan and her shortly after they'd arrived at the hospital. Raleigh had only heard bits and pieces of Warren's side of the conversation, but he'd told them that he was fine and there was no reason for them to come and get him. Whether or not they would stay away was anyone's guess.

"Helen is okay with you being here?" Thea asked.

There was plenty of hesitation in her voice. But it was a good question. Raleigh wanted to know the same thing. Warren had put enough strain on his marriage without adding more. Just his being here could be *more* in Helen's eyes.

Warren took his time answering. "Helen's worried

about me, but she knows why I need to be here. Because of Thea and you."

There it was again. The confusion swirled with all the other things Raleigh was feeling.

"I know," Warren added a moment later. He no doubt saw the mixed emotions on Raleigh's face. "You don't want me to worry about you, but you're my son, and worry comes with the territory of being a father. And for the record, I worried about you even before my relationship with your mother came to light. I know I wasn't involved in your life, but I loved you," he said in a mumble.

Raleigh wasn't sure he wanted to hear that love thing. But at least it didn't twist at him the way it usually did when he thought about Warren being his father. Maybe that was a start. Thea must have thought so because she managed a very short, very slight smile.

The silence settled among them for several long moments before Warren shook his head again. "I should have figured out it was Simon and should have stopped him before it came down to this."

Raleigh gave a frustrated sigh because he felt the same way.

Thea, however, huffed, and this time when she lifted her head from Raleigh's shoulder, there was no trace of a smile. "I could have missed it in the job description, but a badge or a former badge doesn't give you ESP. Simon hid his true self from a lot of people, and he's the only person to blame for what happened. The. Only. Person," she emphasized.

Raleigh looked at her, their eyes connecting, and he was relieved to see that what she'd said wasn't lip service. That was big of her since he'd come damn close to letting her die tonight.

At least the babies hadn't been around for this particular attack, and now that Simon and his hired guns were dead, they were out of danger. Soon, Hannah's baby would be reunited with her birth parents—something they were eager for. Sonya's daughter might be a little trickier. According to the last call Raleigh had gotten from Miguel, they would still need the DNA results before handing over the child that Hannah had delivered.

Raleigh's phone dinged, indicating he had another text message. He'd gotten a lot of them in the hour that they'd been at the hospital since his mom's ranch was now a crime scene that had to be processed. Or at least it would be once the fire department and medical examiner cleared out and took the bodies to the morgue.

"It's from Miguel," Raleigh told Thea when she glanced at his phone. It wasn't the best of news, but it was what he'd expected. "They managed to put out the fire, but most of Mom's house was destroyed."

"Alma's stronger than she looks. She'll get through this and will rebuild," Warren said, and then his forehead bunched up when he glanced at Raleigh. "Sorry."

Raleigh wasn't sure exactly what the apology was for. Maybe because Warren didn't want to remind him that he knew enough about Alma to make comments like that. But it was the truth. His mom was strong, especially under pressure.

First though, she had to stay alive.

"If it's all right, I'd like to be the one to call Hannah's kin," Warren continued a moment later, and he was talking to Raleigh. "I want to tell them who was responsible for her death. It won't be much comfort to them because it won't bring her back, but at least they'll know."

Raleigh nodded, and it was a reminder that he needed to tell Sonya's relatives, as well.

"So, what will happen with you two?" Warren asked.

The question threw Raleigh, and it caused Thea to pull back her shoulders. She looked at him. Raleigh looked at her. And he realized he didn't have a clue what the answer was. But he knew what he wanted to happen.

He wanted to put the past behind them and be with Thea.

Raleigh wasn't even sure that was possible though.

He didn't get a chance to start figuring it out, either, because he saw Dr. Jacobs, the surgeon, making his way toward them. Thea, Warren and he all stood, and Raleigh could tell they were doing what he was—trying to steel himself up for whatever the news might be.

"Alma made it through surgery just fine," Dr. Jacobs immediately said.

Raleigh hadn't expected the relief to hit him so hard, but it nearly knocked the breath out of him. It did the same to Thea because she practically sagged against him. He looped his arm around her waist in case her legs felt as unsteady as his did.

"The bullet didn't hit anything vital, and I was able to remove it with only a small incision," the doctor went on. "She'll have to stay in the hospital a couple of days, of course, but I expect her to make a full recovery."

"When can I see her?" Raleigh asked.

"You can pop into recovery for just a second or two. She's woozy but awake. Follow me," the doctor instructed. Dr. Jacobs started to move but then stopped and looked at Thea and Warren. "I can only allow immediate family in the recovery room, but if you're close to Alma, you'll be able to see her from the observation window."

Warren shook his head. "I'll just be going. I need

to get home." He hugged Thea. "I'm not offering you a ride," he added to her, and even though Warren had whispered it, Raleigh still heard it. "Stay here and work things out with Raleigh."

That sounded like approval for a relationship between Thea and him. Not that Raleigh needed approval from Warren. But it still felt good to get it.

Warren stepped back from Thea and extended his hand to Raleigh. Again, it wasn't much, just a small gesture, but it felt like they were moving in the right direction. Raleigh shook his hand, and judging from the way Warren smiled, it seemed as if Raleigh had handed him the moon. Warren tipped his hat to Dr. Jacobs and headed out while Thea and he followed the doctor down the hall.

"Your mother might not be so happy to see me," Thea muttered, suddenly sounding uncomfortable.

"She's alive. We're alive. That'll make her happy."

Raleigh meant that, too, but he wasn't sure what he'd see when they approached the recovery room. His mother had just been shot. And had killed a man. She might not bounce back from that anytime soon.

Thea stopped at the window while Raleigh went in, but Alma lifted her hand and motioned for Thea to join him.

"Immediate family only," the doctor reminded Alma.

"Thea's practically family," Alma insisted. "Or she should be."

Coming on the heels of Warren's *So, what will happen with you two* question, this felt like matchmaking. Badly timed matchmaking at that. Thea might still be in shock, and he didn't want to press her with Warren's question or anything else.

Thea walked into the room, her steps slow and cautious. "How are you feeling?" she asked his mother.

His mother managed to eke out a smile, though it was clear she was weak and sleepy from the drugs. "Better now that you two are here." The smile didn't last though, and there were tears in her eyes when she looked at Raleigh. "I had to kill Simon. If I hadn't—"

"None of us would be here," Raleigh interrupted. "You saved our lives. Warren's, too." He debated if he should add more about that, but his mother appeared to be waiting for him to continue. "He stayed here until he found out you were out of the woods, and then he went home."

No need to add that he was going home to his wife. Alma knew that. And she nodded. "Good." And it seemed genuine.

Love had definitely given her a kick in the teeth, but maybe one day she could put aside her feelings for Warren and find someone who didn't make her part of his secrets and lies. Of course, without those secrets and lies, Raleigh wouldn't exist.

"The house is gone, I suppose?" Alma asked.

He hadn't planned to bring it up, but since she had, Raleigh nodded. "I'll do the insurance paperwork to get the rebuild started, and you can stay with me until it's done."

"Thea won't mind if I'm there?" his mother pressed.

"Of course not," Thea jumped to answer. "There's no reason for me to mind." In fact, she said it so fast that it made Raleigh wonder if Thea had plans to avoid his place altogether.

Alma took Thea by the hand and inched her closer to the bed. "You'll always be close to Warren. I would never want to change that. I just want you to know that

I'll welcome you, too. I mean, it's as plain as the nose on my face that you're in love with my son."

Thea pulled in her breath, and Raleigh thought some of the color drained from her face. She didn't get a chance to respond though because the doctor tapped his watch. "Your time's up. You can visit Alma in the morning, after we've moved her out of recovery."

Raleigh nodded and then brushed a kiss on his mom's cheek. "Get some rest."

"Tell her you love her," his mom countered, and she quickly closed her eyes, no doubt a ploy so he wouldn't argue with her.

Yeah, she was definitely matchmaking.

Raleigh didn't say anything until they were out of the recovery room and back in the hall that led to the waiting area. "Sorry about what my mom said."

Thea stopped and looked at him. Actually, she glared a little. "I'm not sorry. If she hadn't brought it up, I would have. I'm in love with you." But she immediately continued without giving him a chance to respond. "It's okay if you don't feel the same way. No pressure. But I'm tired of pretending that it's only an attraction between us. For me, it's a whole lot more."

Since it sounded as if she was getting a little angry—and because she wouldn't let him get a word in edgewise—he pulled her to him and kissed her. He made sure it was way too long and way too hot for a hospital hallway. But he'd wanted to make a point. Unfortunately, the point-making got a little clouded when Thea moved right into that kiss.

Thea and he kept it up until he heard someone clear their throat. A nurse, who was smiling at them but had her eyebrow raised. Raleigh knew her. She was Betsy

Fay Millard, and she was a close friend of his mother's. Which meant Alma would soon know about this.

And would no doubt approve.

Betsy Fay hitched her thumb to the room next to them. "It's empty if you two need to work something out." She winked at them and strolled away.

Raleigh supposed he should be a little embarrassed about kissing Thea like that in a public place, but embarrassment wasn't a barrier to what he needed to get done. He took Thea into the room and kissed her again, all the while trying to figure out how to tell her the most important thing he'd ever have to tell her.

The second kiss lasted as long as he could make it last until they both needed air. And when they broke away from each other, Thea looked up at him and smiled. That was it. She didn't say anything. Didn't have to. Because he could see in her eyes every drop of the love she felt for him.

Man, it was amazing.

And just like that, everything suddenly felt right, as if all the pieces of his life had lined up the way they should. That made it a whole lot easier for him to say what was on his mind.

"I love you, Thea." Raleigh didn't have to think about it—he meant it with all his heart.

"Took you long enough," she joked. Some tears watered her eyes, but since she was smiling, he thought that was a good thing. She wadded up a handful of his shirt and pulled him back to her.

Raleigh made sure the third kiss was one they would both remember.

* * * * *

Nicole Helm grew up with her nose in a book and the dream of one day becoming a writer. Luckily, after a few failed career choices, she gets to follow that dream—writing down-to-earth contemporary romance and romantic suspense. From farmers to cowboys, Midwest to *the* West, Nicole writes stories about people finding themselves and finding love in the process. She lives in Missouri with her husband and two sons and dreams of someday owning a barn.

Books by Nicole Helm

Harlequin Intrigue

A Badlands Cops Novel
South Dakota Showdown
Covert Complication
Backcountry Escape
Isolated Threat
Badlands Beware
Close Range Christmas

Carsons & Delaneys
Wyoming Cowboy Justice
Wyoming Cowboy Protection
Wyoming Christmas Ransom

Visit the Author Profile page at
Harlequin.com for more titles.

WYOMING
COWBOY RANGER

Nicole Helm

For anyone who found the courage to go home again, and those who had the bravery to stay.

Chapter 1

Jen Delaney loved Bent, Wyoming, the town she'd been born in, grown up in. She was a respected member of the community, in part because she ran the only store that sold groceries and other essentials within a twenty-mile radius of town.

From her position crouched on the linoleum while she stocked shelves, she looked around the small town store she'd taken over at the ripe age of eighteen. For the past ten years it had been her baby with its narrow aisles and hodgepodge of necessities.

She'd always known she'd spend the entirety of her life happily ensconced in Bent and her store, no matter what happened around her.

The reappearance of Ty Carson didn't change that knowledge so much as make it…annoying. No, annoying would have been just his being in town again. The fact their families had somehow intermingled in the last year was…a catastrophe.

Her sister, Laurel, marrying Ty's cousin Grady had been a shock, very close to a betrayal, though it was hard to hold it against Laurel when Grady was so head over heels for her it was comical. They both glowed with love and happiness and impending parenthood.

Jen tried not to hate them for it.

She could forgive Cam, her oldest brother, for his serious relationship with Hilly. Hilly was biologically a Carson, but she'd only just found that out. Besides, Hilly wasn't like other Carsons. She was so sweet and earnest.

But Dylan and Vanessa… Her business-minded, sophisticated older brother *impregnating* and marrying snarky bad girl Vanessa Carson… *That* was a nightmare.

And none of it was fair. Jen was now, out of nowhere, surrounded by Carsons and Delaneys intermingling—which went against everything Bent had ever stood for. Carsons and Delaneys hated each other. They didn't fall in love and get married and have *babies*.

And still, she could have handled all that in a certain amount of stride if it weren't for *Ty* Carson. Everywhere she turned he seemed to be right there, his stoic gaze always locked on *her*, reminding her of a past she'd spent a lot of time trying to bury and forget.

When she'd been seventeen and the stupidest girl alive, she would have done anything for Ty Carson. Risked the Delaney-Carson curse that, even with all these Carson-Delaney marriages, Bent still had their heart set on. She would have risked her father's wrath over daring to connect herself with a *Carson*. She would have given up anything and everything for Ty.

Instead he'd made promises to love her forever, then

disappeared to join the army—which she'd found out only a good month after the fact. He hadn't just broken her heart—he'd crushed it to bits.

But Ty was a blip of her past she'd been able to forget about, mostly, for the past ten years. She'd accepted his choices and moved on with her life. For a decade she had grown into the adult who didn't care at all about Ty Carson.

Then Ty had come home for good, and all she'd convinced herself of faded away.

She was half convinced he'd returned simply to make her miserable.

"You look angry. Must be thinking about me."

Her head whipped up, the jolt of surprise having nothing on the white-hot flash of fury. "I never think about you, Tyler." She definitely wasn't about to admit she *had* been.

His cocksure grin faded somewhat. He hated his full first name with a passion she'd certainly never understood, but it was one of the few tools in her arsenal she had to get under his unflappable demeanor.

He wasn't the only person who made her want to lash out, but considering what he'd done to her, she didn't make an effort to curb that impulse like she did with everyone else.

She slowly rose from where she'd been crouched, dusting her hands off by slapping them together. "Don't you have anything better to do than stalk me?" she asked haughtily, sailing past him in the narrow aisle with as much grace as she could muster.

"Don't flatter yourself, babe."

Babe. Oh, she'd like to knock his teeth out. Instead she scooted behind the checkout counter and smiled sweetly at him. "Then might I kindly suggest you make your purchases."

"You really think I'd be talking to you if I didn't have to be? I've got ample time to corner you if I wanted to at a family gathering with all the recent Carson-Delaney insanity going around."

She narrowed her eyes at him. He'd always been tall, rangy, dangerous. Age only enhanced all of those things. It was hardly fair he looked even better now than he had then. Certainly unfair he was talking to her as if *she'd* been the one to disappear in the middle of the night a decade ago.

"So what is it you want?" she demanded, but the fact he had a point had fear sneaking past her Ty-defenses. "There's not more trouble, is there?" Bent had been a beacon for it lately.

Laurel and Dylan and even Vanessa dang Carson might be going around town yapping they didn't believe in curses or love solved curses or *whatever*, but trouble after trouble didn't lie. Jen was convinced there had to be *something* to the old curse that said a Carson and Delaney falling in love only spelled trouble.

"No trouble," Ty said casually. "Just a concern. We'll call it a gut feeling."

Develop those off army rangering, did you? She bit her tongue so the words wouldn't escape and reveal how many scraps of information she'd collected about him over the years.

"How can *I* help?" *Mr. Army Ranger should take care of his gut feelings himself, shouldn't he?*

"I just need you to give me a heads-up if you get any new people in the store. You can even send the info through Hilly or Addie, if you'd rather."

Jen raised her chin. It'd be a cold day in hell before she gave this heartless, careless jerk any clue she still had feelings for him. "I don't need to go through anyone, but surely you don't need to know every single stranger I get in here."

"And just how many strangers do you typically get in here?" Ty asked drily.

"Enough."

He didn't respond right away, though she could tell by the tiniest firming of his mouth that he was irritated with her. It nearly made her smile. Ty was not an easy man to irritate—at least not visibly.

"This isn't about us," he said in low, heavy tones.

Any twitch of a smile died. *Us.* They did not acknowledge *us*, and hadn't since his return. There'd been no mention that they'd ever sworn their love for each other. They'd been stupid teenagers, yes, but she'd so believed those words.

"We've had enough trouble lately," Ty said, and she hated that she could see the stiffness in his posture. Anyone else wouldn't have noticed the change, but she knew him too well even all these years later to miss that slight tightening in the way he held himself. "If there's going to be more, I want to head it off at the pass. You run the most visited place in Bent. All I'm asking is for you to—"

"Yes, I understand what you're asking," she replied primly. "Consider it done. Now, feel free to leave." Because she hated him here. Hated breathing the same air as him. Hated looking into those blue eyes she knew too well, because his build could change, the skin around his eyes could crinkle with the years, but the sharp blue of tropical ocean would always be the exact same.

And it would always hurt, no matter how much she tried to exorcise that pain.

He rapped his knuckles against her counter lightly, his lips curved into something like a wry smile. "See you around, Jen."

Not if I can help it.

Ty couldn't explain the feeling that needled along his spine. It had nothing to do with the heavy weight that settled in his stomach. The needling was his gut feeling, honed as an army ranger, that told him the strange, threatening letters he'd been receiving weren't a prank or a joke.

The hard ball of weight was all Jen. Regrets. Guilt. Things he'd never, ever expected to feel, but adulthood had changed him. The army and army rangers had changed him. All the regrets he swore to himself at eighteen to never, ever entertain swamped him every time he saw her.

He tried not to see her, but his family was making it even harder than this small town.

All that was emotional crap he could at least pretend to ignore or will away. Which was exactly what he could not do with the latest letter that had been mixed in with the other mail to Rightful Claim, the bar his cousin owned and where Ty worked.

Vague. Ominous. Unsigned. And addressed to him. He had his share of enemies in Bent. Being a Carson in this town lent itself toward Delaney enemies everywhere he went. But though he'd love to pin it on a Delaney or a crony of theirs, it wasn't.

This was something outside, which meant it likely connected to his time in the army. Yeah, he'd made a few enemies there, too. He wasn't a guy who went looking for trouble. In fact, he could get along with just about anyone.

Until he couldn't.

He blew out a breath as he crossed Main. Away from the prim and tidy Delaney side of the street, to the right side. The rough-and-tumble Carson side with Rightful Claim at the end—with its bright neon signs and assurance that nothing in this town would ever be truly civilized like the Delaneys over there wanted.

Except the lines weren't so clear anymore, were they?

Dylan Delaney was standing in the garage opening to Carson Cars & Bikes. Vanessa and her swell of a baby bump stood next to him, grinning happily up at the man she used to hate.

What was *wrong* with his cousins? He could give a pass to his brother. Noah's wife was barely a Delaney. Oh, somewhere along the line, but Addie hadn't grown up here. Dylan and Laurel? Born and bred rule-abiding proper Delaney citizens, and somehow Vanessa and Grady were head over heels in dumb.

Ty should know, shouldn't he? He'd been there first. He'd just had the good sense to get the hell out of that mess while he could.

But that only conjured images of Jen, who hadn't had the decency to change in his near decade away. Once upon a time he'd been stupid enough to count the freckles on her nose and commit that number to memory.

It wasn't the first time he wished he could medically remove the part of his brain still so in tune to that long past time, and it probably wouldn't be the last.

He didn't nod or greet Dylan as he passed and felt only moderately guilty for being rude. Until Vanessa's voice cut through the air.

"Hey, jerkoff."

He heaved out a sigh and slowly turned to face her. Her baby bump was so incongruous to the sharp rest of her. "Yes, Mrs. Delaney," he replied.

She didn't even flinch, just slid her arm around Dylan's waist. As though a Carson and a Delaney— opposites in every possible way—could be the kind of lifetime partners real marriages were made out of.

If he could erase four years of his adolescent life, it would have been funny. He would have had a heck of a time making fun of all of the fallen Carsons. But since he'd given all *that* up once upon a time, and no one had any clue, all this wedded bliss and the popping out of babies was hard to swallow.

"You coming to the baby shower?" Vanessa demanded. Marriage and pregnancy hadn't softened her any. At least there was that.

"Do I look like the kind of man who goes to baby showers?"

"Oh, don't be a wuss. It's coed."

"It's co-no."

"Noah's coming."

Hell.

"You're way more of a baby shower guy than Noah."

"I take offense to that."

She grinned. "Good. I'll count you down for a yes."

"I don't think—"

"Give him a break, Van," Dylan said, his arm resting across her shoulders, as if just a few months ago they hadn't hated each other's guts. "It's only because Jen's going to be there."

Ty stiffened, fixing Dylan with an icy look. "What's Jen got to do with anything?"

Vanessa's smile went sly, but she nodded agreeably to her husband's words. "It's no secret you two *hate* each other." She enunciated the word *hate* as if it didn't mean what it ought.

But it darn well had to. "I can't stand the whole lot of you, but I've suffered through a few weddings now—a lot better than the two of you did on that first one," he replied, nodding toward Vanessa's expanding stomach.

Vanessa rubbed her belly. "That was fate."

"That was alcohol. Now, I have things to do."

"One o'clock tomorrow. Don't be late."

He grunted. He could disappear for the night, easily enough. Even his brother wouldn't be able to find him. But Noah would be disappointed if he baled. Worse, Noah's wife, Addie, would be disappointed in him. She'd give him that wounded deer look.

Damn Delaney females.

Ty stalked down the street, edgy and snarling and with nothing to take it out on. He pushed into Rightful Claim knowing he had to rein in his temper lest Grady poke at it. Though Grady owned Rightful Claim, Ty lived above it and worked most nights as a bartender.

He'd been toying around with the idea of convincing Grady to let him buy in as partner. He just wasn't 100 percent sure he wanted to be home for good. He was done with the army rangers, that much was for sure, but that didn't mean he was ready to water the roots that tied him to Bent.

Didn't mean he wasn't. The problem was he wasn't sure. Until he was, he was going to focus on taking it one day at a time.

Grady looked up from his place behind the bar where he was filling the cash register to get it ready for the three o'clock opening. "You got a letter in the mail," Grady offered lightly, nodding toward a pile of envelopes and glossy postcards. "No postage. Odd."

Ty shrugged and snatched up the letter with his name on it. "Women never leave you secret admirer notes, Grady?"

"No, women used to leave me themselves," Grady said with a sharp grin.

"Used to," Ty replied with a snort. "Old married man."

"Ain't half-bad with the right marriage, in my experience."

"Sage advice from the married-for-less-than-a-year. You come talk to me when you've got a few decades under your belt."

"Won't change anything," Grady replied with a certainty that didn't make any sense to Ty. How could anyone possibly be sure? Especially Grady? His mother had been married more times than Ty could count. At least Ty's dad had had the good sense to stop after Mom had died. Focused his making people miserable on his kids instead of on a new woman.

"You okay?" Grady asked casually enough.

"Why wouldn't I be okay?"

"You seem…"

Ty looked up at his cousin and raised an eyebrow.

"Edgy," Grady finished, heeding none of Ty's non-verbal warnings.

"I'm always edgy," Ty said, trying to flash the kind of grin he always flashed. It fell flat, and he knew it.

"No. You're always a little sharp, a little hard, but you're not usually *edgy*."

Ty shrugged. "Just waiting for the curse to hit us tri-fold. Or is it quadruple-fold? Can't keep up with you all."

"If you believe in town curses, it's out-of-your-mind-fold." Grady still stood behind the cash register even though he'd finished his work. "If you've got trouble, you only need to share it, cousin. Mine, cow or woman?"

Ty wanted to smile at the old code they'd developed as kids. But the problem was he didn't know *what* kind of trouble he'd brought home. Whatever trouble it was, though, it was his problem. They'd had enough around here lately, and with Van and Laurel pregnant, Ty wasn't going to make a deal about things.

He was going to handle it. He always handled it.

"Be down for opening," Ty grumbled, dreading the Saturday night crowd. He moved through the bar to the back room, not looking down at the letter clutched in his fist. He walked up the stairs, forcing himself not to break into a jog. When he stepped into his apartment, he ripped open the envelope, trying not to focus on the lack of postage.

He pulled out a small, white piece of paper, eyes hurrying over the neatly printed words.

It must be nice to be home with the people you love— family, sure, but first loves most of all.

It won't be so nice to lose. One or the other.

Ty crumpled the note as his hand curled into a fist. He reared his arm back, ready to hurl it into the trash, but he stopped himself.

He smoothed the note out on the counter and studied it. Whoever was threatening him anonymously would have to be stopped.

Which meant he had to figure out who wanted to

hurt him and was close enough to drop an unstamped letter in his mailbox.

The people you love.

Not on his watch.

Jen Delaney was as pretty as he'd been told. It gave him a little thrill. As did watching her while she hadn't a clue anyone was watching. She stocked shelves, waited on the occasional customer, all while he watched from the viewfinder of his camera.

He'd had to take a break when Ty Carson had sauntered up, but that had given him time to leave the note.

Ty Carson.

Feeling the black anger bubble in his gut, he lowered the camera. He took deep calming breaths, and counted backward from ten just like Dr. Michaels always told him to.

He found his calm. He found his purpose. He slid into the car he'd parked in the little church parking lot. He exchanged his camera for his binoculars.

He could just barely make Jen out through the storefront of Delaney General. She was the perfect target. In every way.

And when he targeted her, he'd make Ty fear. He'd make Ty hurt. He'd ruin his life, step by step.

Just like Ty had ruined his.

On one last breath, he smiled at himself in the rearview mirror. Calm and happy, because he had his plan in place.

Step one: charm Jen Delaney.

It shouldn't be hard. He knew everything about her. Thanks to Ty.

Chapter 2

Saturday evenings at Delaney General were always fairly busy. During the week Jen's crowd was minimal and usually the browsing kind. Weekends were more frantic—trips to grab what had been forgotten over the week. A twelve-pack of beer, sauce for spaghetti already on the stove and, in the case of one nervous young gentleman, a box of condoms.

She'd made one joke about telling his mother. He'd scurried away, beet red. There was *some* joy in living in a small town. Jim Bufford hefted a twenty-four-pack of her cheapest beer onto the checkout counter and grinned at her, flashing his missing bottom tooth. "Care to drink dinner with me, darling?"

"Hmm," she replied, pulling the case over the scanner. Jim had been making this particular offer since she'd turned twenty. Since he made it to just about every female who'd ever worked in Delaney General, she didn't take it personally. "Some other night, Jim. Got my nose to the grindstone here."

He handed over a wad of wrinkled bills and tutted while she made change. "Young pretty thing shouldn't work so hard."

"And a nice man like you shouldn't drink his dinner." She handed him his change and he hefted the case off the counter.

"Yeah, yeah," he grumbled, offering a half-hearted goodbye as he pushed open the door and stepped out. Just a few seconds later the bell on the door tinkled again and someone stepped inside.

She didn't recognize this customer. He wore his cowboy hat low, obscuring most of his face. Still, she could usually recognize her regulars by size, clothes, posture and so on. This was a stranger.

She remembered Ty's words from earlier and an icy dread skittered up her spine, but she smiled. "Good evening."

"Evening," the man returned, a pleasant smile of his own. She couldn't see his eyes, but his smile wasn't off-putting. He was wearing what appeared to be hiking gear and had a fancy-looking camera hanging from his neck. "I don't suppose you carry film?" He lifted the camera and his smile turned sheepish.

"Afraid not."

He sighed. "Didn't expect to use so much. You've got a fascinating town here, ma'am."

"We like to think so." She kept her smile in place. The man was perfectly polite. No different from any other stranger who walked into her store looking for provisions of any kind.

Her palms were sweaty, though, and her heart beat too hard. It was only her and him in the store right now, and Ty had warned her about strangers.

And you're going to trust Ty Carson on anything? No. No, she wasn't, but… Well, there'd been too much trouble lately not to heed his warning. So, she'd be smart. Do what her deputy sister would do in this situation: pay attention to details. The man was tall, maybe around her brother Cam's height. But not broad. He had narrow shoulders, though the way he walked exuded a kind of strength. Like a runner, she supposed. Slim, but athletic. She couldn't determine the exact shade of his hair because of the way the hat was positioned and the way he was angled away from her, but it wasn't dark hair.

"I don't have film, but I've got food and drinks or anything else you might need." She smiled at him, but he still didn't look her way. He examined the store.

"Actually I stopped because I was wondering if you'd mind if I took a few pictures of your store."

"I thought you were out of film."

"I am, which is a shame. But I use my phone for pictures, too. I was using film out here because the ambiance seemed to call for it. I was over at the saloon. I hear the swinging doors are original."

"So they claim," Jen muttered, irritably thinking of Ty.

"Amazing." He meandered over to a row of candy, studied the offerings. "I took way too many pictures. And the boardwalks. The signs. It's like stepping back in time. I've been mostly sticking to ghost towns but the mix of past and present here… It's irresistible."

"So you were out at Cain, then?" she asked, referencing a popular ghost town destination for photographers and adventurers.

He nodded, still keeping his head tilted away from her. "That's what brought me out this way."

"From where?"

He chuckled. "You ask every stranger where they're from?"

She had to work to keep the pleasant smile on her face. She couldn't blow this. "Tend to. We don't get many outsiders."

"Ah. Outsiders. Must be nice to live in a community that protects itself against outsiders. You'd feel…safe. Protected and cared for."

She hadn't felt particularly safe after the craziness of the past year, but she decided to agree anyway. "Very."

He swayed on his feet, trying to brace himself on the shelf and upending some candy before he fell backward onto the floor.

Stunned, Jen rushed forward, but he was already struggling to sit up.

"I'm all right," he said, holding out a hand to keep her back. "Just haven't eaten since breakfast. Got caught up, and I suppose the lack of food caught up with me. I'll be all right."

She grabbed one of the candy bars that had fallen to the ground and ripped it open before she handed it to him. She didn't think he'd gotten caught up. She was starting to think he didn't have any money. She almost felt sorry for him. "Here. Don't worry about paying for it. Just eat."

He took the candy, and then a bite. "You're too kind." He looked up for a second.

Blue eyes. A vibrant blue. Blond hair, wispy and

nearly white really. Not with age, just a very, very light shade of blond. His nose was crooked. To the left.

"Didn't expect to run across someone so young and pretty in a tiny little Wyoming town."

"Uh—"

"Sorry." He looked back down at the candy bar, the brim of his hat hiding everything again. "That's awkward and uncomfortable. Let's blame it on the lack of food. Do you think I could trouble you for a small sip of water?"

Jen jumped to her feet and hurried for the cooler that boasted rows of water bottles. She grabbed one of the larger ones and twisted it open. "Here," she said, returning to his side. "You just take this."

He took a sip and then nodded, using the back of his arm to wipe the water droplets off his mouth. He kept his head down.

Was it purposeful? Was he trying to make sure she couldn't identify him? Was he planning something awful? But she'd seen his eyes and the color of his hair—she only had to remember the details.

He took another bite of the candy bar, then a drink of the water. She racked her brain trying to figure out what to do. How to defend herself if he lunged at her. This could all be an act. A ploy. Weaken her defenses, catch her off guard.

Carefully, Jen leaned slightly away and got to her feet, keeping her eyes on him and her body tense and ready to react.

"Thank you for the kindness," he said, sounding exhausted. But it *could* be acting. "I should be out of your way." He struggled to his feet, swayed again, but righted himself.

He seemed so genuinely thankful and feeble. The man was a mess, and maybe he *was* Ty's threatening stranger, but he wasn't doing anything to put her in danger at the moment.

And why would he? He was probably just after Ty. How could she blame anyone on that front?

"Can I get you anything else? Maybe a sandwich? A bag of chips?" His clear weakness ate at her. A man shouldn't go hungry. Though, she supposed, he could sell that nice camera if he was really that bad off.

"No. No, I'll be fine." He kept his head tilted away, but the corner of his smile was soft and kind as he lifted the water bottle in salute. "I appreciate it, ma'am. Your kindness won't be forgotten." And with that, he walked out of the store. No trouble. No danger.

Leaving Jen unsure about what to do.

Ty didn't often find himself uncomfortable. He'd learned early to roll with whatever punches life threw at him. There'd been quite a few.

But nothing could have prepared him for a baby shower. A Carson-Delaney baby shower. Laurel and Vanessa were laughing over their baby bumps, pastel pink and blue decorations everywhere, and Carsons and Delaneys mingled like there'd never been a feud.

Jen was in a corner talking to Addie and Noah, Addie's toddler trying to crawl up Noah and laughing hysterically when he fell. Noah watched with the patience of a happy man.

Ty had never particularly understood his brother, though he loved him with a fierceness that meant he'd lay down his life for the man. What he did know about Noah was that having Addie and Seth in his life and on his ranch made him happy, and that was all Ty really cared about.

"Delaney Delirium getting to you?"

Ty gave Grady a cool look. "Just trying to understand all this baby business," he said, nodding toward Noah and the way he held Seth easily on his hip.

Grady patted him on the back. Hard. "Sure, buddy."

"You really want to be a dad after the way we grew up?" Ty asked, unable to stop himself. He didn't get it. The way Noah had taken to Addie's nephew that she was guardian and mother to, as if it were easy to step into the role of guardian and father. The way Vanessa and Grady seemed calm and even happy about their impending parenthood.

The Carson generation before theirs had not been a particular parental one. More fists and threats than nurturing happiness.

"Figure I got a pretty good example of what *not* to do," Grady said with a shrug. "And a woman to knock some sense into me when I make mistakes. Besides, we turned out okay in spite of it all."

"And Delaney senior ain't got a problem with his grandchild being raised by a cop and saloon owner?"

"Laurel's father doesn't get a say."

Ty knew it was different for Grady. Ty had been eighteen when Mr. Delaney had flexed his parental and town muscles to make sure Ty got the hell away from his daughter. Grady wasn't a dumb teenager, and neither was Laurel. They could refuse a parent's interference.

Couldn't you have?

He shook his head. Ancient history. No amount of Carson and Delaney comingling was reason to go back there.

Laurel called Grady over and he left Ty in the middle of all this goodwill and pastel baby nonsense. He was somewhere in no-man's land. He almost wished a sniper would take him out.

There were toasts and cake and presents of tiny clothes and board books. No matter that their families had been enemies for over a century, no matter that people in town still whispered about curses and the inevitable terrible ends they would all meet, Carsons and Delaneys sat together celebrating new lives.

Some unknown ache spread through him. He couldn't name it, and he couldn't seem to force it away. It sat in his gut, throbbing out to all his limbs.

Faking his best smile, he went to Vanessa and Grady and made his half-hearted excuses to leave early. No one stopped him, but his family sure watched him slip out the front door. He could feel their eyes, their questions. And worst of all, their pity.

As if being alone was the worst fate a person could face. He'd seen a lot worse. This was fine. And good. Right for him. Alone suited—

"Ty."

There was something his gut did when she said his name. No matter the years, he couldn't seem to control that intrinsic physical reaction to his name forming on her lips. A softening. A longing.

He took a minute to brace himself before he turned around. Jen stood on the porch of Grady and Laurel's cabin. She looked like cotton candy in some lacy, frothy pink thing.

And all too viscerally he could remember what she looked like completely *unclothed*. No matter that he assured himself time changed things—bodies, minds, hearts. It was hard to remember as she approached him with a face that wasn't shooting daggers at him for the first time since he'd arrived home.

"Listen." She looked back at the open door, then took a few more steps toward him on the walk. "I wanted to let you know I had a stranger come in the store last night."

"What?" he demanded, fury easily taking over the ache inside him. *Last night?* "Why didn't you call me? I told you—"

She lifted her chin, her eyes cold as ice. "You told me to let you know. Here I am, letting you know. I don't think he's whatever you're looking for. He was perfectly nice. He just asked to take pictures of the store, and then he—"

"What time did he come in?"

"Well, seven but—"

"He was going to take pictures when it was pitch-black?"

She frowned at that, a line forming between her brows that once upon a time he'd loved tracing with his thumb. Where had *that* memory come from?

"He was hungry. He *fainted.* He was out of it. Confused maybe. And totally polite and harmless."

"Damn it, Jen. I told you to call me. I could have—"

"He didn't *do* anything. I know you're paranoid, but—"

"I am *not* paranoid. You think a man who gets a letter with no postage delivered to where he lives and works is paranoid?"

She tilted her head, studying him, and he realized with a start he'd said too much.

He never said too much.

"What was in the letter?" she asked, her voice calm and her eyes on him.

It was hell, this. Still wanting her. Missing that old tiny slice of his life where she'd been his. He didn't want this, but he couldn't seem to get rid of it. It ate at him, had him dreaming about doing things he couldn't possibly allow himself to do. Every once in a while he'd think…what would just one touch do?

But he knew the answer to that.

She audibly swallowed and looked away, a faint blush staining her cheeks. She felt it, too, and yet…

"It doesn't matter," he grumbled, trying to find his usual center of calm. His normal, everyday clear-eyed view of the world and of this problem he had. "What did he look like? Better yet—I want to see your security tape."

Her eyes flashed anger and frustration. "You are *not* looking at my security tape."

"Why not?"

"It's an invasion of my customers' privacy."

He snorted. "I don't care that Mary Lynn Jones bought a pack of Marlboros even though her husband thinks she quit or that little Adam Teller was buying condoms because he talked his way into Lizzie Granger's pants."

Jen's mouth twitched, but then she firmed it into a scowl. "How do you know all that?"

"I pay attention, babe."

Her scowl deepened and she folded her arms across her chest. "Blond hair, blue eyes. About the same height as Cam. I'm not sure what that'd be in feet and inches, but I imagine you would. Skinny, but strong, like a marathon runner. He wore hiking clothes and boots, all in tan, and a big, fancy camera around his neck. Topped it off with a Stetson. Said he was taking pictures of ghost towns and happened upon Bent."

It was more to go on than he thought he'd get out of her, but still not enough to ring any bells. "Tattoos? Scars? Something off about him?"

She shook her head. "Not that I could see."

"I want the tape, Jen. If someone is…" He didn't want to tell her. Didn't trust her to keep it a secret and let him handle it, but he needed to see the man himself. Needed to identify him so he could neutralize this threat. "I'm getting letters. They're not threatening exactly, but they're not…not. I know you don't care about me, but your family is all tangled up with mine now." He gestured at the whole irritating lot of them. "Don't you want to protect what's yours?"

"Of course I do."

That sharp chin of hers came up, defiant and angry. Her temper used to amuse him. Now it just made that ache center in his heart.

But that wasn't the problem at hand. "Then let me see the tape. If I recognize him, I'll know what to do. If I don't, then maybe you're right and it's harmless coincidence." He didn't believe that, but he'd let her think he did.

She was quiet and stiff for humming seconds, then finally she sighed. "Oh, fine. I suppose you want to go now?"

He only raised an eyebrow.

She rolled her eyes. "Let me get my purse and say my goodbyes." She stalked back inside, grumbling about irritating, stubborn males the whole way up.

All Ty could do was pray he'd recognize whoever was on that tape and everything would be over.

Jen stepped out of her tiny little sedan, dressed all in pink, her dark hair in pretty waves around her shoulders.

Sweet. Just like Ty had said. She'd been wary of him last night when he'd first walked into the store. He'd seen it in her eyes, but the feigned hunger and stumble had softened her. She'd given him food and water. Good-hearted, she was indeed.

He smiled, watching as Jen stood there in front of her store. When a motorcycle roared into view, his smile died.

Even before the man took off his helmet, he knew who it was. He watched Jen. She didn't seem *happy* to see Ty, but nor did she seem surprised or *un*happy.

He scowled, watching as Ty strode over to Jen. They exchanged a few words and then Jen unlocked the store and stepped inside, Ty right behind her.

She didn't flip the sign from Closed to Open.

He narrowed his eyes. The rage that slammed into him was sudden and violent, but he'd learned a thing or two about how to handle it. Hone it.

Ty would get his. He *would*.

So, patience would be the name of the game. And another letter.

This time in blood.

Chapter 3

Jen set her purse down on her desk in the back room of the store and tried not to sigh. Why was she getting involved in this?

Don't you want to protect what's yours?

It grated all over again. That he could even ask her that. She would have protected *him*, sacrificed for *him*, and he'd left her alone and confused and so broken-hearted she'd...

She booted up her computer, stabbing at the buttons in irritation. She'd eradicate the past if she could, but since she couldn't she had to find a better way of managing her reaction to it in Ty's presence.

Looming over her like some hulking specter. She flicked a glance over her shoulder and up. "Do you mind?"

His eyes were hard and his mouth was harder. He

was taking this so seriously, and that irritated her. Ty was never serious. Oh, deep down he was, but he usually masked it with lazy smiles and sarcastic remarks.

But whatever this was had him giving no pretense of humor.

She focused on the computer and brought up the security footage. She ignored the flutter of panic in her throat, dismissed it as foolish. Whatever was going on was Ty's problem, and once she showed him the footage he'd realize that and leave her alone.

She fast-forwarded through the day, moving the cursor to around seven when the man had come in. She zipped through her conversation with Jim and his case of beer, then hit Play when the door opened after Jim's exit.

They both watched in silence, heads nearly together as they studied the video.

"You can't see him," Ty said flatly, his breath making the hair at her ear dance. She ignored the shiver of reaction and made sure her voice was even before she spoke.

"Give it a second."

They continued to watch, and Jen could only hope Ty was so focused on the video he didn't notice the goose bumps on her arm or the way her breathing wasn't exactly even.

She had to fight viciously against the memories that wanted to worm their way into her consciousness. Memories of them together. Close like this. Not at *all* clothed like this.

But it was silence around them, heavy, pregnant silence, and she didn't dare look to see if Ty was keeping his eyes on the computer. Of course he was. That's what they were here for.

"You can't see his face," Ty repeated.

Jen peered at the form on the screen. She saw herself, watching the man's entrance. And everywhere the man moved, his hat obscured his face from the camera.

"He did it on purpose."

"How would he have known where the camera is?" Jen returned. It was so natural, the way the stranger on the video kept his head down. She wanted to believe Ty was overreacting, but an uncomfortable feeling itched along her spine.

"He did it on purpose," Ty said in that same flat tone. "Keep watching. We'll get a glimpse when he falls."

But as the man on the screen pitched forward into the candy, and then staggered back before falling to the ground, his face remained completely hidden by the hat.

Jen frowned at that. But surely a man who fell over didn't *purposefully* shield himself from a security camera. It was just coincidence.

"Rewind it," Ty ordered.

She opened her mouth to tell him not to order her around, but then huffed out a breath. Why bother arguing with a brick wall? She moved the cursor back to the man's entrance, then slowed down the time.

Nothing changed. You couldn't see the guy's face. But she let Ty watch. She turned to study him. He was so close her nose all but brushed his cheek. If he noticed, he didn't show it. His gaze was flat and blank, seeing nothing but the computer screen.

His profile could be so hard. *He* could be so hard, but there'd been softness and kindness underneath that mask all those years ago. Did it still exist? Or had military life sucked it out of him? Were any of the parts of him that she loved still in there, or were they all gone?

Horrified with that thought, she blinked at the sting-ing in her eyes. Stupid. It didn't matter one way or the other. Yes, he'd broken her heart years ago, but she'd gotten over it. She'd moved on. And he definitely had.

So, her brain needed to stop taking detours to the past.

"He faked that fall," Ty said, as if it was fact, not just his insane opinion on the matter.

"You're being paranoid."

He turned his head so fast she startled back. His eyes were blazing blue, and no matter how tightly he held his jaw, his mouth was soft. She knew exactly what it would feel like on hers.

What the hell was wrong with her? She closed her eyes against the heated wave of embarrassment.

"I am not being paranoid," he said, his voice low and controlled. "I'm being rational. I'm putting all the dots together. That man didn't fall because he was starving. Did you see that fancy camera? He can afford to eat."

She opened her eyes, irritation exceeding embarrass-ment and old stupid feelings. "That doesn't mean—"

"And furthermore," Ty said, getting in her face no matter how she leaned away in her chair, "even if he *did* fall, he kept his face away from that camera for a reason. I *know* it. Now, you want to prove it, you watch hours of your own security tape and see if that happens with any other person."

He held her gaze, though after a while some of that furious, righteous anger softened into something else. Something… *Something* as his blue eyes roamed her face, settled on her mouth.

Jen shot out of the chair, ignoring the fact she bumped into him, and then scrambled away. "I…have to open the store," she stuttered. "Everyone's expecting me to open at three." She was being foolish, but her heart was hammering in her throat and she had to get out of this tiny room where Ty loomed far too large.

He stood, blocking the door, still as a rock, eyeing her carefully. "You have to be careful, Jen."

She fisted her hands on her hips. "He isn't after me. Now let me out."

"He came in here. He talked to you. There's something purposeful in that."

"What do *I* have to do with your threatening letters?"

He heaved out a breath. "Look." He shook his head, crossed his arms over his chest. He looked at the ceiling, then dropped his arms and shoved his hands in his pockets.

She raised her eyebrows. Nerves? No, not exactly, but definitely discomfort. She wasn't sure she'd ever seen Ty something like unsure.

"I have a feeling this ties to someone I was in the military with," he said, sounding disgusted with himself.

"Again, what does that have to do with me?"

"If it's someone I knew? Someone I bunked with? They would have listened to me talk about home, about my family, about…" He nodded in her direction.

She could only blink at him. He'd talked about *her*? After leaving her like she was garbage you dumped on the side of the road? It didn't make any sense.

"I can't tell anything from that tape, but I've got threatening letters and a strange man in your store, so I've got to think of the obvious conclusion here. You could be in danger."

"That's absurd," she responded. It had to be.

He stepped forward, and before she could sidestep

him, he took her by the chin. Her whole body zoomed off into some other dimension she hadn't been to in a very long time. She could only stare at him, while his big, rough hand held her face in place.

"I need you to be careful." He was so solemn, so serious.

Her throat constricted and her heart beat so hard she was sure her whole body vibrated from the violence of it.

His grip on her chin softened, his fingertip moving along the line of her jaw. She wanted to melt into a puddle, but she wasn't seventeen anymore, and with that fission of delight she was reminded she *hated* Ty Carson.

She slapped his hand away, raising her chin at him, trying for regal instead of panicked. "Don't manhandle me."

He only raised an eyebrow.

"I don't know what you want from me," she said, with more feeling than she should have shown him.

"I want you to be aware. Take precautions. Keep yourself safe and protected, and if that man comes in your store again, I want you to call me immediately." He moved out of the way of the door and her exit. "It's that simple."

Simple? Sure. As if anything to do with Ty Carson was *simple*.

Ty walked out of the general store knowing he'd overplayed his hand. Disgusted with himself for getting wrapped up in old feelings and memories and not focusing on the task at hand, he stalked to his motorcycle.

But he couldn't eradicate the look of Jen's brown eyes, wide on his, her mouth open in shock as he'd held her face. The flutter of pulse. It felt as though in that moment a million memories had arced between them.

He tried to shake it off. They weren't the same people. He had regrets, sure. He should have handled everything with her father differently. But he hadn't and there was no reason to beat himself up over it. You couldn't change the past.

And he couldn't change the fact being a soldier and away from home for nearly a decade with only sporadic visits when on leave had altered him. He wasn't the same teenager who'd run off when the right pressure was applied. Even though Jen had stayed in Bent, she wasn't the same girl.

They were different people, and if there was still a physical attraction it would be best if they both ignored it.

But even more important than that, he had to protect her from whatever was going on. He wasn't sure how to do that yet, but he knew he had to figure it out.

He almost ran right into someone, so lost in his own irritable thoughts. He opened his mouth to apologize, until he recognized the middle-aged man before him.

Mr. Delaney's eyes went from the store, to Ty, and then went hard and flat. "I hope you know what you're doing, Carson."

Funny how time didn't change the utter authority in this man's voice. Jen's father thought he owned the *world*, and Ty was sick with regret for ever being a part of that certainty.

"Know what I'm doing? Hmm." Ty smiled. "I suppose I always do."

"You'll watch your step where my daughter is concerned."

Ty raised an eyebrow and looked back at the store himself. Then he let his smile widen into a wolfish grin.

"I got rid of you once, Tyler. I don't know why I couldn't do it again."

Ty didn't let the violent fury show. He wouldn't give this man the satisfaction. He kept the smile in place, made sure his voice was lazy, but with enough edge to carry a threat. "I seem to recall you fooling around with a married woman, Delaney. I wonder what other dirty skeletons are rattling around in your closet. More torrid connections to other Carsons? Or are your kids taking care of that these days?"

It irritated Ty that not even a flicker of that blow hitting showed on Delaney's face, though he knew it was at least a little knock to the man's pride. That it had come out he'd had an affair with a woman who'd been married to someone else. And not just that, a woman who was blood related to Ty himself.

"Your cousins have made my children very happy," Delaney said, surprising the hell out of Ty. "Maybe you shouldn't have run away all those years ago." He smiled pleasantly. "But you did. The kind of running away that isn't so easy to forgive."

Ty kept his smile in place by sheer force of will. He'd faced down his father's fists. He had no trouble facing down Delaney's barbs. "Funny thing about coming back home again." He glanced at the store. "Some things never change, and some people are more forgiving than others."

Finally he got a reaction out of Delaney, though it was only a tightening of his jaw. Still, it was better than nothing. "Impending grandparenthood looks good on you, Delaney. Have a nice day." He patted the man's shoulder, gratified when Delaney jerked away and stalked into the store.

To Jen. Ty sighed. The simple truth was he had more to worry about than Jen or her father. He had to worry about the messages he was receiving, the uncomfortable gut feeling he had that Jen was in danger. Because of him.

The most important thing was keeping her safe. Not because he still had feelings for her, but because it was the right thing to do. The timing of the letter, the mention of first loves and this stranger's appearance in the store were too close to be coincidental or for him to believe Jen wasn't a target.

If this connected to his military days—which were the only days he'd spent away from Bent—and Jen was a target, it would have to be from early in his career. Before the rangers.

He racked his brain for someone he'd wronged, someone he'd had friction with. A few superiors, but nothing personal. Just normal army stuff, and he'd hardly been the only soldier who'd occasionally mouthed off and gotten punished for it. There'd been the man he'd ratted out, but the man on the tape wasn't Oscar. Not even close. Besides, Oscar had to have known his time in the army was limited when he couldn't keep himself out of the booze or drugs.

Ty brought to mind the figure from Jen's security tape. Not even a tingle of recognition. It ate at him, the faceless man manipulating Jen in her own store. It damn near burned him alive to think she'd be a target of something she had nothing to do with.

Target or not, her cooperation or not, he'd keep her safe. He just had to figure out how.

* * *

He didn't mind cutting himself. He rather liked it. Watching the blood well up, drip down. He'd always liked blood. Dr. Michaels said he had to be careful, not to get too caught up in it.

She was right. He only had so much time. Ty would stay at the store for only so long, and it would take time to sneak into Rightful Claim. He had to craft his message quickly, then deliver it with just as much precision and speed.

The paper hadn't worked, so he'd torn off a piece of his T-shirt and concentrated carefully as he used his bloody fingertip to spell out the message.

He admired his work. He supposed blood might tell, giving away his identity, but he wasn't so worried about that. He liked the message of blood too much to worry about the connections.

Besides, by the time blood told, he'd have his revenge.

Chapter 4

Jen had done a lot of pretending in her life. All through high school she'd pretended she wasn't involved with Ty Carson, then after he'd left she'd pretended she wasn't heartbroken. She did her best to pretend Laurel's marriage to Grady and Dylan's marriage to Vanessa didn't bother her. For most of her life, she'd fooled those she loved the most.

She didn't think she'd fooled anyone tonight as she'd pretended to cheerfully spend her evening making dinner for her family at the Delaney Ranch. She'd chattered happily through dinner, then cleaned up diligently, refusing help and earning looks.

Pity looks.

Even though Ty's whole *thing* was giving her the constant creeps and a feeling of being watched, she went home to her apartment above the store after tidying up at Delaney Ranch. She'd rather face off with someone who might be "targeting" her than withstand her family's pity—most especially the in-law Carson portion of her "family."

Jen always passed the storefront on Main before pulling into the alley where stairs led up to her apartment behind the store. No matter what time of day, she always scanned the front to make sure everything was as it should be.

Her heart slammed painfully against her chest at the shadowy figure looming under the awning of the store's front door, highlighted by the faint security lights inside. She whipped her gaze from the door to the road, jerking the wheel to miss the sidewalk she'd been about to careen onto.

Heart pounding, palms sweating, Jen kept driving, taking her normal turn onto the alley. What should she do? Who was lurking outside her store?

It could be anyone. Jim wanted a six-pack. Someone taking an evening stroll. It could be nothing. But it felt like something.

She fished her phone out of her purse, debating whether she should park or keep driving. The person had to have seen her erratic driving. Would whomever it was know who she was? Would the individual walk back here? Threaten her?

"Oh, damn you, Ty Carson." She pushed the car into Park, watching the alley in case anyone appeared. She started to dial Ty, then cursed herself for it. A smart woman didn't call the idiotic, paranoid man who was causing her panic in the first place. A smart woman called the cops.

And lucky for her, her sister was the cops.

Except Laurel was a detective. And pregnant. *Don't you want to protect what's yours?* She cursed Ty all over again, staring at her phone with indecision. Laurel or Ty? Bent County Sheriff's Department or handle this herself?

She looked back up at the alley entrance. There was no sign of anyone. Surely someone nefarious would have run away upon being spotted. She wouldn't be foolish when everyone already pitied her. No.

Quickly and decisively, she got out of her car and hurried to the back door of the store. She watched the alley, fumbling with her keys as she worked to get the door open. Once inside she quickly shut it and locked it behind her, taking a deep breath and trying to steady her shaky limbs.

"You're being ridiculous," she muttered into the empty room. Still, her heartbeat didn't calm and her nerves continued to fray as she moved from the back of the store to the front. At first she didn't see anything, then a shadow moved and she barely held back the impulse to scream.

It was the man who'd fainted in her store.

Despite all the assurances she'd given Ty that the stranger was no one and completely nonthreatening, *this* felt very threatening.

She backed away from the door, pulling her phone out of her purse. Quickly, she dialed the dispatch number for the sheriff's department. When a woman answered, she explained as calmly and concisely as she could that someone was outside her store, and she didn't consider him dangerous but she did have some concerns.

"I'll have a deputy out your way as soon as possible, ma'am."

"Thank you." Jen hit End and then steeled herself to turn around. He was still there, which had her breath coming in quick puffs. He wasn't pounding on the door or the storefront glass. He was simply standing there, same as he had been.

Except, she realized, he was holding something against the window of the door. Unsteady, Jen inched toward the door, realizing it was a piece of paper. He was holding something like a sign against the glass.

In careful print, it read: *I only wanted to thank you for the other day.*

Though the soft security lights from inside the store lit up the boardwalk enough to illuminate him, he had his cowboy hat pulled low. He smiled sheepishly and it sent a tickle of panic through her that his mouth was the only part of him she could make out.

"I called the police," she shouted, wondering if the sound would carry through the glass.

His sheepish smile didn't fade, but he did nod. He pulled a pen out of his pocket and began to write on the paper again. When he flipped it around, she had to squint and step a little closer to read it.

Didn't mean to frighten you. I'll be on my way. See you soon, Jen.

Jen.

He'd written her name, clear as day. Why did he know her name?

He could have overheard it. He could have asked around. Neither made her feel comforted.

She noticed the flash of red and blue lights. She

craned her head to see the cruiser's progress with some relief easing away the panic.

But when she looked back at the door the man was gone, and dread pooled inside her stomach.

None of it was threatening, and yet she felt threatened. Chilled to the bone. She hugged herself as she waited for the deputy to get out of his cruiser and walk up to the door.

She forced herself to smile at him when she opened the door to him. Thanks to her sister's position with the sheriff's department, she knew most of the deputies. Thomas better than most. "Thomas, thanks for coming, but I feel a little silly. He went away without any fuss."

"It's no problem, Jen. Better safe than sorry, and you know your sister would have my butt if I didn't check it out. Now, why don't you tell me everything that happened."

She sighed, knowing it would all get back to Laurel, and she'd have to answer a thousand questions. Knowing Laurel would tell Grady, who'd undoubtedly mention it to Ty. She'd have to tell Ty herself in that case.

She faced that with about as much dread as she had the stranger at her door.

Ty yawned, feeling unaccountably tired for an early Sunday night. Rightful Claim closed down at midnight rather than two, and he should have felt revved.

Instead, the lack of sleep over the past few days was getting to him. Was he getting old? He shook his head, pushing his apartment door open.

Something fluttered at his feet and he knew immediately it would be another note. He bent down to pick it up, but the odd shape and color of the letters stopped him midcrouch. Icy cold settled in his gut and spread through his limbs.

It was blood. Even as he warned himself it could be fake, he knew. It was blood. A message written in blood.

It wasn't hard to access the part of his brain he'd spent a decade honing in the army and the army rangers. It clicked into place like a machine switched on.

He stood to his full height, taking a careful step backward. The less he disturbed the scene, the better chance he had of nipping this all in the bud before anyone got hurt.

Jen. He pulled the phone out of his pocket and dialed her number. He refused to put her as a contact in his phone, but he knew the number nevertheless. All it had taken was Laurel insisting her wedding party had each other's phone numbers to have it lodged in his brain like a tumor.

It rang, ending on her voice mail message. She was probably asleep, but it didn't assuage his fear. He left a terse message. "Call me. ASAP."

He clicked End and pushed away that jangle of worry. Once he took care of this, he'd make sure she was fast asleep. He'd make sure, wherever she was and whatever she was doing, she was safe and sound.

Safe.

Ty looked at his phone and couldn't believe what he was about to do. He was a Carson and Carsons handled their own stuff, but with Jen involved for whatever reason, he couldn't take that chance.

Because Jen *was* involved, he knew that. Even without reading this new message. He knew the man trying to frighten him would use Jen to do it.

So, he called the Bent County Sheriff's Department.

He explained the situation and was assured someone would be over shortly.

Then he called Jen again, cursing her refusal to answer. *She's asleep and has her phone on silent.*

"Screw it," he muttered, moving out of his apartment and back down the stairs. If he walked around to the front of the saloon, he'd be able to see her store. He knew he should wait for the cops, but if her security lights were on, if he jogged over and checked to make sure her car was in the back lot…

Of course, she might have spent the night at the Delaney Ranch. Jen didn't keep a regular schedule, which was going to be a problem if he was going to keep her safe. Not that he could force her to change anything. She'd only get more erratic if he warned her to stay in one place.

Hardheaded woman.

He stepped outside and his heart all but stopped. The flashing lights of a police cruiser were across the road and down the street, right in front of Delaney General.

Without thinking it through, he was ready to run down the street, bust in and save her from whatever was wrong.

But his name broke through the haze.

"Carson?"

Ty whirled to face the cop walking toward him. Younger guy. Ty didn't like cops, period, but if he had to deal with one he would have preferred Hart. Ty was pretty sure this was the one who'd nearly bungled Addie's kidnapping last year.

"What?" Ty barked. "What's going on over there?"

"Nothing serious. Just a suspicious figure. But you put in a call, too. Something about a note?"

Ty looked at the car down by Delaney General, and then at the too-young deputy trying to be tough.

Ty felt his age for a moment, not in years, but in the decade he'd spent in the military. He remembered what it was like to be young and eager. Foolishly sure of his role in helping people. No doubt this moron had the same conviction, and someday it would be beaten out of him.

Ty tried to keep his voice from being a harsh demand. "So, everyone's okay down there?"

"Looks like it was innocent and harmless. Spooked Ms. Delaney some, but no real threat. We've canvassed the area for a while now, with no evidence of anyone. We were just finishing up when we got your call on the radio. Now, why don't you show me the note."

"Who's with her?"

"Hart."

Ty nodded. That was good. That was fine. Let the police take care of Jen. *Suspicious figure.* Ty looked around Main Street, mostly pitch-black except for the occasional glow from nearby businesses' security lights.

Someone was out there. A suspicious figure.

"Carson?"

"Right. Upstairs. You got stuff to collect it or whatever? I'm pretty sure it's written in blood."

The deputy's eyebrows rose, but he nodded. "I've got everything I need to handle it." He patted his utility belt and then followed Ty around the bar and into the back entrance.

Ty led him to the letter, and the deputy crouched and pulled on rubber gloves as he examined it. "Is this the first letter you've received like this?"

"It's the first one in blood, but it isn't the first one."

The deputy spared him a look. One that said *and you're just now calling the police?* It was only his worry over Jen and her suspicious figure that kept him from kicking the cop out and telling him he'd handle it faster and better.

The deputy picked it up and slid it into what looked like a ziplock bag.

"What's it say?" Ty demanded.

The deputy stood and raised his eyebrows. "You didn't read it?"

"I didn't want to touch it. Blood or fingerprints… You'll be able to get something off it?"

"Should be. Blood could be animal, but there might be something here. Though it'll take some time to send that off for analysis."

"But you will?"

"I'll be recommending it," the deputy returned with a nod. "This is a serious threat." He held up the bag and read through it. "I'd warn you to watch your back, but it won't be your back I'm after."

Jen. He didn't know why this person was fixating on Jen, but he was sure of it. "We need to know who that is."

"You don't have any clues?"

"None. Someone from my army days, maybe? But I'm in the dark. If we can get DNA off that—"

"What about the other letters? Where are they?"

Struggling between his need to do this on his own and his understanding he needed the cops in on this if Jen was going to stay safe, Ty stalked over to the kitchen drawer he'd shoved the other letters in. He grabbed them and held them out to the deputy.

The deputy took them, then nodded toward the door

as footfalls sounded on the stairs. "That'll be Hart. We'll want to consider the connection angle on this. A note to you, a threatening figure at Ms. Delaney's store. Same time frame."

It was indeed Hart, but Ty frowned at Jen walking into the room behind him.

"What's going on?" Jen demanded. "Was he here, too?"

Hart turned to Jen, placed a gentle hand on her shoulder. Gentle enough that Ty's eyes narrowed.

"Jen," Hart said quietly. "Maybe you should calm—"

"Don't you dare tell me to calm down, Thomas." Jen shrugged off his hand and glared at him, then Ty. "Ty seems to think this man is connected—the one sending him threatening notes, and the stranger at my store. And you told me he got another one. Well, it's not okay, and I'm somehow involved. I want to know why."

"We don't know it's the same person," the deputy with the letters said to Hart and Jen. "We only know it's suspicious timing. Do you have an idea of when the letter was dropped off?"

Ty sighed. "I've been bartending since four. Didn't come up till after midnight. I don't know how someone would have broken in without me noticing anything, but it could have happened anytime."

Hart jotted something down on a notepad while the other deputy read through the notes Ty had handed him.

"Excuse us a moment," Hart said, nodding to the other deputy into the hallway. They stood there, conferring in low tones.

Ty studied Jen. She looked calm and collected, pretty as a picture considering it was the middle of the night and she'd called the police over a suspicious figure.

"You and Hart got a thing?" Ty asked, harsher than he'd intended, and if he'd been thinking at all he wouldn't have asked. But the way Hart had touched her raked along his skin like nails on a chalkboard. He didn't like it.

She blinked, looked up at him as though he'd lost his mind. "A thing?"

Ty probably *had* lost his mind, but he wasn't going to let her see that. So he shrugged lazily. "You're the only one I've ever heard call him Thomas. I was starting to think his first name *was* Hart."

"Oh. Well."

"So, you have a thing." He didn't ask it. He stated it. Because of course they did. Delaneys loved their law and order.

Any embarrassment or discomfort she'd had on her face morphed into full-on bristle. "It's none of your business, is it?"

Ty shrugged, forcing the move to be negligent even though his shoulders felt like iron. "It is if he's got a vested interest in keeping you safe. Make it easier for me to trust him anyhow."

"You don't need to worry about me, Tyler."

He tried not to scowl, since she was clearly trying to irritate him, but his name was one of the few things that irritated him no matter how hard he tried to let it go. "If something I did brought you danger, I'll worry about you as much as I want."

She softened at that some. "Ty—"

He didn't want her softening. "You need to stay with your family until this is sorted. The cops might look into it, but they're useless. With the exception of maybe your boyfriend there. This is escalating, and you need to be protected."

"Because heaven forbid I protect myself?"

"Honey, you're Bambi in the woods full of wolves. Stay at that mansion of yours where your brothers can keep an eye on you."

"My *brothers*. Right. Because only men can protect."

"They've got some military experience. That isn't sexism. It's reality."

"The reality is Laurel's a police officer, and I know how to handle myself."

"Laurel's pregnant," Ty responded simply. "You really want her keeping your butt out of trouble?"

"My *butt* is in trouble because of *you*, somehow. You leave without a peep, disappear into thin air, leaving me…" She sucked in a breath and closed her eyes. "You know what? Ancient history doesn't matter. You got me into this mess, and I expect *you* to get me out. Not my brothers, not the police—you."

He looked down at her grimly, then forced himself to smile. "You sure you want that, babe?"

She scowled at him, shaking her hair back like a woman ready to kick some butt. "And why wouldn't I?"

Hart stepped back in, eyeing them both with something like consideration. "We'll take this back to the station, see what kind of analysis we can get. I'd caution you both to be careful, and call me or Deputy McCarthy if you think of anything that might help us figure out the identity of either the suspicious figure or the person writing the notes."

Ty nodded and Jen sent Hart a sweet smile.

"Of course."

"Do you want me to escort you back to your store, Jen?" Hart asked.

Jen sent Ty a killing look, then beamed at Hart. "Thank you, Thomas. I'd appreciate that." She strode over to him, and they walked out of Ty's apartment chatting in low tones.

Deputy McCarthy tipped his hat at Ty. "Call if you think of anything, and we'll be in touch."

Ty only grunted, paying more attention to Hart's and Jen's retreating backs than McCarthy's words.

If she had Hart wrapped around her finger, she'd be fine. Safe. Watched after by more than just her cop sister who was busy growing a human being inside her. He should stop worrying. Jen was a Delaney and would be protected at all costs, regardless of what Ty did.

But no matter how hard he tried to convince himself of that, the worry didn't go away.

He liked watching the police lights flash red and blue. He liked knowing he'd caused a few scenes, and there was a hot lick of thrill at the idea everyone was thinking about him, trying to figure out who he was and what he wanted.

He slunk through the shadows, evading the stupid, useless cops with ease. Watching, always watching.

He'd had a moment of rage when Jen had hurried toward Ty's place with the cop. She'd looked worried.

The cop had touched her.

Now they were walking back out of Ty's. They smiled at each other. The other cop exited shortly thereafter, but the first cop stayed by Jen's side as they walked back to her store.

He followed, melting into the shadows, watching. Jen touched the cop's arm, and he could all but read her lips.

Thank you.

No. This wouldn't do. Jen was his now. His quarry and his to do with whatever he wanted. Part revenge, yes. Hurt Ty. His first objective was always to hurt Ty.

But Jen was pretty and sweet. She had a nice smile. He didn't want her just to hurt Ty anymore, he wanted her. She would be his prize when he tipped the scales back. When he had revenge, he'd have Jen, too.

This cop wouldn't do. Not at all.

Chapter 5

Jen was exhausted when her alarm went off the next morning. Exhausted and then irritated when she knew, without even getting up, that someone was in her apartment.

She might have been scared if she didn't know her family so well, or if she didn't smell what she assumed was Laurel's "famous" omelet—i.e., the only thing she ever bothered to cook.

Jen grabbed her fluffy pink robe that so often brought her comfort and slipped it on as she got out of bed. Summer was beginning to fade, and mornings were colder every day.

Jen moved from her bedroom to the small cramped space of living room and kitchen. "This better be a bad dream," she said, glaring at her sister.

Laurel raised an eyebrow at her as she flipped the omelet in the skillet. "You're telling me."

"Thomas shouldn't have called you." She'd known he would, but he *shouldn't* have. It was at least a small part of the reason the few dates she'd been on with him hadn't worked out. He all but idolized her sister as a police officer, and whether it was petty or not, Jen had never been completely comfortable with it.

"Hart knew better than to keep it from me. I'd have heard about it when I got into the station later, if not before." Laurel turned her attention back to the eggs, and her tone was purposefully mild. "I thought it didn't work out between you two."

Laurel was only ten months older than her, and they'd grown up not just as sisters, but also as friends. Still, ever since high school there'd been this Ty-sized distance between them. Because Jen hadn't told *anyone* about Ty, even her sister. Jen had always known Laurel felt it, and yet she'd never been able to cross that distance. She'd been too embarrassed.

Jen moved into the kitchen, hating the way all this ancient history swirled around her no matter what she did. "It didn't work out with Thomas."

"Then why do you still call him Thomas?"

"Because I wanted it to." Jen sank into her kitchen chair, giving up on sending her sister home. She raked her hands through her hair. "Can't you tell your husband to send his cousin back to wherever he came from and stop ruining my life?"

"So, it didn't work out with Hart because of Ty?"

"No, that isn't what I'm saying." Frowning at Laurel's back, Jen worked through that. "What would Ty have to do with me dating Thomas?"

Laurel shrugged. "I always suspected… Well, something." Laurel moved the omelet onto a plate before turning to face Jen and sliding it in front of her. "Why don't you tell me the truth?"

Jen should. Ty was old news, and it didn't matter now. He'd left. She'd gotten over it. Why not tell her sister? What she'd done in her teens shouldn't be embarrassing in her late twenties. "It's ancient history." History she hated to rehash so much she just couldn't bring herself to.

"Is it?"

"Yes." Jen pushed the plate back at Laurel. "Eat some of this, preggo."

Laurel grimaced and placed a hand to her stomach. "No. Eggs are an emphatic no right now."

Touched Laurel had made them for her even though she was feeling off about them, Jen gave in. All these twisting emotions were silly. "Ty and I had a secret thing back in high school. But that was forever ago." She wanted to say it had hardly mattered, but she knew she'd never make that lie sound like the truth.

"It seems like there's still—"

"No." Maybe things were still complicated, and maybe the *real* reason things hadn't worked out with Thomas was that because no matter how good-looking or funny or kind he was, he'd never made her feel the way Ty had—still did. But that didn't mean...

She didn't know what anything meant anymore.

"Do they know who wrote Ty those letters?" Because she could tell herself she didn't care, and that it was his problem, but the fact Ty Carson had called the police last night made her worry for him. It was so out of character he must be beyond concerned.

"No, and that's why I'm here. Jen, the last letter is in

blood, and every letter points at someone who doesn't want to hurt Ty, but hurt the people he loves."

Though a cold chill had spread through her at the idea of a note written in blood, Jen attempted to keep her demeanor calm and unmoved. "He doesn't love me."

"Are you so sure about that?"

"Positive. He left. He made sure it was a clean break, and we're both different people now. Whatever feelings are between us are those weird old ones born out of nostalgia, not love. Of that I'm sure." She wanted to be sure.

"Okay, so maybe he doesn't still love you. But maybe whoever is threatening Ty thinks he does. From what Hart told me, Ty thinks it's someone from his army days, which points to someone who knew him when he still had a closer connection to you. It doesn't have to make sense to us, if we're dealing with someone who's deranged. And this stranger sniffing around your store is too much of a coincidence. You need to be careful until the police clear everything up."

Jen frowned. "Ty told me to stay at the ranch. I don't want to."

"As much as I'd usually support a contrary refusal to do anything a Carson ordered—"

Jen jumped to her feet and began to pace. "I'm not being contrary. I'm trying to be *sane*. If this man is really after Ty, and for some reason I'm his target, couldn't someone just tell him I don't mean anything to Ty? Wouldn't it be obvious?"

"So he can turn his attention to someone else? Grady? Vanessa? Noah and Addie and Seth?"

Jen closed her eyes against the wave of fear. "Laurel."

"I know it isn't fair, but the fact of the matter is, what we have to do is find out who this individual is and let the law handle them. Not try to shift his focus, much as I'd love it not to be on you."

Overwhelmed and feeling just a pinch sorry for herself, Jen sank back into the chair. "Why do bad things keep happening here?"

Laurel placed her hand over her slightly rounding stomach. "Maybe bad things need to happen to exorcise old feud demons. Maybe it's just bad luck of the draw, but at the end of every one of these 'bad things,' something really good has come out of it."

"I hope that's pregnancy brain talking because when I think of how badly you all have been hurt over the course of the past year—how many hospital visits I've made, how scared I've been—it isn't worth it."

Laurel reached over and squeezed her arm, still rubbing her stomach with her other hand. "It's been worth it to me. And we're all still here. You will be, too, but I want you to be careful, Jen. I want you to take some precautions. Whoever is behind this has left a lot of clues, has been careless, really. I'm hopeful it's all nipped in the bud before anything bad happens, but that means you watching your step and letting some people protect you until this person is caught."

Jen had worked very hard to never feel inferior to her siblings. They'd all always known exactly what they wanted to be, and had sacrificed to become it. Cam and his exemplary military service, and Laurel and her dedication to the law. Dylan and what they'd all thought was his education, but had turned out to be a secret military service of his own.

Jen had only ever wanted to run the store, and then once upon a time she'd wanted to risk everything for Ty Carson.

But it had never come to fruition and her life had been simple and exactly how she liked it. For ten years she'd had exactly what she'd wanted.

Except Ty.

"Why can't I protect myself every now and then?" Jen asked, not daring to meet her sister's gaze. "Why am I always the one who needs to be sheltered?"

"Because the people who love you are all licensed and trained to carry weapons. Because if there's anything the past year should teach us it's that working together and protecting each other is far better than trying to do it all alone. We're not asking you to hide in a corner while we fight your battles for you, Jen. We're asking you to let your family work *with* you to keep you safe during a dangerous time."

"I hate staying at the ranch."

"Join the club. Look, you can come stay with Grady and me, but…"

Jen wrinkled her nose. "He's asking Ty to come stay with you, isn't he?"

Laurel shrugged. "If it's all old news…"

"I'll stay at the ranch, but I'm still running my store. All my normal hours."

"Of course you are. We'll just want someone here with you while you do."

"Laurel."

Laurel pushed to her feet. "We'll come up with a schedule. You don't need to worry about that. Just be vigilant and don't go anywhere alone. That's all."

"That's all," Jen grumbled. "I enjoy being alone, Laurel."

"Well, for a little while you'll enjoy being safe instead." Laurel pulled Jen into a rare hug since she was not the touchy-feely type. "I have to get ready for work. Cam and Hilly are on Jen duty today. They'll just hang around your store being adorably in love. Give them a hard time about when they're going to get married. You'll have fun."

Jen grunted. "So what you meant by 'we'll figure out a schedule' is you already have."

Laurel ignored that statement and pointed to the eggs. "Eat that." She walked to the front door, all policewoman certainty.

"I wish I could be more like you," Jen muttered, not meaning for Laurel to catch it.

But she clearly did. She stopped in the doorway and turned to face Jen, her forehead lined with concern. "No you don't," she said forcefully. "You're exactly who you should be." Then she flashed a grin. "Besides, if you were more like me, you'd be married to a Carson, and no one wants that."

She left on a laugh, and Jen joined in, feeling somehow a little better for it.

"Over my dead body."

Grady rolled his eyes as he wiped down the scarred bar of Rightful Claim. "You're putting my bar in danger, cousin."

Ty didn't bother to roll his eyes right back. It was such bull he couldn't even pretend to get worked up about it. "I can handle myself, Grady. Lest you forget, I was an army ranger." Methodically, he kept pulling chairs off the tables and placing them on the floor.

"Lest you forget, two Carsons against a nut job are better than one."

"You've got a pregnant wife. Noah's got a wife and a

kid at the ranch. I don't buy you're worried about your bar more than you're worried about that. Living here is the best place for me. Besides, it's all nothing."

Grady shook his head, clearly taking his irritation out on the bar. "My wife's a cop and she—"

"Yeah, funny, that."

Grady didn't rise to that bait. "Laurel's worried, which means I'm worried. You shouldn't be sleeping in that apartment alone."

Ty flashed a grin. "I'll see what I can do."

"Yeah, I'll believe that once you're able to look away from Jen Delaney long enough to hook up with someone."

"Jen Delaney." Ty made a dismissive noise, though his shoulders tensed against his will. "Sure."

Grady clapped him on the back. "Lie to yourself all you want, Ty, but you aren't fooling anyone. Probably including Jen. You're coming home with me tonight, and that's that."

"You're not my type."

Grady just flashed him a grin. "Your type's just changed, pal. Jen's going to stay at the Delaney Ranch, against her will, and you're going to be under Carson and cop surveillance against yours. Laurel thinks they'll catch this guy in a few days. You can survive a few days in the presence of marital bliss."

Ty knew Grady's humorous tone wasn't to be believed. His moves were jerky, and though he wore that easy grin, there was an edge to his gaze Ty knew better than to challenge.

At least until he found the *right* challenge.

Because he wasn't about to put Grady and Laurel in danger. Or Noah and Addie and Seth for that matter. It was good Jen would be staying out at the Delaney Ranch. Cam lived in the cabin on the property, and Dylan was currently residing in the house. Much as Ty didn't trust a Delaney as far as he could throw one, both men had been in the military and would protect their own.

Ty couldn't help thinking he'd do a better job of it, and all without bringing any innocent bystanders in. Not that Delaneys were ever really innocent, were they?

Jen is.

Hell. He worked with Grady in silence the rest of their opening routine. He manned the bar while Grady waited tables. The afternoon crowd was sparse, but it slowly got busier and busier as evening inched closer. Even a Monday night could have business booming, especially on a pretty day like today.

Autumn was threatening, and in Wyoming people knew to enjoy the last dregs of summer while they could.

Ty scanned the crowd, that old familiar *bad gut* feeling whispering over his skin. He recognized most of the patrons, but because of the historical atmosphere of the bar they often got strangers in from surrounding towns. It was unusual for him to know *everyone*.

But every stranger's face made him wonder, and every stranger's casual smile made him fear. He thought of all the real danger he'd faced as an army ranger and had never been jittery. Concerned on occasion, but never *nervous*. Determination and right and the mission before him had always given him a center of calm, of certainty.

But Jen had never been unwittingly tied to all those

missions, and as much as he detested himself for being that weak, he knew it was the reason. Fear for *her*.

He had a terrible feeling whoever was doing this knew that, too.

His gaze landed on a stranger in a dark corner. All he could make out was a cowboy hat, pulled low.

Like the man on Jen's tape.

Ty forced himself to keep his gaze moving, keep his moves casual. He took the order of a usual customer, pulled the lever on the beer and glanced again at the man in the corner.

A flash of eye contact, and while he still felt no recognition to this man, he saw the *hate* in that gaze, and more damning, the flash of white-blond hair as Jen had described.

Fighting to keep his cool, and think clearly, he turned to give the beer to the person at the bar. When he quickly turned back to the stranger in the corner—he was gone, and the saloon doors were swinging.

Ty didn't think. Everything around him blanked except getting to that man. If he caught him, this would all be over.

He jumped the bar and ran, ignoring shouts of outrage over spilled beers and Grady's own concerned calling after him. Outside, Ty caught the flash of the man disappearing across the street.

Jen. Her store.

Ty ran as fast as he could, ignoring all else except catching the man who *had* to be responsible for all this. The stranger disappeared behind the buildings on Main, but since Ty had a feeling he knew where the man was running to, he kept his track on the boardwalk.

Once he got to the alley before Delaney General, he

took a sharp turn and all but leaped into the back parking lot. Ty came to a stop, breathing hard, scanning the area around him, but there was nothing.

Nothing. With quick, efficient moves, Ty checked the back door. Locked and he hadn't heard a sound, so it was unlikely the man had beat him here and broken in.

He scanned the dark around him, but there was nothing, not even that gut feeling that warned him someone must be watching. He'd had to have run somewhere else. Ty could search but there were too many options. He could have even stashed a vehicle behind another business on Main and taken the back road out of town.

Ty cursed himself and he cursed the whole situation, but he also came to a conclusion.

He was going to have to do something even more drastic than getting the cops involved. Something no one would approve of, and something that could get him in quite a bit of trouble.

But Ty knew it was the only answer.

Jen had gotten surveillance. Bitterness ate through him like acid at the memory. How dare she protect herself against him and not Ty. She'd let that piece of trash into the back room of her store. Let him talk to her. She hadn't called the cops on Ty.

Red clouded his vision, and he had to be careful or the blood pounding in his ears would get too loud. Too insistent.

He concentrated on the steering wheel underneath his palms as he drove in a deliberate circle around Bent. He thought about Ty chasing after him and losing.

That made him smile. Yes, yes indeed. Ty wasn't

nearly as fast as him, was he? Ty wasn't nearly as smart and strong and brave as he thought, was he?

The comfort at that thought lasted only a moment as he thought about earlier in the day. Jen and her surveillance. Anger came back, swift and addicting. He liked the way rage licked through his system, revved his mind.

Dr. Michaels said it was bad, but he didn't think so. He liked it too much for it to be bad. Didn't he deserve some of what he liked after everything he'd been through?

The man who'd been in Jen's store all day was clearly military, and he carried. He also touched Jen with far too much familiarity. The man guarding her would have to go on the list under the cop.

Yes, that would be good. Ty, the cop, the man in the store. Targets were good. The rage was good, but it had to have targets. Purpose. That's what Dr. Michaels didn't understand.

Maybe she'd go on the list, too. But not yet. Not now. First, he'd deal with the problems in Bent, Wyoming.

He drove down the back road behind the businesses on Main. He looked at the brick of Delaney General, the heavy steel door that would be tough to break into.

He'd have to make his move soon. He preferred to wait. Draw out the anticipation. Level out some of his rage lest he make a mistake.

But they weren't letting him, were they? And they'd be the ones who paid for his mistakes…so why not make a few?

Chapter 6

Jen had never felt particularly at home at the Delaney Ranch, though it was where she'd grown up. Unlike her brothers, she'd never been interested in the ranch work. She'd found the vast landscape unnerving rather than calming.

When she turned eighteen and moved into the apartment above the store, she'd been happier. She felt more herself there, like the building had simply been waiting for her. She liked to think it was the connection to her ancestors who'd run this store rather than raise cattle or protect the town with badge and honor. Like Laurel had always wanted to be a cop, Jen had always wanted her store.

So, waking up on the Delaney Ranch grated. But she did what she always did when she had to be here and didn't want to be—she made herself useful. It was the one thing that softened her feelings toward the place. Making meals or cleaning up. Laurel used to make fun of her "überdomesticity" but Jen found comfort in the tangible things she could do.

Surprisingly, Vanessa was the first person to enter the kitchen. Well, *stumble* was a better term for it. She was bleary-eyed, with messy hair, and she spoke only one word. "Coffee."

"Decaf?" Jen asked sweetly.

"Don't make me hurt you this early in the morning. I am allowed one cup of coffee per day and I will darn well take it."

Jen hid a smile and pulled down a mug. Though she knew Vanessa would just as soon do everything for herself, Jen didn't have any issue waiting on people. Especially pregnant people. "Sit," she ordered, pouring the coffee herself.

Vanessa lowered herself into a chair at the table and grasped the mug carefully when Jen set it in front of her. "Thanks. I don't suppose you're taking breakfast orders?"

"Only for pregnant women. The men around here get cold cereal as far as I'm concerned."

"Turns out I like you, Jen Delaney. I'm starving and the sound of everything makes my stomach turn."

Jen chatted with Vanessa over some possibilities until they came to something Vanessa thought she could stomach. Jen poured coffee for Dylan and then Dad when they arrived, but they both hurried out over some early meeting at the bank.

Dylan, of course, gave Jen a stern warning not to head to the store until Cam came over to escort her. She rolled her eyes at him, but then he kissed Vanessa's cheek and rested his hand on her belly and everything in Jen softened.

And sharp Vanessa Carson-Delaney softened, too.

"He'll be such a good dad," Jen said, more to herself than Vanessa.

"I'm counting on it. I don't have much in the way of good role models on the whole parenting thing." She shrugged philosophically. "Though I guess Dylan doesn't either."

Jen slid into the seat across from Vanessa with her own breakfast. "Doesn't it bother you, living here?"

"It's nice digs," Vanessa replied before taking a tentative bite of the oatmeal Jen had put together. "Apparently pregnancy has put your dad on his best behavior around me. Not much to complain about."

"Well, I'm glad, then."

"Gee, I think you mean that. Carsons and Delaneys might start holding hands and singing 'Kumbaya' before you know it."

Jen laughed. Even though it was ridiculous, the idea they were finding some common ground between their two families warmed her.

As long as she didn't think about Ty.

They ate breakfast companionably before Vanessa made her excuses to go take a shower and get ready for work. "Don't worry," Vanessa offered on her way out of the kitchen. "I won't leave till Cam gets here."

Jen huffed out a breath. She hated this babysitting. The stranger going after Ty, or her because of Ty, was hardly going to bust into the house and take her away. If he really was the stranger in her store, he'd already had ample opportunity to do that.

She cleaned up breakfast, glancing at her phone when

it trilled. She frowned at the fact the text was from Ty of all people. Her frown turned into a scowl when she saw what he'd texted.

High Noon

It was their old code. Back in the days before they'd had cell phones, he'd simply leave a little note somewhere she'd see it, and that's all it would say for her to know to sneak out the back of the house and meet him at *their* tree.

She shoved the phone back on the counter. She was *not* responding to that. Not at all.

She focused on cleaning, and if occasionally she happened to crane her head toward the window, she stopped herself before she took a look toward the old gnarled tree in the backyard.

If Ty had something to say to her, he could come to the front door.

Her phone trilled again.

Come on, Jen. I need to talk to you.

Baloney. She wiped her hands off on a dish towel, then typed a response. Then talk.

I chased him last night.

She blinked down at those words, then swore. Oh, that man. Was he a moron? Did he have any sense of keeping *himself* safe? Chased him! And what him? Were they sure the note leaver and the man at her store were even the same person?

She shoved her phone into her pocket, then stalked

to the front door. She yanked on boots, muttering the whole way. She marched out the front and around the back, a far cry from the teenager who would have snuck around, doing anything to avoid being seen by her family or the ranch hands.

She didn't care who saw her now, because she was about to give Ty Carson a piece of her mind.

She stalked back to that old tree, determined to hold on to her anger and frustration, but the sight of him turned it to dust. His motorcycle was parked exactly where he always used to park it. Older and more lethal, he still looked windswept and she felt her heart do that long slow roll it had always done because Ty Carson was waiting for her.

Her.

She had to swallow at the lump that formed in her throat, embarrassed enough by the emotion to be irritated all over again. "We aren't in high school," she spat, terrified he'd read the rustiness in her voice as old longing.

If he did, he didn't comment on it. "No, we aren't, but I thought it'd get your attention."

She lifted her chin, wanting to feel lofty and above him. "It didn't."

"But me chasing after the guy did." He patted the motorcycle parked in the grass. "Hop on now. I need to talk to you about what happened. Privately."

"Is this yard not private enough?"

He tossed the helmet at her. She caught it out of reflex.

"Nope." He grinned. "Come on, Jen. You know you want to."

She did, God help her. She'd loved riding on the back

of Ty's motorcycle in the middle of the night back in high school. It had been the most thrilling thing she'd ever done, aside from share herself with him. Ten years later and her life was staid. Boring. *Just the way you like it. You love your life.*

"Just up to the Carson cabin right quick, then I'll bring you back."

The fact he was so calm confused her. The fact she was tempted upset her. "They'll wonder where I am. They're worried enough."

"So tell them," he said, nodding toward the phone in her pocket. "This isn't cloak-and-dagger."

"Then why do we have to go somewhere else?"

Ty gave her a bland look. "You should really try to be more difficult, Jen. This back-and-forth is so much fun."

"I'm not getting on your motorcycle."

"All right. We can take your car."

She wanted to punch him, but it'd do about as much good as arguing with him. His body was as thick as his skull. "Fine. Just fine." She pulled her phone out and texted Cam and Vanessa that she was with Ty, and she'd let them know the minute she was back. Then she jerked the helmet onto her head and glared at him as she fastened it. "Let's get this over with."

She caught the boyish grin on his face, hated her body's shivering, *lustful* reaction to it. He swung his leg over the bike, waited for her to take her spot.

Your rightful spot.

She was making a mistake. She *knew* she was making a mistake, and yet she clambered onto the motorcycle just like she used to. She wrapped her arms around his waist just like she used to, and he walked the bike a ways down the hill until they were far enough away from the house for the roar of the engine not to reach anyone.

And *oh* the motorcycle roared and the wind whipped through her hair. She wanted to press her cheek to the leather at his back. She wanted to cry. It still felt like flying. It still felt *wonderful.* But she was old enough to understand it was having her arms around Ty, not the machine between her legs.

It was like traveling back in time, visiting with someone who'd died, knowing you'd have to go back to the living all too soon. She was too desperate for that feeling to let it go, even knowing pain awaited her on the other side.

He drove too fast, took turns too sharply, and through it all she held on to him, biting her lip to keep from laughing into the wind.

When he reached the Carson cabin and cut the engine, it took her a moment to pull herself together and release him, then swing herself off the motorcycle. Took her far too many moments to wipe the grin off her face.

She sighed at the tiny clearing and the ramshackle cabin no one lived in but the Carson family used off and on. So many firsts in that cabin, though it had clearly had some repairs over the years. Uneasily, she remembered that last year Noah and Addie had fought off mobsters from Addie's past at this very place.

"Isn't it awful to be back here?"

Ty shrugged. "I don't care to remember Noah being shot, but he's all right now. Lots of shady crap happened here over the years. Such is life as a Carson. Besides, Addie's fixed it all up and they come up here. I figure they can take it, so can I."

She pulled off her helmet and hung it on the handle of the parked bike. "So, what did you want to talk about?"

His gaze was on the cabin, his expression…haunted. Was it what had happened to Noah here or was it that ride that felt like going back in time?

She didn't want to know.

"Let's go inside."

"Ty—"

He walked up to the door, pulling a key out of his pocket and ignoring all her protests.

She could ignore his demands. She could be petulant and wait outside and refuse to do any number of things.

But with a sigh, she followed him inside.

Step one had been easy enough. Ty was a little surprised. Oh, he figured he still knew Jen well enough to press the right buttons, but it had all been so easy.

Now came the hard part. He had to get her phone off her. Once he had that, it'd be easy enough to keep her here. Safe and sound and under his supervision. There was the potential that someone would figure out where he'd taken her, but he had to hope they realized what he was doing was for Jen's safety.

And if they had to move elsewhere, well, he'd figure that out, too.

She'd probably consider it "kidnapping." He preferred to think of it as "safekeeping." She'd thank him eventually. Well, probably not ever to his face, but philosophically she might realize he did what was right.

Maybe.

Regardless, he *was* right. So, he had to go about getting her phone off her. "Why don't you have a seat."

Eyebrows furrowed, she looked around the room. Addie's redecorating had made it look family friendly and inviting instead of what it used to be—a place to hide from the law or trouble.

Now it looked like a cozy cottage instead of an out-law hideout. Ty couldn't say he liked the change, but with Noah and Grady all domesticated now, who was he to complain? They'd bring their kids up here and teach them to hunt, or have sleepovers with their cousins or second cousins. Make a nice little Carson-Delaney future on old Carson land. On old Delaney land.

Ty glanced at Jen, who'd taken a seat on the sky blue couch Addie had gotten to brighten up the living room. But Jen was the real thing that brightened the room. Her long, wispy brown hair and her pixie face, tawny brown eyes with flecks of green. She had a dainty, fairy-like quality to her and he felt like an oaf.

She looked so right there it hurt, like someone had shoved a knife right in his heart. He was halfway surprised to look down and see nothing there except his jacket.

Shoving his hands in his pockets, he ordered himself to focus. Get her phone away from her, and then keep her safe until the cops caught this lunatic. It'd be a few days, tops, he was almost sure of it.

If it was more, well, they'd reevaluate then.

He crossed to the couch, sat next to her. She raised an eyebrow at him, but he needed the proximity to get to her phone. So, he only smiled blandly in response.

Clearly irritated with him, Jen crossed her arms over her chest. "So, you have something to tell me that just had to be done in private?"

"Yes. The stranger that was in your store, he was at Rightful Claim last night."

Immediate concern softened her features, and he was

momentarily distracted by all those things that had made him, of all people, fall for a Delaney in the first place.

Jen had been the softest, sweetest place he'd ever had the pleasure of landing. Growing up with an abusive father, she'd been like a balm. It hadn't mattered that she was a Delaney because she was kind. No matter how Grady or Noah had believed in the feud at the time—and wasn't that a laugh now?—Ty hadn't cared, because someone had loved him with a gentleness he'd never, ever had in his life.

Jen blinked, looked away as a soft blush stained her cheeks. Like she could read his thoughts, or had a few memories of her own.

"Jen—" But whatever ridiculous soft words had bubbled up inside him, desperate to be free, were cut off by the way she looked at him.

Coolly. Detached, she returned his gaze. "You chased him. That's what your text said."

Business. All business. Good thing, too. Best decision he'd ever made had been to get the hell out of Jen Delaney's life. No use playing back over what might have been, or even what still lurked between them. "Yeah. I thought he was heading for your store, but I lost him."

"I stayed out at the ranch last night, so it wouldn't have mattered."

"It matters." In a casual move, he rested his hand on the cushion between them—close enough his finger could gently nudge the phone farther out of her pocket.

She frowned down at his hand, but he kept it there as her gaze returned. He didn't say anything because he was intent on inching his finger close enough to touch the phone that just barely peeked out of the pocket of her jeans.

"Why did you bring me here, Ty? What's going on?"

He used his index finger to nudge the corner of her phone out of her pocket. If he could move it enough, get it at the right angle, it'd fall out once she stood up. Then he'd just have to hope she didn't feel it or notice it for how long it would take him to secret it away.

So, he nudged and spoke. "The cops are on this whole thing, but I'm worried. I don't like that this guy was hanging around your place and Rightful Claim. It feels off."

"Laurel said he's sloppy and they'll get him in no time." But no matter how brave she tried to sound, she chewed on her bottom lip. She shifted slightly, as if she'd felt the move of her phone.

Ty grabbed her hand before she could pat her pocket down. He'd done it out of desperation, but the sizzle of connection shocked him into forgetting all about the phone.

How did her hand fit with his, like a key to a lock? Even now that simple touch was all it took to make him forget his real purpose and remember her. The feel of her. The rightness of her. And how he'd been the one to mishandle it all, ruin it all.

She blinked once, as if coming out of the same dream, and then jerked her hand away. "What is this?" she demanded. She popped to her feet and he was relieved the phone fell right out, and she didn't even notice. She paced as he scooted over and gently nudged the phone deep into the cushions.

Finally she whirled, as if she'd come to some grand determination. "It's time to take me home."

He smiled lazily, knowing it would make her narrow her eyes and curl her hands into fists. "About that."

"Tyler," she warned through clenched teeth.

It amazed him that he couldn't control his negative reaction to his full name when he'd spent a lifetime controlling any and all negative reactions he didn't want to broadcast. But he nearly flinched every time she leveled him with that haughty *Tyler*.

"We're not going anywhere. Not for a while."

She made a sound of outrage, then did exactly what he'd hoped. She stormed for the door.

He took the moment to fish her phone out of the couch and click off the sound before sliding it into the drawer of the coffee table. Even as she wrenched the front door open and stomped outside, he closed and locked the drawer before sauntering after her.

She stalked right over to his motorcycle and then kicked it over. She gave him a defiant look, but he refused to rise to the bait. Barely. No one, *no one* hurt his bike. But he'd give her a pass since he was…well, not kidnapping her.

Exactly.

"Very mature, Jen."

She flipped him off, which did give him enough of a jolt to laugh. He'd forgotten how much he enjoyed her rare flashes of temper.

"I'm calling Laurel. Do you really think—" She stopped as her hands patted every pocket of her jeans. Once, twice, before shoving her hands into each pocket.

She looked up at him with shock in her gaze. It quickly turned to murder as she let out a primal scream and lunged at him.

Chapter 7

Jen couldn't ever remember being so angry. She wanted to take a chunk out of Ty. She wanted to bloody his nose or knee him in the crotch, and if she'd been able to see anything more than the red haze of anger, she might have been strategic enough to do any of those things. Maybe.

But she was too mad, stupid with it, and she launched herself at him, only to be caught and corralled. She landed precisely one punch to his rock-hard chest before he had his arms wrapped around her tight enough she couldn't wriggle her arms free.

She kicked, but he only lifted her off the ground, angling her so her kicks did nothing.

"I hate you," she spat, right in his face.

He only grinned. "Now, now, darling, your hellcat is showing."

She wriggled on an outraged growl, but he only clamped his arms around her tighter so she could barely move at all as he marched her back inside. So she was pressed against the hard wall of muscle that was the love of her life.

He'd brought her up here, stolen her phone and was thwarting all her attempts to unleash her anger.

"This is ridiculous. Insane. You've lost your mind. Do you really think my family won't come up here and—"

"No, I don't think they will," he replied, equitably, as he all too easily moved her to the living room.

She kept wriggling, but it was no use. He was very, *very* strong, and she refused to acknowledge the hot lick of heat that centered itself in her core.

He dumped her on the couch and when she popped to her feet, he nudged her back down, looming over her.

"Stay put."

"Or what?" she demanded, outrage at his behavior and her body's response boiling together into nothing but pure fury. "Going to stalk me? Leave me some threatening letters in blood? You're no better than—"

He all but shoved his face into hers, cutting off not just her words but also her breath. His eyes shone with that fierce battle light that had thrilled her once upon a time, and maybe it still did, though she didn't much feel like being honest with herself right now. She'd rather pretend the shaky feeling in her limbs was fear, not that old desire to soothe the outlaw in him. To love him until he softened.

"Don't compare me to the man doing this, Jen. Not now. Not ever. You may not like my methods, but I'm doing what I have to do to keep *you* safe."

Her heart jittered, and that pulsing heat she remembered so well spread through her belly like a sip of straight whiskey. But she forced herself to be calm, to be disdainful. "I'm only in danger because of you."

He pushed away from the couch then, but not before she caught the flash of hurt in his eyes. Why did it still hurt *her* to cause him pain? Why couldn't she be completely and utterly unaffected by him, his emotions, his muscles or that past they'd shared?

"Yeah, that's true, which is why it's my duty to protect you."

"I have a family full of dutiful protectors. I don't need you."

His back was to her, so she couldn't read how that statement might have affected him. He was silent for the longest time.

She should speak. Demand her phone back and demand to be taken home. Threaten and yell until she got her way.

But she knew how useless that was. A Carson had an idea in his head and she'd never be able to get through that thick skull. She'd have to be sneakier than that. More devious.

Sneaky and devious weren't exactly natural for her like they were for Ty, but hadn't she loved him and watched him for years? Didn't she know how to retreat, circumnavigate and end up with what she wanted?

And if she didn't know how to do that, she'd figure it out. He wasn't going to lock her up here in the Carson cabin like some sort of helpless princess.

Which meant she had to be calm and reasonable in response to his...his...idiocy.

"Ty," she began, her voice like that of a teacher instructing a student. "Be reasonable. You can't take my phone away from me, lock the doors and expect me to stay put. It isn't sensible, and I'm surprised at you. It isn't like you to act without thinking."

He turned to face her, appearing detached and vaguely, disdainfully amused. A trick of his she'd always envied.

"I've thought it through, darling. I know exactly what I'm doing. I was also quite aware you wouldn't like it."

Bristling, Jen curled her fingers into fists, trying to center her frustration there instead of at him. "Laurel won't—"

"Laurel will. Because you'll be safe and out of harm's way, won't you?"

"Like Addie and Noah were?" she returned, knowing it would hit him where it hurt. No matter that she hated to hurt him, she was very aware she needed to.

"This guy isn't the mob," Ty replied, referring to the men who had hurt Noah and Addie here, but Ty had that blank look on his face that belied the emotion hidden underneath.

"You don't know who he is," Jen returned, gentling her tone without realizing it.

He was so *still*. The stillness that had once prompted her to soothe, to love. Because Ty's stillness wasn't the actual reaction. His stillness hid all the myriad reactions inside him. Ever since he'd been a boy she knew he'd developed that skill, a response to an abusive father, and she'd always seen his stillness for that little boy's hurt. She'd always ached over it.

God, she wished she no longer did, but it was there. Deep and painful. It was against every instinct she had to clamp her mouth shut and keep the soothing words inside.

"I can't figure out who he is when you're in danger. I can't *think* when I'm worried about you."

"I'm not your concern."

He scoffed audibly. "Oh, please."

"I haven't been for ten years. You didn't concern yourself with me when you disappeared without a good-bye. You didn't concern yourself with me for ten full years after you just…" It was bubbling up inside her, all the betrayal and the hurt she'd been hiding from him.

"You want to have that out now?" he asked, so cool and stoic it was like being stabbed.

Jen closed her eyes and pressed fingers to her temple. She had to find some semblance of control when it came to him. "No, I don't. It's ancient history."

"Maybe, but ancient history can fester and rot."

She opened her eyes, worked up her steeliest, most determined look. "Mine hasn't."

"Yeah. You and *Thomas* make a real cute couple."

Jen angled her chin. If he thought that, well, she'd use it. She'd use it to protect her heart. "We're very happy."

But his mouth quirked. "You haven't slept together."

Outraged, she stood. "You don't know that."

"Oh, I know it." He took a step toward her, but she would not back down.

She refused to be affected by the large man looming over her. He was not some romantic hero sweeping her off her feet. He was a thick-skulled caveman thinking he knew better than her and casting aspersions on her made-up relationship with a perfectly decent man.

However, she knew Ty well enough to know that

arrogant grin meant he wanted a fight. She wouldn't give him one.

"I guess we'll have to agree to disagree," she said coolly. "Now, I'd appreciate my phone back. You can rest assured if my family agrees, I'll stay put."

"Because you're so good at doing what your family says?"

She smiled, trying to match his arrogance, though she was afraid it only read brittle. "I only made one very regrettable mistake in that regard. I learned never to make it again." She'd been hurt too deeply by the way he'd left her to ever, ever go back to a place where she'd give her whole heart so completely to someone.

She'd been stupid with youth and innocence, but she was older and wiser and she'd *learned*.

"Touché," he returned wryly.

"Now, perhaps we can have an adult conversation."

"I wouldn't count on it, darling."

She wouldn't let him get to her. He wanted to irritate her. He enjoyed it. So, she wouldn't give him the satisfaction. "Just what exactly is your plan? Surely you're aware you'll have to contact my family."

"Surely."

"As much sway as you have over Grady, it's highly unlikely he'll side with you over Laurel."

"Highly unlikely indeed," he returned, clearly mocking her.

Do not snap. Do not snap at this hardheaded moron. "So. What's the plan?"

"The plan is I tell your family we decided to get out of Dodge for a while, so to speak."

"They won't believe that."

He raised an eyebrow. "You came with me willingly, if you recall. What's not to believe?"

"That I didn't discuss it with them first."

Ty grinned at that. "Yeah, they'll have a real hard time believing we went off and did something without getting approval."

She waved a hand. "It's not like they know about us."

Ty blinked at that, some piece of that sentence piercing his impenetrable shell enough to show surprise. "What do you mean?"

"I mean no one knows what happened between us back then. Well, Laurel and I discussed it briefly the other day, but mostly no Delaney knows that there was ever an us, or that I ever did something without approval. They'd be shocked." She forced herself to laugh. "Can you imagine my father's reaction if he knew I'd been seeing you?"

Ty was too still, and not that stillness that covered up an emotional reaction. No, this was something more like a stillness born of horror. It didn't make any sense, and it made her heart pound too hard in her chest.

"Ty…"

He blinked and turned away. "I should call Grady. He'll believe me. We'll hide out here a few days, and if they still haven't caught the guy, we'll reevaluate."

"Ty—"

"I think Hilly will be able to run the store for you well enough. If not, your father will come up with someone. Consider it a vacation. Relax. Enjoy yourself. Take a bath or whatever it is women do."

"Ty," she snapped, vibrating now with unknown emotions, like a premonition. There was too much happening here and his evasion wasn't nearly as tidy as he'd clearly wanted it to be. Dread weighted her limbs, but she had to understand this. Even when her heart shied away from knowing. "Who knew?"

"Knew what? That I'd bring you he—"

"Tyler." She didn't snap this time. It was little more than a whisper, because she had this horrible, horrible weight in her gut she couldn't unload. "Who knew about us before?"

"It's a small town, Jen. I'm sure any number of—"

She stepped forward. While thoughts of violence whirled in her head, she merely placed her hand over his heart with a gentleness she didn't understand. It was hardly the first time her mind and heart were at odds when it came to Ty. "Tell me the truth."

He didn't look at her. He kept his gaze on the wall and his jaw clamped tight. She thought he was refusing to answer her, but as her hand fell from his chest, his throat moved.

"Jen, you said it was ancient history." But his voice was too soft, too gentle. Two things Ty almost never was—now or then.

But she had to know. She had to... There was too much she didn't know or understand and she needed this whole thing to make sense. If it made sense maybe she could lock all these feelings back in the past where they belonged. "And you said ancient history could fester and rot."

He looked down at her then, and it was like looking at the boy she'd loved. Strong and defiant in everything, but in the depth of those blue eyes she could see his storms and his hurts and his desperation to make things *right*.

It was what she'd always loved about him. Then.

Now? Her brain knew a person didn't still love some-one after a ten-year absence, after the betrayal of leaving without a goodbye, and yet her heart...

"Your father knew."

It was a blow. It didn't matter and yet it felt like someone had plowed something into her stomach.

"He threatened you," Jen surmised, a light-headed queasiness replacing the pain. "That's why you left."

Ty laughed bitterly. "Sure, I was scared of the big bad Delaney. Get a grip, Jen. I left because I left."

She knew better, and it occurred to her now the reason she hadn't been able to get over Ty and her love for him was that she knew he hadn't abandoned her without a reason. He had a reason—one he didn't want her to know about.

It was ancient history, and she wanted to forget. But after he'd disappeared, she'd experienced grief as if he'd died, not just left.

Still, she didn't think he was lying, exactly. Ty had never been intimidated by her father. He'd never been scared of his reaction like she had been. She'd wanted to please her father, and she'd wanted to love Ty. She'd known both couldn't exist, so she'd kept them separate.

Or thought she had. Her father had known. Ty had left because her father had known and—Oh, *God*. "He threatened me," she realized, aloud. "You left because he threatened *me*."

"I would have joined the army no matter what." So still. So blank, and yet in his blankness she knew he felt a million things. In his blankness he confirmed her realization. He'd left only because of something Dad had done to threaten her life.

Ty hadn't left to save his own skin, or even simply

because he'd wanted to. He'd left to protect her in some way. She wanted it to ease or heal something inside her, but it didn't. "You could have said goodbye."

"I have to call Grady. I have to—"

"What are you afraid of, Ty? That the truth from a decade ago will change something? I'm not so sure it will. The why of what you did doesn't change what you did, but maybe the truth would give us both some peace."

"Fine. You want truth and peace and moving on?" Temper sizzled, but he kept his hands jammed into his pockets. "Yeah, he threatened you. Said he'd sell the store if I didn't get the hell out and away from you. So, I did. You got your store, and I got the army, and life went the hell on." He jerked his shoulders in a violent shrug. "I figured he would have told you all that at some point."

Her store. Dad had threatened to sell her store. Jen sank onto the couch behind her. No, her father had never told her that. He wouldn't have, for one simple reason. "He wouldn't have sold the store. It was a bluff."

Ty raised a pitying eyebrow. "Sure, darling."

She wouldn't fall apart in front of Ty. Not when he was being so dismissive. Not when it proved what she'd always felt but tried to talk herself out of.

He hadn't left out of malice, or even to save his own skin. He'd left the way he had out of love. It changed nothing in the here and now, but somehow it changed her. Something deep inside her.

She didn't understand the shift, the feeling, but she figured with enough time she would. She glanced up at Ty, who looked like a storm encased in skin.

Time. They needed more time. So, she'd stay until the threat against her—against *them*—was gone. Then…

Well, then she'd figure out the next step.

They'd disappeared. A morning skulking around town and he hadn't seen hide nor hair. They'd tried to escape him.

It was nearly impossible to swim out of the black, bubbling anger threatening to drown him. But he couldn't let it win, because then he wouldn't succeed in his mission. In his revenge.

Using the prepaid phone he'd picked up at a gas station in Fremont, he dialed the old familiar number, trying to focus on the help he would find.

When the perky secretary answered, he tightened his grip on the phone. Some old memory was whispering something to him, but he couldn't understand it with the fury swamping him.

"I need to speak with Dr. Michaels."

There was a pause on the other end, and he snarled. He narrowly resisted bashing the phone against his steering wheel.

"I'm so sorry," the secretary said soothingly. It did nothing to soothe. "I thought we'd contacted all of her patients. Dr. Michaels will be off for quite a bit. We have a temporary—"

"I need to speak with Dr. Michaels. Now." He closed his eyes against the pain in his skull. It smelled like blood, and for a moment he remembered the singing joy of knocking the life out of that uppity doctor.

Hadn't that only been a dream?

Yes, just a dream, sneaking into her house and waiting for her to get home. Just a dream, standing in her closet and waiting for her to open it to hang up her coat.

Stab. Stab. Stab.

A dream.

The secretary was lying, that was all. Covering for her boss who was off *vacationing*. He'd put them both on the list.

On an oath, he hit End on the phone and threw it against the windshield. It thudded but didn't crack the glass like he'd hoped.

He needed to hurt something. Someone. Now.

But he wanted Ty. Jen. So maybe he'd just save up all the anger.

When he found them, they'd pay.

Chapter 8

Ty didn't care for the tightness in his chest, but he wasn't about to let the woman sitting quietly at the small kitchen table see that. She'd already seen too much, disarming him with the gentle way she'd touched his heart and asked him to explain.

Who cared? So old man Delaney had told him he'd sell Jen's dream out from under her if Ty didn't disappear. So, Ty had listened. Didn't make him good or right. It was simply what had happened.

Why'd Jen have to bring it up? How had she not... known for all these years?

"You know, we have bigger fish to fry than our past," he snapped into the edgy silence they'd lapsed into while he'd put together some food for dinner.

"Yes, we do," she agreed easily. Too easily.

He shouldn't look at her. He knew what he'd see and

what he'd feel, but he was helpless to resist a glance. Her expression was placid, reasonable even, but her hands were clasped tightly on the table and there was misery in her eyes.

He'd always known he'd bring her misery. He just hadn't known it would last so long.

"I'm going to call Grady. Tell him we're lying low for a few days."

She didn't look at him as she nodded. "Yes. All right."

She wasn't listening to him. She was lost in a past that didn't—couldn't—matter anymore.

He pulled his phone out of his pocket and dialed Grady's number as he walked into a bedroom. He stepped inside, closed the door and let the pained breath whoosh out of him.

What the hell did he think he was doing? Saving her? It wasn't his job or place. Maybe she was in danger because of him, but that didn't mean...

"You know Laurel's going to kill you, right?"

Ty might have laughed at his cousin's greeting if he didn't feel like he'd swallowed glass. "She should probably hear me out first."

"Good luck with that."

"Which is why I called you, not her," Ty said, keeping his voice steady and certain. "We're just going to lie low for a few days. Let the cops find the guy. Sensible plan if you ask me."

"Since when does a Carson do the sensible thing and leave it to the cops?"

Ty wanted to be amused, but he was all raw edges

and, if he was totally honest with himself, gaping wounds.

But wounds could heal. Would. Once this was all over.

"Your wife seems to have a handle on finding this guy," Ty explained. "Plus, a Delaney is in the line of fire, not me. Let Laurel and her little deputies figure out who this guy is and—"

"Who this guy is that's targeting *you*, Ty. Why aren't you trying to figure out who it is?"

The blow landed, and Ty refused to acknowledge it. "The cops have his DNA now. What am I supposed to do about it?"

"You've got the brain in your head, which I used to think was quite sharp. Now I'm wondering."

It hurt, and Ty would blame it on already being raw. "I don't know who it is. Not sure how I'm supposed to magically figure it out. I'm not a cop. Look. Jen and I will stay out of sight for a few days. Let the law work, much as it pains me. Safest bet all the way around."

"Then what?"

"What do you mean, then what? Then things go back the way they were and everyone's safe."

Grady was silent for too many humming moments. "You can't run away every time you don't know what to do, or how to face what you have to do."

Shocked, knocked back as if the words had been a physical blow, Ty did everything he could to keep his voice low. "Are you calling me a coward?"

"No, Ty, I'm noticing a pattern. One you're better than." He sighed into the phone.

Ty searched for something nasty or dismissive to

say, but Grady's words had hooks, barbs that took hold and tore him open.

"Stay out of town and keep Jen safe if that's what you have to do," Grady said, with enough doubt to have Ty bristling. "I'll convince my wife it isn't such a bad idea. I'll do that for you because I love you, but I think you're better than this. Maybe someday you'll figure that out."

Ty didn't have any earthly idea what to say to that, and he was someone who always knew what to say— even if it was a pithy comment designed to piss someone off.

In the end, he didn't have to say anything. Grady cut the connection and Ty was left in the small bedroom he'd snuck Jen off to for very different reasons their junior year of high school.

Grady didn't understand. He hadn't gotten out of Bent like Ty had. He didn't understand the world out there was different from their isolated little community in Wyoming. He didn't understand that sometimes a man had to get out and let someone else handle the aftermath.

Grady could think it was cowardice, but Ty knew it took a bigger man to do the right thing without concerning himself over his ego. Carsons ran on ego, and Ty had learned not to.

He'd keep Jen safe, and Grady might never understand, but Ty had never needed anyone's understanding. Ever.

Temper vibrated and he ruthlessly controlled it as he stepped back into the cabin's living area.

Jen sat in the same exact place at the kitchen table, looking at the same spot on the wall, fingers still laced together on the glossy wood Addie always kept clean.

She'd barely caten any of the canned chili he'd fixed earlier. She looked like a statue, regal and frozen and far too beautiful to touch without getting his dirty fingerprints all over her.

He shook that thought away. The days of loving her and feeling inferior to her were over. All that was left was keeping her safe from trouble he'd unwittingly brought to her door, and if he had to wade through some past ugly waters to do it, well, he'd survive.

"Grady'll handle Laurel."

Jen's all-too-pulled-together demeanor changed. She looked over her shoulder at him and rolled her eyes. "Handle. You don't have a clue."

"So she's got him wrapped up in her. Doesn't mean he can't handle her."

"Do you pay attention at all? They work because they talk. They don't agree on everything, they don't handle each other, they *communicate*. And sometimes they still don't agree, but they love each other anyway because if you actually try to understand someone else's point of view, even if you don't share it, you're both a lot better off."

"Is that some kind of lecture?"

She snorted. "God, you're such a piece of work."

He flashed his easy grin and didn't understand why everything seemed to curdle in his stomach. "That's what they all say, darling."

She stood carefully, brushing imaginary wrinkles out of her shirt. "I want my phone back."

"Afraid not."

"I've agreed to stay with you. There's no reason for you to keep my property from me."

She'd never used that Delaney disdain on him. Not

back then, and not even in the time since he'd been back now. Snarky sometimes, yes. Irritated, always. But not that cold, haughty voice as if she was a master talking to a servant.

He'd deal with a lot to keep her safe, to keep his own wounded emotions safe and locked away, but there was no way in hell he was putting up with that.

So he kept walking toward her, grinning the grin that made his soul feel black and shriveled. "Make me, darling."

Jen knew of absolutely no one else who made her consider bodily harm on a person more than Ty. Being stuck in this cabin with him for even a few hours was already torture, and she'd shown admirable restraint if she did say so herself.

She would not lower herself to try to physically best him again. There was no point in a shouting match or demanding her phone back. So, she'd take a page out of her father's notebook and play the better-than-thou Delaney.

She didn't *feel* better than anyone, but she supposed that didn't really matter.

"Fine, if you want to play your childish games, keep my phone." She shrugged as if it was of no consequence. "We're not going to sit around here like lumps on logs," she decided. "We're going to do our own detective work. We'll start with a list of people who would have reason to threaten you, and me through you. You'll need to get a piece of paper and a pen so we can write it all down."

"You're not very good at the lady of the manor crap. You'll have to practice."

She raised an eyebrow at him and knew her face

didn't betray a flicker of irritation or hurt. "Lucky for me, I have all the time in the world to do so."

He held her gaze for a long time. Too long to win the staring match. Still, she thought the move to get situated on the couch in the most dismissive manner she could manage was a good enough substitute to staring him down.

Then she simply waited, fixing him with a bland stare of expectation. His jaw worked before he finally gave in and walked over to the kitchen silently. He jerked open a few drawers before pulling out a pad of paper and a pen.

"Thank my sister-in-law for these homey little touches." He returned, dropping the paper and pen on the coffee table in front of her.

"I like Addie," Jen returned.

"She's a Delaney, so I don't know why you wouldn't."

"She makes Noah happy," Jen persisted, wanting *something* to get through that hard shell of his. "She and Seth make Noah as happy as I've ever seen him."

"Your point?"

"Maybe *you* should thank Addie for the homey touches without being so derisive."

He held her gaze, but nothing changed in his expression. "You wanted to make a list?" he said, just the tiniest hint of irritation edging his tone.

She picked up the paper and the pen, because she did want to do this and there was no need to belabor points about love and happiness in this little hell she found herself in. She poised pen on paper and ignored the way her heart hitched. "I suppose my father would be on the list."

Ty heaved out a sigh. "It ain't your father."

"No, it seems unlikely," Jen agreed, doing everything to sound calm and polite. "But we're starting from nothing, which means no stone left unturned. My father dislikes you. He's threatened me to get to you before apparently. He fits."

"He's not the man who's been skulking around your store or my saloon."

"No. He isn't. But that man could be working for my father. It's not out of the realm of possibility."

Ty didn't argue with that, but he paced the small living room area. "I don't recognize him. If he was someone I'd known, someone who knew *me* personally, wouldn't I recognize him? In your tape. In Rightful Claim. There'd be *some* recognition."

She could see the fact he didn't know the man bothered him on a deeper level than she'd originally thought. The fact there was even the smallest ounce of helplessness inside him softened her. She wanted to reach out and touch his hand, something gentle and friendly and reassuring. She even lifted her hand, but then she let it drop back onto her thigh.

"It's not unheard of for someone to pay someone else to enact some sort of revenge or whatever this is."

Ty shook his head. "I saw him, Jen. There in Rightful Claim. He hated me. I saw it on his face. He *hated* me. But I don't know who he is."

She stayed quiet for a few humming seconds, reminding herself it wasn't her job to comfort him. She was angry with him and she would give him no solace in this, no matter how impotent he felt—not something a man like Ty Carson was used to.

Not her problem, and *not* something she was going to care about. "You don't recognize him, but he hates you. So, who hates you? If you just start naming people it might dislodge a memory. It's also possible this man is connected to someone on the list. Sitting here waiting for Laurel to figure it out—"

"I'd settle for any half-brained cop to figure it out, or a lab to get DNA on that blood."

"I'm sure they'd settle for that, too," Jen replied primly. She wanted to defend Laurel, considering her older sister was the strongest, smartest, most dedicated person Jen knew, but it would land against that hard head like a peaceful breeze and fall on deaf ears. "For now, we write a list." She smiled sweetly over at him. "Even if the police figure it out first, you'll have a handy reference for the next time someone tries to…" She trailed off and frowned.

This person wasn't trying to hurt Ty—not physically. The person who wrote the notes, if he was the same person stalking her store, wanted to cause fear. Worry—not for Ty's own welfare, but for hers.

"They don't want to hurt you—they want to cause you pain," Jen muttered, working through the problem aloud.

"I think that's the same thing, darling."

"No. No, it isn't. If they hated you, they'd want to hurt you."

"He *does* hate me, that's what I'm saying."

She waved him away, trying to think and connect the dots she was so close to connecting. "This person you don't recognize hates *you*, but wants to hurt someone he thinks you l-love." She tripped over that l-word a bit, but she hurried past it and didn't look at him. "So, it would make sense that you didn't hurt this individual. You hurt someone *he* loved."

"You really want a list of all the women I've hurt, Jen?"

"It doesn't have to be a woman, Ty. There are lots of different kinds of love. But yes, if you hurt someone enough that they hated you—that someone who loved them might have hated you—then we should put it on the list. Again, my father qualifies."

"It's not your father."

Jen couldn't see it either, but it fascinated her that Ty was so insistent. Ty, who'd always hated her father, and surely still did. But he refused to consider her father might be behind this.

So, she kept poking at it. "Then who is it?"

Ty shook his head, but in his next breath he started naming names, and Jen went to work to write them down.

With the police scanner, the cops were easy to thwart. They only had three on duty in the area at any given time, so he always knew where they were or where they were headed.

The detective was a little bit harder to track, but knowing she was sister to Jen and married to one of Ty's relatives gave him some intel.

He'd followed the detective around a bit in the afternoon on foot. She'd been in her patrol car, but the town was small, and with his radio she was easy to find.

To watch.

To wait.

She looked like Jen. She might do as a substitute. He'd hurt her just a little. Just a little. It'd take the edge off.

He considered it as he got back in his car when he realized her shift was over. He followed, taking a few turns out of her line of sight so she didn't suspect anything. When she turned off the highway, he parked his car along the shoulder. He slapped one of the abandoned-vehicle tags he'd stolen weeks ago on the back window so no one would think twice about his car being there.

Then he walked up the lane, and to the gleaming-new-looking cabin in a little cove of rock and trees. She was pulling things out of the trunk of her police car.

He could do it. Hurt her. Kill her. Spill blood. Right here, right now. She wore a gun, but what were the chances she'd have the reflexes to hurt him first?

Keep your focus. Keep your focus.

Dr. Michaels told him he did better with a goal. And his goal was causing as much emotional and *then* physical harm to Ty Carson as possible. The cop would be a distraction.

But he ached with the need to kill, and Jen's sister was ripe for the killing.

A loud engine sound cut through the quiet, and the cop shouldered her bag and shaded her eyes against the setting sun. A man roared up on a motorcycle. Not Ty as he'd hoped, but the other one. Not the brother, but a cousin, maybe.

People who mattered to Ty. It would be Ty's fault if they were harmed or killed. Ty would have all that guilt, and his would be gone.

He could pick them off in quick succession—bam, bam—and they'd fall to the ground. He wanted it. Needed it. His hand even reached for his side, but he remembered when he came up with nothing that he'd purposefully left his pistol in his car.

"Ty's the target," he whispered, reminding himself this was premature. Have a goal, Dr. Michaels had al-

ways told him. He ignored the tears of rage and disappointment streaming down his cheeks.

The goal was Ty, not these people. Jen was the best
target. A decision he hadn't made lightly.

He'd do everything he wanted to do to Jen and more,
maybe in front of Ty himself. Yes, Ty had secreted her
away, but he'd find them.

He'd find them and they would know true pain, and
Ty would know true guilt.

And him? He'd finally be at peace.

Chapter 9

The world was black and she couldn't breathe. Jen tried to thrash, but her body wouldn't move. She saw blood, smelled it even. But it wasn't her blood. It bathed the floor around her, but she wasn't hurt. So who was?

She sat bolt upright, eyes flying wide, her sister's name on her lips.

But Laurel wasn't in this unfamiliar room with her. There was no blood. Only slabs of wood, bathed gold in the faint light of a lamp on the bedside table.

Jen wasn't alone, though. No Laurel, no blood. She was in a comfortable bed, heart beating so loud she couldn't hear the horrible sound of her ragged breathing. "Ty?"

Still not fully awake, she reached for him, found his hand warm and strong. Something inside her eased, the sharp claws of panic slowly receding with the contact. Ty was holding her hand and she was safe.

"You were dreaming." His voice was flat, but he was there. When they'd decided to call it a night, he'd gone into one bedroom and she'd gone into another. But just now she'd been in the middle of a horrible nightmare she couldn't seem to fully shake, and he was here in this room with her.

Holding her hand.

"Breathe," he ordered, but there was no snap to his tone. A tinge of desperation, but nothing harsh.

So, she sucked in a breath and let it out. She squeezed his hand because it was her anchor. "It was Laurel. She was hurt."

"Laurel is fine."

"I know. It was just a dream." She fisted her free hand to her heart. "It just felt real. So horribly real. I could smell it."

"Just keep breathing."

So she did. She looked around the room, trying to orient herself. The Carson cabin. It looked so different from when they'd been in high school and snuck up here to...

Well, it wouldn't do to think of that, or how good it would feel to curl up into Ty's strong, comforting body and—

Yeah, no. She focused on the room. It was different from how it had been. New furniture, new curtains. Definitely new linens on the bed, and a pretty area rug that softened the harsh wood walls that had stood for over a century.

It smelled the same, though. The slight must of old not-often-used house and laundry detergent. She blinked owlishly at the lamplight, then at Ty.

He was rumpled, and still. So very still, perched on

the edge of that bed like she might bite. But his hand held hers.

It would have amused her, if it didn't make her unbearably sad.

"Good?" he asked abruptly.

She nodded and he withdrew his hand and got to his feet. He shoved his hands into the pockets of his sweatpants and refused to meet her gaze. "Need anything?"

She did, but she didn't know what exactly. Surely not whatever he was offering, or rather, hoping she wouldn't take him up on.

She rubbed her hand over her chest. She'd calmed her breathing and her mind, but she felt clammy and shaken. There'd been so much blood, and it had been real enough to smell it, to feel it.

It was worse, worrying for someone you loved. So much worse than being concerned over your own safety. But it had been only a dream. Laurel was safe and sound at home, with Grady. Jen hadn't had any silly danger dreams last year when Laurel had been facing down *real* danger, so it was foolish to believe her dreams were suddenly premonitions.

"Jen. Do you need anything?"

She shook her head, trying to focus. "No. No, I'm all right." Which wasn't true. At all.

Ty moved swiftly for the door, and that made all the ways she wasn't all right twine together into panic.

"No, that's a lie. I'm not all right. I'm afraid."

He paused at the door. He didn't turn, but he stopped. "Fear's natural," he said quietly, surprising her.

She rarely told anyone in her family when she was afraid. She'd learned at a young age Delaneys weren't supposed to be afraid. They were supposed to *endure*. And if not, she was the weak one to be protected.

Hadn't that been the appeal of Ty Carson? He hadn't treated her like a fragile little girl, or like she was a little beneath him. He'd been curt with her, rough at times, and she'd known, deep down, he'd thought she was a little better than him.

It wasn't true, but she'd known he'd felt that way, and part of her had relished that. A painful thing to realize, to admit to herself. But she'd been a teenager. Didn't she get to cut herself some slack?

Shouldn't she cut *him* some? "You're not going to tell me not to worry about it, that you'll handle it and I'm just fine?"

"No."

She picked at the coverlet over her legs. She knew he didn't want to have this conversation, to listen to her insecurities, but she also knew he would. And she'd feel better for it. "Everyone else does."

"Everyone else... Listen..." He turned to face her, hands still shoved deep in his pockets and a scowl on his face. He looked like he was preparing for a brawl, but she knew that was always how he looked when faced with a conversation he felt like he needed to have even though he didn't want to. "I've been in a lot of real dangerous situations, and a lot that only *felt* dangerous. Nothing I did could erase the fear whether the danger was real or perceived. You learn to hone it. You should be afraid. What's going on is scary."

She wrapped her arms around herself, trying to hold those words to her heart. "As pep talks go, that was surprisingly effective."

"It isn't always the fear that gets us, it's the idea we

can't or shouldn't be afraid. Fear is natural. To fear is to be human."

Human. Such a complex idea she never really considered. In her memories of Ty he was either that perfect paragon of nostalgic first love, or he was the symbol of the way he'd left her. The way she'd thought about him since he'd been back had been one-dimensional. It had been about *her* feelings, and nothing to do with him as a human being.

It wasn't wrong, exactly. It was just more complicated than that. He was human. She was human. Fears, confusions, mistakes.

Whoever was trying to hurt them was human, too, underneath whatever warped thing made a person want to hurt someone. Human and hurting and doing terrible things to alleviate the hurt.

She didn't want that to be her. She'd done no terrible things, but she'd shoved herself farther and farther into a box without ever dealing with the here and now. The feelings that hurt and diminished all that she was.

It was time to stop. "I don't really want to be alone." She didn't admit things like that. She'd never had to. She'd never had to ask for what she wanted or needed— she either got it easily or she kept that want locked away until she forgot about it or learned to live without it.

She'd thought that was being adaptable, learning to live without what life refused to give her. But sitting here in this bed that wasn't hers, a man who wasn't hers lurking by the door, fear and confusion and hurt lying heavy on her heart, she had to wonder.

Was never asking for the things she wanted holding her back? Is that what had kept her comparing every man she'd ever dated with the man of her high school dreams? A fear of asking for more—for what she wanted—for anything.

"Could you stay?" They might have been the scariest words she'd ever voiced. They opened up every fear of rejection she'd ever harbored without fully realizing it.

But if she could live without the thing when she didn't ask, why not be able to live with it when she did? It was the same. Living without was all the same. If she asked, though, she might get something.

Ty eased himself onto the corner of the bed, still keeping a large distance between them. Because he didn't want to be here. He didn't want to stay with her, but she'd asked.

She'd asked, and he stayed.

When Ty woke up to the ringing of his phone, he was stiff and disoriented. A mix of familiar and unfamiliar assaulting his senses. The smell of the cabin, mixed with something fruity. The familiar warmth of the sunlight on his face that always snuck through the crack in the curtains, the unfamiliar warmth of a body next to him.

The phone stopped, and groggily he tried to figure out why he should care. Jen shifted next to him, and when he looked down on her—a completely ill-advised move—her eyes blinked open.

A deep brown with flecks of green that reminded him of the woods they used to sneak off into. That reminded him of the plans he'd let die because he'd been young and stupid. Because for all his ego and bluster, he'd believed, deep down, he wasn't fit to touch her.

As she held his gaze, sleepy but probing, he wasn't sure if he still believed that. Fear was human, he'd said last night. And people were human. No better or worse for their name or their mistakes. Just…human.

Maybe there was something here to…

"Thank you."

Thank God for those two words. It broke the spell. *Thank you* disgusted him enough to swing off the bed. "For what?" he grumbled, already heading for the door. He wanted her gratitude as much as he wanted another hole in the head.

"For staying," she replied simply.

His eyes were on the door, on exit and escape, but the vision of that dark forest that had been theirs haunted him, that little seed of a thought that things could be different now. As adults. "You were scared, and it was my fault," he said disgustedly.

"Yes. Of course. It could have only been done out of guilt."

Surprised, he turned on her. "What other reason would I have?"

She held his gaze, but then shook her head and yawned. She slid out of bed, shuffling toward the door. "I need coffee for this."

Remembering how annoyingly chipper she got after her first cup in her, he lied. "We never have any coffee at the cabin."

She whirled on him so fast, so violently, he actually moved back a step, afraid she was going to punch him.

He held up his hands in surrender, amused in spite of himself. "That was a joke, darling."

Her eyes narrowed, those dainty fingers curling into fists. "Not. Funny." Then she whirled back around and sailed out of the room.

"It was a little funny," he murmured to himself. He

made a move to follow her, since he could use a jolt of caffeine himself. Before he managed to move, his phone rang again.

Frowning, he crossed the room and grabbed it off the nightstand. He didn't recognize the number, so he answered it cautiously.

"Yeah?"

"Would it kill you to answer your phone on the first call?" He recognized Laurel's irritated voice immediately. She must have been calling from the police station.

He sneered a little at that. "What do you want, Deputy?"

"I want to talk to my sister, but first I need to talk to both of you. Speaker on."

Ty strolled into the living room. "I ain't one of your deputies you get to boss around, Laurel."

"No, but I am your cousin-in-law, the detective in charge of this investigation and the woman who could charge you with kidnapping if you don't do what I say."

"I—"

"But beyond all that, Carson. I've got a name for your guy. So, why don't you cooperate so we can actually talk this out."

He wanted to find a comeback for that. A way to defend that kidnapping charge and pretend the rest didn't matter. But a name mattered. "Fine," he ground out, hitting Speaker on his phone and slapping it against the kitchen table.

"Jen? You're all right?"

"Yes," Jen replied, leaning closer to the phone. "I didn't realize Ty was talking to you, but I suppose I should have with all the bickering. How on earth do you and Grady get along?" Jen wondered, looking longingly at the slow-dripping coffee machine. "Your natural bossiness and his natural Carson-ness."

"Somehow it works," Laurel replied. She was in *all*-cop mode right now—even over the phone—and didn't rise to Jen's sisterly teasing bait. "I've got a missing person who matches the description of the man that was in Rightful Claim and what we could see of the customer who fainted on Jen's store tape."

"The blood?" Ty demanded.

"Still waiting on the results, but we have a name to confirm against, so that's a step. The next step—"

"What's the name?"

"The next step will be—"

"I want his name."

Jen placed her hand on his forearm, and it was only then he realized his entire body had hardened, and that he was all but ready to punch a phone. Worse, that her simple touch did ease some of the tension inside him.

"Laurel. Ty just wants to know if he recognizes the name. Let's start with that, then go through all the steps."

"His name is Braxton Lynn. It's not a perfect match since we don't have a clear picture of him, but it's close enough to wonder."

All the tenseness inside Ty leaked out fully, and futility swept in heavily and depressingly in its wake. "I don't know that name." A dead end. No matter how he went through his memory, the name Braxton *or* Lynn didn't ring any bells whatsoever. Someone was after him, ready to hurt the people he…cared for, and he didn't know the face *or* the name.

"Apparently he's from Phoenix, Arizona," Laurel continued. "I've got some calls in with a couple PDs in the area to get more information on him, maybe get a more positive ID. Criminal record on the Braxton name appears clear from what I've been able to search, but he's been missing for three months. Adult, twenty-six, no family looking for him. A foster sister reported the missing person, but it doesn't seem like anyone's too eager or worried to find him."

"I don't know that name," Ty repeated irritably.

"But we discussed something last night that I think is pertinent," Jen interrupted, sounding so equitable he wanted to growl. "Whoever is here might be threatening Ty or me because of a perceived hurt on a loved one. This Braxton might have a family member or friend who *does* have a connection to Ty."

"It's a solid theory," Laurel said, considering it. But then she barreled on, pure cop. "Like I said, I've got calls in trying to get some more background. Since this is all desk work, I'll handle trying to track down more of a profile and I'll keep you both updated. What about Phoenix?"

"What about it?" Ty retorted, repeating the name in his head like an incantation. *Braxton Lynn. Braxton Lynn.* Why didn't he know that name?

"You don't know the name," Laurel said as if it wasn't a failure on his part. "But what about anyone from the area? If it's a connection we're looking for, maybe it's Phoenix."

Ty stomped away from the phone on the table and paced, raking his hands through his hair. Phoenix? Not that he could think of, but Arizona…maybe. Maybe?

He moved back to the table, leaned close enough to talk into the speaker. "I had a buddy back in the army, before I became a ranger." One who'd had reason to hate him, but how could a kid from Phoenix be connected to a soldier from a small town? "Oscar Villanueva. I can't see as how there'd be any connection, but he was from Arizona. Not Phoenix, though. Some place I'd never heard of and can't remember now."

"Okay. You got any contact information for Oscar?"

Just another failure. "No," Ty managed to say, still sounding pissed instead of broken. "No. We lost touch when I got into the rangers." He didn't mention why Oscar might hate him. It wasn't pertinent until they found a connection.

"Okay. I'll dig into that angle. If you think of the name of the town, you let me know. I find any more connections or the blood results come in, I'll give you a call."

"Yeah," Ty returned, gut churning with emotions that would get in the way of clearheaded thinking. He needed all this…stuff inside him out of the way. He needed to compartmentalize like he had back in the army.

Tie it up. Set it aside. Act on fact and order over *feelings.*

"Take care of my sister, Carson, or you'll have a lot more than me to answer to."

Ty scowled at his phone. "She'll take care of herself." He hit End without waiting to hear what Laurel had to say about that.

Jen sighed. "Ty. You shouldn't have said that."

"Why not?" he returned. "You can and do take care of yourself."

He wanted to pace, to expend the frustrated energy inside him, but pacing was wasted. Maybe he'd go lock himself in the bedroom and do as many push-ups and sit-ups as it took to clear his mind.

"Yes, but you know how Laurel worries. How my family worries. You just added to it by—"

"They should get a new hobby, and so should you for that matter. It isn't your job to placate them."

She didn't bristle like he'd thought she would. She moved to the coffeemaker, unerringly finding the right cupboard for the coffee mugs. "It's been a rough year," she said, and though she sounded unshakable, there was a sadness to those words.

But she hardly had the monopoly on hard years. The Carsons had been through their fair share of what the Delaneys had gone through—though a few more Delaneys had landed themselves in the hospital. Carsons, too, though, so… "For mine, too, darling."

"I don't want to fight with you, Ty." She took a sip of coffee, winced, presumably at the heat. "I want to figure this out so I can go home to my store and live my life."

"Funny, I thought we could do that *and* bicker."

Her mouth almost curved, but the sadness remained. "We can, but I don't want to." She held out a hand. "Truce?"

He didn't want to touch her. There'd been too much already, and his brain had taken a few more detours than he cared for. But the less she knew about all that, the better. "Fine. Truce." He shook her hand.

The chill that skittered up his spine had nothing to do with the handshake. He frowned, looking at the door. He wasn't sure what the feeling was, the foreboding signal that something was off.

"I feel it, too," Jen whispered. "What is it?"

"It's your gut," Ty replied, eyeing every possible entrance in the cabin. Not too many windows, but enough. The door would be impossible to penetrate. The secret passageway had been bolted shut after Addie'd had to use it last year.

"My gut says we should get a gun," Jen said, still holding his hand in hers.

"Yeah, your gut ain't half-bad."

It had been easy to track the motorcycle marks once he'd found them. It had taken him longer than he'd wanted to finally discover the trail, but the Delaney Ranch was rather hard to breach even with all its stretching fields and nooks and crannies.

Good security there, plus a parcel of ranch hands always roaming about and a passel of vigilante residents. He'd nearly gotten himself caught three times.

But now, *now* he was following the heavy divot in the grass clearly made when a motorcycle had irresponsibly driven up the east side of the property, and then driven off again on dirt roads.

Irresponsible Ty. Always making mistakes. Including driving up the unpaved road, rather than turning back to the highway.

He could track the land—especially since the sun had seemed to bake the tracks in good, different from the truck tires that also marred the dirt.

He clucked his tongue at Ty's idiocy. Such a shame Ty would make it so easy for him. The laugh bubbled into his throat, escaped and echoed through the trees. He rather liked the sound of it, but he should be more careful. He wouldn't make a stupid mistake like Ty had.

No. Mistakes wouldn't bring him peace or closure. Mistakes weren't his goal. So, he climbed, following the motorcycle track up and up and up.

He was starting to get winded as morning began to dawn in earnest. Mist that had filtered through the trees began to burn off.

The higher he got, the more the trees thickened, but the road remained. Ty's careless tire tracks guiding him. What utter stupidity.

Jen was better off with him, not Ty. She'd see that eventually. She'd be his prize. Oh, he'd have to hurt her to hurt Ty, but she'd understand. Once she knew the whole story, she'd understand. They could build a life together. Because he'd have peace then. Peace and closure.

Hurt Jen. Kill Ty. Live happily ever after?

It wasn't the plan. Dr. Michaels told him he did better with a plan. With a goal. But couldn't plans and goals change? Didn't he deserve a prize? Jen didn't deserve to die.

But she'd run away from him. She'd called the cops on him. She was *with* Ty. Clearly, she needed to be punished. Like Dr. Michaels, who hadn't listened—not close enough.

So, perhaps it would be up to Jen herself. Defend Ty? Die. Let Ty touch her? Die more painfully. He could envision it. The glint of the knife. The smell of the blood. Just like the uppity doctor.

No, no, that had been only a dream. Maybe he'd dream about Jen, too. Dream about her begging for Ty to save her, but he wouldn't. Ty wouldn't be able to. Ty would have to watch her die. Slowly.

He could see it and he needed it. Now. He needed the kill now. Murder sang its siren song. It flowed through his blood. He could *feel* it there, boiling inside him. It needed release. Knife to throat.

He had his knife out in his hand. Maybe he'd use it on himself. Just a little bit. Just to take the edge off.

Then he saw the cabin.

Chapter 10

Jen watched Ty sweep the cabin with military precision. It didn't seem to matter that they hadn't heard anything, that it had been only this cold chill of a feeling that had gone through both of them. Ty was behaving like they were in imminent danger.

Surely it was just coincidence or…something. It unnerved her more than the feeling itself that he'd felt it, too, and that he took it seriously.

People didn't just *feel* things. If they did, her dream last night about Laurel was a lot more ominous. But Laurel had called this morning with a lead and everything had been fine.

Everything *was* fine, because Ty found nothing. He was now perched in what appeared to be an uncomfortable position, looking through the slight gap in the curtain at the front of the cabin.

"Ty, this is silly. There's nothing out there. We're both wired and worried."

"We both felt something," Ty returned, as if that was just a normal thing people experienced. As if a shared feeling of discomfort or unease magically meant someone was out there.

"But that doesn't make any sense, Ty. It can't be possible."

He shrugged, his gaze never leaving the small patch of yard. "In the rangers you learn to roll with the things that don't make sense. It's not like *we* ever made any sense."

"Why not?" she asked before she remembered that this constant mix-up of them and this situation was only going to cause more heartache. She'd had her epiphany last night about asking for what she wanted, but what about things she didn't know if she wanted?

Part of her wanted Ty, but she didn't think it was a very intelligent part of herself.

Ty scoffed at her question. "Aside from the fact we're opposite in just about every way—a Carson and a Delaney. Ring any cursed bells?"

"That's not holding much weight these days."

"That's these days. Besides, we're still opposites."

"And opposites attract."

Ty shook his head, but his gaze was outside and his demeanor was completely unreadable. "There's got to be some common ground for all those differences to rest on. Attraction is easy."

She didn't know why she felt the need to argue with him, only that she did. It made what they'd had before seem...doomed. An unimportant castoff.

It wasn't that. She wouldn't *let* it be that to him. "Then how do you explain Laurel and Grady?"

"Aside from the fact they both love and would protect the people they love with their life, they love Bent. They believe in it. Honestly, deep down, Laurel and Grady have more alike things than different."

Even knowing it was true, even having said the same to her brother Dylan in defending Grady and Laurel—back before he himself had been felled by a Carson—it irked her that Ty of all people recognized it.

"All right. Explain Dylan and Vanessa."

"Again, they might antagonize each other, but it's only because they're so alike deep down. They want the world to see the persona they put forth, not who they actually are."

It had taken her *years* to understand that about Dylan, and Ty said it like it was common knowledge.

But there was one truth he was refusing to acknowledge, and since he was irritating her with his truths, she'd irritate him with hers. "We're the same deep down, too."

He snorted. "I don't think so, darling."

"You don't have to. I know so. You've only ever tried to harden yourself against that gaping need for someone to love and cherish you and let you protect them, and I've hidden myself against the very same thing."

She watched those words land—that stillness, then the slight rotation of shoulders as if he was willing the words to roll off his back.

But truths weren't easy to shrug away. That she knew.

Then everything in him stiffened, and he brought the binoculars he held in one hand to his eyes.

"Don't pretend you see something just to get out of—"

"There. He's out there."

She rolled her eyes and fisted her hands on her hips. She was not this stupid, and it was insulting he thought she was. "You are not going to change the subject by—"

He thrust the binoculars at her. "He's out there."

Frowning at the binoculars, Jen took them hesitantly. "How do you know it's him?"

"Movement."

"It could be an animal," she replied, studying the binoculars in her hands. She didn't want to look out the window. Didn't want to be fooled into thinking something was out there, and what's more, didn't want something—or someone—to actually be out there.

"I know what I saw."

She looked back to find him checking a pistol. She'd had no doubt there were guns hidden throughout the Carson cabin, but it was a bit of a jolt to see him efficiently working with the weapon.

He was serious, though. This was no dramatic attempt at changing the subject. His movements were too economical. His jaw was too tight. In his eyes that fierce protector light she'd always loved.

She swallowed at the mix of fear and love and turned back to the window. Lifting the binoculars with no small amount of trepidation, she studied the small part of the tree line she could make out through the natural gap in the curtain.

"I don't—" But then she did. First it was just a flash, the sun glinting off something metal. Then she could make out the faint movements of something that blended into the trees but was clearly human.

Human. Her breath caught in her throat, and for a full second or two, she was completely frozen in fear, watching the movement of someone.

"See him?"

Jen had to force herself to swallow, and then embarrassingly had to clear her throat in order to speak. "Yes," she managed, but it was little more than a croak. Fear was paralyzing her and it was demoralizing, but she couldn't seem to control it. "What do we do?"

"You stay put. I go out there and shoot him."

"You can't…" She trailed off. If this man was here to harm them, shouldn't Ty shoot him? She watched the figure, then the glint of light. What was the sun reflecting off?

"I'm not going to kill him. I want to know why the hell he's trying to torture you and me. But I'm not going to give him a chance to hurt you either. Stay put."

"I should call Laurel." But she didn't drop the binoculars. She kept thinking she could figure something out if she could only see his face.

Then she did.

And she screamed.

Jen's scream echoed through the cabin almost in time with a crash against the window, but the minute her scream had pierced the air, Ty had lunged.

The window glass shattered above them, pieces raining down on his back. He thought he'd protected Jen from the brunt of it, thanks to the help of the curtain that kept most of the glass contained.

"Are you okay?" he asked, panicked that maybe something had shot through and reached her before he had.

"I'm fine," she said, her voice muffled underneath him. "What was it? A bullet?"

Ty looked at the curtain. There was a slight rip. He checked around the trajectory of the shot and frowned at what he saw.

An arrow piercing the thick area rug. Not just a flimsy Boy Scout arrow, though. This was a three-blade steel broadhead, the kind used for hunting. Which explained its impact on the window.

The window. Ty rolled off Jen, crouched and waited for someone to try to come through the window. When nothing happened, he looked down at Jen.

She was sitting now but looked dazed. "An arrow," she muttered. "That's…weird."

"A stupid, pointless stunt," Ty muttered. Oh, it was an arrow that could do some damage, but he didn't think that had been kill-shot aim. It was more scare tactics.

Ty got to his feet, done with these childish games. He flicked the safety off his pistol and strode for the door.

"Wait. Wait, Ty, there's a note." Jen crawled over to the arrow and cocked her head to read the piece of paper affixed to the back of the arrow.

Ty said something crude about what he could do with the note, but Jen crouched down to read aloud.

"Why don't you come and find me?"

She wrinkled her nose, but Ty barely heard what she'd read aloud. Rage spread through him like a wildfire. He was nothing but heat and hate. She was bleeding. Just a little trickle from a spot on her cheek, but he'd make someone pay for that.

"I'll find him," he said, low and lethal. He reached the door, ready to jerk it open and start shooting. "I'll—"

"Ty." Jen's gentle admonition did nothing to soothe

the riot of fury and worry inside him, but it did stop his forward movement. "He wants you to."

"Yeah, well, I'll give him the fight he wants." His hand was on the knob, but Jen kept talking.

"He doesn't want a fight. He could have had that back in Bent."

"He doesn't want to hurt me, then, or he could have done that, too."

"He wants to hurt you, but he's playing a game. I don't understand it, but it's a game. Come and find me—he wouldn't want you angrily going after him if he didn't have a plan to take you down."

Ty flicked the lock. "Let him try."

"Use your brain," Jen snapped with surprising force as she stalked over from where the arrow stuck out of the rug. She flicked the lock back in place and glared up at him. "He's trying to mess with you, and has been this whole time. Not only does he know we're alone up here, but he knows *us*. We don't know a darn thing about him. You don't even recognize his name. We can't underestimate him."

She'd never have any idea of how those words hurt. He knew, intellectually, she wasn't blaming him for not knowing the name, for not recognizing the man, but he felt the blame anyway.

Who had he let down? Who had he hurt? How had he lured Braxton Lynn to Bent, Wyoming, and Jen Delaney?

"You can't leave me here without my phone. I need to call Laurel," she said, sounding calm and efficient. "And you need to do something about the window. Maybe duct-tape the curtains to the wall? I know it doesn't keep him out, but it seals us in better."

"That could have hit you," he said because he didn't understand her calm. Didn't understand how she could talk about calling the police and duct-taping curtains of all things.

He needed to eliminate the threat now, and she wanted to do housekeeping.

"I know it could have." She rubbed her palm over her heart. "Or you." Her gaze met his. He'd convinced himself that ache in his heart was nostalgia or even remorse. It was sweet memories but had no bearing on the present.

Except looking at her now, knowing she could have been—and still could be hurt by all this—there was nothing *past* about it. He still loved her, deep into his bones. The kind of love time didn't dull or erase. Something all but meant to be, stitched together in whatever ruled this crazy world.

She felt it, too, in the knowledge he could have been hurt. In the realization, if she hadn't beat him to it already, that what they'd had once upon a time lived and breathed in the here and now—no matter how little either of them wanted it.

Or could have it.

He pointed to his phone on the table. "Call Laurel. I have to go out there."

"Ty—"

"Call Laurel." Then he stalked outside, ready to fight.

He hummed to himself. The shattering crash of arrow against window had been satisfying enough to put a little levity in his step.

He didn't think he'd hit anyone—surely he'd have heard a scream of pain or someone would have run out.

But the fear…there had to be fear now. He looked up as he heard something. The door opening.

So, Ty had taken the bait to come after him.

He tsked under his breath. What a foolish man Ty Carson turned out to be.

Bending down, he pulled another trap out of his backpack. Antique bear trap. All steel and menace. He'd brought them lovingly back from rusty relics to shining pieces of beauty.

He hadn't been sure how or where to use them, but he'd hauled them around just the same. Now he set the three he had hefted up the hill at three separate points around the cabin.

The police would be coming soon. Surely they'd called. Gently, reverently, he pulled the trap open and set it. He watched the ragged edges glint in the light of the sun filtering through the trees.

Like a parent caressing a baby's cheek, he drifted his finger down the sharp edge. "You'll do good work for me, won't you?"

Footsteps sounded, faint but getting closer.

He had to melt away now. Luckily he was excellent at disappearing.

And reappearing when the people who deserved pain least expected it.

Chapter 11

Jen hated the fact she was pacing and wringing her hands like some helpless creature. The princess in the tower again. Waiting for Ty to return or the police to show up.

What kind of coward was she?

She fisted her hands on her hips. She was *choosing* the coward's way out because she was used to fading into the background and letting everyone else handle the tough stuff. The scary stuff.

Being used to something wasn't an excuse, though. She wouldn't be stupid. Leave fighting the bad guys to the people with guns they were trained and licensed to carry. It didn't mean she couldn't do *something*.

Protection. She didn't think Ty was going to find anything stomping around out there. If he did, he'd probably get hurt. At first, she shied away from that possibility, but then she stopped herself. No. She had to face facts.

He'd gone off half-cocked after a taunt from an unstable maniac. He'd put himself in danger. Luckily, Laurel was sending deputies up. They would handle whatever mess Ty had gotten himself into.

In the meantime, she needed to handle *her* mess. She was in a cabin all by herself with an unstable maniac on the loose. The man she shouldn't love, but apparently did, was off *proving* something or other. And the police were on their way.

What would they all need?

Coffee for the police. Possibly first aid for Ty. And then, she needed to protect herself.

No. Reverse all that. For once she would put herself first. Find a weapon, or ten. Then the coffee. And the dope gallivanting around the woods with a pistol could fend for himself. She'd do the first aid last.

Or so she told herself. In the end, love won out. It irritated her, but she couldn't have lived with herself if he'd staggered in bleeding like she'd imagined too many times to count already and she didn't have *something*.

Maybe it wasn't so wrong, she decided, placing the first aid kit on the table before going on a gun hunt. Maybe it wasn't about always putting others first or always putting yourself first. Not always about asking for what you wanted, but choosing the when and knowing the why.

Maybe, it was all about *balance*.

Everything with Ty was complicated, but the feeling she had for him was simple. She pawed through a closet, turning that over in her head. Maybe in the midst of this…weirdness, she would focus on the simple.

As if on cue, she found a hunting rifle in the back corner of the closet. The chamber was empty, but she'd seen some boxes of ammunition in the tiny cabinet above the refrigerator when she'd been looking for a first aid kit.

She was no fan of guns, but her father had forced her to go hunting when she'd been a kid. All Delaneys needed to know how to hunt.

She'd hated every second of it, which had made her just another anomaly in the great Delaney clan. The rest of them might not love it, but they were good with guns, good with hunting. Jen had never had the patience or the aptitude.

She sighed heavily, grabbing the box of ammunition. Who knew being vaguely threatened by a stranger would have her rehashing so many of her childhood emotional issues?

Still, it allowed her to load the gun efficiently so she'd gotten something out of it.

She felt safer with the gun in her hand, felt calmer with the first aid kit within reach. But she was still just *waiting*.

Before she could decide what to do about that, something at the door clicked and the door opened. She knew it would be Ty since he obviously had the key, but still she lifted the rifle.

You never knew, after all.

He stepped inside, closing and locking the door behind him before he glanced at her in the kitchen. When she didn't lower the gun, he quirked an eyebrow.

"Gonna shoot me, darling?"

Since she didn't care for his blasé tone, she used one of her own. "Considering it."

"Well, I came back unscathed, so apparently your theory about that note trying to draw me out was incorrect."

"That's what you think," Jen muttered, finally lowering the rifle. Mostly because she heard the distinct sound of a car engine, which she figured had to be the police.

Ty lifted the curtain and looked out the broken glass. He nodded. "Police. You stay here."

"Because?"

"Because."

"No. Let them come to the door. Where we'll all discuss what happened together. Rather than you taking over."

"I wasn't—"

"You were going to go out there and tell them what's what—from your perspective, and that wouldn't be a problem, except I'm the one who actually saw him shoot the arrow. You searched the woods and all, but *I* saw the whole thing happen. They'll come to the door and we'll talk to them together."

She could tell she'd surprised him. He wasn't used to her giving orders. Well, everyone was going to start getting used to it.

A knock sounded and Ty considered it. "Well, I guess you got your way."

"It's not *my* way, Ty. It's the right way." She reached past him and opened the door. She was a little disappointed Hart wasn't the deputy on the other side of the door, but he was currently working nights so it made sense. "Come in, Deputy." She gestured him inside.

"Ms. Delaney."

"I've left the arrow where it landed, and I'm sure you

can see where it made impact with the window." She could feel Ty watch her as she took the deputy through the sequence of events. Still, he didn't interrupt. He didn't try to take over. He simply watched while Jen answered questions and the deputy wrote notes down in his little notebook.

"And you saw all of this, Mr. Carson?"

Ty shook his head. "No. Once I handed the binoculars over to Jen I went to get my pistol."

"The one you're wearing now?"

"Yes." He flashed the man his cocky Carson grin. "Not going to ask me if it's registered, are you?"

The deputy only grunted. Clearly he'd had enough run-ins with Carsons not to press the issue. "So you're getting the pistol—then what?"

Ty walked him through heading for the door, jumping on Jen when he heard the crash. Then her reading the letter aloud and his heading outside.

"And once you were outside, you searched for the man?"

"No. Not searched. I didn't go into the woods or look for tracks, I went to the stables."

Jen frowned. News to her. He'd let her think he was going after whoever had shot the arrow, to hurt him. But he'd gone to the stables?

"There's a hayloft up there," Ty continued. "It's rickety, but if you know where to step you can get up and get a decent view of the surrounding area. I'll admit, I'd planned to go after him, but the stables caught my eye first. I knew I'd be able to see him if he was anywhere close. But I looked all around and I didn't see anyone. There could be tracks, but I didn't want to risk it alone."

Also news to her. The jerk. She'd been worried for no

reason. Maybe she should have given him more credit, but he'd been so angry when he'd huffed off. Was she really supposed to just *expect* him to make smart decisions?

Maybe the answer was yes, but she wasn't about to admit her mistake to him.

"We'll search the woods and see what we can find."

"He isn't there," Ty said flatly.

"No, but he might have left a clue behind. You let us investigate Mr. Carson and we'll—"

Ty said something crude and Jen sighed, stepping forward to smile at the deputy. "Excuse him. He's so grumpy when he hasn't had his nap. Like a toddler." She smiled at the officer, enjoying Ty's disgusted grunt. "Would you like some coffee?"

"No, ma'am, thank you. I'll join Burns out there and we'll see what we can find. If I have any more questions I'll be in touch, and we'll let you know if we find anything. And everything we find gets turned over to your sister and Deputy Hart."

"Why Hart?" Ty demanded.

The deputy eyed Ty with some disdain. "Hart is taking over as detective now that Laurel's on desk duty. He'll handle all investigations with her until she's on maternity leave, then on his own."

Ty grunted irritably. "I'll search with you."

The deputy shook his head and Jen thought Ty would bite it off if he could. So, she moved easily between law and wannabe outlaw and started ushering the police officer to the door.

"Don't worry, I'll keep him occupied while you do your *jobs*." She gave Ty a pointed look at the word, but he only stared back at her, clearly furious. But he let the deputy exit the cabin while he stayed put.

He narrowed his eyes at her once the door was shut.

"What?" she demanded loftily.

"So, you finally decided to use it."

"Use what?"

"That backbone you've been trying to ignore for almost thirty years."

He expected her to be pissed. That was the point after all. Undermine all this annoying confidence and take charge thing she had going on, and make her angry.

But she didn't so much as flinch. She considered.

It was beautiful to watch. This was the woman he'd always known she could be. More like her sister, but still herself. Because she'd only ever needed to stop trying to *please* everyone, including him.

She wasn't trying to please him like she had when they'd been together, and it gave him a perverse thrill. It was always the Jen he'd wanted, because he didn't deserve the girl who'd bent over backward to give everything to him. He'd never deserve her.

"I suppose that is what I decided while you let me believe you were off chasing down a madman, not looking for him from a safe vantage point."

"If I'd seen him, I'd have gone after him."

"But you didn't search the woods. You looked for him from a safe vantage point and then you came back."

Why her repetition of his very intelligent choices irritated him, he didn't know. So he shrugged. "Your point?"

"My point is you want me to believe you're this one thing—you've always wanted me to believe certain things about you, but they're very rarely true." She frowned a little, as if thinking that over. "Even leaving without a goodbye. You came home ten years later, let me believe you were just a careless jerk—even though I'd known you weren't, but the truth was you'd done it to protect me."

"Like you said earlier. I still could have said goodbye." But he couldn't have. Not and actually done it. He hadn't been strong enough then to tell her he was leaving, to be callous and nasty and cut all ties. So, he'd taken the coward's way out.

He'd like to believe as an adult, he would have made different choices, but sometimes, when he looked into her eyes, he figured he'd always take the coward's way out when it came to hurting her.

He wanted to cross to her. Hold her. Tell her all the ways he hadn't been able to face her. Beg her to forgive him.

It unmanned him, all that swirling emotion inside. Worse, the hideous thought she might be able to see it.

"We should—" Jen was cut off by a knock on the door, thank God. "Maybe they found something," she muttered. Ty was closer, so he answered it. But it wasn't one of the deputies. It was Zach Simmons.

Ty had found out about Zach's existence only a few months ago when his aunt, who'd run away long before he'd been born, had come back to town. Zach was technically Ty's cousin, but he hadn't quite warmed to the man. Zach might be a Carson by blood, but he'd been FBI and his dad had been ATF and everything about him screamed *Delaney* to Ty—even if there weren't any Delaney ties.

So he flat out didn't trust the man. "Zach," he greeted coolly.

"Ty. Jen. Laurel called me. Sounded like you two need some security, so I hitched a ride up with a deputy," Zach said, his eyes taking in his surroundings, reminding Ty of a soldier. He wore a big black backpack and was carrying a weapon openly on his hip, and he had eyes that reminded Ty way too much of the father he'd hated. Eyes he saw in the mirror.

"We don't need security." The only reason Ty didn't slam the door in his face was the whole blood-tie thing. It wasn't Zach's fault he had the old bastard's eyes. And he'd been nothing but pleasant enough since he'd moved to Bent to work with Cam Delaney at his new security business.

But Ty didn't trust him.

"I'm pretty sure security is exactly what you need. You might not want it, but you need it," Zach returned evenly. "Laurel insisted. More, my sister insisted. You try saying no to Hilly."

It was that evenness Ty couldn't quite work out. There was a blankness to Zach, a way he kept all personality locked under a very bland shell. But he was a Carson. Even if he'd grown up away from Bent with an ATF agent father, there was Carson blood in there. A man *had* to feel it.

"Ignore him," Jen interrupted, smiling at Zach in a way that had Ty grinding his teeth together. She even took his arm and pulled him into the living room. "There's plenty of room, and I think an extra set of eyes is a good idea."

"Laurel thought so, too. She wants me to move you—"

"No," Ty said, trying for some of Zach's evenness. It came out like a barked order. "We stay where I know the turf."

Zach looked at Jen as if he was expecting her to argue. That was what Ty didn't trust about Zach. He didn't know when to stick with his own.

"I think Ty's right," Jen said, surprising him. "Clearly this man is going to track us wherever we go, and we can hardly be on the run forever. It's best to stay in a familiar place, and protect ourselves." She smiled winsomely at Zach. "Especially with a security expert around."

"I want to set up some cameras then. Nothing invasive. Just your typical security measures for dangerous lunatics lurking in the woods." He pulled the pack off his back and gave it a little pat.

"How much is that going to cost me?" Ty demanded.

Zach arched an eyebrow at him. "I suppose I'd have to give you a family discount. It'll be borrowed equipment—we can take it all down once this is over. Consider the labor my charitable donation to a good cause."

Ty wanted to tell him they didn't need the security again, but that was knee-jerk and stupid. The more footage they had of this Braxton Lynn, the better chance they had of figuring out why he was after Ty.

"I know Laurel's investigating," Zach continued. "And I respect your sister and her work ethic. She'll work on this till she's keeling over, but she's going to investigate like a detective."

"Is there another way?" Jen asked.

"Sure. There's the FBI way, which I'm rather familiar with. There's also the bend-the-rules-so-we-can-get-our-man way. I'm a bit fond of that one." He pulled a laptop out of his backpack and placed it on the table. "Now that I'm not FBI, I'm not beholden to their rules, and I know a lot of ways to get around the bureaucratic red tape."

Ty considered the computer, then the man. He grinned. "Now you're sounding like a Carson. Let's cut some red tape, cousin."

He gave it a full twenty-four hours before he returned to the cabin. He could tell the cops had sniffed around some, but none had come close to his traps.

He was mildly disappointed, he could admit. It was for the best for his plan that no one had stumbled into one, but finding a bloody corpse or someone whose life was spilling out painfully would have lifted his spirits just a tad.

He looked up from the trap he lovingly caressed. He couldn't see the cabin from here, but he knew where it was.

Jen was probably letting Ty touch her in there. No, no. She was too pure for that. Jen Delaney seemed so kind, so good. No, Ty was probably forcing himself upon her. She was a victim, and it was his duty to save her.

He rubbed at the headache that began to drum. No, that was all wrong. Ty needed to pay, but he could do that only through Jen. Ty had irreparably damaged Oscar.

Ty had broken his brother when they'd been in the army. It was the only explanation, and once he'd gotten through to Oscar, Oscar had agreed it was all Ty's fault. Other people were always to blame for Oscar's shortcomings, but he'd come up with a way to fix that. To get Oscar on his side again.

He would break Ty's woman, for Oscar. It was only fair. Sometimes innocents were hurt because bad men roamed the world. Bad men needed to be hurt. They needed to suffer.

Once Ty did, his own suffering would go away.

He looked down at his shaking hands. He was getting too far out of control. The plan was hazy and he wasn't focused on the goal. The goal.

It was all this waiting. All this planning. Vengeance needed to wait and be planned, but a hero acted. A hero did what he came here to do.

He would be Oscar's hero. *Now.*

Chapter 12

The next morning, Jen was happy to make breakfast for the two men she was temporarily sharing a cabin with. She might have discovered her backbone yesterday, or trusted it enough to use it, but she'd long ago decided she'd rather make the meals her way than be waited on.

Zach had spent most of yesterday tapping away on his computer conferring with Ty in low tones about what little they knew about Braxton Lynn, going over the layout of the cabin and where they could feasibly install cameras.

They had a plan for the cameras now, but Zach hadn't been able to find much about the man.

Frustrated, they'd called it a night, and now today was a fresh day. Zach was going to install his surveillance equipment, then try his hand at some hacking.

Jen had felt superfluous. At best. Last night and now,

but she didn't know how to set up cameras or hack into government records, or anything about Braxton or Ty's military past, so she'd had to accept it. This wasn't her time.

But she'd listened, and she'd come up with her own conclusions. She'd always been good at observing people and reading them. If you were going to contort yourself to be what someone else wanted, or try, you had to understand them on some level.

The man after Ty didn't want something as simple as just to hurt him. He wanted to *torture* Ty, terrorize him, using whatever means—family or past lovers—to do it. The question was, why didn't he focus on Ty's family, the most important thing to him?

There was the most obvious reason, one that made Jen's gut burn with shame. She was the easy target. Carsons were rough and tough and harder to threaten. She was weak and easy pickings.

Well, no thank you.

She let Ty and Zach settle into breakfast as she sipped her coffee and watched them eat and discuss. Like she wasn't even there.

No thank you to that, too.

"You're going about this the wrong way," she announced casually, so irritated with them and herself that it didn't even bother her when they both gave her the same patently Carson questioning look. Eyebrow raised, mouth quirked, with just enough disbelief in their gaze to make a person feel stupid.

She refused.

"You're thinking about this like he's after *me*, when we know he's trying to hurt Ty."

"No. He's trying to hurt *you* because of me."

She rolled her eyes. "Let's try to step outside of macho egomaniac land for one second. Yes, he wants to hurt you. But how? Emotionally, not physically."

"So?"

"So? Everything you're planning is physical. And factual. He's not interested in either thing. He doesn't want to physically hurt you. He wants to terrorize you via someone you care about. Even when you're trying to figure out his connection to you, it's only so you know his identity, so you can identify and isolate his threat. But what you need to be doing is trying to understand him."

"How can we understand him if we don't know who he is?" Zach asked reasonably.

"But we do know. We know his name. We know his foster sister reported him missing, but no one's really looking for him. So, what does that tell you?"

"Not a whole lot."

Ty shook his head. "She's right," he said, with no small amount of irritation. "He's alone in the world. No one really cares about him. Which means you can make the reasonable connection that whoever he's looking to avenge *did* care about him, or he thought they did."

"Exactly. And if he's blaming Ty, out to terrorize Ty, he blames Ty for losing this mystery person. Maybe they died, or maybe they left him. Maybe there's something else, but he wants Ty to hurt the way *he* hurts. The key isn't Braxton or me, it's the link."

Both men stared at her, with no small amount of doubt in their expressions. And they were so quiet and military still, Jen fidgeted with her coffee mug. She didn't let herself blurt out the apologies or *at least that's what I think* that filled her brain.

She knew, *knew*, whether they agreed or not, her theory had more merit than the way they were currently going about things.

"I can't discount it," Zach returned, still frowning as if considering and finding her lacking.

No, not *her*. Her theory. She needed to be better about acknowledging that difference.

"But I can't wrap my head around it either. It doesn't make sense why anyone would get it all so mixed up in their head."

"You're trying to reason it out," Ty interrupted. "I think what Jen's saying is it's not the kind of reason that's going to make sense to, well, reasonable people."

"Exactly," Jen said, emboldened by Ty's understanding. "You can't think about facts and reason, you have to think about the emotion. Revenge is led by emotion."

"You have to consider both," Zach countered. "You've got a good point. His motivation isn't one we're necessarily going to understand because clearly he's not well. But if we know who *he* is, identity-wise, we have a better idea of how to deal with his emotion *and* a better shot at finding the missing link. Facts and emotion need a balance."

Jen considered that. "I suppose you're right. Fact informs the emotion side of things, even if it's not a straight line."

Zach grinned at her. "Can you say that again? 'I suppose you're right.' I've never heard any Carson or Delaney or Simmons for that matter say anything remotely admitting I'm right. I think you're the most reasonable person in the whole dang bunch."

Jen flushed with pleasure.

"Maybe you'd like me to leave you two alone," Ty grumbled.

Jen rolled her eyes at him and got to her feet, clearing the breakfast dishes, but Zach was taking them out of her hand before she could make it to the sink.

"I should do that. You made breakfast. I'll clean up."

It was her first instinct to argue, to insist she did the work she knew she could do. But she wasn't here because she could cook or clean. She wasn't here to take care of everyone while they did the important work.

No.

She was here because she'd been put in danger. Maybe Zach and Ty were here to protect her, but that didn't mean she had to take care of everything.

Wow. It was a lightning bolt of a thought. That she didn't have to be the one to clean up all the messes to earn her place here. That she didn't have to bend over backward to do whatever was asked of her simply because everyone else was more qualified to handle the threat against them.

Because the threat was against her, too.

So, she beamed at Zach and let him take the dishes. "Thank you. I'm going to go call Hilly and see how the store is faring." And she was going to spend some time thinking about how when this was all over, she was going to make sure her life changed.

"Sure is a pretty little thing. Good cook, too."

Ty looked at where Zach was cheerfully washing the breakfast dishes. He was so shocked by the casual commentary all he could seem to manage was, "Excuse me?"

Zach shrugged. "Best breakfast I've had in a while."

When Ty only stared, Zach kept yammering on.

"Certainly the prettiest scenery I've had for breakfast in a *long* while. Maybe ever. Something about sweet—"

"That'll be enough," Ty interrupted, pushing away from the table.

"What? Am I breaking some Carson code? Not supposed to admit a Delaney is pretty as a picture and nice to have around? Figured that nonsense was on the way out with the way everyone's pairing off. Carsons and Delaneys seem destined to end up saying 'I do' in this particular point in history." Zach stopped drying a plate, an overly thoughtful expression on his face. "She's a Delaney. Technically I'm a Carson. I suppose—"

"I said, that'll be enough."

Zach surprised him by laughing and turned back to finishing the dishes. "You've got it *bad*."

Ty blinked. "I don't—"

"I don't see much point in denying everything. Everyone seems to know you two had something way back when, and it doesn't take my former FBI training to figure out it's still simmering under the surface." He shrugged negligently as he put away the last plate. "Why don't you do something about it instead of stomping around snarling like a lion with a thorn in its paw?"

It was horrifying to be seen through so easily by someone he barely knew, so he went for derision. "Yeah, let's just forget the unstable maniac shooting arrows at us."

"Haven't seen an arrow yet today. Even unstable maniacs have to rest, and the fact of the matter is, your brain's going to be a lot clearer if you do something other than brood."

"I don't brood."

"You do an excellent imitation of it, then."

"What business is that of yours?" Ty demanded sharply.

Zach raised an eyebrow with enough condescension in his expression to remind Ty irritably of Grady.

"Absolutely none," Zach replied, pleasantly enough. He wiped his hands on a dish towel and nodded toward the door. "I'm going to set up the cameras like we talked about."

How that made Ty feel guilty was beyond him. He had nothing to feel guilty about. Zach might technically be his cousin, but it wasn't like they'd grown up together. He hadn't even known Zach existed until a couple of months ago. Why would he take advice or ribbing from a virtual stranger?

But as Zach stepped outside, his pack with all its surveillance equipment and computer nonsense on his back, Ty felt *awash* in familial guilt—the kind he hadn't entertained for a very long time. He shook his head and walked to the room he'd given over to Zach last night to just have a second of privacy to…something.

But he had to pass by the open door to the room Jen was in, where she was happily making the bed—whistling. Her cheerfulness scraped across every last raw nerve.

He scowled at her back. "Hart. Zach. You really go for the law-and-order type."

She straightened, leveling him with a look he didn't recognize. "I suppose it's better than the idiot, pea-brained jealous-for-no-reason type." She smiled at him, a surprisingly vicious edge to it.

There had to be something a little screwy in him that even as irritation simmered in his gut, he liked the idea of Jen getting a little vicious. "I am not jealous." Which he knew, very well, was the thing someone said when that was exactly the ugly thing worming around in the person's gut.

Zach calling her pretty, even if it was just to mess with him—it made him feral. It made him want to stake some claim he had no business claiming.

"No, not jealous," Jen said with a dismissive edge. "You just have to be snotty anytime another man even acknowledges I exist. Even though *you* don't acknowledge I exist half the time. Wouldn't, if I wasn't being threatened because of something *you* did."

"Is that some kind of complaint? Pretty sure you've been avoiding me as skillfully as I've been avoiding you since I've been home."

"So you admit it, then?"

"Admit what?"

"That you've avoided me."

He couldn't figure her out, or why there was now a headache drumming at his temples and all he really wanted to do was scoop her up and make good use of that freshly made bed. "Why's that an admission? We were both doing it."

She stepped closer, poked him in the chest. "Yeah, we both were. We both were. I thought it was because you didn't care, but what an idiot I was. It was because you felt the same way I did."

He crossed his arms over his chest, trying to look disdainful instead of whatever uncomfortable thing fluttered in his chest, squeezing his lungs. "And what way's that?"

"Hurt. You were hurting just as I was." She searched

his face, so he did everything he could to keep it impassable.

Hurt had always been the enemy. You showed you were hurt, you got knocked around a little extra hard. Literal or metaphorical in his experience with life.

But here she was, calling it what it was, saying they'd both been walking around with it deep inside them. She was cracking away at something inside him, letting something loose he wouldn't name. Couldn't.

"You know what? I wish I *did* go for the 'law and order' type. I wish Hart or Zach were exactly what I wanted out of life. They're both polite. Kind. Good men who want to do the right thing and aren't afraid to admit it. In other words, the antithesis of *you*. But I..." She took a deep breath and squared her shoulders. She looked like she was getting ready to do battle, and he was...

Scared. That thing she was pulling out of him, that feeling a strong, immovable Carson was never supposed to feel over some *woman*. It stole over him, shamed him deeply that he was bone-deep scared of what this slip of a woman was going to say to him.

He allowed himself to recognize the fear, acknowledge it. Even accepted the fact it was worse than any fear he'd had in the army, because death hadn't seemed so bad. At least it would have been a noble one.

There was nothing noble or impressive about being scared of the woman who held your heart. No. So he would not be a coward no matter how he felt like one. He squared, too, and prepared for the blow.

"I love you," she said, and she certainly knew every one of those words was an unerring bullet against his heart. "Yeah, I love you, you big, overbearing moron.

I have always loved you and I always will. And I want to punch you. And I'm still mad at the way you left, but understanding it means I can forgive, and I *do*."

"Don't." He choked it out, rough and telling. But the emotion that clogged his throat, that made his heart feel too big and beating in his chest, was winning against all control. It was this, right here, that had been his reason for leaving her without saying goodbye.

He wouldn't have ever been able to look at her and hide all those things he felt. He wasn't strong enough to hurt her, even for her own good. Not to her face anyway. He'd never be strong enough for that.

"It'd be awful for you, wouldn't it?" she asked, tears swimming and making her eyes look luminous. "If I didn't hold a grudge. If I just forgave you. Because then you'd have to forgive yourself, and that's the one thing you've never been any good at."

"I said stop."

"No, no. I'm done stopping for someone else's comfort." She stepped so close he could smell her, that light feminine scent that always seemed to float around her. He could feel the warmth of her—not just generic body warmth, but that piece of her soul that had drawn him long before he'd been willing to admit souls even existed.

Was he willing to admit that now? He didn't know.

When she touched him, her palm to his heart, he winced. The look she shot him was triumphant. Determined. And so damn strong he thought she might bring him to his knees.

"I love you," she said, her eyes never leaving his. "I *want* you."

He tried to move away, but so much of him was

suddenly made out of lead and her hand fisted in his shirt, keeping him right where he was. In this nightmare where she said things he wanted and shouldn't have.

Couldn't. The word is couldn't.

"And what scares you, what horrifies you, is that you love and want me, too," she continued, hammering every last nail in the coffin that was his self-control. His belief that he could control his life, his emotions, his choices.

"But you know you'd have to forgive yourself for that love. You'd have to look back at seventeen-year-old Ty and think he actually did the best he could in the situation he was given. You'd have to look back at little ten-year-old Ty and forgive him for letting his dad knock him and his brother around, forgive yourself for not killing him when he started knocking Vanessa around, too. There's so much you'd have to stop blaming yourself for to admit you love me, that we deserve each other—then and now."

If there were words to be salvaged out of this nightmare, he didn't have them. She must have taken them all, because they kept pouring out of her.

"I should have said all that to you when you got back into town, because I knew it then even when I didn't know why you left. I've always known it. But I was too afraid to tell you what I knew, what I saw. I wanted to make you comfortable instead of making us…well, what would have endured. But I was seventeen, too. Young and scarred in my own ways, because we *always* are, Ty. All of us. Scarred and scared and uncertain. We're all doing the best we can with what we have."

He closed his eyes, but her other hand came to his cheek. He didn't want to believe her. She had to hate him for what he'd done—because he hated himself for the way he'd left. For the way he'd come back. He couldn't blame the latter on a young man with few choices. He'd been an adult, and he'd continued to act like she didn't matter.

Still, she touched him like forgiveness wasn't just possible. It was done. A given. Something she wouldn't take back.

"Open your eyes, Ty."

He did, because he seemed to have no power here. She was in control. She gave the orders, and he obeyed, excellent soldier that he was.

But it was more than that. No matter how much he didn't want to believe he could have her, no matter how much he knew he didn't deserve her, his heart still wanted.

"I love you," she said, and it didn't hurt so much the second time. "And you love me. That's where we'll start."

So much of his scars and his past fought to win, to deny. But she was touching him, staring at him. Drowning in her eyes, he lost the battle with himself.

"No. This is where we start," he replied, covering her mouth with his.

They didn't know they were being watched.

Chapter 13

It was home. Ty's kiss had always been exactly where Jen belonged, and somehow she had made it happen again.

So she threw herself into it, into him, wrapping herself around him with what she might have called desperation just days ago.

But she wasn't desperate. No. She was determined. She had finally figured out what she wanted, what she was willing to fight for, and it didn't matter if they were hiding out from danger or if they went home to Bent right now.

He was hers.

His hands streaked over her, rough and possessive. She returned the favor. He scraped his teeth across her bottom lip, so she dug her fingernails into his shoulders. Her knees buckled, but he held her up hard against his chest.

And then it all softened, as if all the tension simply leaked out of him. As if he was giving in to more than just the driving attraction that had always been between them. His mouth softened, his hands gentled. He held her as if she was spun glass and kissed her as if she were the center of his universe.

He was giving in to love.

She'd chosen it years ago, but she hadn't been mature enough to understand that. She'd called it fate or divine intervention, but it had been her. Her wanting him, and his wanting her. She'd been afraid of the consequences, but that had only made it more exciting.

Ten years later the excitement wasn't in thwarting her family's expectation, it was in the choice. In the knowledge of all that time, in the changes she'd made inside herself and the changes she hadn't made, he was still where she belonged.

The dull ring of a phone pierced the fog in her brain, but with her body humming and desperate for more of Ty, she didn't really acknowledge it. It couldn't be all that important, could it? Not as important as this.

Except, of course, it might be. Because they were not just realizing and deciding all these big, life-changing things in the midst of a normal day.

She managed to move her mouth away from his, though she kept her arms tight around him, and couldn't resist pressing a kiss to his jaw. "Phone."

"Nah." His hands slid up under her shirt, over the cotton of her bra. Hot and rough, he dragged his fingertips across the peaks of her nipples.

"It could, uh…" What was she talking about? It was hard to remember with need curling low in her stomach.

But the phone kept jangling and somewhere in the fog of desperate lust she understood… "It could be important."

"Why would it—" He managed to lift his head, his expression as dazed as she felt. But he narrowed his eyes. "I guess it could be." But the sound died and they looked at each other, still holding on, still not close enough.

He lowered his mouth. "We'll just forget—"

But it immediately started ringing again and they both sighed. Ty let her go, and she had to sink onto the bed. Her legs simply wouldn't hold her.

He pulled the phone out of his pocket, frowned at the screen, then handed it to her. "Your sister. Why don't you answer it."

Jen cocked her head at the screen as she swiped to answer. "We can talk about why my sister is in your phone as Deputy PITA later." She lifted the receiver to her ear and answered, trying to sound breezy and light.

She was pretty sure she sounded deranged.

"Is everything okay?" Laurel asked without preamble, worry enhancing the demand in her tone. "Are you safe?"

"Safe? Of course. Everything is great. Everything is… Yes."

There was a long, contemplative silence over the phone and Jen had to squeeze her eyes shut and try to get a hold of herself.

But what she really wanted was a hold of Ty and to banish this ache that felt as though it had been growing inside her for a decade.

"You were commandeered to the Carson cabin by your ex—who left you without explanation ten years ago. You're in danger because someone who wants to hurt him thinks hurting you will do the trick. But you're great?"

Though Jen had gotten her breathing somewhat closer to being in control, she couldn't look at Ty or she'd never be able to have a coherent conversation. So, she stared at her lap and focused on the fact Laurel was calling them.

"I'm just making the best out of a bad situation," she offered brightly.

"Is that best in Ty Carson's pants?"

"Laurel!" Jen managed through strangled laughter. It was a little too apt.

"Well, you're panting like you're running away from a bad guy or…"

"Did you call for a reason?" Jen asked primly, wondering just how red her cheeks were and just what Ty would read into her embarrassment over her sister's seeing right through her even over the phone.

"Yes. Actually. I want to talk to both of you on Speaker, and Zach if he's there. I think I'm hoping he's not there or things would be weird."

"He's out putting up some of his surveillance equipment," Jen grumbled.

"Okay, that's fine. You can fill him in. Put me on Speaker. Unless Ty's naked. I don't want to talk to Ty on Speaker if he's naked."

"He's not…" Fumbling with his phone, Jen managed to switch on Speaker. She avoided Ty's steady gaze even though she felt it boring into her. She cleared her throat. "Laurel has some news."

"The DNA on your notes matches Braxton Lynn," Laurel announced. "And here's where things get interesting. We looked into the name you gave us, Ty. Oscar

Villanueva of Minnow, Arizona. Turns out he and Braxton Lynn lived in the same group home for four years."

"He's connected to Oscar," Ty said dully.

Jen reached out and gave his hand a squeeze. Though she didn't know why it should hit him hard, she could tell from that voice devoid of all emotion it *did* hit him.

"Yes. I'm still working on information, but Braxton's behavior became erratic after Oscar left for the army. Bounced around different foster situations, and I wouldn't be surprised if he had some criminal issues, but I don't have any access to juvenile records. Which is why I want you to pass that along to Zach."

"You're telling me you, Ms. Law and Order, know full well Zach is hacking into closed files?" Ty asked incredulously.

"Don't sound so surprised. I *am* married to Grady. Something had to rub off. Besides, I'm not asking him to. I just know he can and probably is. So, give him the name and if he finds anything, I want to know. My men searched the woods. A few footprints, but nothing concrete enough to figure out where he disappeared to, so I want you two to stay put for the time being. Now that we're sure that it's him, we should be able to round him up soon enough."

"Where's Oscar?" Ty asked.

There was no answer, only the slight buzz of a phone connection. Jen looked up, her heart twisting at that blank expression on his face.

"Laurel." Ty's voice was quiet and calm, but Jen could see the tension in him underneath that stoic mask.

"It seems as if Oscar's been in a lot of trouble since he got out of the army," Laurel said gently, and vaguely

Jen noted. "Since he was *kicked* out of the army I should say, but you knew that, didn't you?"

"Yeah, I knew."

"Is it possible that has something to do with Braxton's fixation on you? Oscar, his foster brother, was booted out, and you went into the rangers?"

Jen watched Ty rake his hands through his hair. And there it was—all that guilt he heaped upon himself. "Yeah. Not possible. Probable. I reported Oscar's dependence on drugs and alcohol to our superiors. It directly resulted in Oscar's discharge."

"You didn't think to tell me that a little sooner?" Laurel demanded.

"No, I didn't. I didn't think they could be connected. Or maybe I didn't want them to be. I'll apologize for that, but it doesn't change anything."

"We should focus on Braxton," Jen said. She tried to reach for Ty's hand again, but he moved away from her. Out of reach. "Obviously he blames Ty for something, but Oscar having some trouble with the law—"

"He's in prison."

Jen closed her eyes. She didn't know the man, and yet her heart ached for what this would all do to Ty.

"I have to go," Laurel said, sounding understandably tired. No doubt she was putting in too many hours on top of pregnancy. "Fill Zach in. Keep yourselves safe. Got it?"

"Yeah. Thanks, Laurel," Jen managed. "Keep us updated."

"I will. Stay safe."

The call ended and Jen looked at Ty. He had his back to her, so rigid. Everything about him radiated *do not touch* energy. Her first instinct was to give him space, even as her heart ached to touch him. To soothe.

Her heart had been leading her today, not her instincts. So, she'd be brave enough to follow her heart again. She crossed the room to him, wrapped her arms around him from behind and leaned her cheek against his back.

Ty didn't want her comfort. That was what he told himself. He didn't want soft arms or sweet words. It was better, so much better, when you learned to do without. Because you could forget. You could convince yourself you didn't need it.

God, he needed her. Even something as simple as this hug kept that heavy blackness of guilt from consuming him completely.

But it slithered along the edges. The connection to Oscar made so much sense. He'd thought about Oscar on and off over the years. Ty had always felt bad for the way things had shaken out, but he'd known Oscar was a liability to everyone around him. He thought getting him booted home might be some kind of a favor.

Instead it had been a life sentence. Prison.

How could it not be his fault? His action had directly led to Oscar's discharge. Maybe bad things would have happened to Oscar either way, but it was hard to hold on to that when he could only think of all the ways he could have done it differently.

"Don't," Jen murmured.

He stiffened. "Don't what?" he asked, knowing exactly what she'd say.

She moved to his front and reached up to brush her fingers over his close-cropped hair. "You know what.

Don't blame yourself for someone else's actions. We're too old for that now."

He could have shrugged her off. He could have ignored it all and focused on the task at hand: Braxton Lynn and his fixation on Jen. Instead, faced with her sympathetic brown eyes and her kiss and "I love yous" drifting through his mind, only the truth could spill out.

"I ratted him out, Jen. Now he's in prison. How am I not supposed to draw some conclusions on my guilt?"

"You informed your superiors of a problem because he was a potential threat—not just to others, but to himself."

"How did you…" But he realized she didn't *know* it. She just figured it out. She was always good at that—working out why people felt the way they did, thought the way they did, acted the way they did.

"So, say it."

He didn't want to. Partially because he couldn't believe it and partially because of that same emotion that had jolted him earlier. Fear. But again, he wouldn't let fear win. "It wasn't my fault," he intoned, even though it was a lie.

"Now, work on believing it." She smiled and then lifted on her toes to brush her mouth against his.

She kissed him like she believed he was worthy of it or her. She always had, and he'd figured it for a lack in judgment. A lack he took advantage of because he couldn't help himself.

But her judgment was just fine, and she understood him all too well. Still she loved him. Over years and distance, she loved him and was willing to forgive him. Forgive *him*.

"What are we going to do about this?" he asked, and he didn't have to specify which *this*. She clearly knew. She smiled. "Embrace it."

He watched the man. He still hadn't figured out who this third wheel was, and he didn't like it.

He didn't like anything right now. Through the night he'd managed to drill a hole in the room he'd figured to be a bedroom based on one of the few windows and cheerful curtains.

All while cops had tramped around in the night, loud and stupid, he had worked. It had been so easy to stand in the shadow against the cabin and quietly and carefully drill his hole. Everyone said his old-fashioned tools were pointless. But they were quiet. They were gruesomely effective.

He'd gotten a perfect hole to insert the tiny camera. Modern technology had its place, too. He appreciated the old and the antique of a simpler, better time, but Oscar had taught him how to use the modern, too. He'd taught him to drive when no one in that house had cared about him.

Oscar had been his big brother. They didn't need blood to have a bond.

But then Oscar had left. Tempted away by the army and their lies about bravery and courage and meaning something.

He would have followed. Had planned on it. But then Oscar had gotten thrown out.

Ty's fault.

Oscar had started getting into trouble. Oscar hadn't wanted him around anymore.

Ty's fault.

All of it, all the bad before he'd finally gotten his brother back was Ty's fault.

Maybe he'd been a little grateful for Oscar's prison time, because Oscar didn't have a choice anymore. If Oscar wanted a visit from the outside, it was from him. He didn't tell Oscar that, though. Instead, he told Oscar he would make everything right. Balance the scales so they were brothers again.

Oscar had liked the idea. Liked the idea of hurting anyone who'd harmed him.

First it was the girl in Phoenix. She'd led Oscar on, and then Oscar had had no choice but to hurt her. But Oscar had landed in jail, and the girl had gotten off scot-free.

He'd fixed that, and Oscar had been very appreciative. Oscar had even called him *brother* again.

He had to close his eyes to rid them of the tears that clouded his vision. They'd been brothers again.

And once he paid back Ty for all the ways he'd hurt Oscar, they'd be a real family. For good. No matter what.

He narrowed his eyes at the man walking out of the stables. This stranger was putting up surveillance equipment.

That wouldn't do.

He knelt and pulled the pack off his back and surveyed his weapon options. He wanted to save the bear traps for Ty, though anyone who wandered across them would be fine, but he wouldn't lure this stranger to one. The arrows were for Jen. She needed some comeuppance for the way she'd let Ty touch her.

The gun would probably be too loud. He pulled the pistol out, aimed it, pretended to fire. Then chuckled to himself. He was nothing if not resourceful. Why take out the stranger now when he could get two for the price of one?

And then Jen would be his.

She would need to be punished.

He was starting to ache for that. For her screams. For her blood.

She isn't your focus. She's only a tool to get to Ty.

But if she was only a tool, that meant whatever was left over could be his. Screams, blood and all.

Chapter 14

Jen managed only a few bites of her canned chili dinner. Zach had hacked into the juvenile records system, and his expression was grim as he got ready to tell them what he'd found. It made her stomach churn.

"Unfortunately, this isn't the kind of record I'd want to see knowing said person is out there haunting the woods."

"That bad?"

"It looks like it started small. He's got some vague notes in his foster files about erratic behavior, threats of violence. A few assault charges he was given some leeway on since he was so young and bounced around. Things kind of level off, then spike up again right around the time Oscar would have left for the army. Stalking, assault—mostly against women. It looks like he had mandatory counseling as he got closer to eighteen."

"Clearly it solved all his problems," Ty returned drily.

"Record-wise? It seems to have helped. He doesn't have anything as an adult. Not so much as a speeding ticket. He left the group home as soon as he could. Had trouble keeping a job, but other than that…"

"Mostly against women," Jen murmured, turning that small piece of information over in her mind. It had to be relevant, and possibly the key. "And yet, his anger is directed at Ty, but he's chosen me as a target."

"He views you as weaker. A safer target," Zach offered.

"Yes. His behavior now… He has to know he's going to get in trouble—after years of not getting into any."

"Just because there's no record of it doesn't mean he didn't do anything wrong. It just means he wasn't caught," Ty pointed out.

"It's more likely," Zach agreed. "The lengths to which he's willing to go now doesn't point to an emotionally stable soul, or a man who was rehabilitated, then snapped back."

"If his violence is typically against women, then that's our answer." It explained the lack of action. She was stuck in a cabin with a former army ranger and a former FBI agent, so that would be threatening to Braxton. If they were going to draw him out, end this, it needed to be with someone he didn't find threatening. It just made sense. But then Ty laughed.

Not a real laugh—a harsh, sarcastic sound that had her bristling. "No," he said simply, as if she'd outlined her plan out loud, as if his word was final.

"You don't know what I was going to say."

"Of course I know what you were going to say.

You're a Delaney, aren't you?" He pushed out of his chair and began to pace.

She was surprised enough by the angry strides to be quiet for a few seconds. He wasn't even trying to hide his irritation. It simmered around him plain as day, with every footstep one way and every whirl to pace in the opposite direction. Which wasn't like Ty at all.

"I don't know what being a Delaney has to do with the fact that a woman won't be threatening to him, and we need to draw him out."

"Addie did the same thing, didn't she?" Ty demanded, eyes blazing. "She tried to use herself as bait. And what happened?"

Jen frowned. She hated to think back to the way Addie had been kidnapped and hurt. Terrorized really, but she'd survived. And the man who'd hurt her couldn't anymore. "This isn't the same as the *mob*, Ty. I believe you pointed that out to me just a few days ago when I reminded you that Noah bringing Addie here hadn't exactly worked out for them back then."

"You're not going to be the lure, darling, so get it out of your head."

"Oh, well, you've told me," she replied, letting the sarcasm drip from her tone without trying to soften it any. She pretended to salute him. "Yes, sir. Et cetera."

Zach cleared his throat. "Maybe I could be the tie-breaker?"

They both glared at him with such venom he cleared his throat again. "And maybe I'll leave you two to argue it out. I'll go to my room and, er, watch the surveillance tape."

Jen didn't even watch him go. She turned her glare back to Ty. He was scowling at her.

"Do you think I'm weak?" she demanded.

He didn't even flinch, or hesitate. "No."

She had to admit it soothed her irritation a little bit. Until he kept talking.

"But I think this is my fight. And you know what? Ten years in the military, yeah, I think I've got a little better handle on a psychopath who hates women than you do."

"That's doesn't mean—"

"Yes, it does. You will stay put. You will do as I say."

"Do as you…" Rage tinged her vision red. "You think you can order me around simply because I love you? Well, think again, Mister."

"Are you really going to keep saying that?"

"Yes, I am. I love you a million times over, but you will not boss me around like I'm still seventeen and need a keeper. What we have now is an adult relationship, Ty, and we're going to treat each other like adults."

He stared at her. All that irritable energy that had been pumping off him was gone, somehow wrapped up and shoved beneath this impenetrable veneer.

Then he softened. Not so much visibly—he was still all rigid military muscle, but that fighter's light in his eyes dimmed and he stepped toward her.

"I can't stand the thought of it, Jen," he said, his voice rough as he laid his hands on her shoulders. "You getting hurt in all this."

She didn't smile, though she wanted to. It was almost as if her whole life had been building to this moment—danger mixed with love, hope mixed with fear. "Tell me why," she murmured, leaning into him. "Besides your incessant need to heap guilt upon yourself."

For a hair of a second he went stiff, and honestly it

soothed her as well as the gradual softening, the way his arms came around her. It wasn't *easy* for him to love her. She'd always known that. It was the fact he'd do it anyway that had always meant the world to her. Love meant facing down all his fears and guilt, and he did so. For her.

It made the forgiveness for all that had come before easier and easier. It watered the seeds of determination until fear didn't have room to grow.

They'd come through this because they'd come so far. They'd find a way to work together to get home because now they got to go home together.

"I can't stand the thought of you getting hurt because I love you. Which you said you already knew," he grumbled.

"Doesn't hurt to hear." She sighed. "We're a team. I'm not a person you're protecting," she muttered into his chest. "It's not fair to use love against me to try to keep me safe and locked away."

He kissed her hair. "Who said I was going to be fair?"

"We have to do something. We can't stay shut up here forever. I have to get back to my store. I have to— we have to—get back to our lives. I don't want to wait around for the next note. I want to go home."

He pulled her back, though he held on to her shoulders. He looked into her eyes.

"I'll get you home. I promise you that."

"I don't need you to. I need you to work with me. For the three of us to work as a team so we can *all* go home. I want you to promise me we're in this together, not that you'll get me home."

He pulled a face, but he didn't let her go, didn't move away. So she traced her fingers along his scruffy jaw.

"I need that promise from you, Ty. As much as I need your love. Love might exist without teamwork and communication, but I think we both learned it doesn't *work* without it."

He sighed heavily, clearly struggling to agree, even though there was no way he could disagree. It was their simple truth, whether either of them liked it or not.

"I can't promise not to act instinctively to protect you. I can't promise to let you get hurt if I see a way around it, even if it hurts me. I can't promise you that."

"So, what are you going to promise me?"

"Just how demanding is new Jen going to be?"

She grinned at him, because she liked the idea. New Jen and more *demanding*. No, she'd never demanded things for herself. But now she would. Because life didn't protect the good girls who bent over backward to make other people happy, any more than it protected women who did the opposite. Life was undiscerning, and there was no cosmic reward of safety.

"Yeah, I think new Jen is demanding, but fair."

He swept his hand over the crown of her head. "New Jen's not so bad."

"Uh-huh. So, where's my promise?"

He grunted, but he held on to her shoulders, kept her gaze. "I promise that the three of us work together to get home safely. No secrets, no sacrificial plans. We're going to be smart. And we're going to work together."

Jen rose to her toes and pressed her mouth to his. "That's a fine promise."

He wasn't happy about the promise. In fact, it sat heavy in his gut like a weight through the rest of the evening. Just like the knowledge Oscar was in prison. Just like the knowledge Jen was right.

They couldn't stand around waiting for the guy to make a move. Eventually they had to go home.

It was a surprise to him that Jen had flipped it all on its head. He wanted to go home. He wanted to live that life they'd planned, but with this new version of themselves—strong and smarter and capable of facing down the world. Facing Bent and her father and the incessant ribbing they'd surely get from their siblings and cousins.

He welcomed that.

He'd been a coward. He could admit that now, in the dark on this uncomfortable couch. Grady had been right. He ran away, not from dangerous situations, but from emotions. From love and hope and the things his childhood had taught him were traps.

But his brother, his cousins and Jen had all proved that wrong for him, and it was time to stop being ruled by his past. By the guilt of the abused.

He looked over at the door to the room Jen was in. He'd given Zach the other bedroom since the guy had all sorts of equipment. Besides, didn't he deserve to be the one on the couch since this was all his fault?

But Jen didn't blame him. Not for any of it. She loved him, forgave him and thought they could embrace a future together

It had only taken a threat against her for him to see it, believe it might be possible. There was guilt there, too, and he knew it would be easy to stay on this uncomfortable couch and drown in it. He'd always let himself drown in it, considered his guilt so brave.

But Jen had called it childish, and as much as he wanted to tell himself—and her—that she didn't know what she was talking about, of course she did. She'd always known what she was talking about more than he did.

He rolled off the couch, surprised to find himself as shaky as he'd ever been facing down a dangerous mission.

This wasn't dangerous, but it was daunting. This wasn't life or death, but it was Jen's heart and for that he'd face life or death. He walked to the door to her room. He paused, breathing through the unfamiliar nerves.

If he went into this room, he was making promises he couldn't take back. He was accepting everything Jen had said. He was forgiving himself for a past he'd always blamed himself for.

Can you really do that?

He never thought the answer to that question would be yes, but it was. Because Jen had forgiven him, and she was the best person he knew. She had to be right in her forgiveness, so he'd believe in her, and forgiveness of self would follow.

He turned the knob, slipped into the dark room.

"Oh, Zach, is that you?" she murmured sleepily.

She was lucky he knew better. "You're a real laugh a minute."

She chuckled, so pleased with herself he couldn't help but find himself smiling in the dark. She'd always been his joy in the dark.

"What took you so long?" she demanded.

"I guess I had some things to work out." Even with no light, he knew exactly how many steps to the bed, what side she'd be sleeping on. He toed off his boots and then lowered himself onto the mattress.

She rolled into him, pulling the covers over him. No hesitation. She'd made her decision, and it wouldn't waver. He couldn't either.

He pulled her close, his decision made, no matter where it took them. "I don't take it lightly."

She snuggled in. "I know. I don't either." She pressed a kiss to his jaw. "Make love to me, Ty."

"I figured a rousing game of gin rummy would be more my speed."

"Hmm." She kissed his temple, his cheek, his neck. "Are you sure about that?" she murmured, her hand drifting under his T-shirt.

He rolled her underneath him. "On second thought."

She laughed, tugging at his shirt. "Oh, hurry. It's been too long."

Far too long, so he did exactly what she asked. He hurried. They tugged off each other's clothes with more desperation than nimble fingers. He couldn't get enough of her, worse than the kiss earlier today because she was naked underneath him. His. Always.

They came together on a sigh, and it didn't matter his skin had scars and her curves had changed. They were the same here. Soul to soul. So he held her there, connected completely. So completely it didn't even bother him to feel the wetness of her tears on his shoulder. This was so big, so important, tears seemed vital.

"I love you," she whispered.

He said it back, for the first time without even an ounce of a twinge of guilt or regret, because she'd washed them away, with her love and forgiveness. All that was left in their wake was determination and surety.

So he moved, with slow, sure strokes, drawing her pleasure out with lazy patience. She chanted his name, rained kisses over his face, begged him for more, and still he kept a brutally easy pace.

Then she arched against him, scraping the lobe of his ear between her teeth. "All of you," she said, fingers digging into his arms. "I want all of you."

It unlocked that last piece of himself, and he gave her exactly what she asked for. All of him, every ounce of himself to her. Always and forever her.

They fell over that bright pulsing edge together, entwined tightly in each other. So tightly he was sure it took hours to unwind themselves from each other. Eternity to move off her, though he pulled her to him.

They lay there, breath slowing to normal, hearts eventually calming. And for the very first time in a very long time, he felt something like peace.

But they weren't ready for peace yet. Something evil still lurked out there, and they had to vanquish it before they could have their peace.

"I won't let anything happen to you, and you can get all prickly over that and go on about teamwork, but it doesn't change the simple truth I won't *let* anything happen to you."

She was quiet for a long moment, drawing gentle patterns across his chest. In the end, she didn't respond to that at all. She simply sighed. "I've missed you, Ty."

"I missed you, too, Jen." Never again would he let anything keep them apart that way. Not himself, and certainly not some maniac bent on terror.

Jen will die.

He wanted to carve those words into his skin, but he settled for the tree trunk. It was dark, a blackness that suited everything about his mood. Clouds had rolled in and not even the moon shone.

He couldn't see where he carved, but he carved the words anyway.

Jen will die.

Jen will die.

She'd let Ty touch her, and so she would die.

His hands cramped, and still he carved. Carved and carved trying to get rid of the need to carve the words into his own skin.

It would be her soon enough. The wait would have to be over.

At sunrise, his plan would begin.

Jen will die.

And Ty would watch.

Chapter 15

Jen awoke the next morning with a contentment completely incongruous to the situation she found herself in.

She *knew* she should be worried and focused on the trouble at hand, but Ty's warm body next to her was everything she wanted, and the worry wouldn't win.

If there was anything she'd learned from the past year of troubles and fear for her family, it was that love endured. Hers and Ty's had endured all this time apart, and it would endure whatever danger the universe indiscriminately threw at them.

A few threatening notes and one arrow through a window were hardly going to take away this satisfied contentment, and that was that.

Her stomach growled, more than a little empty after she'd only picked at her dinner last night. She figured the numerous times they'd turned to each other in the night had burned off quite a few calories.

She looked at Ty's face in the dim glow of dawn filtering through the curtains. So strong and stern, even in sleep. It made her smile. It made her want to press her mouth to his. But her stomach was insistent and she figured Ty could use some extra sleep.

She slid out of bed and moved as quietly as possible for the door. The wind was rattling the cabin walls and it seemed to muffle the sound of her footsteps. She opened the door and peeked back at him. He didn't wake up, so she closed the door quietly behind her and went for the kitchen.

There was some bacon in the freezer she could defrost, along with some frozen hash browns she could fry up. She was in the mood for a deliciously filling, greasy breakfast and would be happy to putter about the kitchen for a bit. It would keep her mind occupied and her nerves settled.

She moved quietly around the kitchen, even let herself daydream about once this was all over. Would they spend the night at his place or hers? She couldn't imagine living above Rightful Claim, and not just because it would give her father a heart attack…but so would the alternative.

A Carson tramping around the apartment above the Delaney General Store. The thought made her smile.

A door creaked and she looked up, trying to hide her disappointment when it was Zach coming out of his bedroom door rather than Ty coming out of theirs.

He peered over at what she was doing. "You know you're an angel, right?"

She smiled at him. "An angel of fat."

"I'll take it. First I'm going to head out. One of the cameras is down. Could have been some animal interference, but I want to get it back up and running."

She frowned at Zach as he unlocked the door. "Don't you think you should wait? You shouldn't go out there alone."

"It's a typical malfunction." He held up his phone and tapped the screen. "I've got all the cameras tied in here, so I can look in all directions. I'll know if someone's out there before they know I am. Plus I'm carrying." He patted the gun at his hip. "You can watch me on the video on my computer in my room if you're nervous—I've got everything set up, you just have to walk in. Where's Ty?"

"Uh." He was still in her bed, fast asleep. Even though she wasn't embarrassed of being with Ty per se, it was a little awkward considering they were sharing a cabin with Zach. "He's, uh…" Her bedroom door opened and Ty stepped out, sleep rumpled and shirtless. "There."

"Ah." But Zach didn't say anything else. Just nodded his head and opened the door.

"Where are you going?"

"Jen'll fill you in." With that, he left and closed the door behind him.

Ty frowned, flipping the lock before turning to her. "He leaving us to our own devices?"

"A camera is down. He's going to check it out. Apparently he can see all the feeds on his phone and we shouldn't worry about it, but I don't like it."

"Me neither. I'll get dressed and head out there."

"I don't like that either," Jen muttered, but not loud enough for him to hear. She had no better ideas. Only dread creeping across all those places that had been happy and hopeful just a few moments before.

Ty returned, dressed in jeans and a T-shirt, boots on and laced. He'd fastened on his old Wild West–style holster that seemed more ominous than just part of his personal Carson style today.

"He said we can watch him on his computer. It's all set up. Maybe we should just do that? Zach was an FBI agent. I feel like we should trust him a little."

"Shows what you know. FBI agents are a bunch of pencil pushers," Ty grumbled, but he strode for Zach's room instead of the door. Jen focused on breakfast prep as Ty returned with a laptop. He placed it on the kitchen table so she could see it out of the corner of her eye and he could sit at the table and watch.

On the screen were six boxes. Five of them showed areas around the cabin, but one was completely black.

"That must be the broken one," Ty murmured, sliding into a seat and watching the screen intently.

Then they were quiet, the only sounds Jen cooking up the hash browns and then the bacon. She plated breakfast, all daydreams lost to reality. When she slid into the seat next to Ty, they ate in continued silence, watching the screen of Zach's laptop. Occasionally Zach would appear in one box, then disappear.

The black screen popped back to life, showing a swath of trees moving with the wind.

"That's the view from the back of the cabin, right?" Jen asked. Though she'd lost her appetite to nerves, and now had a vague headache threatening at the base of her head, she forced herself to eat. She didn't want to admit that she was keeping her strength up in case they had to fight or run, but that was exactly the thought that prompted her to eat.

"Yeah, that's the one he fixed up on the roof. West corner." Ty chewed bacon thoughtfully. "I guess it could be as simple as the wind knocking it off. It's been blowing hard half the night."

"Zach said maybe animal interference."

Ty nodded. "That, too."

"It seems...far-fetched it'd be something that simple. That unthreatening."

Ty shrugged. "That's only because we're being threatened. Wind. Animals. Those things happen regardless of human threat."

She studied his profile. On the surface he seemed calm, but there was something about the way he ate. Mechanically, his eyes never drifting from the computer screen. "You're worried."

He flicked her a glance. "I'll worry about everything until this is over."

Yes, they both would. She turned her attention to the computer screen as well, and watched as Zach appeared and then disappeared again. "Maybe we should go out and tell him he fixed it."

"I think he knows. He's just checking the others."

The video flickered and all six sections of the screen went black for a moment before coming back.

Ty narrowed his eyes, moved closer to study the screen. "That look different to you?"

It didn't, but the cold feeling seeping into her skin definitely didn't help matters. "Something isn't right."

"Yeah. You keep watching, I'll go out and check."

"Ty—"

But he held up a hand and pulled a key out of his pocket. He walked over to the couch, stuck the key in the small end table's drawer, and then pulled out her phone. "You keep watch and call or text me if you see anything on the screen I should watch out for."

"But if someone is out there, the ringer—"

He pulled out his phone. "I'll set it to vibrate."

"He could still hear—"

"Do you have a better idea?" Ty asked, and it wasn't laced with heat or derision. It was an honest question. "With Zach out there and something not right? I'm all ears, Jen, but I don't think we have time."

"Go. Be careful. Please."

He brushed a kiss over her cheek as he headed determinedly for the door. Jen didn't beg him to stay, though she wanted to. But she would be strong and she would be smart. She gripped her phone and watched all six boxes on the computer screen.

She was like the control tower. Much as it might feel like she was separate and doing nothing, she had an important function here.

So, she watched, waiting for Zach or Ty to appear. She frowned at the way the wind outside shrieked and made the entire house groan, then looked back at Zach's computer screen. Nothing moved. Not a tree, not a leaf, not a blade of grass.

Oh God. She jumped to her feet. Something was all wrong. She swiped open her phone and punched in Ty's number as she strode for the door.

It didn't ring. Nothing happened. She looked down at the screen. It was black. She hit the home button and tapped the screen, but nothing.

Her phone had died.

And Ty and Zach were out there and the cameras had been tampered with.

Something was off. The knowledge crept along Ty's skin as if he were walking through spider webs. But even when he checked his phone, there was no message from Jen so everything must be all right.

At least where the cameras were. There were spots the cameras didn't reach, so there could still be something wrong. Someone could be lurking, watching.

He walked carefully along the perimeter of the cabin, one hand on his phone and one on the handle of his gun in its holster. He watched the woods and saw nothing but the trees swinging wildly in the tempestuous wind.

Ty realized now, seeing the actual scene before him, that the video had been frozen. No wind. No movement. Which meant Jen wouldn't be able to warn him if anything bad was coming because there was no real-time video feed going to her.

He pulled the gun out of its holster, flicked off the safety and watched. By the time he'd made a full path around the cabin and stables, Zach was nowhere to be found.

Dread pooled, but Ty didn't let worry grow out of it. He'd figure this out, with skills honed from the army and the rangers. He could take on one unbalanced lunatic, and would. Because people's lives were in danger, and it was...

He couldn't allow the guilt anymore. Not with Jen's words and I love yous in his head, but he could say this was his *responsibility*. His purpose was to keep Jen safe. And to find Zach.

Ty might not have felt a particular affinity for Zach, but he wasn't about to let anyone, especially a blood relation, be hurt over something that had to do with him. Besides, maybe Zach was busy kicking butt on his own. Ty would only be backup.

He could hope.

He texted Jen first, tried not to consider how irritated she'd be.

Trouble. Stay put. Call Laurel.

He shoved his phone in his pocket. Jen wouldn't be able to see anything to help him unless the video unfroze, and he didn't consider that likely, but it was still a better shot than having her come out here. Inside the cabin she was safe.

Ty walked the perimeter again, this time making his circle bigger. He searched the trees, paused to listen and wished he'd brought his binoculars.

At one pause before he made it back to the front door again, he heard a rustle. He moved toward it carefully, pretended to veer off in the wrong direction. He did it a few more times, always keeping the location of the first rustle in his mind as he made a very circular path toward it.

He caught sight of something black and ducked behind a tree, but the color didn't move. Carefully, inching forward by avoiding as many dry leaves and twigs as he could, Ty moved toward the color.

The closer he got, the surer he was the figure was human. Zach. Seated on the ground, which wasn't right at all. Ty took another step closer and could see he wasn't just sitting there whiling away the time, he was tied to the tree, his head lolled down, blood dripping from a wound to his temple.

The spurt of fear and need to help had him speeding forward but halfway through the step his military training kicked in. It could be a trick. It could be—

The pain was so quick, so sharp, so absolutely blinding he could only fall with a strangled breath. He landed hard on the unforgiving ground, writhing in pain and trying to stop his body's natural reaction because he had to think.

But it hurt so damn bad thoughts wouldn't form. Knives in his foot, clawing through him. Searing, tearing pain.

But the image of Zach tied to the tree, bloody, flashed into his brain and he bore down to focus. He moved himself into a sitting position and looked down at his foot.

He was caught in a trap of some kind. He focused on his breathing over the panic. He had to keep his head, and he concentrated on the in and out of breathing, and helping Zach, as he eyed the metal clawed onto his foot.

If there was a bright side, and it was a pretty dim one, it was that he'd tripped it so quickly that his thick work boots had taken some of the trauma. Though the blade had sliced through flesh and potentially bone, he wasn't likely to bleed out like he might have if the trap had gotten more of his leg.

Then he heard more than a rustle. Footfall and twigs snapping. He realized he'd dropped his gun in the fall, but that didn't mean he was weaponless. He just had to move for a knife and—

"Tsk. Tsk." The man from Rightful Claim and Jen's store stepped forward, gun trained not on Ty—but on

Zach. "And to think you were an army ranger. What an embarrassment."

Ty swallowed down the pain, the fear, and focused on the mission. Eliminating the threat. So, he flashed a grin. "Well, hi there, Braxton. It's about time."

All that was missing from this joyous scene was a chorus of angels. Everything—everything—had worked out. He almost wanted to cry, but instead he surveyed the man who had caused all his problems.

"Have you been waiting long?" he asked of Ty. Ty's stoic response did nothing to irritate him. Oscar was also very good at appearing unmoved. It was a military thing.

Inside, Braxton *knew*, Ty was scared. In pain.

He studied the bear trap. It hadn't taken quite the chunk out of Ty he might have hoped, but Ty was stuck, and in pain. He wished it was more, but Ty's casual greeting couldn't hide the pale pallor to his face, or the grimace of pain.

It was better that Ty was only marginally hurt, and thus would not just live but stay conscious through what he had planned.

Yes, everything was better this way. He looked at the other man, still unconscious. Alive, but bleeding.

Braxton smiled. This was good. So good. In fact, he realized in this moment that Dr. Michaels had been wrong. So wrong she deserved the beating and stabbing he'd given her. Yes, he remembered it now. Every beautiful plunge into her fragile skin and hard bone.

He hadn't killed her, but he'd done irreparable damage.

It had been right all along. That violence. That payback.

He didn't need what Dr. Michaels had told him. Not focus. Not a *goal*.

He needed only blood.

So, without another word, Braxton walked away, whistling.

The next part of his plan was more blood, and it was already in place.

Chapter 16

Jen had all the weapons she could find piled on the tabletop. Ignoring the way her arms shook, the way her head ached, she tried to figure different ways to carry as many guns and knives as possible on her person.

She refused to think about her dead phone, the dead landline she'd tried. She passed off the wave of dizziness that caught her as cowardly nerves and *refused* to give in to it.

She'd used Zach's computer to send an urgent email to Laurel, Cam, Grady and even the general email for the Bent County Sheriff's Department, but Zach's computer was so foreign to her she didn't have time to try to find an instant messaging service. She needed to protect herself, and she needed a plan.

A plan to protect the men out there trying to protect her.

Zach should be back by now, that was for sure, and the fact Ty wasn't caused her to worry, but she wouldn't worry uselessly. She would act.

Once it was loaded, she shoved a smaller gun into the waistband of her jeans. She fixed a sheathed knife into the side of her boot. One rifle had a strap, so she set it aside, ready and loaded.

She had to steady herself on the table. The dizziness wouldn't go away and the painful throbbing in her head wouldn't stop. For a moment, she thought she'd be sick.

She took a deep breath to center herself. Ty was a former army ranger and Zach was a former FBI agent. There was no way she was going to have to go out there and save their butts. They were either perfectly fine, or taking care of everything.

She could stay where she was. Maybe she was really sick or something.

She shook that ridiculous thought away. She was letting emotional nerves turn into physical responses, and she wouldn't be that weak or cowardly.

She would take precautions, go outside and search for Zach and Ty, armed to the teeth, and hope to God Laurel read her email and sent someone to help them.

Even though she was probably overreacting. If she found them out there, fine and in charge, she'd scold them both for scaring her to death.

And if they weren't, she'd fight for them the way they would fight for her. Maybe she wasn't as skilled, but she knew how to use a gun and she knew how to use her brain. Cowering inside wasn't acceptable. Not now.

Slowly, feeling sluggish and worse with every step, she hid the guns and knives she'd collected that she couldn't carry. But this time when she hid them, she put them places she would know where to get them. Places she might be able to reach if she needed to. Under couch cushions and under the sink in the bathroom.

More and more, she couldn't seem to think past the painful throbbing in her head. It was a heck of a time for her first migraine, but she wouldn't give in. Because Ty and Zach still weren't back and they should be.

They should be. So, even if things were fine, she had every right to be worried. To act. She gripped the table for a second, righting herself and breathing through the pain. She glanced at the computer screen, the six frozen boxes.

Except they weren't frozen anymore. Trees moved, grass swayed, and on one of the blocks, she saw two figures.

She swayed on her feet, nearly passed out, but it was Ty. Ty, caught in something. He couldn't seem to move his foot as he reached forward, fiddling with something around his foot. Zach was limp and clearly tied up. Since the feed was in black and white, she could only hope the smudge on his face was…anything except the blood it looked like it could be. Had to be if he was tied up.

No one showed up on any of the other screens, and Braxton or whoever had hurt them was nowhere to be seen. But they were hurt, and that made her decision.

She had to get to them. Save them. There was *no* choice. She slung the rifle over her shoulder and sprinted to the door. She fell forward, somehow grabbing onto the knob and keeping herself upright. She twisted, fought against the fog and the dizziness, then remembered she had to unlock the door.

It took too long to manage it. Why was fear making

her so sluggish? Why couldn't she be strong and brave? She *had* to be. Zach and Ty were hurt and they needed her. She had to be brave.

She managed to twist the knob and push the door open.

To a man.

She screamed. Or thought she did. But the next thing she knew she was on the floor, looking up into Braxton Lynn's face. He looked the same as he had in her store, but it reminded her more of when he'd held the note up to her door than when he'd thanked her for the candy bar.

Something was missing in his eyes, something human. His pleasant smile was all wrong. She was on the floor. She had to reach for her gun, but her limbs were so heavy. So heavy. They didn't move.

"Oopsie," Braxton said cheerfully, nudging her legs out of the way of the door with his boot before he closed the door and flipped the lock. "Looks like someone has themselves a little carbon monoxide poisoning. Isn't that a shame?"

Poison. God, it all made sense now, even as the black crept through her mind and she lost her tenuous grasp on consciousness.

Ty gritted his teeth against the pain, against the dull edge of shock trying to win. It couldn't. Zach was bleeding and Jen was on her own. Vulnerable and no doubt that madman was heading right toward her.

The way Braxton had simply studied the trap on Ty's foot, peered at Zach's limp body, then walked away, whistling, was all Ty needed to know to understand he was going for Jen now. That he didn't expect Ty or Zach to die. No, he wanted them alive for whatever was next.

Ty had to stop it. He had to escape this.

He'd tried to use whatever he could reach to pry the jaws of the trap open, but everything had broken off. He'd tried to pull the chain holding the trap down, but that had sent such a jolt of pain through him he'd almost passed out.

There had to be a way out of this. Had to be. He simply refused any scenario where he didn't free his foot and go save Jen.

Maybe she'd save herself. She was armed, and clearly stronger than Braxton gave her credit for if he thought the only thing that had kept her safe thus far had been him and Zach. Ty would believe Jen could handle herself, but he'd work like hell to get out of this and make sure she could.

He was about ready to test the give of the chain again when he heard a low sound. He wouldn't have thought it human, but Zach also moved a little, his head lolling, eyelids fluttering.

"Zach," Ty called. "Wake up. Now." They weren't too far apart, but Ty couldn't reach him. Could only watch as he still wavered somewhere just out of reach.

Ty wasn't about to give up on him. He kept talking, kept repeating Zach's name. "Zach. Come on, man. We need you now."

"Hurts," he mumbled. "Can't move."

"You're tied up to a tree. Some kind of head injury. Braxton's got us stuck here and Jen's alone in the cabin. He's going to hurt her if we don't do something. You need to come out of it."

"Can't see. Black."

"Open your eyes," Ty commanded, trying to sound like an officer, not a desperate man shouting at an injured one.

It took another few minutes of talking him through it, repeating the situation over and over again, until Zach's eyes opened and stayed open. Finally, after what felt like eons, he seemed close to himself.

"We have to get out of this," Zach said, looking around the wooded area they'd found themselves in. "I want to believe Jen can take care of herself, but he took us both out."

"It's our own stupid faults. He wouldn't have if we'd stayed inside." Ty leaned forward, trying to reach the chain of the trap to tug at with his hands. If he could reach it, he could pull it off whatever it was attached to and maybe walk with the damn thing on his foot.

"No, he would have gotten us. I've dealt with enough criminals and unbalanced individuals to know he's determined, and he won't stop until he gets what he wants, or someone stops him."

"I'll stop him," Ty said, a swear, a promise.

"And me." Zach rolled his shoulders. "The knots aren't great and he didn't tie my legs. I can get out of it. I just…" Zach swore, twisting his body one way and then the other. Ty might have been impressed if steel claws weren't digging into his foot. "I can get out of it," Zach said more firmly this time. He maneuvered his body this way and that, grimacing and wincing, but never losing consciousness again.

"How long had I been out?" he asked, then hissed in pain.

"Too damn long."

"I don't remember how it happened."

Ty recognized the disgust of failure and guilt in Zach's tone and knew it wouldn't serve them any. "Well, since I currently have my foot caught in what appears to be a bear trap, I can't cast stones. He's gone after Jen. We've got to—"

Zach stood, the ropes falling to the ground.

"How the hell'd you do that, Houdini?"

"I told you the knots sucked. Now let's see what we've got here." He crouched in front of Ty's leg, squeezed his eyes shut for a second and swore a few more times. "Little bastard gave me a concussion."

"Let's give him a lot worse. Get me out of this thing."

It took too long, that much Ty knew. Like Ty, Zach used a variety of natural objects to try to pry the trap open.

"You should go."

Zach raised an eyebrow at Ty. "You want me to leave you here stuck in a nineteenth-century bear trap?"

"I've gotta believe Jen can ward off this guy, but I also believe two is better than one. Go. Help her and—"

Something clicked and the bear trap opened. It was almost as painful as the going in had been. His vision dimmed, but he focused on the hard ground beneath him and Zach's hand on his shoulder.

"Found the release mechanism. Can you walk?"

"Hell if I know. Let's find out." He took Zach's outstretched hand and got to his feet, putting pressure only on the good one. He had to have broken bones on top of the puncture wounds that were currently oozing blood.

"I could carry you."

Ty snorted. "You and what army? You've got a concussion and I'm not exactly a lightweight. Just give me an arm."

Zach did so, winding his arm around Ty, and Ty did the same. He took a tentative step with it, not putting full weight on. His good leg nearly buckled, but Zach kept him upright.

It would have to do. They moved slowly, and Ty swore, repeatedly, with every step of his injured foot, but kept stepping forward with Zach's help. "Toward the cabin," he said with gritted teeth.

"You aren't going to be much help."

Ty pointed to the gun that had fallen when the trap had gotten him. "The hell I'm not."

Zach bent to pick it up as Ty balanced on one foot. Ty took it from him and shoved it in its holster. "You got your phone on you?"

"No. He's got it. You?"

Ty paused. Much as it galled him to waste time, he pulled his phone out of his pocket and hit Laurel's number. He motioned Zach for them to keep walking as he used his free hand to hold the phone to his ear.

"T—"

He didn't even let her get his name out. "Get as many deputies up here as you can. Plus Grady and Noah." Cursing his bad luck, he added, "And Dylan and Cam. Everybody. Anybody."

"They're already on their way. We got an email from Jen. I tried to call but her phone goes straight to voice mail and the cabin phone line is dead. We've got some car trouble, but we're working on it. Someone should be there in ten minutes. You don't sound so good."

"Minor injuries. Have an ambulance ready, but don't send it up here yet."

"Is Jen okay?" Laurel demanded. Since Ty didn't know how to answer that, he didn't. "Gotta focus." He hit End and shoved his phone in his pocket. "Cavalry's coming," he said through gritted teeth.

"Good. I've got a bad feeling we're going to need it. We've still got a ways to go."

Too much of a ways. "Go ahead."

"How are you going to—"

He leaned against a tree and handed the gun to Zach. "You run hard as you can. I'll be behind you. Just make sure she's safe. Help her if she's not. We don't have the time for me."

Zach nodded once. "I'll see what I can do." Then he was off.

It about killed Ty to watch Zach run off, knowing Jen's fate was in his hands. No. Her own hands and Zach's hands and all the help they had coming.

He didn't even consider waiting. He braced himself, then took off after Zach in the fastest limping job he could manage. Maybe he wouldn't save the day, but he wasn't going to take the chance that he wouldn't need to.

He'd do whatever he could, fight through any pain, suffer any consequences to be sure Jen was safe.

It was freezing in the cabin, even with the fire crackling in the hearth. The windows were open since he had to air out all that carbon monoxide he'd poured inside. He'd gotten a bit of a headache himself when he put the straitjacket on Jen.

And everyone said his odd collection of things would be a waste.

He laughed, pleased all over again at the genius. He wished he'd thought of the carbon dioxide sooner. It would have saved him some trouble.

But he'd been able to use his bear trap. Ty's blood was on it now. Worth it. Everything was worth blood.

Jen moaned, moving weakly against the straitjacket that tied her arms behind her and her body to the couch. He watched her slowly drift to consciousness from his position by the window, breathing in fresh air.

He wanted to watch the fear creep into her. Wanted to see the panic on her face when she realized where she was. When she realized he'd immobilized her completely. When she realized no one could or would help her now because he was the only one here.

He laughed again, and her eyes flew open. Pretty eyes. Such a shame to squeeze until they popped right out.

Would that be bloody? Hmm.

He thought for a second about focus, about goals, about what Dr. Michaels had always told him.

But she'd been wrong. Leaning into the black was so much better. Hadn't everything gotten better since he'd stabbed the good doctor? Once he was done with Ty, he'd go back and finish the job.

Revenge. It wasn't just for Oscar anymore, and though a part of him felt guilty, a part of him was too excited about what was to come.

Blood. Blood. Blood. Ty's suffering would be for Oscar. Jen's blood would be for him.

Her eyes darted around the room as she swallowed and moved, trying to escape the straitjacket. She wouldn't be able to, but it'd be fun to watch her try. Fun to watch her scream and beg.

He'd watch for as long as that thrilled him, then he'd kill her. Just like Dr. Michaels, but he'd finish the job. Leave her ripped apart and bloody for Ty to find.

He frowned a little. It would be possible someone else would find her first, and that wouldn't do. No, Ty had to be the one who stepped into all the glorious blood he'd soon shed.

He still had some work to do to perfect his plan.

He watched her struggle against the bonds he'd put on her, and smiled. He'd have the perfect view to do just that.

Chapter 17

Jen pretended to slip back into unconsciousness so she could think. She tried to remember what had happened or how she'd ended up immobile on the couch.

Her arms were wrapped uncomfortably around her body, but she couldn't move out of the position. It was like she was tied together, fastened to the couch.

Panic came, though she tried to fight it. She wanted to pretend like she was still unconscious but she just... she couldn't. She writhed and tried to free her hands, move her arms only a little, but she couldn't.

She sobbed out a breath, was afraid she wouldn't be able to suck in another. She opened her eyes as she desperately tried to move her limbs. What had he done to her? Why couldn't she move even her arms?

She blinked once, then twice, thought maybe she was hallucinating before she came to the conclusion that her eyes were not deceiving her.

He'd put her in an honest-to-goodness straitjacket.

"Worked out that it fit almost perfectly."

She jerked at his voice, even though she knew he'd been there. It wasn't that he spoke that gave her a start, it was how...conversational he sounded.

"One of my foster mothers used to put me in it. I kept it. A token of the time."

"That's horrible," Jen replied. Talking helped ease some of her panic. If she could focus on Braxton, on talking, she could take her mind off the fact that she couldn't move.

"It was horrible. And now it's horrible for you."

"Th-that doesn't seem very f-fair," Jen managed. She tried to ignore the fact she couldn't move. Because she had to be able to get out of this, or at least stall...whatever he was going to do to her. The longer she could keep him from hurting her, the better shot she had of someone coming to save her. Them.

God. Ty. Zach. They were all tied up in some fashion or another now. She didn't understand how one lone, crazy man had been able to best all three of them.

Except no. He hadn't bested them yet. She had to believe there was a way out of this. As long as she believed, there was a chance.

"Fair?" He laughed, and there was no edge or bitterness to the sound. He seemed genuinely amused. "You don't actually think life is *fair*, do you?"

She wouldn't answer that—not with the awful joyful gleam in his ice-blue eyes. "I-it's Braxton, right? You're Braxton."

He tilted his head and studied her. "Are we going to be friends now, Jen? You were nice enough to give me a candy bar, right? You're going to be nice enough to talk to me. Soften me up and maybe I'll let you go."

She closed her eyes and breathed. She thought about Ty. If he were in her place, he wouldn't panic. He wouldn't cry. Sure, he had military training she didn't, but she could be as tough as him when push came to shove. When she had to be.

"I know you're going to hurt me because you think it'll hurt Ty, but—"

He laughed again, louder, but it had an edge to it now that had her swallowing at the lump in her throat.

"Now you're going to lie to me?" he demanded, still standing over by the window. "You're going to lie there, in a *straitjacket*, and tell me Ty doesn't care about you. Oh, Jen, you're stupider than I gave you credit for. You think I don't know you let him touch you? You think I don't know everything that went on in that room last night?"

Horror waved through her, a crawling sensation of disgust crept along her skin as he pointed to the bedroom she'd shared with Ty.

"You…"

"Amazing what you can learn from watching people on video. Your third wheel friend knows that, doesn't he? Don't worry. It was dark. I couldn't really see anything, but I know what you did. I know what you said. Love is such a powerful motivator, don't you think? When you love someone, you want to hurt the people who hurt them."

"No. You want to heal the hurt in them, not punish the person who hurt them."

Braxton laughed bitterly. "Oh, aren't you full of it."

"No, I'm not." Was she really arguing with a homicidal maniac? It was probably pointless and stupid, but it kept her attention off the horrible sensation of forced immobility. "If someone hurt Ty, I would want to help Ty, not worry about stupid, selfish revenge."

"Stupid?" he repeated in a low, dangerous tone. "Selfish?"

"Yes, stupid. And selfish on both parts. I would want him okay, not someone else hurt. And Ty would never want me to hurt people *for* him. If he had a problem, he'd deal with it himself. I know you're trying to... You think this means you cared about your brother—"

"Cared?" He almost screamed the word but then he seemed to shake himself. He turned away from her, muttering something she couldn't hear. Then he repeated her words, till he was just muttering the word *himself* over and over again. As if he was working out a math problem, but every word he uttered was simply *himself*.

"You've given me an idea, Jen." He turned back to her, affable and pleasant again. "An interesting idea. Do you think Ty would sacrifice his own life for yours? Or would he hurt you to save his own skin? Which one's love?"

Without knowing what Braxton was planning, thinking, she didn't want to give him any answer. So she simply swallowed.

Braxton finally moved away from the window, but he moved toward her and that was when she realized he had a very large knife in his hand.

"Do knives make you nervous, Jen?" he asked, sounding almost concerned, almost human. He twisted the knife one way and then another. When he knelt next to the couch, she whimpered no matter how she tried not to make a noise.

Braxton smiled, brandishing the knife above her head. "You're terrified. My, my. I quite like them. Anything sharp really. Blood is so…interesting. So soothing. Would Ty shed his own to save you yours?"

A tear slipped over. She could feel it trail down her cheek. Braxton pointed the sharp tip of the knife at it. She squeezed her eyes shut as the tip of the knife touched the teardrop and pierced her skin. It hurt, but she couldn't move. She was stuck, the tip of the blade cutting into her skin.

"Blood and tears." He made a considering noise, but the knife eased off her cheek. She felt something trickle down her chin—tears or blood or both—and tried to believe she would survive this.

But she didn't have any idea how.

The cabin came into view, and with it, Zach standing behind the stables. Ty's body was becoming slowly numb. He welcomed it, as long as it didn't interfere with his ability to move forward.

"He's got the windows open," Zach said by way of greeting.

Ty glared at Zach when he finally reached him. "Then get in there and—"

"I scoped it out. We need to work this together. I go in guns blazing, not only do I end up dead, but she might, too. We'll have to find a way to draw him out."

"The concussed and the mangled foot?"

"If it's all we got. I'd like to wait for the cops."

Fury, fear and sheer frustration welled up inside Ty like a tidal wave destroying all the numb. "Wait for… Are you—"

"I said I'd like to, not that I would." Zach scanned the trees, calm and sure. Ty might have been reassured if he wasn't so scared. "What's taking them so long?"

Ty tried not to think about all the worst-case scenarios. The wind having knocked down trees to block the road, Braxton having men working for him, happily picking off cops as they came.

He couldn't think about it now. He had to get to Jen. "What's the situation inside?"

Zach eyed him and Ty knew in a moment it was terrible, but before he could start forward, Zach spoke in clear, concise military tones.

"She's tied up. I need you to be prepared for that. He's got the door booby-trapped, but the windows are open. I don't see any traps, but I've got to believe he's got something going on there. He's bested us once, so we can't let him do it again. We have to be more careful than we were. Smarter."

"Tied up where? How?"

Zach scrubbed a hand over his face, smearing some of the blood across his cheek accidentally. "On the couch. I can't be sure, but I think he's got her in a straitjacket."

Ty swore and moved forward, but Zach grabbed his arm again, this time giving it a good yank.

"You're not new to this," he snapped, his voice firm. "You know dangerous situations, and people who would do anything to prove their point. You know the dangers and everything that could go wrong. You have to forget it's Jen for right now."

"That's bull. Why did I do all those things in the army? Because they were supposed to keep the people I loved here safe. Why'd you get kicked out of the FBI, Zach? Because you cared about your family more than you cared about procedure. So, don't give me that crap right now."

"I'm not talking about arbitrary procedure. I'm talking about a plan that prioritizes getting Jen out of there without getting anyone hurt."

"I'll get hurt. Ten times over." He'd go to hell and back and enjoy the ride.

"You think she'd want that?"

"I think I don't care." But it poked at some of his certainty. She wouldn't want that. It'd hurt her, and that was the last thing Ty wanted. She was already being hurt, far too much. His fault, and his guilt was talking. She wouldn't want that either. "What kind of booby traps?"

"The door's got some kind of trip wire. My instinct is explosives. Potentially enough to blow this whole clearing to hell."

Ty fought the fatigue and pain going on inside his body to think. *Think*. Jen had tried to understand Braxton, tried to understand his emotions. She'd been right, and he needed to think like she had.

"He incapacitated us, but didn't kill us," Ty said. "He could have. Easily."

"Yeah."

"He wants to torture Jen, but he wants me alive to see it. Whatever trap he's got going on in there isn't big scale because that'd ruin it. End it. He wants me to suffer—if we all die, I don't suffer."

"Okay. Okay. I'll give you that. But two things we have to keep in mind. First, I don't think he cares if *he* gets hurt as long as he gets revenge, so that's not a threat to him. Second, if you go in there, he hurts Jen. The closer you are to her with him the more likely he is to do something to her."

Zach was right. It burned, but Zach was right. The minute Ty stepped foot in that cabin, Jen was in at least twice as much danger. Which meant he had to do something that went against every fiber of his being.

He had to trust someone else with Jen's safety. He had to put it all in someone else's hands. He had to trust, and he had to believe, in someone aside from himself—not just Zach, but Jen, too.

Guilt told him this was all his fault and he should take responsibility for it. Guilt told him he couldn't let Zach get even more hurt when this was Ty's own fight.

But Jen... Here, in that cabin, she'd forgiven him everything—his faults, his choices, the things he'd done or not done. Everything he'd hated himself for, she'd washed away with forgiveness. And she always had.

She'd told him to let it go, to forgive himself, and he had tried, or had believed he might someday. But in this moment, he had to. Because if he didn't, Jen would more than likely die.

"You'll go in," Ty said, having no trouble snapping into army ranger mode. "There's a secret passageway on the opposite side of the cabin, but it's been sealed. Still, with the right timing, the right tools, you can either unseal it or create enough noise he comes out."

Zach nodded.

"If I situate myself in the hayloft, I've got the perfect position to pick him off if he comes out the door."

Zach rose an eyebrow and nodded toward Ty's foot. "How you going to get up there?"

"Carefully," Ty replied. Zach held out the gun Ty had given him and Ty took it. "You'll be unarmed."

"You're better off with the gun. You can pick him off through a window, we end this. Besides, he took my gun and my phone, but I've still got my knife." Zach motioned to his boot. "Vanessa gave me that idea."

"Thank God for Vanessa and her arsenal. Let's go." He motioned Zach to follow him back into the woods. Zach offered an arm, but Ty shook his head. Walking hurt like nothing he'd ever experienced, but Jen's life hung in the balance. He'd deal.

They moved through the cover of the trees to the opposite side of the cabin. Braxton couldn't know he was out here and free, or Jen and Zach were in even more danger.

Ty moved up the side of the cabin and showed Zach the secret passage and where it had been sealed.

Zach pulled out the knife. "This should do the trick. If not, I'll start banging away, try to lure him out."

Ty nodded. "I doubt he knows who you are, so hurting Jen to get to you won't matter to him, hopefully. He might think you're of some emotional connection to me, though. He might even know you're my cousin, my blood. So he could hurt you again, to get to me. We can't discount that."

"Yeah, I haven't let a man best me twice in this lifetime. I don't plan to start now."

"That's the Carson spirit." Ty studied the clearing, the cabin. "I'll be in the hayloft, out of sight, but if you get him out the front door, I can take him out. Jen's the priority."

Zach nodded, already prying at the seal on the door. "You should get out of sight now. I'll see what I can do here, but no matter what, I'll get her out. That's a promise."

Like Jen had chosen to forgive him, love him, Ty chose to believe Zach. He clapped him on the shoulder. "Take care of yourself, cousin." And then he limped for the stables, gun at the ready.

* * *

Blood and tears, but Ty wasn't here. Should he kill her and then bring Ty to the aftermath? Better for him to watch. He'd get the blood, and the revenge. Oscar wanted the revenge. He wanted the blood.

But she was right there and all it would take was a few minutes. He could cut her to ribbons and it would be done. Right now. No more waiting.

Why did he have to wait?

"Braxton, I know you want to hurt me…"

Her voice was so sweet he wished she'd stop talking. It wasn't like the doctor's voice. The doctor had always been so cold. So condescending. Jen sounded afraid of him.

He liked that.

"Could you let me out of this thing? I don't care if you tie me up again. I just can't lie like this."

He walked back over to her. She wanted out, and maybe that would suit his purposes. Maybe a little fight would make this all sit right. He'd had to fight the doctor. Element of surprise, yes, but she'd tried to push him off.

He'd liked that. The way she'd hit and begged and still he'd plunged the knife into her skin.

His stomach jumped with anticipation, even more so when Jen's fear shone in her eyes like tears.

"You want out?"

She swallowed visibly. "Just a little? I know you have to keep me tied up, but if I could just move a little. My circulation and I… I…"

Desperation. He liked it on her. Fear and desperation. It was what he wanted from Ty, but maybe he'd practice on sweet Jen. He held the knife over her head again, watched as she squeezed her eyes shut and braced herself for another cut.

The one from before was just a little dot now, a little smear of blood and tears down her cheek and chin.

Pleasure spurted through him, dark and wonderful. If only this moment could last.

"Cut yourself," he said.

"What?"

He liked the way she paled. Fear. He liked her fear so much. It was better than a shot of whiskey. Better than the drugs Oscar had liked so much that Braxton had never understood.

Why do drugs when you could make someone afraid? When the power of that could stir everything inside you?

"I'll free one arm. If you take the knife and cut yourself. More than I did on your face." He wondered if it would be more or less satisfying to watch her cause herself pain, or if it would be better for him to do it. Her hurting herself would cause Ty more pain, he thought, but the blood on her face made him wonder if he cared. "Maybe your wrist. It'd take a while for one wrist to bleed out."

"But…"

"One wrist. Then I decide if I do the rest, or you do. One wrist. Then we get Ty. I'd like to get a better look at Ty's blood, too. Maybe so would you."

"Braxton—"

He laid the flat of the blade against her cheek. "Sweet Jen didn't do anything to deserve this, but you love a monster. Maybe you're a monster, too. Monsters need to bleed, Jen. Isn't that what all the fairy tales tell us?"

But she didn't answer. She only cried.

Chapter 18

Jen would scold herself for crying later. For now, it was the release of fear she'd needed to center herself. "Okay, Braxton," she said, opening her eyes and making sure to look at him, to try to be a person to him. "I'll cut my wrist if you let me have one arm."

One arm would be all she'd need. There was a pistol in the cushion of the couch, unless he'd found it when she'd been unconscious. But she'd take the chance— had to.

Zach and Ty were stuck and she had to be able to save herself, and them.

Braxton could hurt her, *would* hurt her, but as long as he didn't kill her she had a shot. And he wouldn't kill her as long as Ty was somewhere else, so there was some bright side to his being stuck.

She just needed to get to that gun, and she just

needed it to be there. One arm. All she needed was one arm. Didn't matter if she had to cut herself to do it.

She breathed in and out, trying to accept the fact she would have to do it. She'd have to cut her own flesh and…

She had to convince him to free her arm first. She had to actually get him to do it before she worried about pressing a sharp blade to her wrist.

An involuntary shudder moved through her, but she forced herself to look at Braxton and tried to treat him like a human being even though whatever made someone humane was clearly missing in him.

"I've killed before, Jen, you know," he said, so simply, so *conversationally* the way you'd tell someone you didn't care for pizza. He stared at her intently, looking for a reaction.

She didn't know what kind he wanted. If she did, she'd act it out and give it to him. She'd go along with whatever he wanted. "I'm sorry," she whispered.

"Sorry?"

It wasn't the answer he wanted, but what was? What could she say to just make him untie her?

No time for panic. Breathe in. Breathe out. As long as Ty isn't here, you have time.

But did Ty have time? Did Zach?

She couldn't think about them.

"Are you going to let me go? Please? I'm going to have a panic attack."

He laid the flat of his blade against her cheek like he'd done before, and again she couldn't hide her response. A shudder, a wince and more tears welling behind her eyelids.

She opened her eyes when he did nothing. He was

grinning. Finally, it started to make sense. He wanted her to be afraid. He wanted her to shudder and wince at the idea of his killing people, over the idea and possibility he could kill her.

"Panic attack. I might like to watch that."

He was never going to let her go. He was going to torture her until... When?

"But I'd like to see your blood more," he continued. He pressed the knife against her cheek until she hissed out a breath when it lightly scored her chin.

He leaned in closer, his face so close to hers she could feel his breath against the blood dripping down her neck.

"Please let me out," she whispered, letting her fear and her tears run free, since that's what he wanted from her anyway. Fear and tears and blood. "Please. I just need to sit up or move my arm. Please. Anything."

He didn't lean away, though he did pull the knife off her skin. But then he replaced it with something much worse.

His tongue.

A groan mixed with a scream tore from her throat as she struggled to move her face, her body, her entire being away from him as he licked the blood off her face.

But he only made a considering noise, as if he was mulling over the taste of her blood.

Shudders racked her body and true fear crept through everything. She didn't know how to fight insanity. She didn't know how to escape. A tiny part of her wondered if death wouldn't just be easier.

The thought passed. Ty was out there, trapped. Zach was trapped and probably hurt. Her entire family was

412 *Wyoming Cowboy Ranger*

trying to solve the mystery of Braxton Lynn. Someone would make it here eventually and help her.

Ty was counting on her. He'd left her alone thinking she could handle anything that came her way, so she would. She *would*.

If she believed that, she could endure anything.

Anything.

"Please, Braxton. Just a break from the straitjacket. Besides, if you take all this fabric off you'll be able to cut me wherever you want."

"I want to watch you cut yourself, Jen. A test. Which do I like better? Inflicting pain? Or making you inflict pain on yourself? I get blood either way."

"Then just free my arms. Please. *Please.*"

He sighed heavily. "Fine. But only because I want the experiment. It's important to find out what makes you feel the best, isn't it?" He undid some strap, then rolled her to the side so her back was to him. "I thought I liked revenge. Doing something for my brother. Ty was supposed to be Oscar's brother, but he ratted him out. Did you know that about the man you let touch you? That he's no better than a cowardly tattletale?"

She bit her tongue against the need to defend Ty. He wanted her fear and her desperation, but she doubted he'd care for her anger.

There were sounds, the gradual loosening of the fabric holding her arms around her. She nearly wept with relief, but then Braxton paused.

"If you try anything, this is my plan. Cut you to ribbons. Bathe this room in your blood. Then bring Ty in to see your mangled corpse that he should have been brave enough and smart enough to save. One attempt at escape, one look at the door, one wrong move—you're dead, and he sees it *all*."

She didn't suppress this shudder since she knew he liked it. If she gave him everything he liked, maybe he'd make a mistake—get too excited. No matter what, as long as she did what he said, he'd keep her alive. She wouldn't be the sacrifice he made to hurt Ty.

Braxton pushed her up into a sitting position. He held the strap of one arm tight around his fist. He tugged the other sleeve off. "I'm going to give you the knife. You're going to slice your wrist. If you do all that, I won't put the straitjacket back on."

Jen nodded, and her arm that was now free shook. Even if she could muster up the guts or strength to cut herself, she wasn't sure her limbs would cooperate. Still, Braxton slowly pressed the handle of the knife into her palm—holding her other arm still by the straps on the jacket.

With his hand now free, he pulled a gun out of his pocket. Everything inside her sank. It was the gun she'd hidden in the couch.

"Hope you weren't planning on using this." He smiled indulgently.

She shook her head even though that's exactly what her plan had been. Still, he'd given her a knife. Maybe he had the gun pointed at her, but she had a weapon, too. If he let go of her other arm, she could knock him down.

She just needed the right moment.

But he just kept smiling, like he knew every move she'd make and had a counterplan for it. He didn't take the straitjacket off her completely. Instead, he pushed the sleeve still on her arm up, revealing her wrist and adjusting his hold onto her forearm.

"Cut yourself. And don't wimp out. A real cut. I want to see blood *gush*. I like knives better, but if I have to shoot you to get blood, I'll do it. So, pick your poison."

Jen briefly considered letting him shoot her. It might be better for her in the long run. But she had a knife now. He'd untied her. Her feet were still fastened together, but she had a weapon and she wasn't tethered to the couch any longer.

"Go on now."

She nodded, arms still shaking as she slowly brought the knife to where he held her wrist out for her. She'd only have to lunge forward, right in the gut. He'd shoot her, but he'd be hurt, too. Wouldn't it be worth it?

"Do it now," Braxton ordered, jerking her wrist toward the knife. "Or I'll put you back in. I'll carve that pretty face of yours all up while your arms are tied around you. Would you prefer that, Jen?"

No, she wouldn't, but she was afraid he was going to do it anyway. But first, she'd cut herself. It excited him, and if he leaned down to lick her wrist like he'd done with her face, she'd have the best chance to stab him where it would do the most damage.

She closed her eyes and pressed the blade to her wrist, inhaling sharply to give herself one last second before she inflicted pain.

But then she heard something. Like a door being opened somewhere. She kept her eyes closed, even as hope soared through her. She had to cut herself and keep Braxton's attention.

"What the hell was that?" Braxton demanded as she opened her eyes.

He not only looked away, he turned, which gave her the opportunity to strike.

* * *

A scream tore through the air. Ty immediately jumped from the hayloft. He saw stars, the pain in his foot so bright and burning he nearly lost consciousness.

When a gunshot sounded, Ty didn't care about the pain. He ran.

He stopped for a moment at the window, but he couldn't see anything. It'd have to be the door—regardless of booby traps.

Zach was reaching the door just as Ty rounded the corner.

"Was just about in when I heard it. I'll kick in the door. Stay to the side. We'll give it a minute, me in first since I've got two good feet, then you follow and shoot."

Ty nodded.

Zach reared back and kicked. It didn't open the door, but it jarred it, so Zach kicked again. This time it splintered, and opened weakly.

Almost immediately there was another gunshot.

They both swore, but there was no time to consider the ramifications of Braxton's shooting at them. Zach went in first, a low roll that hopefully got him some cover. Ty moved in, weapon drawn.

Braxton stood behind the couch, his arm wrapped around Jen's throat. She was limp and lifeless, blood smeared all over her face. Braxton held the barrel of the gun to her head and grinned.

Jen was too close for comfort, but they simply didn't have another option. Ty aimed and fired.

Braxton jerked back and Jen fell to the floor. Zach and Ty moved forward as a unit. Red bloomed on Braxton's shirt and he touched the wound and smiled. "Look at all that blood," he murmured, transfixed by the sight of his own fingers drenched in his own blood.

Then his eyes rolled back and he collapsed in a heap. Ty didn't think he was dead—he'd probably just passed out.

"I'll tie him up," Zach said.

Ty tossed him his phone. "Call Laurel again and find out what the damn holdup is. We need that ambulance." He looked down at Jen. Her face was covered in blood and she was so pale and lifeless everything inside him went cold. He fell to his knees next to her and nearly wept when her eyes fluttered open.

"You're okay," she murmured.

"Where are you bleeding, darling?" She tried to move, but he stopped her, afraid she'd hurt herself more. "I don't see where you're bleeding from."

"He smeared it all over me. He…" She shuddered, closing her eyes again. "S'okay, though. Have to."

"Have to *what*?"

"Get shot. It's like… It's like. Laurel and Cam and Dylan, they all did."

"Baby, shh. Just tell me where—"

"But then it'll be okay, right? Because they did, but now it's good. We'll be good, because I got shot. It's the answer to the curse. It'll be okay."

She wasn't making any sense, but he didn't care. "Yeah, it'll be okay. It has to be." It had to be. With shaking hands, he moved his fingers over her, trying to find the wound. It had to be on her back, but he was loath to turn her over. But there was bleeding that had to be stopped.

"My arm," she mumbled. "Hurts. Under my arm."

He didn't know which one she was talking about, so

gently he lifted the one closest to him, but she shook her head sluggishly.

He lifted the other one, found the bleeding, gaping wound right under her armpit. Not fatal, thank God, but they needed to stop the bleeding. Get her safe.

"Stabbed him, but he shot me."

Ty nearly wept right there, but he held it together and took the first aid kit Zach handed him.

"We have to get her to a hospital," he said, opening the case and pulling out all the bandages inside. He handed half to Zach to start unwrapping.

"How? On your bike?"

Ty shook his head, pressing the first pad of gauze to her wound. She hissed out a breath, but her eyes remained closed and her breathing was getting too shallow for his comfort. "What did Laurel say?"

"Trees down everywhere. Their cars were tampered with. The ambulance is trying to get up here, but without a road—"

"We'll carry her to it, then." Ty wrapped more bandages, as many as he could manage, as tight as he could manage, around her arm.

"I don't know if you recall the fact your foot is torn to hell."

"You'll carry, then. We have to get her to that ambulance. We'll bandage her up and get her out of here."

"What about him?"

Ty didn't even glance back at Braxton's body. "He can rot in hell."

Chapter 19

"I convinced him to let my arms free."

"How did you do that?" Thomas asked gently.

Jen sat in the hospital bed, tired and a little off from the drugs they'd given her, but she'd felt up to giving her statement to the police. She wanted to get it all out and over with, before the nurses let her family back in, before she saw Ty.

She wanted to get rid of all the ugliness so it could be behind her. "He told me he'd let my arms loose if I cut myself for him."

Thomas raised an eyebrow as he wrote that down on his notepad.

"He was obsessed with blood. He seemed to lose his grasp on reality or humanity with every passing moment. The need for revenge against Ty sort of faded into…bloodlust I guess." She shuddered again, was pretty sure she'd flash back to Braxton whenever she saw blood.

But she was alive and Braxton… "Thomas, is Braxton…"

"He made it to the hospital, but he'd lost too much blood."

"Braxton said…" She swallowed against the wave of nausea—didn't know if it had to do with the drugs or everything else. "He said he'd killed people."

Thomas nodded solemnly. "Laurel's been in touch with the authorities in Arizona. They've been able to connect him to an attack on his therapist, along with a murder of one of Oscar Villanueva's victims."

She slumped in her bed, far too aware that she could have easily been another of his murder victims.

"Do you want to stop for now? I can come back—"

"No. I want it over with."

"All right. So, he untied you?"

"Yes, and then there was this noise and I took the moment of distraction to stab him, but he had a gun and he shot me. I'm not sure he meant to, it was more of an impulse response. I mean, he wanted to hurt me, but I don't think he wanted to kill me yet. But things get fuzzy from there."

"You don't remember Zach and Ty coming in?"

"No. No, it just kind of goes blank. I remember talking to Ty in the cabin. He was trying to figure out how I was hurt. Will Ty be in trouble, since I can't remember?"

"No. We have Zach's statement, cut-and-dried self-defense. Ty will be fine."

Jen nodded, closing her eyes against the fatigue.

"You should rest, Jen. I've got enough to build the

case and file everything. I may need to ask you a few more questions in the future, depending on how everything goes, but we're mostly done."

Jen grimaced but she nodded. "All right." She tried to smile. "Thank you."

Thomas paused on his way out of the hospital room. "I'm… I wish we could have done more."

Jen shook her head and sighed. "You did what you could. We all did. And now it's over."

Thomas nodded and slipped out the door. Jen allowed herself a moment of quiet, of release. They'd all done the best they could, and now it was over. Everyone she loved was safe, and she'd survived.

Everything was going to be okay.

It was an emotional acceptance because there had been a moment there, before she'd managed to convince him to take the straitjacket off, and for a second there after he'd shot her, where she'd been certain she was going to die.

But she was alive.

She heard the door swish open, and opened her eyes to see Ty. He had a crutch under one arm, and a medical boot on the foot.

She hadn't seen him since the ambulance, and she'd been in and out at that point. But he'd held her hand the whole way to the hospital.

"You should've told Hart to scram."

She held out her good arm to him. "I wanted it over. Did you sneak back here or are you allowed?"

He managed a smile. "Which do you think?" He moved over to her, relying on the crutch. She scooted to the side of the bed so he could slide onto it next to her.

They didn't say anything else. He just wrapped his

arms around her and she leaned into the strong wall of his chest.

She thought she might cry, but she didn't. Instead, she just breathed. It was over, and she had this. Everything was okay.

She hadn't realized she'd said it out loud until Ty spoke.

"Yeah it is," he said before kissing her temple. "You know when they'll spring you?"

"Tomorrow they said. They didn't let you out already?"

"Discharged and all." He fidgeted irritably. "I'll have to have some surgery later, but they want some of the wounds to heal first."

"Not everyone can say they have a limp because of a bear trap."

"Making jokes already? I'm impressed, darling." He kissed her again, and his grip on her never loosened.

"I don't want to think about horrible things, or be angry or sad or scared for at least a month."

"Let's shoot for a year."

"Maybe two."

He laughed, but then he just held her, so she held him back. "It really is okay," she whispered. "And there's a lot of okay left to get."

"I know. It's going to take me a little while to… Hell, I thought you were dead, Jen."

She pressed her forehead into his neck. "But I'm not. Which means we have a lot of plans to make. So, you think on that."

The door opened again, and her whole family poured in. A nurse started mounting objections, but Grady easily sweet-talked her out of the room.

Hilly rushed over and gave her a hug, while Dylan insisted Vanessa take a seat. Zach hovered in the background, but Jen motioned him over.

"Glad you're okay, Jen," he offered.

She gently touched the bandage on his temple. "Thank you for everything."

He shrugged, clearly uncomfortable, and then he quickly moved away as her father came over and gave her a hug. Laurel perched herself on the little sliver of bed at the end.

"Well, here we are again," Jen said, opting for cheerful. "But you know, it's over now. We all got shot, and we'll all get our happily-ever-afters."

"Oh, for heaven's sake," Laurel muttered. "There's *no curse*."

"Not anymore," Jen agreed, grinning when Laurel rolled her eyes.

"What about Zach?" Hilly asked. "He's a Carson."

"I'm a Simmons," Zach replied firmly.

"No, Hilly's right. Zach's one of us," Grady replied. "But we're out of Delaneys for him to pair up with."

"Eh, you never know when one will pop out of the woodwork," Vanessa returned with a grin. "Watch your back, Zach."

He scoffed, but Jen rather liked the idea. And she liked having everyone around, talking as if things were normal. As if she wasn't hooked up to a hospital bed, as if nothing had terrorized any of them over the course of the past year.

It was nice. It was...perfect really. A cleansing moment to put everything about yesterday behind her.

She tried to hide the yawns, the exhaustion, but

pretty soon Laurel was shooing everyone out, assuring Jen they'd all be back tomorrow.

Ty didn't budge.

When her family was gone, she snuggled into him, ready for a nice long sleep.

"They'll make you leave," she murmured into his chest.

Ty only held on tighter. "Like hell, darling."

Epilogue

Ty cursed the crutch that had been a part of his life for too many months now. The surgery had been successful, but healing was annoying.

"You're pushing yourself too hard," Jen insisted as they walked across a stretch of rocky land at the edge of Carson property.

They'd been staying out at the Carson Ranch, where there weren't as many stairs to navigate as there were at his apartment above Rightful Claim and hers above the store.

Still, he was antsy to have a space of his own, to be done with healing and get on with living.

So, they'd start living. "What do you think?" he asked, waving a hand to encompass the stretch of field in front of them, the mountains sparkling in the blue-sky distance.

She smiled up at him, confusion written in her expression. She was the most beautiful woman he'd ever known, and she was all his. His faults and errors were no longer the black marks that held down his soul. Because in Jen he always had a place to find his salvation, and love.

"It's a pretty view," she offered.

"How'd you like a kitchen window looking out over that view?"

The confusion left her features, and something else he couldn't quite name replaced it. A certainty—the sure sign of a Jen Delaney plan in the works.

He found he quite liked going along with Jen Delaney's plans.

"I don't think I'd like it, I think I'd love it. But before you go getting ideas, there's one thing you're going to have to do first."

He dug around in his pocket, pulled out the velvet box and popped it open. Pleased that he'd managed to surprise her, he pulled the ring out and held it in the light so it sparkled. "This what you had in mind?"

She nodded wordlessly, tears already falling over her cheeks. He wiped one away, then took her hand.

"So, what do you say, Jen Delaney. Ready to promise your life to a Carson?"

"I always have been," she whispered, grinning at him, urging him to put the ring on her finger.

He slid it on easily, but kept her hand in his. "Anything else before we break ground?"

She took a deep, shaky breath. "I want lots of babies," she said, and though her voice wavered, her smile didn't. "Babies and forever. That should do it."

"We can start working on the babies thing right now if you're up to it."

She laughed, the sound carrying on the wind as it filled up his soul, because that was what his second chance with Jen had done—filled the empty places inside him, washed away the guilt he'd carried for so long.

Love and trust were that powerful, and he'd never let himself forget it.

He kissed her hands, looked into her eyes, and gave her the one thing he knew she'd never expect. The words. "I love you. I can't remember a time I didn't. I don't want to ever remember a time I didn't."

More tears spilled over, and she lightly wrapped her arms around his neck, careful not to move him so he had to put undue pressure on his foot. "I love you with everything I am," she whispered. "I always will. We can survive anything, so we will."

"Yeah, we will."

Always.

* * * * *

IF YOU ENJOYED THIS BOOK
WE THINK YOU WILL ALSO LOVE

HARLEQUIN

INTRIGUE

Seek thrills. Solve crimes. Justice served.

Dive into action-packed stories that will keep you
on the edge of your seat. Solve the crime
and deliver justice at all costs.

6 NEW BOOKS AVAILABLE EVERY MONTH!

"The crime scene unit is out at your house," Daniel went on after glancing through his texts. "They've found two sets of footprints outside your office window. There are some drag marks, too. So maybe the guy had drugged Mandy before he got there, revived her enough so she could walk at least part of the way and then gave her a second dose of the drug once he got her inside."

Of course, the killer could have incapacitated the woman in other ways, smothering or a blow to the head, but it didn't really matter. He'd gotten Mandy into Kara's house, murdered her and staged the body. Maybe as a threat to Kara to tell her to back off her investigation into the missing and dead surrogates, maybe just to torment her.

The tormenting was definitely working.

HIEXP45518

She shook her head. "I didn't hear anything to let me know someone was in my house."

At the moment, he considered that a good thing. "If you had, you might have gone inside to check things out and been killed."

Daniel hoped that was a warning she'd take to heart. He didn't want Kara setting up any more traps for this snake. She certainly didn't jump to defend what she'd done. Nope. Her emotions went in the other direction. Her eyes filled with tears.

"Oh, God. Daniel, I'm so sorry."

Hell. He'd hoped she would be able to keep the aftermath of all of this at bay. Apparently not. Those tears didn't spill down her cheeks, but she was blinking hard to keep them from falling.

Daniel figured this was a mistake the size of Texas, but he went to her and pulled her into his arms. Kara practically sagged against him, her head landing on his shoulder. He didn't want to notice how well she fit. Didn't want to notice her scent, which he immediately took in. Or the soft, breathy sigh she made.

But he noticed.

Don't miss
Safeguarding the Surrogate *by Delores Fossen,*
available July 2021 wherever
Harlequin Intrigue books and ebooks are sold.

Harlequin.com

Love Harlequin romance?

DISCOVER.

Be the first to find out about promotions,
news and exclusive content!

Facebook.com/HarlequinBooks

Twitter.com/HarlequinBooks

Instagram.com/HarlequinBooks

Pinterest.com/HarlequinBooks

YouTube.com/HarlequinBooks

ReaderService.com

EXPLORE.

Sign up for the Harlequin e-newsletter and
download a free book from any series at
TryHarlequin.com

CONNECT.

Join our Harlequin community to
share your thoughts and connect
with other romance readers!
Facebook.com/groups/HarlequinConnection

HARLEQUIN

Heartfelt or thrilling, passionate or uplifting—Harlequin is more than just happily-ever-after.

With twelve different series to choose from and new books available every month, you are sure to find stories that will move you, uplift you, inspire and delight you.

HNEWS2021